BODY DOUBLE

A Novel

TESS GERRITSEN

DOUBLEDAY LARGE PRINT
HOME LIBRARY EDITION

BALLANTINE BOOKS • NEW YORK

A Ballantine Book
Published by The Random House Publishing Group

ISBN 0-7394-4578-2

Manufactured in the United States of America

This Large Print Book carries the
Seal of Approval of N.A.V.H.

To Adam and Danielle

ACKNOWLEDGMENTS

Writing is lonely work, but no writer truly labors alone. I'm lucky to have had the help and support of Linda Marrow and Gina Centrello at Ballantine Books, Meg Ruley, Jane Berkey, Don Cleary and the superb team at the Jane Rotrosen Agency, Selina Walker at Transworld, and—most important of all—my husband Jacob. Warmest thanks to you all!

BODY DOUBLE

PROLOGUE

That boy was watching her again.

Fourteen-year-old Alice Rose tried to focus on the ten exam questions on her desk, but her mind was not on freshman English; it was on Elijah. She could feel the boy's gaze, like a beam aimed at her face, could feel its heat on her cheek, and knew she was blushing.

Concentrate, Alice!

The next question on the test was smudged from the mimeograph machine, and she had to squint to make out the words.

Charles Dickens often chooses names that match his characters' traits. Give some examples and describe why the names fit those particular characters.

Alice chewed her pencil, trying to dredge up an answer. But she couldn't think while *he* was sitting at the next desk, so close that she could inhale his scent of pine soap and wood smoke. Manly smells. Dickens, Dickens, who cared about Charles Dickens and Nicholas Nickleby and boring freshman English when gorgeous Elijah Lank was looking at her? Oh my, he was *so* handsome, with his black hair and blue eyes. Tony Curtis eyes. The very first time she'd ever seen Elijah, that's what she'd thought: that he looked exactly like Tony Curtis, whose beautiful face beamed from the pages of her favorite magazines, *Modern Screen* and *Photoplay.*

She bent her head forward, and as her hair fell across her face, she cast a furtive glance sideways through the curtain of blond strands. Felt her heart leap when she confirmed that he was, indeed, looking at her, and not in that disdainful way that all the other boys in school did, those mean boys who made her feel slow and dim-witted. Whose ridiculing whispers were always just out of earshot, too soft for her to make out their words. She knew the whispers were about her, because they were always looking at her as they did it. Those were the same boys who'd taped the photo of a cow to her locker, who mooed if she accidentally brushed against them in the hallway. But Elijah—he was looking at her in a different way altogether. With smoldering eyes. Movie star eyes.

Slowly she raised her head and stared back, not through a protective veil of hair this time, but with frank acknowledgment of his gaze. His test paper was already completed and turned facedown, his pencil put away in his desk. His full attention was focused on her, and she could scarcely breathe under the spell of his gaze.

He likes me. I know it. He likes me.

Her hand lifted to her throat, to the top button of her blouse. Her fingers brushed across her skin, leaving a trail of heat. She thought of Tony Curtis's molten gaze on Lana Turner, a look that could make a girl go tongue-tied and wobble-kneed. The look that came just before the inevitable kiss. That's when the movies always went out of focus. Why did that have to happen? Why did it always go fuzzy, just at the moment when you most wanted to see . . .

"Time's up, class! Please turn in your test papers."

Alice's attention snapped back to her desk, to the mimeographed test paper, half the questions still unanswered. Oh, no. Where had the time gone? She *knew* these answers. She just needed a few more minutes . . .

"Alice. Alice!"

She looked up and saw Mrs. Meriweather's hand held out.

"Didn't you hear me? Time to turn in your test."

"But I—"

"No excuses. You've got to start *listening*, Alice." Mrs. Meriweather snatched up Alice's exam and moved on down the aisle. Though Alice could barely hear their murmurs, she knew the girls right behind her were gossiping about her. She turned and saw their heads bent together, their hands shielding their mouths, muffling giggles. *Alice can read lips, so don't let her see we're talking about her.*

Now some of the boys were laughing, too, pointing at her. What was so funny?

Alice glanced down. To her horror she

saw that the top button had fallen off her blouse, which was now gaping open.

The school bell rang, announcing dismissal.

Alice snatched up her book bag and hugged it to her chest as she fled the classroom. She didn't dare look anyone in the eye, just kept walking, head down, tears building in her throat. She dashed into the restroom and locked herself in a stall. As other girls came in and stood laughing, primping in front of the mirrors, Alice hid behind the latched door. She could smell all their different perfumes, could feel the whoosh of air each time the door swung open. Those golden girls, with their brand-new sweater sets. They never lost buttons; they never came to school wearing hand-me-down skirts and shoes with cardboard soles.

Go away. Everyone please just go away.

The door finally stopped whooshing open.

Pressed up against the stall door, Alice strained to hear if anyone was still in the room. Peeking out through the crack, she saw no one standing in front of the mirror.

Only then did she creep out of the bathroom.

The hallway was deserted as well, everyone gone for the day. There was no one to torment her. She walked, shoulders hunched self-protectively, down the long corridor with its battered lockers and wall posters announcing the Halloween dance in two weeks. A dance she would certainly not be going to. The humiliation of last week's dance still stung, and would probably always sting. The two hours of standing alone against the wall, waiting, hoping a boy would ask her onto the floor. When a boy had at last approached her, it was not to dance. Instead he'd suddenly doubled over and thrown up on her shoes. No more dances for her. She'd been in this town only two months, and already she wished her mother would pack them up and move them again, take them someplace where they could start over. Where things would finally be different.

Only, they never are.

She walked out the school's front entrance, into the autumn sunshine. Bending over her bicycle, she was so intent on opening the lock that she didn't hear the footsteps. Only as his shadow fell across her face did she realize Elijah was standing beside her.

"Hello, Alice."

She jerked to her feet, sending her bike crashing onto its side. Oh god, she was an idiot. How could she be so clumsy?

"That was a hard exam, wasn't it?" He spoke slowly, distinctly. That was one more thing she liked about Elijah; unlike the other kids, his voice was always clear, never muddled. And he always let her see his lips. He knows my secret, she thought. Yet he still wants to be my friend.

"So did you finish all the questions?" he asked.

She bent down to pick up her bike. "I knew the answers. I just needed more time." As she straightened, she saw that his gaze had dropped to her blouse. To the gap left by the missing button. Flushing, she crossed her arms.

"I've got a safety pin," he said.

"What?"

He reached in his pocket and pulled out a pin. "I'm always losing buttons myself. It's kind of embarrassing. Here, let me fasten it for you."

She held her breath as he reached for her blouse. She could barely suppress her trembling as he slipped his finger beneath the fabric to close the pin. Does he feel my heart pounding? she wondered. Does he know I'm dizzy from his touch?

When he stepped back, her breath flew out. She looked down and saw that the gap was now modestly pinned shut.

"Better?" he asked.

"Oh. Yes!" She paused to compose herself. Said, with queenly dignity: "Thank you, Elijah. That's very thoughtful of you."

A moment passed. Crows cawed, and the autumn leaves were like bright flames engulfing the branches above.

"You think you could help me with something, Alice?" he asked.

"With what?"

Oh, stupid, stupid answer. You should just have said yes! Yes, I'll do anything for you, Elijah Lank.

"I've got this project I'm doing for biology. I need a partner to help me with it, and I don't know who else to ask."

"What kind of project is it?"

"I'll show you. We've got to go up by my house."

His house. She'd never been to a boy's house.

She nodded. "Let me drop my books off at home."

He pulled his bike from the rack. It was almost as battered as hers, the fenders going rusty, the vinyl peeling off the seat. That old bike made her like him even more. We're a real pair, she thought. Tony Curtis and me.

They rode to her house first. She didn't invite him in; she was too embarrassed to let him see the shabby furniture, the paint peeling off the walls. She just ran inside, dumped her book bag on the kitchen table, and ran out.

Unfortunately, her brother's dog, Buddy, did as well. Just as she came out the front door, he scampered out in a blur of black and white.

"Buddy!" she yelled. "You come back here!"

"He doesn't listen very well, does he?" said Elijah.

"Because he's a stupid dog. *Buddy!*"

The mutt glanced back, tail wagging, then trotted off down the road.

"Oh, never mind," she said. "He'll come

home when he's ready." She climbed onto her bike. "So where do you live?"

"Up on Skyline Road. You ever been up there?"

"No."

"It's kind of a long ride up the hill. Think you can make it?"

She nodded. *I can do anything for you.*

They pedaled away from her house. She hoped that he'd turn onto Main Street, past the malt shop where the kids always hung out after school playing the jukebox and sipping their sodas. *They'll see us go riding by together,* she thought, *and wouldn't that set the girls' tongues wagging? There goes Alice and Elijah-with-the-blue-eyes.*

But he didn't lead her down Main Street. Instead, he turned up Locust Lane, where there were hardly any houses, just the backside of a few businesses and the employee parking lot for the Neptune's Bounty Cannery. Oh, well. She was riding with him, wasn't she? Close enough behind him to watch his thighs pumping, his rear end perched on the seat.

He glanced back at her, and his black hair danced in the wind. "You doing okay, Alice?"

"I'm fine." Though the truth was, she was getting out of breath because they had left the village and were starting to climb up the mountain. Elijah must ride his bike up Skyline every day, so he was used to it; he seemed hardly winded, his legs moving like powerful pistons. But she was panting, pushing herself onward. A flash of fur caught her eye. She glanced sideways and saw that Buddy had followed them. He looked tired too, his tongue hanging way out as he ran to keep up.

"Go home!"

"What did you say?" Elijah glanced back.

"It's that stupid dog again," she panted. "He won't stop following us. He's gonna— gonna get lost."

She glared at Buddy, but he just kept trotting along beside her in his cheerful dumb dog way. Well, go ahead, she thought. Tucker yourself out. I don't care.

They kept moving up the mountain, the road winding in gentle switchbacks. Through the trees she caught occasional glimpses of Fox Harbor far below, the water like battered copper in the afternoon sunlight. Then the trees became too thick, and she could see only the forest, clothed in brilliant reds and oranges. The leaf-strewn road curved ahead of them.

When at last Elijah pedaled to a stop, Alice's legs were so tired she could barely stand without trembling. Buddy was nowhere in sight; she only hoped he could find his own way home, because she sure wasn't going to go looking for him. Not now, not with Elijah standing here, smiling at her, his eyes glittering. He leaned his bike up against a tree and hoisted his book bag over his shoulder.

"So where's your house?" she asked.

"It's that driveway there." He pointed down the road, to a mailbox rusting on a post.

"Aren't we going to your house?"

"Naw, my cousin's home sick today. She was throwing up all night, so let's not go in the house. Anyway, my project's out here, in the woods. Leave your bike. We're gonna have to walk."

She propped her bike up next to his and followed him, her legs still wobbly from the ride up the mountain. They tramped into woods. The trees were dense here, the ground thickly carpeted by leaves. Gamely she followed him, waving at mosquitoes. "So your cousin lives with you?" she asked.

"Yeah, she came to stay with us last year. I guess it's permanent now. Got nowhere else to go."

"Your parents don't mind?"

"It's just my dad. My mom's dead."

"Oh." She didn't know what to say about that. Finally murmured a simple "I'm sorry," but he didn't seem to hear her.

The undergrowth became thicker, and brambles scratched her bare legs. She had trouble keeping up with him. He was pulling ahead of her, leaving her with her skirt snagged on blackberry canes.

"Elijah!"

He didn't answer. He just kept moving ahead like a bold explorer, his book bag slung over his shoulder.

"Wait!"

"Do you want to see this or don't you?"

"Yes, but—"

"Then come *on.*" His voice had taken on an impatient edge and it startled her. He stood a few yards ahead, looking back at her, and she noticed that his hands were clenched into fists.

"Okay," she said meekly. "I'm coming."

A few yards farther, the woods suddenly opened up into a clearing. She saw an old stone foundation, all that remained of a long-gone farmhouse. Elijah glanced back at her, his face dappled by afternoon light.

"It's right here," he said.

"What is?"

He bent down and pulled aside two wooden boards, revealing a deep hole. "Take a look in there," he said. "I spent three weeks digging that."

Slowly she approached the pit and stared inside. The afternoon light was slanting low behind the trees, and the bottom of the hole was in shadow. She could make out a layer of dead leaves, which had accumulated at the bottom. A rope was curled over the side.

"Is this to trap a bear, or something?"

"It could. If I laid some branches over it, to hide the opening, I could catch a lot of things. Even a deer." He pointed into the hole. "Look, you see it?"

She leaned in closer. Something gleamed faintly in the shadows below; chips of white that peeked out from beneath the scattering of leaves.

"What is it?"

"That's my project." He reached for the rope and pulled.

At the bottom of the pit, leaves rustled, boiled up. Alice stared as the rope went taut, as Elijah hauled up something from the shadows. A basket. He pulled it out of the hole and set it on the ground. Brushing aside the leaves, he revealed what had gleamed white at the pit's bottom.

It was a small skull.

As he picked off the leaves, she saw clumps of black fur and spindly ribs. A knobby chain of spine. Leg bones as delicate as twigs.

"Isn't that something? It doesn't even smell anymore," he said. "Been down there almost seven months now. Last time I checked it, there was still some meat on it. Neat how even that disappears. It started to rot real fast after it got warm, back in May."

"What is it?"

"Can't you tell?"

"No."

Picking up the skull, he gave it a little twist, pulling it off the spine. She flinched as he thrust it toward her.

"Don't!" she squealed.

"Meow!"

"Elijah!"

"Well, you did ask what it was."

She stared at hollow eye sockets. "It's a cat?"

He pulled a grocery sack out of his book bag and began placing the bones in the sack.

"What are you going to do with the skeleton?"

"It's my science project. From kitty to skeleton in seven months."

"Where did you get the cat?"

"Found it."

"You just *found* a dead cat?"

He looked up. His blue eyes were smiling. But these were no longer Tony Curtis eyes anymore; these eyes scared her. "Who said it was dead?"

Her heart was suddenly pounding. She took a step back. "You know, I think I have to go home now."

"Why?"

"Homework. I've got homework."

He was on his feet now, had sprung there effortlessly. The smile was gone, replaced by a look of quiet expectation.

"I'll . . . see you at school," she said. She backed away, glancing left and right at woods that looked the same in every direction. Which way had they come from? Which way should she go?

"But you just got here, Alice," he said. He was holding something in his hand. Only as he raised it over his head did she see what it was.

A rock.

The blow sent her to her knees. She crouched in the dirt, her vision almost black, her limbs numb. She felt no pain, just dumb disbelief that he had hit her. She started to crawl, but could not see where she was going. Then he grabbed her ankles and yanked her backward. Her face scraped against the ground as he dragged her by her feet. She tried to kick free, tried to scream, but her mouth filled with dirt and twigs as he pulled her toward the pit. Just as her feet dropped over the edge, she grabbed a sapling and held on, her legs dangling into the hole.

"Let go, Alice," he said.

"Pull me up! Pull me up!"

"I said, let *go*." He lifted a rock and brought it down on her hand.

She shrieked and lost her grip. Slid feet-first into the hole, landing on a bed of dead leaves.

"Alice. Alice."

Stunned by the fall, she looked up at the circle of sky above, and saw the silhouette of his head, leaning forward, peering down at her.

"Why are you doing this?" she sobbed. *"Why?"*

"It's nothing personal. I just want to see how long it takes. Seven months for a kitty. How long do you think it'll take you?"

"You can't do this to me!"

"Bye-bye, Alice."

"Elijah! *Elijah!*"

The wooden boards slid across the opening, eclipsing the circle of light. Her last glimpse of sky vanished. This isn't real, she thought. This is a joke. He's just trying to scare me. He'll leave me down here for a few minutes, and then he'll come back and let me out. Of course he'll come back.

Then she heard something thud onto the well cover. *Rocks. He's piling rocks on top.*

She stood up and tried to climb out of the hole. Found a dry wisp of vine that immediately disintegrated in her hands. She clawed at the dirt, but could not find a handhold, could not pull herself even a few inches without sliding back. Her screams pierced the darkness.

"Elijah!" she shrieked.

Her only answer was stones thudding onto wood.

ONE

*Pesez le matin que vous n'irez peut-être
pas jusqu'au soir,
Et au soir que vous n'irez peut-être pas
jusqu'au matin.
Be aware every morning that you may not
last the day,
And every evening that you may not last the
night.*

—ENGRAVED PLAQUE IN THE
CATACOMBS OF PARIS

A row of skulls glared from atop a wall of intricately stacked femurs and tibias. Though it was June, and she knew the sun was shining on the streets of Paris sixty feet above her, Dr. Maura Isles felt chilled as she walked down the dim passageway, its walls lined almost to the ceiling with human remains. She was familiar, even intimate, with death, and had confronted its face countless times on her autopsy table, but she was stunned by the scale of this display, by the sheer number of bones stored in this network of tunnels beneath the City of Light. The one-kilometer tour took her through only a small section of the catacombs. Off-limits to tourists were numerous side tunnels and bone-filled chambers, their dark mouths gaping seductively behind locked gates. Here were the remains of six million Parisians who had once felt the sun on their faces, who had hungered and thirsted and loved, who had felt the beating of their own hearts in their chests, the rush of air in and out of their lungs. They could never have imagined that one day their bones would be unearthed from their cemetery resting places, and moved to this grim ossuary beneath the city.

That one day they would be on display, to be gawked at by hordes of tourists.

A century and a half ago, to make room for the steady influx of dead into Paris's overcrowded cemeteries, the bones had been disinterred and moved into the vast honeycomb of ancient limestone quarries that lay deep beneath the city. The workmen who'd transferred the bones had not carelessly tossed them into piles, but had performed their macabre task with flair, meticulously stacking them to form whimsical designs. Like fussy stonemasons, they had built high walls decorated with alternating layers of skulls and long bones, turning decay into an artistic statement. And they had hung plaques engraved with grim quotations, reminders to all who walked these passageways that Death spares no one.

One of the plaques caught Maura's eye, and she paused among the flow of tourists to read it. As she struggled to translate the words using her shaky high school French, she heard the incongruous sound of children's laughter echoing in the dim corridors, and the twang of a man's Texas accent as he muttered to his wife. "Can you believe this place, Sherry? Gives me the goddamn creeps . . ."

The Texas couple moved on, their voices fading into silence. For a moment Maura was alone in the chamber, breathing in the dust of the centuries. Under the dim glow of the tunnel light, mold had flourished on a cluster of skulls, coating them in a greenish cast. A single bullet hole gaped in the forehead of one skull, like a third eye.

I know how you died.

The chill of the tunnel had seeped into her own bones. But she did not move, determined to translate that plaque, to quell her horror by engaging in a useless intellectual puzzle. Come on, Maura. Three years of high school French, and you can't figure this out? It was a personal challenge now, all thoughts of mortality temporarily held at bay. Then the words took on meaning, and she felt her blood go cold . . .

Happy is he who is forever faced with the hour of his death
And prepares himself for the end every day.

Suddenly she noticed the silence. No voices, no echoing footsteps. She turned and left that gloomy chamber. How had she fallen so far behind the other tourists? She was alone in this tunnel, alone with the dead. She thought about unexpected power outages, about wandering the wrong way in pitch darkness. She'd heard of Parisian workmen a century ago who had lost their way in the catacombs and died of starvation. Her pace quickened as she sought to catch up with the others, to rejoin the company of the living. She felt Death pressing in too closely in these tunnels. The skulls seemed to stare back at her with resentment, a chorus of six million berating her for her ghoulish curiosity.

We were once as alive as you are. Do you think you can escape the future you see here?

When at last she emerged from the catacombs and stepped into the sunshine on Rue Remy Dumoncel, she took in deep breaths of air. For once she welcomed the noise of traffic, the press of the crowd, as if she had just been granted a second chance at life. The colors seemed brighter, the faces friendlier. My last day in Paris, she thought, and only now do I really appreciate the beauty of this city. She had spent most of the past week trapped in meeting rooms, attending the International Conference of Forensic Pathology. There had been so little time for sightseeing, and even the tours arranged by the conference organizers had been related to death and illness: the medical museum, the old surgical theater.

The catacombs.

Of all the memories to bring back from Paris, how ironic that her most vivid one would be of human remains. That's not healthy, she thought as she sat at an outdoor café, savoring one last cup of espresso and a strawberry tart. In two days, I'll be back in my autopsy room, surrounded by stainless steel, shut off from sunlight. Breathing only the cold, filtered air flowing from the vents. This day will seem like a memory of paradise.

She took her time, recording those memories. The smell of coffee, the taste of buttery pastry. The natty businessmen with cell phones pressed to their ears, the intricate knots of the scarves fluttering around women's throats. She entertained the fantasy that surely danced in the head of every American who had ever visited Paris: What would it be like to miss my plane? To just linger here, in this café, in this glorious city, for the rest of my life?

But in the end, she rose from her table and hailed a taxi to the airport. In the end she walked away from the fantasy, from

Paris, but only because she promised herself she would someday return. She just didn't know when.

Her flight home was delayed three hours. That's three hours I could have spent walking along the Seine, she thought as she sat disgruntled in Charles de Gaulle. Three hours I could have wandered the Marais or poked around in Les Halles. Instead she was trapped in an airport so crowded with travelers she could find no place to sit. By the time she finally boarded the Air France jet, she was tired and thoroughly cranky. One glass of wine with the in-flight meal was all it took for her to fall into a deep and dreamless sleep.

Only as the plane began its descent into Boston did she awaken. Her head ached, and the setting sun glared in her eyes. The headache intensified as she stood in baggage claim, watching suitcase after suitcase, none of them hers, slide down the ramp. It grew to a relentless pounding as she later waited in line to file a claim for her missing luggage. By the time she finally stepped into a taxi with only her carry-on bag, darkness had fallen, and she wanted nothing more than a hot bath and a hefty dose of Advil. She sank back in the taxi and once again drifted off to sleep.

The sudden braking of the vehicle awakened her.

"What's going on here?" she heard the driver say.

Stirring, she gazed through bleary eyes at flashing blue lights. It took a moment for her to register what she was looking at. Then she realized that they had turned onto the street where she lived, and she sat up, instantly alert, alarmed by what she saw. Four Brookline police cruisers were parked, their roof lights slicing through the darkness.

"Looks like some kind of emergency going on," the driver said. "This is your street, right?"

"And that's my house right down there. Middle of the block."

"Where all the police cars are? I don't think they're gonna let us through."

As if to confirm the taxi driver's words, a patrolman approached, waving at them to turn around.

The cabbie stuck his head out the window. "I got a passenger here I need to drop off. She lives on this street."

"Sorry, bud. This whole block's cordoned off."

Maura leaned forward and said to the driver, "Look, I'll just get out here." She handed him the fare, grabbed her carry-on bag, and stepped out of the taxi. Only moments before, she'd felt dull and groggy; now the warm June night itself seemed electric with tension. She started up the sidewalk, her sense of anxiety growing as she drew closer to the gathering of bystanders, as she saw all the official vehicles parked in front of her house. Had something happened to one of her neighbors? A host of terrible possibilities passed through her mind. Suicide. Homicide. She thought of Mr. Telushkin, the unmarried robotics engineer who lived next door. Hadn't he seemed particularly melancholy when she'd last seen him? She thought, too, of Lily and Susan, her neighbors on the other side, two lesbian attorneys whose gay rights activism made them high-profile targets. Then she spotted Lily and Susan standing at the edge of the crowd, both of them very much alive, and her concern flew back to Mr.

Telushkin, whom she did not see among the onlookers.

Lily glanced sideways and saw Maura approaching. She did not wave but just stared at her, wordless, and gave Susan a sharp nudge. Susan turned to look at Maura, and her jaw dropped open. Now other neighbors were turning to stare as well, all their faces registering astonishment.

Why are they looking at me? Maura wondered. What have I done?

"Dr. Isles?" A Brookline patrolman stood gaping at her. "It is—it is *you,* isn't it?" he asked.

Well, that was a stupid question, she thought. "That's my house, there. What's going on, officer?"

The patrolman huffed out a sharp breath. "Um—I think you'd better come with me."

He took her by the arm and led her through the crowd. Her neighbors solemnly parted before her, as though making way for a condemned prisoner. Their silence was eerie; the only sound was the crackle of police radios. They reached a barrier of yellow police tape, strung between stakes, several of them pounded into Mr. Telushkin's front yard. *He's proud of his lawn and he's not going to be happy about that,* was her immediate and utterly inane thought. The patrolman lifted the tape and she ducked under it, crossing into what she now realized was a crime scene.

She knew it was a crime scene because she spotted a familiar figure standing at the center of it. Even from across the lawn, Maura could recognize homicide detective Jane Rizzoli. Now eight months pregnant, the petite Rizzoli looked like a ripe pear in a pantsuit. Her presence was yet another bewildering detail. What was a Boston detective doing here in Brookline, outside her usual jurisdiction? Rizzoli did not see Maura approaching; her gaze was fixed instead on a car parked at the curb in front of Mr. Telushkin's house. She was shaking her head, clearly upset, her dark curls springing out in their usual disarray.

It was Rizzoli's partner, Detective Barry Frost, who spotted Maura first. He glanced at her, glanced away, and then did a sudden double take, his pale face whipping back to stare at her. Wordlessly he tugged on his partner's arm.

Rizzoli went absolutely still, the strobelike

flashes of blue cruiser lights illuminating her expression of disbelief. She began to walk, as though in a trance, toward Maura.

"Doc?" Rizzoli said softly. "Is that you?"

"Who else would it be? Why does everyone keep asking me that? Why do you all look at me as though I'm a ghost?"

"Because . . ." Rizzoli stopped. Gave a shake of her head, tossing unkempt curls. "Jesus. I thought for a minute you *were* a ghost."

"What?"

Rizzoli turned and called out: "Father Brophy?"

Maura had not seen the priest standing off by himself at the periphery. Now he emerged from the shadows, his collar a slash of white across his neck. His usually handsome face looked gaunt, his expression shell-shocked. *Why is Daniel here?* Priests were not usually called to crime scenes unless a victim's family requested counsel. Her neighbor Mr. Telushkin was not Catholic, but Jewish. He would have no reason to request a priest.

"Could you please take her into the house, Father?" Rizzoli said.

Maura asked: "Is anyone going to tell me what's going on?"

"Go inside, Doc. Please. We'll explain later."

Maura felt Brophy's arm slip around her waist, his firm grasp clearly communicating that this was not the time for her to resist. That she should simply obey the detective's request. She allowed him to guide her to her front door, and she registered the secret thrill of the close contact between them, the warmth of his body pressed against hers. She was so aware of him standing beside her that her hands were clumsy as she inserted the key into her front door. Though they had been friends for months, she had never before invited Daniel Brophy into her house, and her reaction to him now was a reminder of why she had so carefully maintained a distance between them. They stepped inside, into a living room where the lamps were already on, lit by automatic timers. She paused for a moment near the couch, uncertain of what to do next.

It was Father Brophy who took command.

"Sit down," he said, pointing her to the couch. "I'll get you something to drink."

"You're the guest in my house. I should be offering you the drink," she said.

"Not under the circumstances."

"I don't even know what the circumstances are."

"Detective Rizzoli will tell you." He left the room and came back with a glass of water—not exactly her beverage of choice at that moment, but then, it didn't seem appropriate to ask a priest to fetch the bottle of vodka. She sipped the water, feeling uneasy under his gaze. He sank into the chair across from her, watching her as though afraid she might vanish.

At last she heard Rizzoli and Frost come into the house, heard them murmuring in the foyer to a third person, a voice Maura didn't recognize. Secrets, she thought. Why is everyone keeping secrets from me? What don't they want me to know?

She looked up as the two detectives walked into the living room. With them was a man who introduced himself as Brookline Detective Eckert, a name she'd probably forget within five minutes. Her attention was completely focused on Rizzoli, with whom she had worked before. A woman she both liked and respected.

The detectives all settled into chairs, Rizzoli and Frost facing Maura across the coffee table. She felt outnumbered, four to one, everyone's gazes on her. Frost pulled out his notepad and pen. Why was he taking notes? Why did this feel like the start of an interrogation?

"How are you doing, Doc?" Rizzoli asked, her voice soft with concern.

Maura laughed at the trite question. "I'd be doing a lot better if I knew what was going on."

"Can I ask you where you've been tonight?"

"I just got home from the airport."

"Why were you at the airport?"

"I flew in from Paris. From Charles de Gaulle. It was a long flight, and I'm not in the mood for twenty questions."

"How long were you in Paris?"

"A week. I flew there last Wednesday." Maura thought she detected a note of accusation in Rizzoli's brusque questions, and her irritation was now building toward anger. "If you don't believe me, you can ask my secretary, Louise. She's the one who booked the flight for me. I was there for a meeting—"

"The International Conference of Forensic Pathology. Is that correct?"

Maura was taken aback. "You already know?"

"Louise told us."

They've been asking questions about me. Even before I got home, they were talking to my secretary.

"She told us your plane was supposed to land at five P.M. at Logan," said Rizzoli. "It's now nearly ten o'clock. Where've you been?"

"We had a late departure from Charles de Gaulle. Something about extra security checks. The airlines are so paranoid, we were lucky just to get off the ground three hours late."

"So your departure was three hours delayed."

"I just told you that."

"What time did you land?"

"I don't know. About eight thirty."

"It took you an hour and a half to get home from Logan?"

"My suitcase didn't show up. I had to file a claims form with Air France." Maura stopped, suddenly at her limit. "Look, goddamn it, what is this all about? Before I answer any more questions, I have a right to know. Are you accusing me of something?"

"No, Doc. We're not accusing you of anything. We're just trying to figure out the time frame."

"Time frame for what?"

Frost said, "Have you received any threats, Dr. Isles?"

She looked at him in bewilderment. "What?"

"Do you know anyone who might have reason to hurt you?"

"No."

"You're sure?"

Maura gave a frustrated laugh. "Well, is anyone *ever* sure?"

"You must have had a few cases in court where your testimony pissed off someone," said Rizzoli.

"Only if they're pissed off by the truth."

"You've made enemies in court. Perps you've helped convict."

"I'm sure you have too, Jane. Just by doing your job."

"Have you received any specific threats? Any letters or phone calls?"

"My phone number's unlisted. And Louise never gives out my address."

"What about letters sent to you at the medical examiner's office?"

"There's been the occasional weird letter. We all get them."

"Weird?"

"People writing about space aliens or conspiracies. Or accusing us of trying to cover up the truth about an autopsy. We just put those letters in the screwball file. Unless there's an overt threat, in which case we refer it to the police."

Maura saw Frost scribble in his notebook, and she wondered what he had written. By now she was so angry, she wanted to reach across the coffee table and snatch the notebook out of his hands.

"Doc," said Rizzoli quietly, "do you have a sister?"

The question, so out of the blue, startled Maura and she stared at Rizzoli, her irritation suddenly forgotten. "Excuse me?"

"Do you have a sister?"

"Why are you asking that?"

"I just need to know."

Maura released a sharp breath. "No, I don't have a sister. And you know that I'm adopted. When the hell are you going to tell me what this is all about?"

Rizzoli and Frost looked at each other.

Frost closed his notebook. "I guess it's time to show her."

Rizzoli led the way to the front door. Maura stepped outside, into a warm summer night that was lit up like a garish carnival by the flashing lights from the cruisers. Her body was still functioning on Paris time, where it was now four A.M., and she saw everything through a haze of exhaustion, the night as surreal as a bad dream. The instant she emerged from her house, all faces turned to stare at her. She saw her neighbors gathered across the street, watching her across the crime scene tape. As medical examiner, she was accustomed to being in the public eye, her every move followed by both police and media, but tonight the attention was somehow different. More intrusive, even frightening. She was glad to have Rizzoli and Frost flanking her, as though to shield her from curious eyes as they moved down the sidewalk, toward the dark Ford Taurus parked at the curb in front of Mr. Telushkin's house.

Maura did not recognize the car, but she

did recognize the bearded man standing beside it, his thick hands gloved in latex. It was Dr. Abe Bristol, her colleague from the M.E.'s office. Abe was a man of hearty appetites, and his girth reflected his love of rich foods, his belly spilling over his belt in flabby excess. He stared at Maura and said, "Christ, it's uncanny. Could've fooled me." He nodded toward the car. "I hope you're ready for this, Maura."

Ready for what?

She looked at the parked Taurus. Saw, backlit by the flashing lights, the silhouette of a figure slumped over the steering wheel. Black splatters obscured the windshield. *Blood.*

Rizzoli shone her flashlight on the passenger door. At first, Maura did not understand what she was supposed to be looking at; her attention was still focused on the blood-spattered window, and the shadowy occupant in the driver's seat. Then she saw what Rizzoli's Maglite beam was shining on. Just below the door handle were three parallel scratches, carved deep into the car's finish.

"Like a claw mark," said Rizzoli, curling her fingers as though to trace the scar.

Maura stared at the marks. Not a claw, she thought as a chill ran up her back. *A raptor's talon.*

"Come around to the driver's side," said Rizzoli.

Maura asked no questions as she followed Rizzoli around the rear of the Taurus.

"Massachusetts license plate," Rizzoli said, her flashlight beam sweeping across the rear bumper, but it was just a detail mentioned in passing; Rizzoli continued around to the driver's side of the car. There she paused and looked at Maura.

"This is what got us all so shook up," she said. She aimed her flashlight into the car.

The beam fell squarely on the woman's face, which stared toward the window. Her right cheek rested against the steering wheel; her eyes were open.

Maura could not speak. She gaped at the ivory skin, the black hair, the full lips, slightly parted, as though in surprise. She reeled backward, her limbs suddenly boneless, and she had the dizzying sense that she was floating away, her body no longer anchored to the earth. A hand grasped her arm, steadying her. It was Father Brophy, standing right behind her. She had not even noticed he was there.

Now she understood why everyone had been so stunned by her arrival. She stared at the corpse in the car, at the face illuminated by Rizzoli's flashlight beam.

It's me. That woman is me.

TWO

She sat on the couch, sipping vodka and soda, the ice cubes clattering in her glass. To hell with plain water; this shock called for sterner medicine, and Father Brophy had been understanding enough to mix her a strong drink, handing it to her without comment. It's not every day you see yourself dead. Not every day you walk onto a crime scene and encounter your lifeless doppelgänger.

"It's just a coincidence," she whispered. "The woman looks like me, that's all. A lot of women have black hair. And her face—how can you really see her face in that car?"

"I don't know, Doc," said Rizzoli. "The resemblance is pretty scary." She sank into the easy chair, groaning as the cushions swallowed up her heavily pregnant frame. Poor Rizzoli, thought Maura. Women who are eight months pregnant should not be dragging themselves through homicide investigations.

"Her hairstyle is different," said Maura.

"A little longer, that's all."

"I have bangs. She doesn't."

"Don't you think that's sort of a superficial detail? Look at her face. She could be your sister."

"Wait till we see her with more light. Maybe she won't look like me at all."

Father Brophy said, "The resemblance is there, Maura. We all saw it. She looks exactly like you."

"Plus, she's sitting in a car in your neighborhood," added Rizzoli. "Parked practically in front of your house. And she had this lying on the back seat." Rizzoli held up an evidence bag. Through the transparent plastic, Maura could see it contained an article torn from *The Boston Globe.* The headline was large enough for her to read it even from across the coffee table.

RAWLINS INFANT WAS BATTERED BABY, MEDICAL EXAMINER TESTIFIES.

"It's a photo of *you,* Doc," said Rizzoli.

"The caption says 'Medical Examiner Dr. Maura Isles leaves the courtroom after testifying in Rawlins trial.'" She looked at Maura. "The victim had this in her car."

Maura shook her head. "Why?"

"That's what we're wondering."

"The Rawlins trial—that was almost two weeks ago."

"Do you remember seeing that woman in the courtroom?"

"No. I've never seen her before."

"But she's obviously seen *you.* In the newspaper, anyway. And then she shows up here. Looking for you? Stalking you?"

Maura stared at her drink. The vodka was making her head float. Less than twenty-four hours ago, she thought, I was walking the streets of Paris. Enjoying the sunshine, savoring the scents drifting from the street cafés. How did I manage to take a wrong turn into this nightmare?

"Do you keep a firearm, Doc?" asked Rizzoli.

Maura stiffened. "What kind of question is that?"

"No, I'm not accusing you of anything. I just wondered if you have a way to defend yourself."

"I don't have a gun. I've seen the damage they can do to a human body, and I won't have one in my house."

"Okay. Just asking."

Maura took another sip of vodka, needing liquid courage before she asked the next question: "What do you know about the victim?"

Frost pulled out his notebook, flipping through it like some fussy clerk. In so many ways, Barry Frost reminded Maura of a mild-mannered bureaucrat with his pen always at the ready. "According to the driver's license in her purse, her name is Anna Jessop, age forty, with an address in Brighton. Vehicle registration matches the same name."

Maura's head lifted. "That's only a few miles from here."

"The residence is an apartment building. Her neighbors don't seem to know much about her. We're still trying to reach the landlady, to let us into the unit."

"Does the name Jessop ring any bells?" asked Rizzoli.

She shook her heard. "I don't know anyone by that name."

"Do you know anyone in Maine?"

"Why do you ask?"

"There was a speeding ticket in her purse. Looks like she got pulled over two days ago, driving south on the Maine Turnpike."

"I don't know anyone in Maine." Maura took a deep breath. Asked: "Who found her?"

"Your neighbor Mr. Telushkin made the call," said Rizzoli. "He was out walking his dog when he noticed the Taurus parked at the curb."

"When was that?"

"Around eight P.M."

Of course, thought Maura. Mr. Telushkin walked his dog at precisely the same time every night. Engineers were like that, precise and predictable. But tonight he had encountered the unpredictable.

"He didn't hear anything?" Maura asked.

"He said he'd heard what he thought was a car backfiring, maybe ten minutes before that. But no one saw it happen. After he found the Taurus, he called nine-one-one. Reported that someone had just shot his neighbor, Dr. Isles. Brookline Police responded first, along with Detective Eckert here. Frost and I arrived around nine."

"Why?" Maura said, finally asking a question that had occurred to her when she'd first spotted Rizzoli standing on her front lawn. "Why are you in Brookline? This isn't your beat."

Rizzoli glanced at Detective Eckert.

He said, a little sheepishly, "You know, we only had one homicide last year in Brookline. We thought, under the circumstances, it made sense to call in Boston."

Yes, it did make sense, Maura realized. Brookline was little more than a bedroom community trapped within the city of Boston. Last year, Boston PD had investigated sixty homicides. Practice made perfect, with murder investigations as well as anything else.

"We would have come in on this anyway," said Rizzoli. "After we heard who the victim was. Who we thought it was." She paused. "I have to admit, it never even occurred to me that it might *not* be you. I took one look at the victim and assumed . . ."

"We all did," said Frost.

There was a silence.

"We knew you were due to fly home this evening from Paris," said Rizzoli. "That's what your secretary told us. The only thing that didn't make sense to us was the car. Why you'd be sitting in a car registered to another woman."

Maura drained her glass and set it on the coffee table. One drink was all she could handle tonight. Already, her limbs were numb and she was having trouble focusing. The room had softened to a blur, the lamps casting everything in a warm glow. This is not real, she thought. I'm asleep in a jet somewhere over the Atlantic, and I'll wake up to find the plane has landed. That none of this has happened.

"We don't know anything yet about Anna Jessop," said Rizzoli. "All we do know— what we've all seen with our own eyes—is that whoever she is, she's a dead ringer for you, Doc. Maybe her hair's a little longer. Maybe there's a few differences here and there. But the point is, we were fooled. All of us. And we *know* you." She paused. "You can see where I'm going with this, can't you?"

Yes, Maura could, but she didn't want to say it. She just sat staring at the glass on the coffee table. At the melting ice cubes.

"If we were fooled, anyone else could have been as well," said Rizzoli. "Including whoever fired that bullet into her head. It was just before eight P.M. when your neighbor heard the backfire. Already getting dark. And there she was, sitting in a parked car just a few yards from your driveway. Anyone seeing her in that car would assume it's you."

"You think I was the target," said Maura.

"It makes sense, doesn't it?"

Maura shook her head. "None of this makes sense."

"You have a very public job. You testify at homicide trials. You're in the newspaper. You're our Queen of the Dead."

"Don't call me that."

"It's what all the cops call you. What the press calls you. You know that, don't you?"

"It doesn't mean I like that nickname. In fact, I can't stand it."

"But it does mean you're noticed. Not just because of what you do, but also because of the way you look. You know the guys notice you, don't you? You'd have to be blind not to see it. Nice-looking woman always gets their attention. Right, Frost?"

Frost gave a start, obviously not expecting to be put on the spot, and his cheeks reddened. Poor Frost, so easily caught in a blush. "It's only human nature," he admitted.

Maura looked at Father Brophy, who did not return her gaze. She wondered if he, too, was subject to the same laws of attraction. She wanted to think so; she wanted to believe that Daniel was not immune to the same thoughts that went through her head.

"Nice-looking woman in the public eye," said Rizzoli. "Gets stalked, attacked in front of her own residence. It's happened before. What was the name of that actress out in L.A.? The one who got murdered."

"Rebecca Schaefer," said Frost.

"Right. And then there's the Lori Hwang case here. You remember her, Doc."

Yes, Maura remembered it, because she had performed the autopsy on the Channel Six newscaster. Lori Hwang had been on the air only a year when she was shot to death in front of the studio. She'd never realized she was being stalked. The perp had been watching her on TV and had written a few fan letters. And then one day he had waited outside the studio doors. As Lori had stepped out and walked toward her car, he had fired a bullet into her head.

"That's the hazard of living in the public

eye," said Rizzoli. "You never know who's watching you on all those TV screens. You never know who's in the car right behind yours when you drive home from work at night. It's not something we even think about—that someone might be following us. Fantasizing about us." Rizzoli paused. Said, quietly: "I've been there. I know what it's like to be the focus of someone's obsession. I'm not even that much to look at, but it happened to me." She held out her hands, revealing the scars on her palms. The permanent souvenirs of her battle with the man who had twice almost taken her life. A man who still lived, though trapped in a quadriplegic's body.

"That's why I asked whether you'd received any strange letters," said Rizzoli. "I was thinking about her. Lori Hwang."

"Her killer was arrested," said Father Brophy.

"Yes."

"So you're not implying it's the same man."

"No, I'm just pointing out the parallels. A single gunshot wound to the head. Women in public jobs. It just makes you think." Rizzoli struggled to her feet. It took some effort to push herself out of the easy chair. Frost was quick to offer her his hand, but she ignored it. Though heavily pregnant, Rizzoli was not one to reach for assistance. She hoisted her purse over her shoulder and gave Maura a searching look. "Do you want to stay somewhere else tonight?"

"This is my house. Why would I go anywhere else?"

"Just asking. I guess I don't need to tell you to lock your doors."

"I always do."

Rizzoli looked at Eckert. "Can Brookline PD watch the house?"

He nodded. "I'll make sure a patrol car comes by every so often."

"I appreciate that," said Maura. "Thank you."

Maura accompanied the three detectives to the front door and watched them walk to their cars. It was now after midnight. Outside, the street had been transformed back into the quiet neighborhood she knew. The Brookline PD cruisers were gone; the Taurus had already been towed away to the crime lab. Even the yellow police tape had been removed. In the morning, she thought, I'll wake up and think I imagined the whole thing.

She turned and faced Father Brophy, who was still standing in her foyer. She had never felt more uneasy in his company than at this moment, the two of them alone in her house. The possibilities surely swirled in both their heads. *Or just mine? Late at night, alone in your bed, do you ever think of me, Daniel? The way I think of you?*

"Are you sure you feel safe staying here alone?" he asked.

"I'll be fine." *And what's the alternative? That you spend the night with me? Is that what you're offering?*

He turned toward the door.

"Who called you here, Daniel?" she asked. "How did you know?"

He looked back at her. "Detective Rizzoli did. She told me . . ." He paused. "You know, I get calls like this all the time from the police. A death in the family, someone needs a priest. I'm always willing to respond. But this time . . ." He paused. "Lock your doors, Maura," he said. "I don't ever want to go through another night like this one."

She watched him walk out of her house

and climb into his car. He did not immediately start the engine; he was waiting to make sure that she was safely inside for the night.

She closed the door and locked it.

Through the living room window, she watched Daniel drive away. For a moment she stared at the empty curb, feeling suddenly abandoned. Wishing, at that moment, that she could call him back. And what would happen then? What did she want to happen between them? Some temptations, she thought, are best kept beyond our reach. She scanned the dark street one last time, then stepped away from the window, aware that she was framed by the light in her living room. She closed the curtains and went from room to room, checking the locks and the windows. On this warm June night, she would normally sleep with her bedroom window open. But tonight, she left the windows closed and turned on the air conditioner.

In the early morning she awakened, shivering from the chill air blowing out the vent. Her dreams had been of Paris. Of strolling under blue skies, past buckets of roses and star-gazer lilies, and for a moment, she did not remember where she was. Not in Paris any longer, but in my own bed, she realized. And something terrible has happened.

It was only five A.M., yet she felt wide awake. It's eleven A.M. in Paris, she thought. There the sun is shining and if I were there now, I would already have had my second cup of coffee. She knew that jet lag would catch up with her later today, that this burst of early morning energy would be gone by afternoon, but she could not force herself to sleep any longer.

She rose and got dressed.

The street in front of her house looked the same as it always had. The first streaks of dawn lit the sky. She watched the lights come on in Mr. Telushkin's house next door. He was an early riser, usually heading off to work at least an hour before she did, but this morning, she'd been the first to awaken, and she saw her neighborhood with fresh eyes. Saw the automatic sprinklers come on across the street, water hissing circles on the lawn. She saw the paperboy cycle past, baseball cap turned backward, and heard the thump of *The Boston Globe* hitting her front porch. Everything seems the same, she thought, but it's not. Death has paid a visit to my neighborhood, and everyone who lives here will remember it. They will look out their front windows at the curb where the Taurus was parked, and shudder at how close it came to touching any one of us.

Headlights swung around the corner, and a vehicle drove along the street, slowing down as it approached her house. A Brookline police cruiser.

No, nothing is the same, she thought as she watched the cruiser drive past.

Nothing ever is.

She arrived at work before her secretary did. By six, Maura was at her desk, tackling the large stack of transcribed dictations and lab reports that had accumulated in her in-box during the week she had been at the Paris conference. She was already a third of the way through when she heard footsteps, and she looked up to see Louise standing in the doorway.

"You're here," Louise murmured.

Maura greeted her with a smile. *"Bonjour! I thought I'd get an early start on all this paperwork."*

Louise just stared at her for a moment, then she came into the room and sat down in the chair facing Maura's desk, as though she was suddenly too tired to stand. Though fifty years old, Louise always seemed to have twice the stamina of Maura, who was ten years younger. But this morning, Louise looked drained, her face thin and sallow under fluorescent lights.

"Are you all right, Dr. Isles?" Louise asked quietly.

"I'm fine. A little jet-lagged."

"I mean—after what happened last night. Detective Frost sounded so sure it was you, in that car . . ."

Maura nodded, her smile fading. "It was like being in the Twilight Zone, Louise. Coming home to find all those police cars in front of my house."

"It was awful. We all thought . . ." Louise swallowed and looked down at her lap. "I was so relieved when Dr. Bristol called me last night. To let me know it was a mistake."

There was a silence, heavy with reproach. It suddenly dawned on Maura that she should have been the one to call her own secretary. She should have realized that Louise was shaken, and would want to hear her voice. I've been living alone and unattached for so long, she thought, that it doesn't even occur to me that there are people in this world who might care what happens to me.

Louise stood up to leave. "I'm so glad to see you back, Dr. Isles. I just wanted to tell you that."

"Louise?"

"Yes?"

"I brought you a little something back from Paris. I know this sounds like a lame excuse, but it's packed in my suitcase. And the airline lost it."

"Oh." Louise laughed. "Well, if it's chocolate, my hips certainly don't need it."

"Nothing caloric, I promise." She glanced at the clock on her desk. "Is Dr. Bristol in yet?"

"He just got here. I saw him in the parking lot."

"Do you know when he's doing the autopsy?"

"Which one? He has two today."

"The gunshot from last night. The woman."

Louise gave her a long look. "I think that one is second on his schedule."

"Do they know anything more about her?"

"I don't know. You'll have to ask Dr. Bristol."

THREE

Although she had no autopsies on her own schedule that day, at two o'clock Maura headed downstairs and changed into a scrub suit. She was alone in the women's locker room, and she took her time removing her street clothes, folding her blouse and slacks and placing them in a tidy pile inside the locker. The scrubs felt crisp against her bare skin, like freshly laundered sheets, and she found comfort in the familiar routine of tightening the trouser drawstrings and tucking her hair into a cap. She felt contained and protected by laundered cotton, and by the role she donned along with the uniform. She glanced in the mirror, at a reflection as cool as a stranger's, all emotions shielded from sight. She left the locker room, walked down the hall, and pushed into the autopsy suite.

Rizzoli and Frost were already standing beside the table, both of them gowned and gloved, their backs obstructing Maura's view of the victim. It was Dr. Bristol who first spotted Maura. He stood facing her, his generous girth filling the extra-large surgical gown, and he met her gaze as she entered the room. His eyebrows pinched into a frown above the surgical mask, and she saw the question in his eyes.

"I thought I'd drop in to watch this one," she said.

Now Rizzoli turned to look at her. She, too, was frowning. "Are you sure you want to be here?"

"Wouldn't you be curious?"

"But I'm not sure I'd want to watch. Considering."

"I'm just going to observe. If that's okay with you, Abe."

Bristol shrugged. "Well hell, I guess I'd be curious, too," he said. "Join the party."

She moved around to Abe's side of the table and at her first unobstructed view of the corpse, her throat went dry. She had seen her share of horrors in this lab, had gazed at flesh in every stage of decay, at bodies so damaged by fire or trauma that the remains could scarcely be categorized as human. The woman on the table was, in the scope of her experience, remarkably intact. The blood had been washed away, and the bullet's entry wound, in the left scalp, was obscured by her dark hair. The face was undamaged, the torso marred only by dependent mottling of the skin. There were fresh puncture marks in the groin and neck, where the morgue assistant Yoshima had drawn blood for lab tests, but the torso was otherwise untouched; Abe's scalpel had yet to make a single slice. Had the chest already been split open, the cavity exposed, the body would have struck her as a far less disturbing sight. Opened corpses are anonymous. Hearts and lungs and spleens are merely organs, so lacking in individuality that they can be transplanted, like spare auto parts, between bodies. But this woman was still whole, her features startlingly recognizable. Last night, Maura had seen the corpse fully clothed and in shadow, lit only by the beam of Rizzoli's Maglite. Now the features were harshly lit by autopsy lamps, the clothes stripped off to reveal the naked torso, and those features were more than merely familiar.

Dear god, that's my own face, my own body, on the table.

Only she knew just how close the resemblance was. No one else in that room would have seen the shape of Maura's bare breasts, the curve of her thighs. They knew only what she allowed them to see, her face, her hair. They could not possibly know that the similarities between her and this corpse were as intimate as the flecks of reddish brown in the pubic hair.

Maura looked at the woman's hands, the fingers long and slender like her own. A pianist's hands. The fingers had already been inked. Skull and dental X-rays had been completed as well; the dental panograph was now displayed on the light box, two white rows of teeth glowing in a Cheshire cat's grin. Is that how my X-rays would look? she wondered. Are we the same, right down to the enamel on our teeth?

She asked, in a voice that struck her as unnaturally calm, "Have you learned anything else about her?"

"We're still checking on that name, Anna

Jessop," said Rizzoli. "All we have so far is that Massachusetts driver's license, issued four months ago. It says she's forty years old. Five foot seven, black hair, green eyes. A hundred twenty pounds." Rizzoli eyed the corpse on the table. "I'd say she fits that description."

So do I, thought Maura. I'm forty years old and five foot seven. Only the weight is different; I weigh a hundred twenty-five. But what woman doesn't lie about her weight on her driver's license?

She watched, wordless, as Abe completed his surface exam. He jotted occasional notations on the preprinted diagram of a female body. Bullet wound in the left temple. Dependent mottling of the lower torso and thighs. Appendectomy scar. Then he set down the clipboard and moved to the foot of the table to collect vaginal swabs. As he and Yoshima rotated the thighs to expose the perineum, it was the corpse's abdomen that Maura focused on. She stared at the appendectomy scar, a thin white line tracing across ivory skin.

I have one, too.

Swabs collected, Abe moved to the instrument tray and picked up the scalpel.

The first cut was almost unbearable to watch. Maura actually lifted her hand to her chest, as though she could feel the blade slice into her own flesh. This was a mistake, she thought as Abe made his Y incision. I don't know if I can watch this. But she remained rooted to her spot, trapped by appalled fascination as she saw Abe reflect back the skin from the chest wall, swiftly peeling it away as though skinning game. He worked unaware of her horror, his attention focused only on the task of opening up the torso. An efficient pathologist can complete an uncomplicated autopsy in under an hour, and at this stage of the postmortem, Abe wasted no time on needlessly elegant dissection. Maura had always thought Abe a likable man, with his hearty appetite for food and drink and opera, but at this moment, with his bulging abdomen and his neck thick as a bull's, he looked like a fat butcher, his knife tearing through flesh.

The skin of the chest was now flayed open, the breasts concealed beneath the peeled-back flaps, the ribs and muscles exposed. Yoshima leaned forward with pruning shears and cut through the ribs. Each snap made Maura wince. How easily a human bone is cracked, she thought. We think of our hearts as protected within a sturdy cage of ribs, yet all it takes is the squeeze of a handle, the scissoring of blades, and one by one, the ribs surrender to tempered steel. We are made of such fragile material.

Yoshima snipped through the last bone, and Abe sliced the last strands of gristle and muscle. Together they removed the breastplate, as though lifting off the lid of a box.

Inside the open thorax, the heart and lungs glistened. Young organs, was Maura's first thought. But no, she realized; forty years old wasn't so young, was it? It was not easy to acknowledge that, at age forty, she was at the halfway mark in her life. That she, like this woman on the table, could no longer be considered young.

The organs she saw in the open chest appeared normal, without obvious signs of pathology. With a few swift cuts, Abe excised the lungs and heart and placed them in a metal basin. Under bright lights he made a few slices to view the lung parenchyma.

"Not a smoker," he said to the two detectives. "No edema. Nice healthy tissue."

Except for the fact it was dead.

He dropped the lungs back into the basin, where they formed a pink mound, and he picked up the heart. It rested easily in his massive hand. Maura was suddenly aware of her own heart, thumping in her chest. Like this woman's heart, it would fit in Abe's palm. She felt a twinge of nausea at the thought of him holding it, turning it over to inspect the coronary vessels as he was doing now. Though mechanically just a pump, the heart sits at the very core of one's body, and to see this one so exposed to view made her own chest feel hollow. She took a breath, and the scent of blood made her nausea worse. She turned away from the corpse and found herself meeting Rizzoli's gaze. Rizzoli, who saw too much. They had known each other almost two years now, had worked enough cases together to have developed the highest regard for each other as professionals. But along with that regard came a measure of respectful wariness. Maura knew just how acute were Rizzoli's instincts, and as they looked at each other across the table, she knew that the other woman must surely see how close Maura was to bolting from the room. At the unspoken question in Rizzoli's eyes, Maura simply squared her jaw. The Queen of the Dead reasserted her invincibility.

She focused, once again, on the corpse.

Abe, oblivious to the undercurrent of tension in the room, had sliced open the heart's chambers. "Valves all look normal," he commented. "Coronaries are soft. Clean vessels. Geez, I hope my heart looks this good."

Maura glanced at his enormous belly and doubted it, knowing his passion for foie gras and buttery sauces. Enjoy life while you can, was Abe's philosophy. Indulge your appetites now, because we all end up, sooner or later, like our friends on the table. What good are clean coronaries if you've lived a life deprived of pleasures?

He set the heart in the basin and went to work on the contents of the abdomen, his scalpel slicing deep, through peritoneum. Out came the stomach and liver, spleen and pancreas. The odor of death, of chilled organs, was familiar to Maura, yet this time so disturbing. As if she was experiencing an autopsy for the very first time. No longer the jaded pathologist, she watched Abe cut with scissors and knife, and the brutality of the procedure appalled her. Dear god, this is what I do every day, but when my scalpel cuts, it's through the unfamiliar flesh of strangers.

This woman does not feel like a stranger.

She slipped into a numb void, watching Abe work as though from a distance. Fatigued by her restless night, by jet lag, she felt herself recede from the scene unfolding on the table, retreating to some safer vantage point from which she could watch with dulled emotions. It was just a cadaver on the table. No connection, no one she knew. Abe quickly freed the small intestines and dropped the coils into the basin. With scissors and kitchen knife, he gutted the abdomen, leaving only a hollow shell. He carried the basin, now heavy with entrails, to the stainless steel countertop, where he lifted out the organs one by one for closer examination.

On the cutting board, he slit open the stomach and drained the contents into a smaller basin. The smell of undigested food made Rizzoli and Frost turn away, their faces grimacing in disgust.

"Looks like the remains of supper here,"

said Abe. "I'd say she had a seafood salad. I see lettuce and tomatoes. Maybe shrimp . . ."

"How close to the time of death was her last meal?" asked Rizzoli. Voice oddly nasal, her hand over her face, blocking the smells.

"An hour, maybe more. I'm guessing she ate out, since seafood salad's not the kind of meal I'd fix for myself at home." Abe glanced at Rizzoli. "You find any restaurant receipts in her purse?"

"No. She could've paid cash. We're still waiting for her credit card info."

"Jesus," said Frost, still averting his gaze. "This just about kills any appetite I ever had for shrimp."

"Hey, you can't let that bother you," said Abe, now slicing into the pancreas. "When you get right down to it, we're all made up of the same basic building blocks. Fat, carbohydrates, and protein. You eat a juicy steak, you're eating muscle. You think I'd ever swear off steak, just because that's the tissue I dissect every day? All muscle has the same biochemical ingredients, but sometimes it just smells better than at other times." He reached for the kidneys. Made neat slices into each, and dropped small tissue samples into a jar of formalin. "So far, everything looks normal," he said. He glanced at Maura. "You agree?"

She gave a mechanical nod but said nothing, suddenly distracted by the new set of X-rays that Yoshima was now hanging on the light box. They were skull films. On the lateral view, the outline of soft tissue could be seen, like a semitransparent ghost of a face in profile.

Maura crossed to the light box and stared at the star-shaped density, startlingly bright against the softer shadow of bone. It had lodged up against the skull table. The bullet's deceptively small entrance wound in the scalp gave little indication of the damage this devastating projectile could do to the human brain.

"Jesus," she murmured. "It's a Black Talon bullet."

Abe glanced up from the basin of organs. "Haven't seen one of those in a while. We'll have to be careful. Metal tips on that bullet are razor-sharp. They'll cut right through your glove." He looked at Yoshima, who had worked at the M.E.'s office longer than any of the current pathologists, and who served as their institutional memory.

"When's the last time we had a vic come in with a Black Talon?"

"I'd guess it was about two years ago," said Yoshima.

"That recent?"

"I remember Dr. Tierney had the case."

"Can you ask Stella to look it up? See if that case got closed. Bullet's unusual enough to make you wonder about any linkage."

Yoshima stripped off his gloves and went to the intercom to buzz Abe's secretary. "Hello, Stella? Dr. Bristol would like a search for the last case involving a Black Talon bullet. It would have been Dr. Tierney's . . ."

"I've heard of them," said Frost, who'd moved to the light box for a closer look at the X-ray. "First time I've had a vic with one."

"It's a hollow point, manufactured by Winchester," said Abe. "Designed to expand and cut through soft tissue. When it penetrates flesh, the copper jacket peels open to form a six-pointed star. Each tip's as sharp as a claw." He moved to the corpse's head. "They were taken off the market in '93, after some nut out in San

Francisco used them to kill nine people in a mass shooting. Winchester got such bad publicity, they decided to stop production. But there are still a few out there in circulation. Every so often, one'll turn up in a vic, but they're getting pretty rare."

Maura's gaze was still on the X-ray, on that lethal white star. She thought of what Abe had just said: *Each tip's as sharp as a claw.* And she remembered the scratch marks left on the victim's car. *Like the claw mark of a raptor's talon.*

She turned back to the table, just as Abe completed his scalp incision. In that brief instant, before he peeled the skin flap forward, Maura found herself unavoidably staring at the dead woman's face. Death had mottled the lips to a dusky blue. The eyes were open, the exposed corneas dry and clouded by exposure to air. The eye's bright gleam during life is merely the light's reflection off moist corneas; when the lids no longer blink, when the cornea is no longer bathed in fluid, the eyes turn dry and dull. It's not the departure of the soul that drains the appearance of life from one's eyes; it's simply the cessation of the blink reflex. Maura gazed down at the two clouded bands across the cornea, and for an instant she imagined the eyes as they must have looked while alive. It was a startling glimpse into the mirror. She had the sudden, vertiginous thought that in fact *she* was the one lying on the table. That she was watching her own corpse being autopsied. Didn't ghosts linger in the same places they frequented while alive? This is my haunt, she thought. The autopsy lab. This is where I'm doomed to spend eternity.

Abe peeled the scalp forward and the face collapsed like a rubber mask.

Maura shuddered. Looking away, she noticed that Rizzoli was once again watching her. *Is she looking at me? Or at my ghost?*

The whir of the Stryker saw seemed to drill straight into her marrow. Abe cut through the dome of exposed skull, preserving the segment where the bullet had punched through. Gently, he pried off and removed the cap of bone. The Black Talon tumbled out of the open cranium and clattered into the basin Yoshima was holding beneath it. It gleamed there, its metal points splayed open like the petals of a lethal blossom.

The brain was mottled with dark blood.

"Extensive hemorrhage, both hemispheres. Just what you'd expect from the X-rays," Abe said. "The bullet entered here, left temporal bone. But it didn't exit. You can see it there, in the films." He pointed to the light box, where the bullet stood out as a bright starburst, resting against the inner curve of the left occipital bone.

Frost said, "Funny how it ended up on the same side of the skull it entered."

"There was probably ricochet. The bullet punched into the cranium and bounced back and forth, slicing through brain. Expending all its energy on the soft tissue. Like spinning the blades of a blender."

"Dr. Bristol?" It was his secretary, Stella, on the intercom.

"Yeah?"

"I found that case with the Black Talon. Victim's name was Vassily Titov. Dr. Tierney did the autopsy."

"Who was the detective on that case?"

"Um . . . here it is. Detectives Vann and Dunleavy."

"I'll check with them," said Rizzoli. "See what they remember about it."

"Thanks, Stella," called Bristol. He looked

at Yoshima, who had the camera ready. "Okay, snap away."

Yoshima began to take photos of the exposed brain, capturing a permanent record of its appearance before Abe removed it from its bony house. Here is where a lifetime's worth of memories were laid down, Maura thought, as she gazed at the glistening folds of gray matter. The ABC's of childhood. Four times four is sixteen. The first kiss, the first lover, the first heartbreak. All are deposited, as packets of messenger RNA, into this complex collection of neurons. Memory was merely biochemistry, yet it defined each human being as an individual.

With a few nicks of the scalpel, Abe freed the brain and carried it in both hands, as though bearing treasure, to the countertop. He would not dissect it today; instead he would let it soak in a basin of fixative, to be sectioned later. But he needed no microscopic examination to see the evidence of trauma; it was there, in the bloody discoloration on the surface.

"So we've got the entrance wound here, in the left temple," said Rizzoli.

"Yes, and the skin hole and cranial hole line up perfectly," said Abe.

"That's consistent with a straight shot into the side of the head."

Abe nodded. "The perp probably pointed right through the driver's window. And the window was open, so there was no glass to distort the trajectory."

"So she's just sitting there," said Rizzoli. "Warm night. Window down. Eight o'clock, it's getting dark. And he walks up to her car. Just points the gun and fires." Rizzoli shook her head. "Why?"

"Didn't take the purse," said Abe.

"So not a robbery," said Frost.

"Which leaves us with a crime of passion. Or a hit." Rizzoli glanced at Maura. There it was again—that possibility of a targeted killing.

Did he hit the right target?

Abe suspended the brain in a bucket of formalin. "No surprises so far," he said, as he turned to perform the neck dissection.

"You'll be running tox screens?" asked Rizzoli.

Abe shrugged. "We can send one off, but I'm not sure it's necessary. The cause of death is right up there." He nodded toward the light box, where the bullet stood out against the cranial shadow. "You have any reason to want a tox screen? Did CST find any drugs or paraphernalia in the car?"

"Nothing. The car was pretty tidy. I mean, except for the blood."

"And all of it is from the victim?"

"It's all B positive, anyway."

Abe glanced at Yoshima. "You typed our gal yet?"

Yoshima nodded. "It matches. She's B positive."

No one was looking at Maura. No one saw her chin snap up, or heard her sharp intake of breath. Abruptly she turned so they could not see her face, and she untied her mask, pulling it off with a brisk tug.

As she crossed to the trash can, Abe called out: "You bored with us already, Maura?"

"This jet lag is getting to me," she said, shrugging off the gown. "I think I'm going to go home early. I'll see you tomorrow, Abe."

She fled the lab without a backward glance.

The drive home went by in a blur. Only as she reached the outskirts of Brookline did her brain suddenly unlock. Only then did she break out of the obsessive loop of thoughts that kept playing in her head. *Don't think about the autopsy. Put it out of your mind. Think about dinner, about anything but what you saw today.*

She stopped at the grocery store. Her refrigerator was empty, and unless she wanted to eat tuna and frozen peas tonight, she needed to shop. It was a relief to focus on something else. She threw items into her cart with manic urgency. Far safer to think about food, about what she would cook for the rest of the week. *Stop thinking about blood spatters and women's organs in steel basins. I need grapefruits and apples. And don't those eggplants look good?* She picked up a bundle of fresh basil and greedily inhaled its scent, grateful that its pungency swept away, if only for the moment, all the remembered smells of the autopsy lab. A week of bland French meals had left her starved for spices; tonight, she thought, I'll cook a Thai green curry so hot it will burn my mouth.

At home she changed into shorts and a T-shirt and threw herself into preparing dinner. Sipped chilled white Bordeaux as she sliced chicken and onions and garlic. The steamy fragrance of jasmine rice filled the kitchen. No time to think of B positive blood and black-haired women; the oil's smoking in the pot. Time to sauté the chicken, add the curry paste. Pour in the can of coconut milk. She covered the pot to let it simmer. Looked up at the kitchen window and suddenly caught a reflection of herself in the glass.

I look like her. Exactly like her.

A chill swept through her, as though the face in the window was not a reflection, but a phantom staring back. The lid on the pot rattled from the rising steam. Ghosts trying to get out. Desperate to get her attention.

She turned off the burner, crossed to the telephone, and dialed a pager number she knew by heart.

A moment later, Jane Rizzoli called. In the background, Maura could hear a phone ringing. So Rizzoli was not at home yet, but probably sitting at her desk in Schroeder Plaza.

"I'm sorry to bother you," said Maura. "But I need to ask you something."

"Are you okay?"

"I'm fine. I just want to know one more thing about her."

"Anna Jessop?"

"Yes. You said she had a Massachusetts driver's license."

"That's right."

"What's the birth date on her license?"

"What?"

"Today, in the autopsy lab, you said she was forty years old. What day was she born?"

"Why?"

"Please. I just need to know."

"Okay. Hold on."

Maura heard the shuffling of pages, then Rizzoli came back on the line. "According to that license, her birthday's November twenty-fifth."

For a moment, Maura did not say anything.

"You still there?" asked Rizzoli.

"Yes."

"What's the problem, Doc? What's going on?"

Maura swallowed. "I need you to do something for me, Jane. It's going to sound crazy."

"Try me."

"I want the crime lab to run my DNA against hers."

Over the line, Maura heard the other telephone finally stop ringing. Rizzoli said, "Tell me that again. Because I don't think I heard you right."

"I want to know if my DNA matches Anna Jessop's."

"Look, I agree there's a strong resemblance—"

"There's more."

"What else are you talking about?"

"We both have the same blood type. B positive."

Rizzoli said, reasonably: "How many other people have B positive? It's like, what? Ten percent of the population?"

"And her birthday. You said her birthday's November twenty-fifth. Jane, so is mine."

That news brought dead silence. Rizzoli said softly: "Okay, you just made the hairs on the back of my arms stand up."

"You see why I want it, now? Everything about her—from the way she looks, to her blood type, to her date of birth . . ." Maura paused. "She's *me*. I want to know where she comes from. I want to know who that woman is."

A long pause. Then Rizzoli said, "Answering that question is turning out to be a lot harder than we thought."

"Why?"

"We got back a credit report on her this afternoon. Found out that her MasterCard account is only six months old."

"So?"

"Her driver's license is four months old. The plates on her car were issued only three months ago."

"What about her residence? She had an address in Brighton, right? You must have spoken to her neighbors."

"We finally got hold of the landlady late last night. She says she rented it out to Anna Jessop three months ago. She let us into the apartment."

"And?"

"It's empty, Doc. Not a stick of furniture, not a frying pan, not a toothbrush. Someone had paid for cable TV and a phone line, but no one was there."

"What about the neighbors?"

"Never saw her. They called her 'the ghost.'"

"There must be some prior address. Another bank account—"

"We've looked. We can't find *anything* on this woman that dates back earlier."

"What does that mean?"

"It means," said Rizzoli, "that until six months ago, Anna Jessop didn't exist."

FOUR

When Rizzoli walked into J. P. Doyle's, she found the usual suspects gathered around the bar. Cops, most of them, trading the day's war stories over beer and peanuts. Located right down the street from Boston PD's Jamaica Plain substation, Doyle's was probably the safest watering hole in the city. Make one false move, and a dozen cops would be on you like a New England Patriots' pile-on. She knew this crowd, and they all knew her. They parted to let the pregnant lady through, and she saw a few grins as she waddled in among them, her belly leading the way like a ship's prow.

"Geez, Rizzoli," someone called out. "You putting on weight or what?"

"Yeah." She laughed. "But unlike you, I'll be skinny by August."

She made her way toward Detectives Vann and Dunleavy, who were waving at her from the bar. Sam and Frodo—that's what everyone called the pair. The fat Hobbit and the skinny one, partners so long they acted like an old married couple, and probably spent more time with each other than they did with their wives. Rizzoli seldom saw the two apart, and she figured it was only a matter of time before they started dressing in matching outfits.

They grinned and saluted her with identical pints of Guinness.

"Hey, Rizzoli," said Vann.

"—you're late," said Dunleavy.

"Already on our second round—"

"—You want one?"

Jesus, they even finished each other's sentences. "It's too noisy in here," she said. "Let's go in the other room."

They headed into the dining area, toward her usual booth beneath the Irish flag. Dunleavy and Vann slid in opposite her, sitting cozily side by side. She thought of her own partner, Barry Frost, a nice guy, even a swell guy, but with whom she had absolutely nothing in common. At the end of the day, she went her way, Frost went his. They liked each other well enough, but she didn't think she could stand much more togetherness than that. Certainly not as much as these two guys.

"So you've got yourself a Black Talon vic," said Dunleavy.

"Last night, out in Brookline," she said. "First Talon since your case. That was what, two years ago?"

"Yeah, about."

"Closed?"

Dunleavy gave a laugh. "Nailed tight as a coffin."

"Who was the shooter?"

"Guy named Antonin Leonov. Ukrainian immigrant, two-bit player, trying to go big league. Russian mob would've taken him out eventually, if we hadn't arrested him first."

"What a moron," snorted Vann. "He had no idea we were watching him."

"Why were you?" she asked.

"We got a tip he was expecting a delivery from Tajikistan," said Dunleavy. "Heroin. Big one. We were on his tail for almost a week, and he never spotted us. So we follow him to his partner's house. Vassily Titov. Titov must've pissed off Leonov or something. We watch as Leonov goes into Titov's house. Then we hear gunshots, and Leonov comes back out."

"And we're waiting for him," said Vann. "Like I said, a moron."

Dunleavy raised his Guinness in a toast. "Open and shut. Perp's caught with the weapon. We're there to witness it. Don't know why he even bothered to plead innocent. Took the jury less than an hour to come back with the verdict."

"Did he ever tell you how he got hold of those Black Talons?" she asked.

"You kidding?" said Vann. "He wouldn't tell us anything. Hardly spoke any English, but he sure as hell knew the word *Miranda.*"

"We brought a team in to search his house and business," said Dunleavy. "Found, like, eight boxes of Black Talons stored in his warehouse, can you believe it? Don't know how he got his hands on so many, but he had quite a stash." Dunleavy shrugged. "So that's the scoop on Leonov. I don't see how he connects with your shooting."

"There've been only two Black Talon

shootings here in five years," she said. "Your case and mine."

"Yeah, well, there's probably a few bullets still floating around out there on the black market. Hell, check eBay. All I know is, we nailed Leonov, and good." Dunleavy downed his pint. "You've got yourself a different shooter."

Something she had already concluded. A feud between small-time Russian mobsters two years ago did not seem relevant to the murder of Anna Jessop. That Black Talon bullet was a dead link.

"You'll lend me that file on Leonov?" she asked. "I still want to look it over."

"On your desk tomorrow."

"Thanks, guys." She slid out of the booth and hauled herself to her feet.

"So when're you popping?" asked Vann, nodding at her belly.

"Not soon enough."

"The guys, they have a bet going, you know. On the baby's sex."

"You're kidding."

"I think we're up to seventy bucks it's a girl, forty bucks it's a boy."

Vann giggled. "And twenty bucks," he said, "is on *other.*"

* * *

Rizzoli felt the baby give a kick as she let herself into her apartment. Settle down in there, Junior, she thought. It's bad enough you treated me like a punching bag all day; now you're going to keep it up all night as well? She didn't know if she was carrying a boy, girl, or other; all she knew was that this kid was eager to be born.

Just stop trying to kung-fu your way out, okay?

She threw her purse and keys on the kitchen counter, kicked off her shoes by the door, and tossed her blazer over a dining room chair. Two days ago her husband, Gabriel, had left for Montana as part of an FBI team investigating a paramilitary weapons cache. Now the apartment was sliding back into the same comfortable anarchy that had reigned here before their marriage. Before Gabriel had moved in and instilled some semblance of discipline. Leave it to an ex-Marine to rearrange your pots and pans in order of size.

In the bedroom, she caught a glimpse of her reflection in the mirror. She scarcely recognized herself, apple-cheeked and sway-backed, her belly bulging beneath maternity stretch pants. When did I disappear? she thought. Am I still there, hidden somewhere in that distorted body? She confronted that stranger's reflection, remembering how flat her belly had once been. She did not like the way her face had plumped up, the way her cheeks had turned as rosy as a child's. The glow of pregnancy, Gabriel had called it, trying to reassure his wife that she did not, in fact, look like a shiny-nosed whale. That woman there is not really me, she thought. That's not the cop who can kick down doors and blow away perps.

She flopped on her back onto the bed and spread both arms across the mattress like a bird taking flight. She could smell Gabriel's scent in the sheets. I miss you tonight, she thought. This was not the way marriage was supposed to be. Two careers, two work-obsessed people. Gabriel on the road, her alone in this apartment. But she'd known, going into it, that it would not be easy. That there'd be too many nights like this one, when his job, or hers, would keep them apart. She thought of calling him again, but they had already talked twice that morning, and Verizon was stealing enough of her paycheck as it was.

Oh, what the hell.

She rolled sideways, pushed herself off the bed, and was about to reach for the phone on the nightstand when it suddenly rang. Startled, she looked at the caller ID readout. An unfamiliar number—not Gabriel's.

She picked up the receiver. "Hello?"

"Detective Rizzoli?" a man asked.

"Yes it is."

"I apologize for the late hour. I just got back into town this evening, and—"

"Who's calling, please?"

"Detective Ballard, Newton PD. I understand you're lead investigator on that shooting last night, out in Brookline. A victim named Anna Jessop."

"Yes, I am."

"Last year, I caught a case here. It involved a woman named Anna Jessop. I don't know if it's the same person, but—"

"You said you're with Newton PD?"

"Yes."

"Could you identify Ms. Jessop? If you viewed the remains?"

A pause. "I think I need to. I need to be sure it's her."

"And if it is?"

"Then I know who killed her."

Even before Detective Rick Ballard pulled out his ID, Rizzoli could have guessed the man was a cop. As she walked into the reception area of the M.E.'s building, he immediately rose to his feet, as though at attention. His eyes were a direct and crystalline blue, his brown hair clipped in a conservative cut, and his shirt was pressed with military neatness. He had the same quiet air of command that Gabriel possessed, the same rock-solid gaze that seemed to say, *In a pinch, you can count on me.* He made her wish, just for an instant, that she was slim-waisted again, and attractive. As they shook hands, as she looked at his ID, she felt him studying her face.

Definitely a cop, she thought.

"You ready to do this?" she asked. When he nodded, she glanced at the receptionist. "Is Dr. Bristol downstairs?"

"He's finishing up an autopsy right now. He said you can meet him down there."

They took the elevator to the basement level and walked into the morgue anteroom, where cabinets held supplies of shoe covers and masks and paper caps. Through the large viewing window they could see into the autopsy lab, where Dr. Bristol and Yoshima were at work on a gaunt, gray-haired man. Bristol spotted them through the glass and he waved in greeting.

"Ten minutes more!" he said.

Rizzoli nodded. "We'll wait."

Bristol had just made the scalp incision. Now he peeled the scalp forward over the cranium, collapsing the face.

"I always hate this part," said Rizzoli. "When they start messing with the face. The rest, I can handle."

Ballard didn't say anything. She looked at him and saw that his back was now rigid, his face grimly stoic. Since he was not a homicide detective, he probably did not make many visits to the morgue, and the procedure now going on beyond that window must surely strike him as appalling. She remembered the first visit she'd ever made here as a police cadet. She'd been part of a group from the academy, the only woman among the six brawny cadets, and the men had all towered over her. Everyone had expected the girl to be the squeamish one, that she'd be the one who'd turn away during the autopsy. But she had planted herself front and center, had watched the entire procedure without flinching. It was one of the men, the most strapping among them, who had paled and stumbled off to a nearby chair. She wondered if Ballard was about to do the same. Under fluorescent lights, his skin had taken on a sickly pallor.

In the autopsy room, Yoshima began sawing the cranium open. The whir of blade against bone seemed to be more than Ballard could deal with. He turned from the window, fixing his gaze instead on the boxes of gloves stacked up in various sizes on the shelf. Rizzoli actually felt a little sorry for him. It had to be humiliating when you were a tough-looking guy like Ballard, to let a girl cop see you going rubber-kneed.

She shoved a stool his way, then pulled one up for herself. Gave a sigh as she sat down. "Nowadays, I'm not so good at standing on my feet too long."

He sat down too, looking relieved to be

focused on anything other than that whining bone saw. "Is that your first?" he asked, pointing to her belly.

"Yep."

"Boy or girl?"

"I don't know. We'll be happy either way."

"That's how I felt when my daughter was born. Ten fingers and toes, that's all I was asking for . . ." He paused, swallowing hard, as the saw continued to whine.

"How old is your daughter now?" asked Rizzoli, trying to distract him.

"Oh, fourteen, going on thirty. Not a barrel of laughs right now."

"Rough age for girls."

"See all my gray hairs coming in?"

Rizzoli laughed. "My mom used to do that. Point to her head and say, 'These gray hairs are all *your* fault.' I have to admit, I wasn't nice to be around when I was fourteen. It's the age."

"Well, we've got some problems going on, too. My wife and I separated last year. Katie's getting pulled in different directions. Two working parents, two households."

"That's gotta be hard on a kid."

The whine of the bone saw mercifully ceased. Through the window, Rizzoli saw

Yoshima remove the skullcap. Saw Bristol free up the brain, cupping it gently in both hands as he extracted it from the cranium. Ballard kept his gaze averted from the window, his attention focused on Rizzoli.

"It's hard, isn't it?" he said.

"What is?"

"Working as a cop. Your condition and all."

"At least no one expects me to kick down any doors these days."

"My wife was a rookie when she got pregnant."

"Newton PD?"

"Boston. They wanted to yank her right off patrol. She told them being pregnant was an advantage. Said perps are a lot more courteous."

"Perps? They're never courteous to me."

In the next room, Yoshima was sewing the corpse's incision closed with needle and suture, a macabre tailor stitching together not fabric, but flesh. Bristol stripped off his gloves, washed his hands, then lumbered out to meet his visitors.

"Sorry for the delay. Took a little longer than I expected. The guy had tumors all over his abdomen and never saw a doctor.

So instead, he gets me." He reached out with a beefy hand, still damp, to greet Ballard. "Detective. So you're here to take a look at our gunshot."

Rizzoli saw Ballard's face tighten. "Detective Rizzoli asked me to."

Bristol nodded. "Well, let's go then. She's in the cold room." He led them across the autopsy lab, through another doorway to the large refrigeration unit. It looked like any walk-in meat locker, with temperature dials and a massive stainless steel door. Hanging on the wall beside it was a clipboard with the log of deliveries. The name of the elderly man on whom Bristol had just finished the postmortem was there on the list, delivered at eleven p.m. last night. This was not a roster one wanted to be on.

Bristol opened the door and wisps of condensation drifted out. They stepped inside, and the smell of chilled meat almost made Rizzoli gag. Since becoming pregnant, she had lost her tolerance for foul odors; even a whiff of decay could send her reeling for the nearest sink. This time she managed to hold back the nausea as she gazed with grim resolve at the row of gurneys in the cold room. There were five body bags, their contents shrouded in white plastic.

Bristol walked up the row of gurneys and scanned the various tags. He stopped at the fourth one. "Here's our girl," he said, and unzipped the bag low enough to reveal the upper half of the torso, the Y-incision stitched together with mortician's suture. More of Yoshima's handiwork.

As the plastic parted, Rizzoli's gaze wasn't on the dead woman, but on Rick Ballard. He was silent as he stared down at the corpse. The sight of Anna Jessop seemed to freeze him in place.

"Well?" said Bristol.

Ballard blinked, as though snapping out of his trance. He released a breath. "It's her," he whispered.

"You're absolutely sure?"

"Yes." Ballard swallowed. "What happened? What did you find?"

Bristol glanced at Rizzoli, a silent request for her go-ahead to release the information. She gave a nod.

"Single gunshot, left temple," Bristol said, pointing to the entrance wound in the scalp. "Extensive damage to the left temporal as well as both parietal lobes, from intracranial ricochet. Massive intracranial bleed."

"That was the only wound?"

"Correct. Very quick, very efficient."

Ballard's gaze had drifted to the torso. To the breasts. It was not a surprising male response, when confronted with a nude young woman, but Rizzoli was nonetheless disturbed by it. Alive or dead, Anna Jessop had a right to her dignity. Rizzoli was relieved when Dr. Bristol matter-of-factly zipped the bag shut, granting the corpse its privacy.

They walked out of the cold room and Bristol swung the heavy refrigerator door shut. "Do you know the names of next of kin?" he asked. "Anyone we need to notify?"

"There are none," said Ballard.

"You're sure of that."

"She has no living . . ." His voice abruptly faded. He had gone stock-still, and was staring through the window, into the autopsy lab.

Rizzoli turned to see what he was looking at, and knew immediately what had caught his attention. Maura Isles had just walked into the lab, carrying an envelope of X-rays. She crossed to the viewing box, clipped up films, and turned on the light. As she stood gazing at images of shattered limb bones, she did not realize that she was being watched. That three pairs of eyes were staring at her through the window.

"Who is that?" Ballard murmured.

"That's one of our M.E.'s," said Bristol. "Dr. Maura Isles."

"The resemblance is scary, isn't it?" said Rizzoli.

Ballard gave a startled shake of his head. "For a moment I thought . . ."

"We all did, when we first saw the victim."

In the next room, Maura slid the films back into the envelope. She walked out of the lab, never realizing she'd been observed. How easy it is, to stalk another person, thought Rizzoli. There is no such thing as a sixth sense that tells us when others are staring at us. We don't feel the stalker's gaze on our backs; only at the instant when he makes his move do we realize he's there.

Rizzoli turned to Ballard. "Okay, you've seen Anna Jessop. You've confirmed you knew her. Now tell us who she really was."

FIVE

The ultimate driving machine. That's what all the ads called it, what Dwayne called it, and Mattie Purvis was steering that powerful machine down West Central Street, blinking back tears and thinking: You have to be there. Please, Dwayne, be there. But she didn't know if he would be. There was so much about her husband that she didn't understand these days, as if some stranger had stepped into his place, a stranger who scarcely paid attention to her. Scarcely even looked at her. *I want my husband back. But I don't even know how I lost him.*

The giant sign with PURVIS BMW beckoned ahead; she turned into the lot, passing rows of other gleaming ultimate machines, and spotted Dwayne's car, parked near the showroom door.

She pulled into the stall next to his and turned off her engine. Sat for a moment, breathing deep. Cleansing breaths, just like they'd taught her in Lamaze class. The class Dwayne had stopped coming to a month ago, because he thought it was a waste of his time. *You're the one having the baby, not me. Why do I need to be there?*

Uh-oh, too many deep breaths. Suddenly light-headed, she reeled forward against the steering wheel. Accidentally bumped the horn and flinched as it gave a loud blare. She glanced out the window and saw one of the mechanics looking at her. At Dwayne's idiot wife, honking her horn for nothing. Flushing, she pushed open the door, eased her big belly out from behind the steering wheel, and walked into the BMW showroom.

Inside it smelled like leather and car wax. An aphrodisiac for guys, Dwayne called it, this banquet of scents that now made Mattie faintly nauseated. She paused among the sexy sirens of the showroom: this year's new models, all sensuous curves and chrome, gleaming under spotlights. A man

could lose his soul in this room. Run his
hand over a metallic blue flank, stare too
long at his reflection in a windshield, and
he'd begin to see his dreams. He'd see the
man he *could* be if only he owned one of
these machines.

"Mrs. Purvis?"

Mattie turned and saw Bart Thayer, one
of her husband's salesmen, waving at her.
"Oh. Hi," she said.

"You looking for Dwayne?"

"Yes. Where is he?"

"I think, uh . . ." Bart glanced toward the
back offices. "Let me check."

"That's okay, I can find him."

"*No!* I mean, uh, let me get him, okay?
You should sit down, take a load off. In
your condition, you shouldn't be standing
around too much." Funny thing for Bart to
say; he had a belly bigger than hers.

She managed a smile. "I'm only pregnant, Bart. Not crippled."

"So when's the big day?"

"Two weeks. That's when we think it's
due, anyway. You never know."

"Ain't that the truth. My first son, he didn't
want to come out. Born three weeks late
and he's been late for everything ever

since." He winked. "Let me get Dwayne for you."

She watched him walk toward the back offices. Trailed after him, just far enough to watch him knock on Dwayne's door. There was no response, so he knocked again. At last the door opened and Dwayne stuck his head out. He gave a start when he spotted Mattie waving at him from the showroom.

"Can I talk to you?" she called out to him.

Dwayne stepped right out of his office, closing the door behind him. "What are you doing here?" he snapped.

Bart looked back and forth at the couple. Slowly he began to sidle away toward the exit. "Uh, Dwayne, I think I'll just take a little coffee break now."

"Yeah, yeah," muttered Dwayne. "I don't care."

Bart fled the showroom. Husband and wife looked at each other.

"I waited for you," Mattie said.

"What?"

"My OB appointment, Dwayne. You said you were coming. Dr. Fishman waited twenty minutes, and then we couldn't wait any longer. You missed seeing the sonogram."

"Oh. Oh, Jesus. I forgot." Dwayne ran his hand over his head, smoothing back his dark hair. Always fussing over his hair, his shirt, his tie. When you're dealing with a high-end product, Dwayne liked to say, you have to look the part. "I'm sorry."

She reached in her purse and pulled out a Polaroid. "Do you even want to take a look at the picture?"

"What is it?"

"It's our daughter. That's a picture of the sonogram."

He glanced at the photo and shrugged. "Can't see much of anything."

"You can see her arm here, and her leg. If you look real hard, you can almost see her face."

"Yeah, cool." He handed it back. "I'll be home a little late tonight, okay? There's a guy coming by at six for a test drive. I'll catch dinner on my own."

She put the Polaroid back in her purse and sighed. "Dwayne—"

He gave her a quick peck on the forehead. "Let me walk you out. C'mon."

"Can't we go out for coffee or something?"

"I've got customers."

"But there's no one else in the show-room."

"Mattie, *please.* Just let me do my job, okay?"

Dwayne's office door suddenly opened. Mattie's head swiveled around as a woman stepped out, a lanky blonde who quickly ducked across the hall, into another office.

"Who's that?" said Mattie.

"What?"

"That woman who was just in your of-fice."

"Oh. Her?" He cleared his throat. "New hire. I thought it was about time we brought in a saleswoman. You know, diversify the team. She's turned into a real asset. Moved out more cars last month than Bart did, and that's saying something."

Mattie stared at Dwayne's closed door, thinking: That's when it started. Last month. That's when everything changed between us, when the stranger moved into Dwayne's body.

"What's her name?" she asked.

"Look, I've really got to get back to work."

"I just want to know her name." She turned and looked at her husband and, in that instant, she saw raw guilt in his eyes, as glaring as neon.

"Oh, Jesus." He turned away. "I don't need this."

"Uh, Mrs. Purvis?" It was Bart, calling from the showroom doorway. "Did you know you have a flat tire? The mechanic just pointed it out to me."

Dazed, she turned and stared at him. "No. I . . . I didn't."

"How can you *not* notice you have a flat tire?" Dwayne said.

"It might have—well, it seemed to handle a little sluggishly, but—"

"I don't believe this." Dwayne was already heading for the door. Walking away from me as always, she thought. And now he's angry. How did everything suddenly become my fault?

She and Bart followed him to her car. Dwayne was crouched down by the right rear wheel, shaking his head.

"Can you believe she didn't notice this?" he said to Bart. "Look at this tire! She shredded the fucking tire!"

"Hey, it happens," said Bart. He gave Mattie a sympathetic glance. "Look, I'll ask Ed to slip on a new one. No problem."

"But look at the rim, it's all screwed up. How many miles you think she drove on this thing? How can anyone be that dense?"

"C'mon, Dwayne," said Bart. "It's no big deal."

"I didn't know," said Mattie. "I'm sorry."

"Did you drive it like this all the way from the doctor's office?" Dwayne glanced at her over his shoulder, and the anger she saw in his eyes scared her. "Were you daydreaming or what?"

"Dwayne, *I didn't know.*"

Bart patted Dwayne on the shoulder. "Maybe you should lighten up a little, how 'bout it?"

"Stay the hell out of this!" snapped Dwayne.

Bart retreated, hands lifted in submission. "Okay, okay." He shot a last glance at Mattie, a look of *good luck, honey,* and walked away.

"It's only a tire," said Mattie.

"You must've been throwing sparks all down the road. How many people you think saw you driving around like this?"

"Does it matter?"

"*Hello!* This is a *Beemer.* When you're driving a machine like this, you're upholding an image. People see this car, they expect the driver to be a little smarter, a little more hip. So you go clanking around on a bare rim, it *ruins* the image. It makes every other Beemer driver look bad. It makes *me* look bad."

"It's only a tire."

"Stop saying that."

"But it is."

Dwayne gave a snort of disgust and rose to his feet. "I give up."

She swallowed back tears. "It's not about the tire. Is it, Dwayne?"

"What?"

"This fight is about us. Something's wrong between *us.*"

His silence only made things worse. He didn't look at her, but turned, instead, to watch the mechanic walking toward them.

"Hey," the mechanic called out. "Bart said I should go ahead and change that tire."

"Yeah, take care of it, will you?" Dwayne paused, his attention shifting to a Toyota that had just driven into the lot. A man climbed out and stood eyeing one of the BMWs. Bent close to read the dealer's sticker on the window. Dwayne smoothed back his hair, gave his tie a tug, and started walking toward the new customer.

"Dwayne?" said Mattie.

"I got a client here."

"But I'm your *wife.*"

He spun around, his gaze suddenly, shockingly, poisonous. *"Don't. Push it. Mattie."*

"What do I have to do to get your attention?" she cried. "Buy a car from you? Is that what it takes? Because I don't know any other way." Her voice broke. "I don't know any other way."

"Then maybe you should just stop trying. Because I don't see the point anymore."

She watched him walk away. Saw him pause to square his shoulders, put on a smile. His voice suddenly boomed out, warm and friendly, as he greeted the new client on the lot.

"Mrs. Purvis? Ma'am?"

She blinked. Turned to look at the mechanic.

"I'll need your car keys, if you don't mind. So I can move her into the bay and get that tire on." He held out a grease-stained hand.

Wordless, she gave him her key ring, then turned to look at Dwayne. But he did not even glance her way. As if she was invisible. As if she was nothing.

She scarcely remembered driving home.

She found herself sitting at the kitchen table, still holding the keys, the day's mail stacked in front of her. On top was the credit card bill, addressed to Mr. and Mrs. Dwayne Purvis. Mr. and Mrs. She remembered the first time someone had called her Mrs. Purvis, and the joy she'd felt at hearing the name. Mrs. Purvis, Mrs. Purvis.

Mrs. Nobody.

The keys spilled to the floor. She dropped her head in her hands and began to cry. Cried as the baby kicked inside her, cried until her throat ached and the mail was soaked with her tears.

I want him back the way he was. When he loved me.

Through the stuttering of her own sobs, she heard the squeal of a door. It came from the garage. Her head shot up, hope blooming in her chest.

He's home! He's come home to tell me he's sorry.

She jumped up so quickly that her chair tipped over. Giddy, she opened the door and stepped into the garage. Stood blinking in the gloom, bewildered. The only car parked in the garage was hers.

"Dwayne?" she said.

A strip of sunlight caught her eye; the door leading to the side yard was ajar. She crossed the garage to close it. She had just pushed it shut when she heard a footfall behind her, and she froze, heart thumping. Knew, in that instant, that she was not alone.

She turned. Halfway around, darkness met her.

SIX

Maura stepped from the afternoon sunshine into the cool gloom of the Church of Our Lady of Divine Light. For a moment she could see only shadows, the vague outlines of pews, and the silhouette of a lone woman parishioner seated at the front, her head bowed. Maura slipped into a pew and sat down. She let the silence envelop her as her eyes adjusted to the dim interior. In the stained glass windows above, glowing with richly somber hues, a woman with swirling hair gazed adoringly at a tree from which hung a bloodred apple. Eve in the Garden of Eden. Woman as temptress, seducer. Destroyer. Staring up at the window, she felt a sense of disquiet, and her gaze moved to another. Though she had been raised by

Catholic parents, she did not feel at home in the church. She gazed at the jewel-toned images of holy martyrs framed in these windows, and though they might now be enshrined as saints, she knew that, as living flesh and blood, they could not have been flawless. That their time on earth was surely marred by sins and bad choices and petty desires. She knew, better than most, that perfection was not human.

She rose to her feet, turned toward the aisle, and paused. Father Brophy was standing there, the light from the stained glass casting a mosaic of colors on his face. He had approached so quietly that she hadn't heard him, and now they faced each other, neither one daring to break the silence.

"I hope you're not leaving already," he finally said.

"I just came to meditate for a few minutes."

"Then I'm glad I caught you before you left. Would you like to talk?"

She glanced toward the rear doors, as though contemplating escape. Then she released a sigh. "Yes. I think I would."

The woman in the front pew had turned

and was watching them. And what does she see? Maura wondered. The handsome young priest. An attractive woman. Intent whispers exchanged beneath the gazes of saints.

Father Brophy seemed to share Maura's uneasiness. He glanced at the other parishioner, and he said: "It doesn't have to be here."

They walked in Jamaica Riverway Park, following the tree-shaded path that led alongside the water. On this warm afternoon, they shared the park with joggers and cyclists and mothers pushing baby strollers. In such a public place, a priest walking with a troubled parishioner could hardly stir gossip. This is how it always has to be between us, she thought as they ducked beneath the drooping branches of a willow. No hint of scandal, no whiff of sin. What I want most from him is what he can't give me. Yet here I am.

Here we both are.

"I wondered when you'd come by to see me," he said.

"I've wanted to. It's been a rough week."

She stopped and gazed at the river. The whish of traffic from the nearby road obscured the sound of the rushing water. "I'm feeling my own mortality these days."

"You haven't before?"

"Not like this. When I watched that autopsy last week—"

"You watch so many of them."

"Not just watch them, Daniel. I *perform* them. I hold the scalpel in my hand and I cut. I do it almost every day at work, and it never bothered me. Maybe it means I've lost touch with humanity. I've grown so detached that I don't even register it's human flesh I'm slicing. But that day, watching it, it all became personal. I looked at her and I saw myself on the table. Now I can't pick up a scalpel without thinking about her. About what her life might have been like, what she felt, what she was thinking when . . ." Maura stopped and sighed. "It's been hard going back to work. That's all."

"Do you really have to?"

Perplexed by the question, she looked at him. "Do I have a choice?"

"You make it sound like indentured servitude."

"It's my job. It's what I'm good at."

"Not, in itself, a reason to do it. So why do you?"

"Why are you a priest?"

Now it was his turn to look perplexed. He thought about it for a moment, standing very still beside her, the blueness of his eyes muted in the shadows cast by the willow trees. "I made that choice so long ago," he said, "I don't think about it much anymore. Or question it."

"You must have believed."

"I still believe."

"Isn't that enough?"

"Do you really think that faith is all that's required?"

"No, of course not." She turned and began walking again, along a path dappled with sunlight and shade. Afraid to meet his gaze, afraid that he'd see too much in hers.

"Sometimes it's good to come face-to-face with your own mortality," he said. "It makes us reconsider our lives."

"I'd rather not."

"Why?"

"I'm not big on introspection. I grew so impatient with philosophy classes. All those questions without answers. But physics and chemistry, I could understand. They were comforting to me because they taught principles that are reproducible and orderly." She paused to watch a young woman on Rollerblades skate past, pushing a baby in a stroller. "I don't like the unexplainable."

"Yes, I know. You always want your mathematical equations solved. That's why you're having such a hard time with that woman's murder."

"It's a question without an answer. The sort of thing I hate."

She sank onto a wooden bench facing the river. Daylight was fading, and the water flowed black in the thickening shadows. He too sat down, and although they didn't touch, she was so aware of him, sitting close beside her, that she could almost feel his heat against her bare arm.

"Have you heard any more about the case from Detective Rizzoli?"

"She hasn't exactly been keeping me in the loop."

"Would you expect her to?"

"As a cop, no. She wouldn't."

"And as a friend?"

"That's just it, I thought we *were* friends. But she's told me so little."

"You can't blame her. The victim was

found outside your house. She has to wonder—"

"What, that I'm a suspect?"

"Or that you were the intended target. It's what we all thought that night. That it was you in that car." He stared across the river. "You said you can't stop thinking about the autopsy. Well, I can't stop thinking about that night, standing in your street with all those police cars. I couldn't believe any of it was happening. I *refused* to believe."

They both fell silent. Before them flowed a river of dark water, and behind them, a river of cars.

She asked, suddenly: "Will you have dinner with me tonight?"

He didn't answer for a moment, and his hesitation made her flush with embarrassment. What a foolish question. She wanted to take it back, to replay the last sixty seconds. How much better to have just said good-bye and walked away. Instead, she'd blurted out that ill-considered invitation, one that they both knew he shouldn't accept.

"I'm sorry," she murmured. "I guess it's not such a good—"

"Yes," he said. "I'd like to very much."

*   *   *

She stood in her kitchen dicing tomatoes for the salad, her hand jittery as it gripped the knife. On the stove simmered a pot of coq au vin, wafting out steam fragrant with the scents of red wine and chicken. An easy, familiar meal that she could cook without consulting a recipe, without having to stop and think about it. She could not cope with any meal more complicated. Her mind was completely focused on the man who was now pouring two glasses of pinot noir.

He placed one glass beside her on the counter. "What else can I do?"

"Not a thing."

"Make the salad dressing? Wash lettuce?"

"I didn't invite you here to make you work. I just thought you'd prefer this to a restaurant, where it's so public."

"You must be tired of always being in the public's eye," he said.

"I was thinking more about you."

"Even priests eat out at restaurants, Maura."

"No, I meant . . ." She felt herself flush and renewed her efforts with the tomato.

"I guess it would make people wonder," he said. "If they saw us out together." He watched her for a moment, and the only sound was her knife blade rapping against the cutting board. What does one do with a priest in the kitchen? she wondered. Ask him to bless the food? No other man could make her feel so uneasy, so human and flawed. And what are your flaws, Daniel? she wondered as she slid the diced tomatoes into a salad bowl, as she tossed them with olive oil and balsamic vinegar. Does that white collar give you immunity to temptation?

"At least let me slice that cucumber," he said.

"You really can't relax, can you?"

"I'm not good at sitting idle while others work."

She laughed. "Join the club."

"Would that be the club for hopeless workaholics? Because I'm a charter member." He pulled a knife from the wooden block and began to slice the cucumber, releasing its fresh, summery fragrance. "It comes from having to help out with five brothers and a sister."

"Seven of you in the family? My god."

"I'm sure that's what my dad said every time he heard there was another one on the way."

"So where were you in that seven?"

"Number four. Smack in the middle. Which, according to psychologists, makes me a natural born mediator. The one always trying to keep the peace." He glanced up at her with a smile. "It also means I know how to get in and out of the shower really fast."

"And how do you go from sibling number four to being a priest?"

He looked back down at the cutting board. "As you might expect, a long story."

"One you don't want to talk about?"

"My reasons will probably strike you as illogical."

"Well, it's funny how our biggest decisions in life are usually the least logical. The person we choose to marry, for instance." She took a sip of wine and set the glass back down. "I certainly couldn't defend my own marriage on the basis of logic."

He glanced up. "Lust?"

"That would be the operative word. That's how I made the biggest mistake of my life. So far, that is." She took another sip of wine. *And you could be my next big mis-*

take. If God wanted us to behave, He shouldn't have created temptation.

He slid the sliced cucumbers into the salad bowl and rinsed the knife. She watched him standing at the sink, his back to her. He had the tall, lean build of a long-distance runner. Why do I put myself through this? she wondered. Of all the men I could be attracted to, why does it have to be this one?

"You asked why I chose the priesthood," he said.

"Why did you?"

He turned to look at her. "My sister had leukemia."

Startled, she didn't know what to say. Nothing seemed appropriate.

"Sophie was six years old," he said. "The youngest one in the family, and the only girl." He reached for a dish towel to dry his hands, and neatly hung it back on the rack, taking his time, as though he needed to measure his next words. "It was acute lymphocytic leukemia. I suppose you could call it the good kind, if there's any such thing as a good leukemia."

"It's the one with the best prognosis in children. An eighty percent survival rate." A true statement, but she was sorry the instant after she'd said it. The logical Dr. Isles, responding to tragedy with her usual helpful facts and heartless statistics. It was the way she'd always coped with the messy emotions of those around her, by retreating into her scientist's role. A friend just died of lung cancer? A relative left quadriplegic from a car accident? For every tragedy she could cite a statistic, drawing reassurance in the crisp certainty of numbers. In the belief that behind every horror, there is an explanation.

She wondered if Daniel thought her detached, even callous, for her response. But he did not seem to take offense. He simply nodded, accepting her statistic in the spirit she had offered it, as a simple fact.

"The five-year survival rates weren't quite so good back then," he said. "By the time she was diagnosed, she was pretty sick. I can't tell you how devastating it was, to all of us. To my mother, especially. Her only girl. Her baby. I was fourteen then, and I was the one who kind of took over keeping an eye on Sophie. Even with all the attention she got, all the coddling, she never acted spoiled. Never stopped being the sweetest kid you could imagine." He still wasn't looking at Maura; he was gazing at the floor, as though unwilling to reveal the depth of his pain.

"Daniel?" she said.

He took a deep breath, straightened. "I'm not sure how to tell this story to a seasoned skeptic like you."

"What happened?"

"Her doctor informed us that she was terminal. In those days, when a doctor renders his opinion, you accept it as gospel. That night, my parents and brothers went off to church. To pray for a miracle, I guess. I stayed behind in the hospital, so Sophie wouldn't be alone. She was bald by then. Lost it all with the chemotherapy. I remember her falling asleep in my lap. And me praying. I prayed for hours, made all sorts of crazy promises to God. If she had died, I don't think I would have set foot in church again."

"But she lived," said Maura softly.

He looked at her and smiled. "Yes, she did. And I kept all those promises I made. Every single one. Because that day, He was listening to me. I don't doubt it."

"Where is Sophie now?"

"Happily married, living in Manchester.

Two adopted kids." He sat down facing her across the kitchen table. "So here I am."

"Father Brophy."

"Now you know why I made the choice."

And was it the right one? she wanted to ask, but didn't.

They refilled their wineglasses. She sliced crusty French bread and tossed the salad. Ladled steaming coq au vin into serving bowls. The way to a man's heart is through his stomach; was that what she was trying to reach, what she really wanted? Daniel Brophy's heart?

Maybe it's because I can't have him that I feel safe wanting him. He's beyond my reach, so he can't hurt me, the way Victor did.

But when she'd married Victor, she'd thought he could never hurt her either.

We're never as impervious as we think.

They had just finished their meal when the ringing of the doorbell made them both stiffen. Innocent though the evening had been, they exchanged uneasy glances, like two guilty lovers caught in the act.

Jane Rizzoli was standing on Maura's front porch, black hair frizzed to an unruly mass of curls in the humid summer air.

Though the night was warm, she was dressed in one of the dark business pantsuits she always wore to work. This was not a social call, thought Maura, as she met Rizzoli's somber gaze. Glancing down, she saw that Rizzoli was carrying a briefcase.

"I'm sorry to bother you at home, Doc. But we need to talk. I thought it'd be better to see you here, and not at your office."

"Is this about the case?"

Rizzoli nodded. Neither one of them had to specify which case they were talking about; they both knew. Though she and Rizzoli respected each other as professionals, they had not yet crossed that line into a comfortable friendship, and tonight, they regarded each other with a measure of uneasiness. Something has happened, Maura thought. Something that has made her wary of me.

"Please come in."

Rizzoli stepped into the house and paused, sniffing the scent of food. "Am I interrupting your dinner?"

"No, we just finished."

The *we* did not escape Rizzoli's notice. She gave Maura an inquiring look. Heard footsteps and turned to see Daniel in the hallway, carrying wineglasses back to the kitchen.

"Evening, Detective!" he called.

Rizzoli blinked in surprise. "Father Brophy."

He continued into the kitchen, and Rizzoli turned back to Maura. Though she didn't say anything, it was clear what she was thinking. The same thing that woman parishioner had been thinking. *Yes, it looks bad, but nothing has happened. Nothing except dinner and conversation. Why the hell must you look at me like that?*

"Well," said Rizzoli. A lot of meaning was crammed into that one word. They heard the sound of clattering china and silverware. Daniel was loading the dishwasher. A priest at home in her kitchen.

"I'd like to talk to you in private, if I could," said Rizzoli.

"Is that really necessary? Father Brophy is my friend."

"This is going to be tough enough to talk about as it is, Doc."

"I can't just tell him to leave." She stopped at the sound of Daniel's footsteps emerging from the kitchen.

"But I really should go," he said. He glanced at Rizzoli's briefcase. "Since you obviously have business to discuss."

"Actually, we do," said Rizzoli.

He smiled at Maura. "Thank you for dinner."

"Wait," said Maura. "Daniel." She stepped outside with him, onto the front porch, and closed the door behind her. "You don't have to leave," she said.

"She needs to talk to you in private."

"I'm so sorry."

"Why? It was a wonderful evening."

"I feel as if you're being chased out of my house."

He reached out and grasped her arm in a warm and reassuring squeeze. "Call me whenever you need to talk again," he said. "No matter what the hour."

She watched him walk toward his car, his black clothes blending into the summer night. When he turned to wave good-bye, she caught a glimpse of his collar, one last glimmer of white in the darkness.

She stepped back into the house and found Rizzoli still standing in the hallway, watching her. Wondering about Daniel, of course. She wasn't blind; she could see that something more than friendship was growing between them.

"So can I offer you a drink?" asked Maura.

"That'd be great. Nothing alcoholic." Rizzoli patted her belly. "Junior's too young for booze yet."

"Of course."

Maura led the way down the hall, forcing herself to play the proper hostess. In the kitchen she dropped ice cubes into two glasses and poured orange juice. Added a splash of vodka to hers. Turning to set the drinks on the kitchen table, she saw Rizzoli take a file folder from her briefcase and set it on the kitchen table.

"What's that?" asked Maura.

"Why don't we both sit down first, Doc? Because what I'm gonna tell you may be kind of upsetting."

Maura sank into a chair at the kitchen table; so did Rizzoli. They sat facing each other, the folder lying between them. A Pandora's box of secrets, thought Maura, staring at the file. Maybe I don't really want to know what's inside.

"Do you remember what I told you last week, about Anna Jessop? That we could find almost no records on her that went back more than six months? And the only residence we had for her was an empty apartment?"

"You called her a phantom."

"In a sense, that's true. Anna Jessop didn't really exist."

"How is that possible?"

"Because there was no Anna Jessop. It was an alias. Her real name was Anna Leoni. About six months ago, she took on an entirely new identity. Started closing her accounts, and finally moved out of her house. Under the new name, she rented an apartment in Brighton that she never intended to move into. It was just a blind alley, in case anyone managed to learn her new name. Then she packed up and moved to Maine. A small town, halfway up the coast. That's where she's been living for the last two months."

"How did you learn all this?"

"I spoke to the cop who helped her do it."

"A cop?"

"A Detective Ballard, out in Newton."

"So the alias—it wasn't because she was running from the law?"

"No. You can probably guess what she was running from. It's an old story."

"A man?"

"Unfortunately, a very wealthy man. Dr. Charles Cassell."

"I don't know the name."

"Castle Pharmaceuticals. He founded it. Anna was a researcher in his company. They became involved, but three years later, she tried to leave him."

"And he wouldn't let her."

"Dr. Cassell sounds like the kind of guy you don't just walk out on. She ended up in a Newton ER one night with a black eye. From there, it got seriously scary. Stalking. Death threats. Even a dead canary in her mailbox."

"Jesus."

"Yeah, that's true love for you. Sometimes, the only way you can stop a man from hurting you is to shoot him—or to hide. Maybe she'd still be alive if she'd chosen the first option."

"He found her."

"All we have to do is prove it."

"Can you?"

"We haven't been able to talk to Dr. Cassell yet. Quite conveniently, he left Boston the morning after the shooting. He's been traveling on business for the past week, and isn't expected home till tomorrow." Rizzoli lifted the glass of orange juice to her lips, and the clatter of ice cubes jarred Maura's nerves. Rizzoli set the drink back down and was silent for a moment. She seemed to be buying time, but for what? Maura wondered.

"There's something else about Anna Leoni you need to know," Rizzoli said. She pointed to the file on the table. "I brought that for you."

Maura opened the folder and felt a jolt of recognition. It was a color photocopy of a wallet-sized photo. A young girl with black hair and a serious gaze was standing between an older couple whose arms enfolded her in a protective embrace. She said, softly: "That girl could be me."

"She was carrying that in her wallet. We believe that's Anna at around ten years old, with her parents, Ruth and William Leoni. They're both dead now."

"These are her parents?"

"Yes."

"But . . . they're so old."

"Yes, they were. The mother, Ruth, was

sixty-two years old when that photo was taken." Rizzoli paused. "Anna was their only child."

An only child. Older parents. I know where this is going, thought Maura, and I'm afraid of what she's about to tell me. This is why she really came tonight. It's not just about Anna Leoni and her abusive lover; it's about something far more startling.

Maura looked up at Rizzoli. "She was adopted?"

Rizzoli nodded. "Mrs. Leoni was fifty-two the year Anna was born."

"Too old for most agencies."

"Which is why they probably had to arrange a private adoption, through an attorney."

Maura thought of her own parents, now both dead. They too had been older, in their forties.

"What do you know about your own adoption, Doc?"

Maura took a deep breath. "After my father died, I found my adoption papers. It was all done through an attorney here in Boston. I called him a few years ago, to see if he would tell me my birth mother's name."

"Did he?"

"He said my records were sealed. He refused to release any information."

"And you didn't pursue it?"

"I haven't, no."

"Was the attorney's name Terence Van Gates?"

Maura went dead silent. She didn't have to answer the question; she knew Rizzoli could read it in her stunned gaze. "How did you know?" Maura asked.

"Two days before her death, Anna checked into the Tremont Hotel, here in Boston. From her hotel room, she made two phone calls. One was to Detective Ballard, who was out of town at the time. The other was to Van Gates's law office. We don't know why she contacted him—he hasn't returned my calls yet."

Now the revelation is coming, thought Maura. The real reason she's here tonight, in my kitchen.

"We know Anna Leoni was adopted. She had your blood type and your birth date. And just before she died, she was talking to Van Gates—the attorney who handled *your* adoption. An amazing set of coincidences."

"How long have you known all this?"

"A few days."

"And you didn't tell me? You kept it from me."

"I didn't want to upset you if it wasn't necessary."

"Well, I *am* upset that you waited this long."

"I had to, because there was one more thing I needed to find out." Rizzoli took a deep breath. "This afternoon, I had a talk with Walt DeGroot in the DNA lab. Earlier this week, I asked him to expedite that test you requested. This afternoon, he showed me the autorads he'd developed. He did two separate VNTR profiles. One was Anna Leoni's. The other was yours."

Maura sat frozen, braced for the blow she knew was about to fall.

"They're a match," said Rizzoli. "The two genetic profiles are identical. "

SEVEN

The clock on the kitchen wall ticked. The ice cubes slowly melted in the glasses on the table. Time moved on, but Maura felt trapped in that moment, Rizzoli's words looping endlessly in her head.

"I'm sorry," said Rizzoli. "I didn't know how else to tell you. But I thought you had a right to know that you have a . . ." Rizzoli stopped.

Had. I had a sister. And I never even knew she existed.

Rizzoli reached across the table and grasped Maura's hand. It was unlike her; Rizzoli was not a woman who easily gave comfort or offered hugs. But here she was, holding Maura's hand, watching her as though she expected Maura to crumble.

"Tell me about her," Maura said softly. "Tell me what kind of woman she was."

"Detective Ballard's the one you should talk to."

"Who?"

"Rick Ballard. He's in Newton. He was assigned to her case after Dr. Cassell assaulted her. I think he got to know her pretty well."

"What did he tell you about her?"

"She grew up in Concord. She was briefly married, at twenty-five, but it didn't last. They had an amicable divorce, no kids."

"The ex-husband's not a suspect?"

"No. He's since remarried, and he's living in London."

A divorcée, like me. Is there a gene that preordains failed marriages?

"As I said, she worked for Charles Cassell's company, Castle Pharmaceuticals. She was a microbiologist, in their research division."

"A scientist."

"Yeah."

Again, like me, thought Maura, gazing at her sister's face in the photo. So I know that she valued reason and logic, as I do. Scientists are governed by intellect. They take

comfort in facts. We would have understood each other.

"It's a lot to absorb, I know it is," said Rizzoli. "I'm trying to put myself in your place,
and I really can't imagine. It's like discover-
ing a parallel universe, where there's another version of you. Finding out she's been
here all this time, living in the same city. If
only . . ." Rizzoli stopped.

*Is there any phrase more useless than "if
only"?*

"I'm sorry," said Rizzoli.

Maura breathed deeply and sat up
straight, indicating she was not in need of
hand-holding. That she was capable of
dealing with this. She closed the folder and
slid it back to Rizzoli. "Thank you, Jane."

"No, you keep it. That photocopy's meant
for you."

They both stood up. Rizzoli reached into
her pocket and laid a business card on the
table. "You might want this, too. He said
you could call him with any questions."

Maura looked down at the name on the
card: RICHARD D. BALLARD, DETECTIVE. NEWTON
POLICE DEPARTMENT.

"He's the one you should talk to," said
Rizzoli.

They walked together to the front door, Maura still in control of her emotions, still playing the proper hostess. She stood on the porch long enough to give a good-bye wave, then she shut the door and went into the living room. Stood there, listening as Rizzoli's car drove away, leaving only the quiet of a suburban street. All alone, she thought. Once again I'm all alone.

She went into the living room. From the bookshelf, she pulled down an old photo album. She had not looked at its pages in years, not since her father's death, when she'd cleaned his house a few weeks after the funeral. She had found the album on his nightstand, and had imagined him sitting in bed on the last night of his life, alone in that big house, gazing at the photos of his young family. The last images he would have seen, before turning off the light, would have been happy faces.

She opened the album and gazed at those faces now. The pages were brittle, some of the photos nearly forty years old. She lingered over the first one of her mother, beaming at the camera, a dark-haired infant in her arms. Behind them was a house that Maura did not remember, with

Victorian trim and bow windows. Underneath the photo, her mother, Ginny, had
written in her characteristically neat hand:
Bringing Maura home.

There were no pictures taken in the hospital, none of her mother in pregnancy. Just
this sudden, sharp image of Ginny smiling
in the sunshine, holding her instant baby.
She thought of another dark-haired baby,
held in another mother's arms. Perhaps, on
that very same day, a proud father in another town had snapped off a photo of his
new daughter. A girl named Anna.

Maura turned the pages. Saw herself
grow from a toddler to a kindergartener.
Here on a brand-new bicycle, steadied by
her father's hand. There at her first piano
recital, dark hair gathered back with a green
bow, her hands poised on the keys.

She turned to the last page. Christmas.
Maura, about seven years old, standing
flanked by her mother and father, their arms
intertwined in a loving weave. Behind them
was a decorated tree, sparkling with tinsel.
Everyone smiling. A perfect moment in
time, thought Maura. But they never last;
they arrive and then they vanish, and we

can't bring them back; we can only make new ones.

She'd reached the end of the album. There were others, of course, at least four more volumes in the history of Maura, every event recorded and catalogued by her parents. But this was the book her father had chosen to keep beside his bed, with the photos of his daughter as an infant, of himself and Ginny as energetic parents, before the gray had crept into their hair. Before grief, and Ginny's death, had touched their lives.

She gazed down at her parents' faces and thought: How lucky I am that you chose me. I miss you. I miss you both so much. She closed the album and stared through tears at the leather cover.

If only you were here. If only you could tell me who I really am.

She went into the kitchen and picked up the business card that Rizzoli had left on the table. On the front was printed Rick Ballard's work number at the Newton PD. She flipped over the card and saw he'd written his home number as well, with the words: "Call me anytime. Day or night. —R.B."

She went to the phone and dialed his

home number. On the third ring, a voice answered: "Ballard." Just that one name, spoken with crisp efficiency. This is a man who gets right down to business, she thought. He's not going to welcome a call from a woman in emotional meltdown. In the background she could hear a TV commercial playing. He was at home, relaxing; the last thing he'd want was to be bothered.

"Hello?" he said, now with a note of impatience.

She cleared her throat. "I'm sorry to call you at home. Detective Rizzoli gave me your card. My name is Maura Isles, and I . . ." *And I what? Want you to help me get through this night?*

"I was expecting you to call, Dr. Isles," he said.

"I know I should have waited till morning, but—"

"Not at all. You must have a lot of questions."

"I'm having a really hard time with this. I never knew I had a sister. And suddenly—"

"Everything's changed for you. Hasn't it?" The voice that had sounded brusque only a moment before was now so quiet, so sympathetic, that she found herself blinking back tears.

"Yes," she whispered.

"We should probably meet. I can see you any day next week. Or if you want to meet in the evening—"

"Could you see me tonight?"

"My daughter's here. I can't leave right now."

Of course he has a family, she thought. She gave an embarrassed laugh. "I'm sorry. I wasn't thinking straight—"

"So why don't you come here, to my house?"

She paused, her pulse hammering in her ear. "Where do you live?" she asked.

He lived in Newton, a comfortable suburb west of metropolitan Boston, scarcely four miles from her home in Brookline. His house was like all the other homes on that quiet street, undistinguished but well kept, yet another boxy home in a neighborhood where none of the houses were particularly remarkable. From the front porch, she saw the blue glow of a TV screen and heard the monotonous throb of pop music. MTV—not at all what she expected a cop to be watch-ing.

She rang the bell. The door swung open and a blond girl appeared, dressed in ripped blue jeans and a navel-baring T-shirt. A provocative outfit for a girl who could not be much older than fourteen, judging by the slim hips and the barely-there breasts. The girl didn't say a thing, just stared at Maura with sullen eyes, as though guarding the threshold from this new interloper.

"Hello," said Maura. "I'm Maura Isles, here to see Detective Ballard."

"Is my dad expecting you?"

"Yes, he is."

A man's voice called out: "Katie, it's for me."

"I thought it was Mom. She's supposed to be here by now."

Ballard appeared at the door, towering over his daughter. Maura found it hard to believe that this man, with his conservative haircut and pressed Oxford shirt, could be the father of a pubescent pop-tart. He held out his hand to shake hers in a firm grip. "Rick Ballard. Come in, Dr. Isles."

As Maura stepped into the house, the girl

turned and walked back to the living room, flopping down in front of the TV.

"Katie, at least say hello to our guest."

"I'm missing my show."

"You can take a moment to be polite, can't you?"

Katie sighed loudly, and gave Maura a grudging nod. "Hi," she said, and fixed her gaze back on the TV.

Ballard eyed his daughter for a moment, as though debating whether it was worth the effort to demand some courtesy. "Well, turn down the sound," he said. "Dr. Isles and I need to talk."

The girl grabbed the remote and aimed it like a weapon at the TV. The volume barely dropped.

Ballard looked at Maura. "Would you like some coffee? Tea?"

"No, thank you."

He gave an understanding nod. "You just want to hear about Anna."

"Yes."

"I have a copy of her file in my office."

If the office reflected the man, then Rick Ballard was as solid and reliable as the oak desk that dominated the room. He chose not to retreat behind that desk; instead he pointed her toward a sofa, and he sat in an armchair facing her. No barriers stood between them except a coffee table, on which a single folder rested. Through the closed door, they could still hear the manic thump of the TV.

"I have to apologize for my daughter's rudeness," he said. "Katie's been going through a hard time, and I'm not quite sure how to deal with her these days. Felons, I can handle, but fourteen-year-old girls?" He gave a rueful laugh.

"I hope my visit isn't making things worse."

"This has nothing to do with you, believe me. Our family's going through a tough transition right now. My wife and I separated last year, and Katie refuses to accept it. It's led to a lot of fights, a lot of tension."

"I'm sorry to hear that."

"Divorce is never pleasant."

"Mine certainly wasn't."

"But you did get past it."

She thought of Victor, who had so recently intruded upon her life. And how, for a brief time, he had lured her into thoughts of reconciliation. "I'm not sure one ever gets past it," she said. "Once you've been married to someone, they're always part of your life, good or bad. The key is to remember the good parts."

"Not so easy, sometimes."

They were silent for a moment. The only sound was the TV's irritating pulse of teen defiance. Then he straightened, squaring his broad shoulders, and looked at her. It was a gaze she could not easily turn away from, a gaze that told her she was the sole focus of his attention.

"Well. You came to hear about Anna."

"Yes. Detective Rizzoli told me you knew her. That you tried to protect her."

"I didn't do a good enough job," he said quietly. She saw a flash of pain in his eyes, and then his gaze dropped to the file on the coffee table. He picked up the folder and handed it to her. "It's not pleasant to look at. But you have a right to see it."

She opened the folder and stared at a photograph of Anna Leoni, posed against a stark white wall. She was wearing a paper hospital gown. One eye was swollen almost shut, and the cheek was bruised purple. Her intact eye gazed at the camera with a stunned expression.

"That's the way she looked when I first

met her," he said. "That photo was taken in the ER last year, after the man she'd been living with struck her. She'd just moved out of his home in Marblehead, and was renting a house here, in Newton. He showed up at her front door one night and tried to talk her into coming back. She told him to leave. Well, you don't *tell* Charles Cassell to do anything. That's what happened."

Maura heard the anger in his voice, and she looked up. Saw that his mouth had tightened. "I understand she pressed charges."

"Hell, yes. I coached her through it every step of the way. A man who hits a woman understands only one thing: punishment. I was going to make damn sure he faced the consequences. I deal with domestic abuse all the time, and it makes me angry every time I see it. It's like flipping a switch inside me; all I want to do is nail the guy. That's what I tried to do to Charles Cassell."

"And what happened?"

Ballard gave a disgusted shake of his head. "He ended up in jail for one lousy night. When you have money, you can buy yourself out of just about anything. I hoped that would be the end of it—that he'd stay away from her. But this is a man who's not used to losing. He kept calling her, showing up on her doorstep. She moved twice, but each time he found her. She finally took out a restraining order, but it didn't stop him from driving past her house. Then, around six months ago, it started to get deadly serious."

"How?"

He nodded at the file. "It's there. She found it wedged in her front door one morning."

Maura turned to a photocopied sheet. On it were only two typed words centered on a blank sheet of paper.

You're dead.

Fear whispered up Maura's spine. She imagined waking up one morning. Opening her front door to pick up the newspaper, and seeing this single sheet of white paper flutter to the ground. Unfolding it to read those two words.

"That was only the first note," he said. "There were others that came afterwards."

She turned to the next page. It had the same two words.

You're dead.

And turned to a third, and a fourth sheet.

You're dead.
You're dead.

Her throat had gone dry. She looked at Ballard. "Wasn't there something she could do to stop him?"

"We tried, but we could never prove he actually wrote those. Just like we couldn't prove he was the one who scratched her car or slashed her window screens. Then one day she opened her mailbox. Inside was a dead canary with its neck broken. That's when she decided she wanted to get the hell out of Boston. She wanted to disappear."

"And you helped her."

"I never stopped helping her. I was the one she called whenever Cassell came by to harass her. I helped her get the restraining order. And when she decided to leave town, I helped her do that, too. It's not easy to just disappear, especially when someone with Cassell's resources is looking for you. Not only did she change her name, she set up a fake residence under that new name. She rented an apartment and never moved in—it was just to confuse anyone tracking her. The idea is that you go someplace else entirely, where you pay for everything in cash. You leave behind everything and everyone. That's the way it's supposed to work."

"But he found her anyway."

"I think that's why she came back to Boston. She knew she wasn't safe up there anymore. You know she called me, don't you? The night before?"

Maura nodded. "That's what Rizzoli said."

"She left a message on my answering machine, told me she was staying at the Tremont Hotel. I was in Denver, visiting my sister, so I didn't hear the message till I got home. By then, Anna was dead." He met Maura's gaze. "Cassell will deny he did it, of course. But if he managed to track her to Fox Harbor, then there has to be someone in that town who's seen him. That's what I plan to do next—prove that he was up there. Find out if anyone remembers him."

"But she wasn't killed in Maine. She was killed in front of *my* house."

Ballard shook his head. "I don't know where you come into this, Dr. Isles. But I don't believe Anna's death had anything to do with you."

They heard the chime of the doorbell. He

made no move to rise and answer it, but remained in his chair, his gaze on her. It was a gaze so intent she couldn't turn away, could only stare back, thinking: I want to believe him. Because I cannot bear to think that her death was somehow my fault.

"I want Cassell put away," he said. "And I'll do everything I can to help Rizzoli do it. I watched the whole thing unfold, and I knew from the very beginning how it was going to end. Yet I couldn't stop it. I owe it to her, to Anna," he said. "I need to see this through to the end."

Angry voices suddenly drew her attention. In the other room, the TV had gone silent, but Katie and a woman were now exchanging sharp words. Ballard glanced toward the door as the voices rose to shouts.

"What the hell were you thinking?" the woman was yelling.

Ballard stood up. "Excuse me, I should probably find out what the fuss is all about." He walked out, and Maura heard him say: "Carmen, what's going on?"

"You should ask your daughter that question," the woman answered.

"Give it a rest, Mom. Just give it a *fucking rest.*"

"Tell your father what happened today. Go on, tell him what they found in your locker."

"It is *not* a big deal."

"*Tell* him, Katie."

"You are totally overreacting."

"What happened, Carmen?" said Ballard.

"The principal called me this afternoon. The school did a random locker check today, and guess what they found in our daughter's locker? A joint. How the hell does that look? Here she's got two parents in law enforcement, and she's got drugs in her locker. We're just lucky he's letting us deal with it ourselves. What if he'd reported it? I can just see having to arrest my own daughter."

"Oh, Christ."

"We have to deal with this together, Rick. We have to agree on how to handle it."

Maura rose from the couch and went to the door, unsure of how to politely make her exit. She did not want to intrude on this family's privacy, yet here she was, listening to an exchange she knew she shouldn't be hearing. I should just say good-bye and go, she thought. Leave these beleaguered parents alone.

She walked into the hall and paused as she approached the living room. Katie's mother glanced up, startled to see an unexpected visitor in the house. If the mother was any indication of what Katie would one day look like, then that sullen teenager was destined to be a statuesque blonde. The woman was almost as tall as Ballard, with the rangy leanness of an athlete. Her hair was tied back in a casual ponytail, and she wore no trace of makeup, but a woman with her stunning cheekbones needed little enhancement.

Maura said, "Excuse me for interrupting."

Ballard turned to her, and gave a weary laugh. "I'm afraid you're not exactly seeing us at our best. This is Katie's mom, Carmen. This is Dr. Maura Isles."

"I'm going to leave now," said Maura.

"But we hardly got a chance to talk."

"I'll call you another time. I can see you have other things on your mind." She nodded to Carmen. "Glad to meet you. Good night."

"Let me walk you out," said Ballard.

They stepped out of the house, and he gave a sigh, as though relieved to be away from the demands of his family.

"I'm sorry to intrude on that," she said.

"I'm sorry you had to listen to it."

"Have you noticed we can't stop apologizing to each other?"

"You have nothing to apologize for, Maura."

They reached her car and paused for a moment.

"I didn't get to tell you much about your sister," he said.

"Next time I see you?"

He nodded. "Next time."

She slid into her car and closed the door. Rolled down her window when she saw him lean down to talk to her.

"I will tell you this much about her," he said.

"Yes?"

"You look so much like Anna, it takes my breath away."

She could not stop thinking of those words as she sat in her living room, studying the photo of young Anna Leoni with her parents. All these years, she thought, you were missing from my life, and I never realized it.

But I must have known; on some level I must have felt my sister's absence.

You look so much like Anna, it takes my breath away.

Yes, she thought, touching Anna's face in the photo. It takes my breath away, too. She and Anna had shared the same DNA; what else had they shared? Anna had also chosen a career in science, a job governed by reason and logic. She too must have excelled in mathematics. Had she, like Maura, played the piano? Had she loved books and Australian wines and the History Channel?

There is so much more I want to know about you.

It was late; she turned off the lamp and went to her bedroom to pack.

EIGHT

Pitch black. Head aching. The scent of wood and damp earth and . . . something else that made no sense. Chocolate. She smelled chocolate.

Mattie Purvis opened her eyes wide, but she might as well have kept them tightly closed because she could see nothing. Not a glimmer of light, not a wisp of shadow on shadow. *Oh god, am I blind?*

Where am I?

She was not in her own bed. She was lying on something hard, and it made her back ache. The floor? No, this wasn't polished wood beneath her, but rough planks, gritty with dirt.

If only her head would stop pounding.

She closed her eyes, fighting off nausea.

Trying, even through the pain, to remember how she could have arrived at this strange, dark place where nothing seemed familiar. Dwayne, she thought. We had a fight, and then I drove home. She struggled to retrieve the lost fragments of time. She remembered a stack of mail on the table. She remembered crying, her tears dripping onto envelopes. She remembered jumping up, and the chair hitting the floor.

I heard a noise. I went into the garage. I heard a noise and went into the garage, and . . .

Nothing. She could remember nothing after that.

She opened her eyes. It was still dark. Oh, this is bad, Mattie, she thought, this is very, very bad. Your head hurts, you've lost your memory, and you're blind.

"Dwayne?" she called. She heard only the whoosh of her own pulse.

She had to get up. She had to find help, had to find a phone at the very least.

She rolled onto her right side to push herself up, and her face slammed up against a wall. The impact bounced her right onto her back again. She lay stunned, her nose throbbing. What was a wall doing here? She reached out to touch it and felt more rough wooden planks. Okay, she thought, I'll just roll the other way. She turned to the left.

And collided with another wall.

Her heartbeat thudded louder, faster. She lay on her back again, thinking: walls on both sides. This can't be. This isn't real. Pushing up off the floor, she sat up, and slammed the top of her head. Collapsed, once again, onto her back.

No, no, no!

Panic seized her. Arms flailing, she hit barriers in every direction. She clawed at the wood, splinters digging into her fingers. Heard shrieks but did not recognize her own voice. Everywhere, walls. She bucked, thrashed, her fists pummeling blindly until her hands were bruised and torn, her limbs too exhausted to move. Slowly her shrieks faded to sobs. Finally, to stunned silence.

A box. I am trapped in a box.

She took a deep breath and inhaled the scent of her own sweat, her own fear. Felt the baby squirm inside her, another prisoner trapped in a small space. She thought of the Russian dolls her grandmother had once given her. A doll inside a doll inside a doll.

We're going to die in here. We're both going to die, my baby and me.

Closing her eyes, she fought back a fresh wave of panic. *Stop. Stop this right now. Think, Mattie.*

Hand trembling, she reached toward her right side, touched one wall. Reached to her left. Touched another wall. How far apart was that? Maybe three feet wide, maybe more. And how long? She reached behind her head and felt a foot of space. Not so bad in that direction. A little room there. Her fingers brushed against something soft, just behind her head. She tugged it closer and realized it was a blanket. As she unrolled it, something heavy thudded onto the floor. A cold metal cylinder. Her heart was pounding again, this time not with panic, but with hope.

A flashlight.

She found the switch and flicked it on. Released a sharp breath of relief as a beam of light slashed the darkness. *I can see, I can see!* The beam skimmed across the walls of her prison. She aimed it toward the ceiling and saw there was barely enough head room for her to sit up, if she kept her head cocked.

Big-bellied and clumsy, she had to squirm to push herself up to a sitting position. Only then could she see what was at her feet: a plastic bucket and a bed pan. Two large jugs of water. A grocery sack. She wriggled toward the sack and looked inside. That's why I smelled chocolate, she thought. Inside were Hershey bars, packets of beef jerky, and saltine crackers. And batteries—three packages of fresh batteries.

She leaned back against the wall. Heard herself suddenly laugh. A crazy, frightening laugh that wasn't hers at all. It was a madwoman's. *Well, this is dandy. I have everything I need to survive except . . .*

Air.

Her laughter died. She sat listening to the sound of her own breathing. Oxygen in, carbon dioxide out. Cleansing breaths. But oxygen runs out eventually. A box can hold only so much. Didn't it already seem staler? Plus she had panicked—all that thrashing around. She had probably used up most of the oxygen.

Then she felt the cool whisper in her hair. She looked up. Aiming the flashlight just over her head, she saw the circular grate. It was only a few inches in diameter, but wide enough to bring in fresh air from above. She stared at that grate, bewildered. I am trapped in a box, she thought. I have food, water, and air.

Whoever had put her in here wanted to keep her alive.

NINE

Rick Ballard had told her that Dr. Charles Cassell was wealthy, but Jane Rizzoli had not expected *this.* The Marblehead estate was surrounded by a high brick wall, and through the bars of the wrought-iron gate, she and Frost could see the house, a massive white Federal surrounded by at least two acres of emerald lawn. Beyond it glittered the waters of Massachusetts Bay.

"Wow," said Frost. "This is all from pharmaceuticals?"

"He started off by marketing a single weight-loss drug," said Rizzoli. "Within twenty years, he built up to *that.* Ballard says this is not the kind of guy you ever want to cross." She looked at Frost. "And if you're a woman, you sure as hell don't leave him."

She rolled down her window and pushed the intercom button.

A man's voice crackled over the speaker: "Name, please?"

"Detectives Rizzoli and Frost, Boston PD. Here to see Dr. Cassell."

The gate whined open, and they drove through, onto a winding driveway that brought them to a stately portico. She parked behind a fire-engine-red Ferrari— probably the closest her old Subaru would ever get to celebrity cardom. The front door swung open even before they could knock, and a burly man appeared, his gaze neither friendly nor unfriendly. Though dressed in a polo shirt and tan Dockers, there was nothing casual about the way this man was eyeing them.

"I'm Paul, Dr. Cassell's assistant," he said.

"Detective Rizzoli." She held out her hand, but the man did not even glance at it, as though it was not worth his attention.

Paul ushered them into a house that was not at all what Rizzoli had expected. Though the exterior had been traditional

Federal, inside she found the decor starkly modern, even cold, a white-walled gallery of abstract art. The foyer was dominated by a bronze sculpture of intertwining curves, vaguely sexual.

"You do know that Dr. Cassell just got home from a trip last night," said Paul. "He's jet-lagged and not feeling well. So if you could keep it short."

"He was away on business?" said Frost.

"Yes. It was arranged over a month ago, in case you're wondering."

Which didn't mean a thing, thought Rizzoli, except that Cassell was capable of planning his moves ahead of time.

Paul led them through a living room decorated in black and white, with only a single scarlet vase to shock the eye. A flat-screen TV dominated one wall, and a smoked-glass cabinet contained a dazzling array of electronics. A bachelor's dream pad, thought Rizzoli. Not a single feminine touch, just guy stuff. She could hear music and she assumed it was a CD playing. Jazz piano chords melted together in a mournful walk down the keys. There was no melody, no song, just notes blending in wordless lament. The music grew louder as Paul led them toward a set of sliding doors. He opened them, and announced:

"The police are here, Dr. Cassell."

"Thank you."

"Would you like me to stay?"

"No, Paul, you can leave us."

Rizzoli and Frost stepped into the room, and Paul slid the doors shut behind them. They found themselves in a space so gloomy that they could barely make out the man seated at the grand piano. So it had been live music, not a CD playing. Heavy curtains were drawn over the window, blocking out all but a sliver of daylight. Cassell reached toward a lamp and switched it on. It was only a dim globe shaded by Japanese rice paper, but it made him squint. A glass of what looked like whiskey sat on the piano beside him. He was unshaven, his eyes bloodshot—not the face of a cold corporate shark, but of a man too distraught to care what he looked like. Even so, it was an arrestingly handsome face, with a gaze so intense it seemed to burn its way into Rizzoli's brain. He was younger than she had expected a self-made mogul to be, perhaps in his late forties. Still young enough to believe in his own invincibility.

"Dr. Cassell," she said, "I'm Detective Rizzoli, Boston PD. And this is Detective Frost. You do understand why we're here?"

"Because he sicced you on me. Didn't he?"

"Who?"

"That Detective Ballard. He's like a god-damn pit bull."

"We're here because you knew Anna Leoni. The victim."

He reached for his glass of whiskey. Judging by his haggard appearance, it was not his first drink of the day. "Let me tell you something about Detective Ballard, before you go believing everything he says. The man is a genuine, class-A asshole." He downed the rest of his drink in a single gulp.

She thought of Anna Leoni, her eye swollen shut, her cheek bruised purple. *I think we know who the real asshole is.*

Cassell set the empty glass down. "Tell me how it happened," he said. "I need to know."

"We have a few questions, Dr. Cassell."

"First tell me what happened."

This is why he agreed to see us, she thought. He wants information. He wants to gauge how much we know.

"I understand it was a gunshot wound to the head," he said. "And she was found in a car?"

"That's right."

"That much I already learned from *The Boston Globe.* What kind of weapon was used? What caliber bullet?"

"You know I can't reveal that."

"And it happened in Brookline? What the hell was she doing there?"

"That I can't tell you, either."

"Can't tell me?" He looked at her. "Or you don't know?"

"We don't know."

"Was anyone with her when it happened?"

"There were no other victims."

"So who are your suspects? Aside from me?"

"We're here to ask *you* the questions, Dr. Cassell."

He rose unsteadily to his feet and crossed to a cabinet. Took out a bottle of whiskey and refreshed his glass. Pointedly he did not offer his visitors a drink.

"Why don't I just answer the one question you came to ask," he said, settling back onto the piano bench. "No, I did not kill her. I haven't even seen her in months."

Frost asked: "When was the last time you saw Ms. Leoni?"

"It would have been sometime in March, I think. I drove by her house one afternoon. She was out on the sidewalk, getting her mail."

"Wasn't that after she took out the restraining order against you?"

"I didn't get out of my car, okay? I didn't even speak to her. She saw me and went right into the house without saying a word."

"So what was the point of that drive-by?" said Rizzoli. "Intimidation?"

"No."

"Then what?"

"I just wanted to see her, that's all. I missed her. I still . . ." He paused and cleared his throat. "I still miss her."

Now he's going to say that he loved her.

"I loved her," he said. "Why would I hurt her?"

As if they'd never heard a man say that before.

"Besides, how could I? I didn't know where she was. After she moved, that last time, I couldn't find her."

"But you tried?"

"Yes, I tried."

"Did you know she was living in Maine?" asked Frost.

A pause. He looked up, frowning. "Where in Maine?"

"A little town called Fox Harbor."

"No, I didn't know that. I assumed she was somewhere in Boston."

"Dr. Cassell," said Rizzoli, "where were you last Thursday night?"

"I was here, at home."

"All night?"

"From five P.M. on. I was packing for my trip."

"Can anyone verify that you were here?"

"No. Paul had the night off. I freely admit I have no alibi. It was just me here, alone with my piano." He banged the keyboard, playing a dissonant chord. "I flew out the next morning. Northwest Airlines, if you want to check."

"We will."

"The reservations were made six weeks ago. I had meetings already planned."

"That's what your assistant told us."

"Did he? Well, it's true."

"Do you keep a gun?" asked Rizzoli.

Cassell went very still, his dark eyes searching hers. "Do you honestly think I did it?"

"Could you answer the question?"

"No, I do not have a gun. Not a pistol or a rifle or a pop-gun. And I didn't kill her. I didn't do *half* the things she accused me of."

"Are you saying she lied to the police?"

"I'm saying she exaggerated."

"We've seen the photo of her taken in the ER, the night you gave her a black eye. Did she exaggerate that charge as well?"

His gaze dropped, as though he could not bear her accusatory look. "No," he said quietly. "I don't deny hitting her. I regret it. But I don't deny it."

"What about repeatedly driving past her house? Hiring a private detective to follow her? Showing up on her doorstep, demanding to speak to her?"

"She wouldn't answer any of my calls. What was I supposed to do?"

"Take a hint, maybe?"

"I don't sit back and just let things *happen* to me, Detective. I never have. That's why I own this house, with that view out there. If I really want something, I work hard for it. And then I hold on to it. I wasn't going to just let her walk out of my life."

"What was Anna to you, exactly? Just another possession?"

"Not a possession." He met her gaze, his eyes naked with loss. "Anna Leoni was the love of my life."

His answer took Rizzoli aback. That simple statement, said so quietly, had the honest ring of truth to it.

"I understand you were together for three years," she said.

He nodded. "She was a microbiologist, working in my research division. That's how we met. One day she walked into a board meeting to give us an update on antibiotic trials. I took one look at her, and I thought: *She's the one.* Do you know what it's like, to love someone so much, and then watch them walk away from you?"

"Why did she?"

"I don't know."

"You must have an idea."

"I don't. Look at what she had here! This house, anything she wanted. I don't think I'm ugly. Any woman would've been thrilled to be with me."

"Until you started hitting her."

A silence.

"How often did that happen, Dr. Cassell?"

He sighed. "I have a stressful job . . ."

"Is that your explanation? You slapped your girlfriend because you had a hard day at the office?"

He did not answer. Instead he reached for his glass. And that, no doubt, was part of the problem, she thought. Mix a hard-driving executive with too much booze, and you get a girlfriend with black eyes.

He set the glass down again. "I just wanted her to come home."

"And your way of convincing her was to cram death threats in her door?"

"I didn't do that."

"She filed multiple complaints with the police."

"Never happened."

"Detective Ballard says it did."

Cassell gave a snort. "That moron believed everything she told him. He likes playing Sir Galahad, it makes him feel important. Did you know he showed up here once, and told me that if I ever touched her again, he'd beat the shit out of me. I think that's pretty pitiful."

"She claimed you slashed her window screens."

"I didn't."

"Are you saying she did it herself?"

"I'm just saying I didn't."

"Did you scratch her car?"

"What?"

"Did you mark up her car door?"

"That's a new one to me. When did that supposedly happen?"

"And the dead canary in her mailbox?"

Cassell gave an incredulous laugh. "Do I *look* like somebody who'd do something that perverted? I wasn't even in town when that supposedly happened. Where's the proof it was me?"

She regarded him for a moment, thinking: Of course he denies it, because he's right; we can't prove he slashed her screens or scratched her car or put a dead bird in her mailbox. This man didn't get where he is by being stupid.

"Why would Anna lie about it?" she said.

"I don't know," he said. "But she did."

TEN

By noon Maura was on the road, yet one more weekender caught in traffic as it streamed north like migratory salmon out of a city where the streets were already shimmering with heat. Trapped in their cars, their children whining in backseats, vacationers could only inch grimly northward toward the promise of cool beaches and salt air. That was the vision Maura held on to as she sat in traffic, gazing at a line of cars that stretched all the way to the horizon. She had never been to Maine. She knew it only as a backdrop in the L.L. Bean catalogue, where tanned men and women wore parkas and hiking boots while, at their feet, golden retrievers lolled on the grass. In the world of L.L. Bean, Maine was the land of forests and misty shores, a mythical place too beautiful to exist except as a hope, a dream. I am sure to be disappointed, she thought as she stared at sunlight glaring off the unending line of cars. But that's where the answers lie.

Months ago, Anna Leoni had made this same journey north. It would have been a day in early spring, still chilly, the traffic not nearly as heavy as today. Driving out of Boston, she too would have crossed the Tobin Bridge and then headed north on Route 95, toward the Massachusetts–New Hampshire border.

I am following in your footsteps. I need to know who you were. It's the only way I'll learn who I am.

At two, she crossed from New Hampshire into Maine, where the traffic magically dissolved, as though the ordeal up till then had been merely a test, and now the gates were opening to admit the worthy. She stopped only long enough to pick up a sandwich at a rest stop. By three, she had left the interstate and was traveling on Maine's Route 1, hugging the coast as she continued north.

You came this way, too.

The views Anna saw would have been different, the fields just turning green, the trees still bare. But surely Anna had passed that same lobster roll shack, had glanced at the same junk dealer's yard where eternally rusting bed frames were displayed on the lawn, and had reacted, like Maura, with an amused shake of the head. Perhaps she too had pulled off the road in the town of Rockport to stretch her legs and had lingered beside the statue of André the seal while she gazed over the harbor. Had shivered as the wind blew in a chill from the water.

Maura climbed back into her car and continued north.

By the time she passed the coastal town of Bucksport and turned south, down the peninsula, sunlight was already slanting lower over the trees. She could see fog rolling in over the sea, a gray bank of it, advancing toward shore like a hungry beast swallowing up the horizon. By sunset, she thought, my car will be enveloped in it. She had made no hotel arrangements in Fox Harbor, had left Boston with the quaint idea that she could simply pull into a seaside motel somewhere and find a bed for the night. But she saw few motels along this rugged stretch of coast, and those she did pass all displayed NO VACANCY signs.

The sun dipped even lower.

The road made an abrupt curve, and she gripped the wheel, barely managing to stay in her lane as she rounded a rocky point, past scraggly trees on one side, the sea on the other.

Suddenly there it was—Fox Harbor, nestled in the shelter of a shallow inlet. She had not expected it to be such a small town, little more than a dock, a steepled church, and a string of white buildings facing the bay. In the harbor, lobster boats bobbed at their moorings like staked prey, waiting to be swallowed up by the incoming fog bank.

Driving slowly down Main Street, she saw tired front porches in need of paint, windows where faded curtains hung. Clearly this was not a wealthy town, judging by the rusting trucks in the driveways. The only late-model vehicles she saw were in the parking lot of the Bayview Motel, cars with license plates from New York and Massachusetts and Connecticut. Urban refugees who'd fled hot cities for lobster and a glimpse of paradise.

She pulled up in front of the motel registration office. First things first, she thought; I need a bed for the night, and this looked like the only place in town. She got out of her car and stretched stiff muscles, inhaled damp and briny air. Though Boston was a harbor town, she seldom smelled the sea at home; the urban smells of diesel and car exhaust and hot pavement contaminated every breeze that blew in from the harbor. Here, though, she could actually taste the salt, could feel it cling like a fine mist to her skin. Standing in that motel parking lot, the wind in her face, she felt as if she'd suddenly emerged from a deep sleep, and was awake again. Alive again.

The motel's decor was exactly as she'd expected it would be: sixties wood paneling, tired green carpet, a wall clock mounted in a ship's wheel. No one was manning the counter.

She leaned forward. "Hello?"

A door creaked open and a man appeared, fat and balding, delicate spectacles perched like a dragonfly on his nose.

"Do you have any rooms for the night?" Maura asked.

Her question was met with dead silence.

The man stared at her, jaw sagging open, his gaze riveted on her face.

"Excuse me," she said, thinking that he had not heard her. "Do you have any vacancies?"

"You . . . want a room?"

Didn't I just say that?

He looked down at his registration book, then back at her. "I'm, uh, sorry. We're full up for the night."

"I've just driven all the way up from Boston. Is there some place in town I might find a room?"

He swallowed. "It's a busy weekend. There was a couple came in just an hour ago, asking for a room. I called around, had to send them all the way up to Ellsworth."

"Where's that?"

"About thirty miles."

Maura looked up at the clock mounted in the ship's wheel. It was already four forty-five; the search for a motel room would have to wait.

She said, "I need to find the office for Land and Sea Realty."

"Main Street. It's two blocks down, on the left."

*   *   *

Stepping through the door into Land and Sea Realty, Maura found yet another deserted reception room. Was no one in this town manning his post? The office smelled like cigarettes, and on the desk, an ashtray overflowed with butts. Displayed on the wall were the firm's property listings, some of the photos badly yellowed. Clearly this was not a hot real estate market. Scanning the offerings, Maura saw a tumble-down barn (PERFECT FOR A HORSE FARM!), a house with a sagging porch (PERFECT HANDYMAN SPECIAL!), and a photo of trees—that was it, just trees (QUIET AND PRIVATE! PERFECT HOUSE LOT!). Was there anything in this town, she wondered, that wasn't *perfect*?

She heard a back door open and turned to see a man emerge, carrying a dripping coffee carafe, which he set on the desk. He was shorter than Maura, with a square head and close-cropped gray hair. His clothes were far too large for him, the shirtsleeves and trouser cuffs rolled up as though he was wearing a giant's hand-me-downs. Keys rattling on his belt, he swaggered over to greet Maura.

"Sorry, I was out back washing the coffee pot. You must be Dr. Isles."

The voice took Maura aback. Though it was husky, no doubt from all those cigarettes in the ashtray, it was clearly a woman's. Only then did Maura notice the swell of breasts under that baggy shirt.

"You're . . . the person I spoke to this morning?" Maura asked.

"Britta Clausen." She gave Maura a brisk, no-nonsense handshake. "Harvey told me you'd gotten into town."

"Harvey?"

"Down the road, Bayview Motel. He called to let me know you were on the way." The woman paused, giving Maura the once-over. "Well, I guess you don't need to show me any ID. No doubt, looking at you, whose sister you are. You wanna drive up to the house together?"

"I'll follow you in my car."

Miss Clausen sorted through the key ring on her belt and gave a satisfied grunt. "Here it is, Skyline Drive. Police are all finished going through it, so I guess I can walk you through."

*　　*　　*

Maura followed Miss Clausen's pickup
truck up a road that suddenly curved away
from the coast and wound up a bluff. As
they climbed, she caught glimpses of the
coastline, the water now obscured beneath
a thick blanket of fog. The village of Fox
Harbor vanished into the mists below. Just
ahead of her, Miss Clausen's brake lights
suddenly flared, and Maura barely had time
to hit her own brakes. Her Lexus skidded
across wet leaves, coming to a stop with its
bumper kissing a Land and Sea Realty for
sale sign staked in the ground.

Miss Clausen stuck her head out the window. "Hey, you okay back there?"

"I'm fine. I'm sorry, I wasn't paying attention."

"Yeah, that last curve takes you by surprise. It's this driveway, off to the right."

"I'm right behind you."

Miss Clausen gave a laugh. "Not *too*
close behind, okay?"

The dirt road was hugged so closely by
trees, Maura felt as though she was driving
through a tunnel in the woods. It opened up
abruptly to reveal a small cedar-shingled
cottage. Maura parked beside Miss
Clausen's pickup truck and stepped out of

the Lexus. For a moment she stood in the silence of the clearing and stared at the house. Wooden steps led to a covered porch where a swing hung motionless in the still air. In a small shade garden, foxgloves and daylilies struggled to grow. On all sides the forest seemed to press in, and Maura found herself breathing more quickly, as though trapped in a small room. As though the air itself was too close.

"It's so quiet here," said Maura.

"Yeah, it's a ways from town. That's what makes this hill such a good value. Real estate boom's gonna move up this way, you know. Few years from now, you're gonna see houses all up and down this road. This is the time to buy."

Because it's *perfect,* Maura expected her to add.

"I'm having a house lot cleared right next door," said Miss Clausen. "After your sister moved in, I figured it was time to get these other lots ready. You see one person living up here, it gets the ball rolling. Pretty soon everyone's looking to buy in the neighborhood." She gave Maura a thoughtful look. "So what kind of doctor are you?"

"A pathologist."

"That's like, what? You work in a lab?"

This woman was starting to irritate her. She answered, bluntly: "I work with dead people."

That answer didn't seem to disturb the woman in the least. "Well, you must have regular hours, then. Lot of weekends off. A summer place might interest you. You know, the lot next door's gonna be ready to build on soon. If you ever thought of owning a little vacation place, you'll never find a cheaper time to invest."

So this was what it felt like to be trapped with a time-share salesman. She said, "I'm really not interested, Miss Clausen."

"Oh." The woman huffed out a breath, then turned and stomped up onto the porch. "Well, just come on in, then. Now that you're here, you can tell me what to do with your sister's things."

"I'm not really sure I have that authority."

"I don't know what else to do with it all. I sure don't want to pay for storing them. I've got to empty out the house if I ever want to sell it or rent it out again." She rattled through her keys, looking for the right one. "I manage most of the rental units in town, and this place hasn't been the easiest one to fill. Your sister, she signed a six-month lease, you know."

Is that all Anna's death means to her? Maura wondered. No more rent checks, a property in need of a new tenant? She did not like this woman with her clanking keys and her acquisitive stare. The real estate queen of Fox Harbor, whose only concern seemed to be bringing in her quota of monthly checks.

At last Miss Clausen pushed open the door. "Go on in."

Maura stepped inside. Though there were large windows in the living room, the closeness of the trees, and the late afternoon hour, filled the house with shadow. She saw dark pine floors, a worn area rug, a sagging couch. The faded wallpaper had green vines lacing across the room, adding to Maura's sense of leafy suffocation.

"Came completely furnished," said Miss Clausen. "I gave her a good price, considering that."

"How much?" asked Maura, staring out the window at a wall of trees.

"Six hundred a month. I could get four times that, if this place was closer to the water. But the man who built it, he liked his privacy." Miss Clausen gave the living room a slow, surveying look, as though she hadn't really seen it in a while. "Kind of surprised me when she called to ask about the place, especially since I had other units available, down by the shore."

Maura turned to look at her. Daylight was fading, and Miss Clausen had receded into the shadows. "My sister asked specifically about this house?"

Miss Clausen shrugged. "I guess the price was right."

They left the gloomy living room and started down a hallway. If a house reflected the personality of its occupant, then something of Anna Leoni must linger within these walls. But other tenants had also claimed this space, and Maura wondered which knickknacks, which pictures on the wall had belonged to Anna, and which had been left by others before her. That pastel painting of a sunset—surely not Anna's. No sister of mine would hang something so hideous, she thought. And that odor of stale cigarettes permeating the house—surely it had not been Anna who smoked. Identical twins are often eerily alike; wouldn't Anna have shared Maura's aversion to cigarettes?

Wouldn't she, too, sniffle and cough at the first whiff of smoke?

They came to a bedroom with a stripped mattress.

"She didn't use this room, I guess," said Miss Clausen. "Closet and dressers were empty."

Next came a bathroom. Maura went in and opened the medicine cabinet. On the shelves were Advil and Sudafed and Ricola cough drops, brand names that startled her by their familiarity. These were the same products she kept in her own bathroom cabinet. Right down to our choice of flu medicines, she thought, we were identical.

She closed the cabinet door. Continued down the hall to the last doorway.

"This was the bedroom she used," said Miss Clausen.

The room was neatly kept, the bedcovers tucked in, the dresser top free of clutter. *Like my bedroom,* thought Maura. She went to the closet and opened the door. Hanging inside were slacks and pressed blouses and dresses. Size six. Maura's size.

"State police came in last week, gave the whole house a going-over."

"Did they find anything of interest?"

"Not that they told me. She didn't keep much in here. Lived here only a few months."

Maura turned and looked out the window. It was not yet dark, but the gloom of the surrounding woods made nightfall seem imminent.

Miss Clausen was standing just inside the bedroom door, as though waiting to charge a toll before she'd let Maura exit. "It's not such a bad house," she said.

Yes it is, thought Maura. It's a horrid little house.

"This time of year, there's nothing much left to rent. Everything's pretty much taken. Hotels, motels. No rooms at the inn."

Maura kept her gaze on the woods. Anything to avoid engaging this distasteful woman in any further conversation.

"Well, it was just a thought. I guess you found a place to stay tonight, then."

So that's what she's trying to get at. Maura turned to look at her. "Actually, I don't have a place to stay. The Bayview Motel was full."

The woman responded with a tight little smile. "So's everything else."

"They told me there were some vacancies up in Ellsworth."

"Yeah? If you want to drive all the way up there. Take you longer than you think in the dark. Road winding all over the place." Miss Clausen pointed to the bed. "I could get you some fresh linens. Charge you what the motel would have. If you're interested."

Maura looked down at the bed, and felt a cold whisper up her spine. *My sister slept here.*

"Oh, well. Take it or leave it."

"I don't know . . ."

Miss Clausen gave a grunt. "Seems to me you don't have much of a choice."

Maura stood on the front porch and watched the taillights of Britta Clausen's pickup truck disappear into the dark curtain of trees. She lingered a moment in the gathering darkness, listening to the crickets, to the rustle of leaves. She heard creaking behind her, and turned to see the porch swing was moving, as though nudged by a ghostly hand. With a shudder, she stepped back into the house and was about to lock the door when she suddenly went very still.

Felt, once again, that whisper of a chill against her neck.

There were four locks on the door.

She stared at two chains, a sliding latch, and a dead bolt. The brass plates were still bright, the screws untarnished. *New locks.* She slid all the bolts home, inserted the chains into their slots. The metal felt icy against her fingers.

She went into the kitchen and flipped on the lights. Saw tired linoleum on the floor, a small dining table with chipped Formica. In the corner, a Frigidaire growled. But it was the back door she focused on. It had three locks, brass plates gleaming. She felt her heart starting to thump faster as she fastened the locks. Then she turned and was startled to see yet another bolted door in the kitchen. Where did that one lead?

She slid open the bolt and opened the door. She saw narrow wooden stairs leading down into darkness. Cool air rose from below, and she smelled damp earth. The back of her neck was prickling.

The cellar. Why would anyone want to lock the door to the cellar?

She closed the door, slid the bolt shut.

That's when she realized this lock was different; it was rusted, old.

Now she felt the need to check that all the windows were bolted as well. Anna had been frightened so badly that she had turned this house into a fortress, and Maura could still feel that fear permeating every room. She tested the kitchen windows, then moved to the living room.

Only when she was satisfied that the windows were all secure in the rest of the house did she finally begin exploring the bedroom. Standing before the open closet, she gazed at the clothes inside. Sliding the hangers across the pole, she eyed each garment, noting they were precisely her size. She pulled a dress from its hanger—a black knit, with the clean, simple lines that she herself favored. She imagined Anna standing in a department store, lingering over this dress on the rack. Checking the price tag, holding up the garment against her body as she gazed into a mirror, thinking: This is the one I want.

Maura unbuttoned her blouse, removed her slacks. She stepped into the black dress, and as she pulled up the zipper, she felt the fabric close over her curves like a second skin. She turned to face the mirror. This is what Anna saw, she thought. The same face, the same figure. Did she, too, deplore the thickening of her hips, the signs of impending middle age? Did she too turn sideways, to check the flatness of her belly? Surely all women who try on new dresses perform an identical ballet in front of a mirror. Turn this way, turn that. Do I look fat from behind?

She paused, her right side to the mirror, staring at a strand of hair that clung to the fabric. She plucked it off and held it up to the light. It was black like hers, but longer. A dead woman's hair.

The ringing telephone made her jerk around. She went to the nightstand and paused, heart pounding, as the phone rang a second time, a third, each jangle unbearably loud in that silent house. Before it could ring a fourth time she picked up the receiver.

"Hello? Hello?"

There was a click, and then the dial tone.

Wrong number, she thought. That's all it is.

Outside, the wind was picking up, and even through the closed window she heard the groan of swaying trees. But inside the house, it was so silent she could hear her own heartbeat. Is this what your nights were like? she wondered. In this house, surrounded by dark woods?

That night, before she climbed into bed, she locked the bedroom door, then propped a chair against it as well. She felt a little sheepish doing so. There was nothing to be afraid of, yet she felt more threatened here than in Boston, where the predators were human and far more dangerous than any animal that might lurk among these woods.

Anna was afraid here, too.

She could feel that fear, still lingering in this house with its barricaded doors.

She bolted awake to the sound of screeching. Lay gasping for breath, heart thudding. Only an owl, no reason to panic. She was in the woods, for god's sake; of course she'd hear animals. Her sheets were soaked in sweat. She had locked the window before going to bed, and the room now felt stifling, airless. I can't breathe, she thought.

She rose and slid open the window.

Stood taking in deep breaths of fresh air as she stared out at the trees, their leaves silvered by moonlight. Nothing moved; the woods had once again gone silent.

She returned to bed and this time slept soundly until dawn.

Daylight changed everything. She heard birdsong, and looking out her window, saw two deer cross the yard and bound off into the woods, white tails flashing. With sunlight streaming into the room, the chair she'd propped up against the door last night now struck her as irrational. I won't be telling anyone about this, she thought, as she pulled it aside.

In the kitchen she made coffee from a bag of ground French roast she found in the freezer. Anna's coffee. She poured hot water through the filter as she inhaled the steamy fragrance. She was surrounded by Anna's purchases. The microwave popcorn and packages of spaghetti. The expired cartons of peach yogurt and milk. Each item represented a moment in her sister's life when she had paused before a grocery store shelf and thought: I need this, too. And then later, upon the return home, she had emptied sacks and put away these choices. When Maura looked at the contents of the cabinets, it was her sister's hand she saw, stacking the cans of tuna on the flowered shelf paper.

She carried her coffee mug outside to the front porch and stood sipping from it as she surveyed the yard where sunlight dappled the little garden patch. Everything is so green, she marveled. The grass, the trees, the light itself. In the high canopy of branches, birds sang. I can see now why she might want to live here. Why she would want to wake up every morning to the smell of the woods.

Suddenly the birds rose flapping from the trees, startled by a new sound: the low rumble of machinery. Though Maura could not see the bulldozer, she could certainly hear it through the woods, sounding annoyingly close. She remembered what Miss Clausen had told her, that the lot next door was being cleared. So much for a peaceful Sunday morning.

She went down the steps and circled around to the side of the house, trying to see the bulldozer through the trees, but the woods were too thick, and she could not catch even a glimpse of it. But looking down, she did spot animal tracks, and remembered the two deer she had seen through her bedroom window that morning. She followed them along the side of the house, noticing other evidence of their visit in the chewed leaves of the hostas planted against the foundation, and marveled at how bold those deer had been, grazing right up against the wall. She continued toward the back, and came to a halt at another set of tracks. These were not from deer. She stood very still for a moment. Her heart began to thud, and her hands went clammy around the mug. Slowly, her gaze followed the tracks toward a soft patch of dirt beneath one of the windows.

A boot's imprints were pressed into the soil where someone had stood, peering into the house.

Into her bedroom.

ELEVEN

Forty-five minutes later, a Fox Harbor police cruiser came bouncing down her dirt road. It pulled up in front of the cottage, and a cop climbed out. He was in his fifties, bull-necked, his blond hair going bald on top.

"Dr. Isles?" he said, offering her a meaty handshake. "Roger Gresham, chief of police."

"I didn't know I'd get the chief himself."

"Yeah, well, we were planning to drive up here anyway when your call came in."

"We?" She frowned as another vehicle, a Ford Explorer, came up the driveway and pulled up next to Gresham's cruiser. The driver stepped out and waved at her.

"Hello, Maura," said Rick Ballard.

For a moment she just looked at him,

startled by his unexpected arrival. "I had no idea you were here," she finally said.

"I drove up last night. When did you get in?"

"Yesterday afternoon."

"You spent the night in this house?"

"The motel was full. Miss Clausen—the rental agent—offered to let me sleep here." She paused. Added on a defensive note, "She did say the police were finished with it."

Gresham gave a snort. "Bet she charged you for the night, too. Didn't she?"

"Yes."

"That Britta, she's something else. She'd charge ya for air if she could." Turning toward the house, he said: "So where did you see those footprints?"

Maura led the men past the front porch and around the corner of the house. They stayed to the side of the path, scanning the ground as they moved. The bulldozer had fallen silent, and now the only sounds were their footfalls on the carpet of leaves.

"Fresh deer tracks here," said Gresham, pointing.

"Yes, there were a pair of deer that came through here this morning," said Maura.

"That could explain those tracks you saw."

"Chief Gresham," said Maura, and sighed. "I *can* tell a boot print from a deer track."

"No, I mean some guy might've been out here hunting. Out of season, you understand. Followed those deer outta the woods."

Ballard suddenly halted, his gaze fixed on the ground.

"Do you see them?" she asked.

"Yes," he said. His voice was strangely quiet.

Gresham squatted down beside Ballard. A moment passed. Why didn't they say something? A wind stirred the trees. Shivering, she looked up at the swaying branches. Last night, someone had come out of those woods. He had stood outside her room. Had stared in her window while she slept.

Ballard glanced up at the house. "Is that a bedroom window?"

"Yes."

"Yours?"

"Yes."

"Did you close your curtains last night?" He looked over his shoulder at her, and she knew what he was thinking: *Did you treat them to an inadvertent peep show last night?*

She flushed. "There aren't any curtains in that room."

"Those are too big to be Britta's boots," said Gresham. "She's the only person who'd be tramping around up here, checking on the house."

"Looks like a Vibram sole," said Ballard. "Size eight, maybe nine." His gaze followed the prints back toward the woods. "Deer tracks overlie them."

"Which means he came through here first," said Maura. "Before the deer did. Before I woke up."

"Yes, but how long before?" Ballard straightened and stood peering through the window into her bedroom. For a long time he did not say anything, and once again she grew impatient with their silence, anxious to hear a reaction—any reaction—from these men.

"You know, it hasn't rained here in close to a week," said Gresham. "Those boot prints may not be all that fresh."

"But who'd be walking around here, looking in windows?" she asked.

"I can call Britta. Maybe she had a man up to work on the place. Or someone peeked in there 'cause they were curious."

"Curious?" asked Maura.

"Everyone up here's heard about what happened to your sister, down in Boston. Some folks might want to peek into her house."

"I don't understand that kind of morbid curiosity. I never have."

"Rick here tells me you're a medical examiner, right? Well, you must have to deal with the same thing I do. Everyone wanting to know the details. You won't believe how many folks have asked me about the shooting. Don't you think some of these busybodies might want to take a peek inside her house?"

She stared at him in disbelief. The silence was suddenly broken by the crackle of Gresham's car radio.

"Excuse me," he said, and headed back to his cruiser.

"Well," she said. "I guess that pretty much dispenses with my concerns, doesn't it?"

"I happen to take your concerns very seriously."

"Do you?" She looked at him. "Come inside, Rick. I want to show you something."

He followed her back up the steps to the front porch, and into the house. She swung the door shut and pointed to the array of brass locks.

"That's what I wanted you to see," she said.

He frowned at the locks. "Wow."

"There's more. Come with me."

She led him into the kitchen. Pointed to more gleaming chains and bolts barring the back door. "These are all new. Anna must have had them installed. Something scared her."

"She had reason to be afraid. All the death threats. She didn't know when Cassell might turn up here."

She looked at him. "That's why you're here, isn't it? To find out if he did?"

"I've been showing his photograph around town."

"And?"

"So far, no one remembers seeing him. But it doesn't mean he wasn't here." He pointed to the locks. "Those make perfect sense to me."

Sighing, she sank into a chair at the

kitchen table. "How could our lives have turned out so differently? There I was, getting off a plane from Paris while she . . ." She swallowed. "What if I'd been raised in Anna's place? Would it all have turned out the same? Maybe she'd be the one sitting here now, talking to you."

"You're two different people, Maura. You may have her face, her voice. But you're not Anna."

She looked up at him. "Tell me more about my sister."

"I'm not sure where to start."

"Anything. Everything. You just said I sound like her."

He nodded. "You do. The same inflections. The same pitch."

"You remember her that well?"

"Anna wasn't a woman you'd easily forget," he said. His gaze held hers. They stared at each other, even as footsteps came thumping into the house. Only when Gresham had walked into the kitchen did she finally break off eye contact and turn to look at the police chief.

"Dr. Isles," said Gresham. "I wonder if you could do me a little favor. Come up the road with me a ways. There's something I need you to look at."

"What sort of thing?"

"That was dispatch on the radio. They got a call from the construction crew right up the road. Their bulldozer turned up some—well, some bones."

She frowned. "Human?"

"That's what they're wondering."

Maura rode with Gresham in the cruiser, with Ballard following right behind them in his Explorer. The trip was barely worth climbing into the car for, just a short curve up the road, and there the bulldozer was, sitting in a freshly cleared lot. Four men in hard hats stood in the shade next to their pickup trucks. One of them came forward to meet them as Maura, Gresham, and Ballard climbed out of the vehicles.

"Hey, Chief."

"Hey, Mitch. Where is it?"

"Out near the bulldozer. I spotted that bone, and I just shut my engine right down. There used to be an old farmhouse here, on this lot. Last thing I want to do is dig up some family graveyard."

"We'll just have Dr. Isles here take a look before I make any calls. I'd hate to have the M.E. drive all the way over from Augusta for a bunch of bear bones."

Mitch led the way across the clearing. The newly churned-up soil was an obstacle course of ankle-snagging roots and over-turned rocks. Maura's pumps were not de-signed for hiking, and no matter how care-fully she picked her way across the terrain, she could not avoid soiling the black suede.

Gresham slapped his cheek. "Goddamn blackflies. They sure found us."

The clearing was surrounded by thick stands of trees; the air was close here and windless. By now, insects had caught their scent and were swarming, greedy for blood. Maura was grateful she'd chosen to wear long pants that morning; her unprotected face and arms were already turning into blackfly feeding stations.

By the time they reached the bulldozer, the cuffs of her trousers were soiled. The sun shone down, sparkling on bits of bro-ken glass. The canes of an old rosebush lay uprooted and dying in the heat.

"There," said Mitch, pointing.

Even before she bent down to look more

closely at it, Maura already knew what it was, lodged there in the soil. She didn't touch it, but just crouched there, her shoes sunk deep in freshly overturned earth. Newly exposed to the elements, the paleness of bone peeked through the crust of dried dirt. She heard cawing among the trees and glanced up to see crows flitting like dark specters among the branches. *They know what it is, too.*

"What do you think?" asked Gresham.

"It's an ilium."

"What's that?"

"This bone." She touched her own, where the pelvis flared against her slacks. She was reminded, suddenly, of the grim fact that beneath skin, beneath muscle, she too was merely skeleton. A structural frame of honeycombed calcium and phosphorus that would endure long after her flesh had rotted. "It's human," she said.

They were silent for a moment. The only sound on that bright June day came from the crows, a gathering flock of them, perched in the trees above, like black fruit among the branches. They stared down with eerie intelligence at the humans, and their caws built to a deafening chorus.

Then, as though on cue, their screeches abruptly stopped.

"What do you know about this place?" Maura asked the bulldozer operator. "What used to be here?"

Mitch said, "There were some old stone walls here. Foundation of a house. We moved all the stones over there, figured someone could use the rocks for something else." He pointed to a pile of boulders near the edge of the lot. "Old walls, that's really nothing unusual. You go walking in the woods, you find a lot of old foundations like this one. Used to be sheep farms all up and down the coast. Gone, now."

"So this could be an old grave," said Ballard.

"But that bone's right up where one of the old walls was standing," said Mitch. "I don't think you'd want to bury dear old Ma so close to the house. Bad luck, I'd think."

"Some people believed it was good luck," said Maura.

"What?"

"In ancient times, an infant buried alive under the cornerstone was supposed to protect the house."

Mitch stared at her. A look of *Who the heck are you, lady?*

"I'm just saying that burial practices change over the centuries," said Maura. "This could very well be an old grave."

From overhead came a noisy flapping. The crows simultaneously rose from the tree, feathers beating the sky. Maura watched them, unnerved by the sight of so many black wings lifting at once, as though by command.

"Weird," said Gresham.

Maura rose to her feet and looked at the trees. Remembered the noise of the bull-dozer that morning, and how close it had seemed. "Which direction is the house from here? The one I stayed in last night?" she asked.

Gresham looked up at the sun to orient himself, then pointed. "That way. Where you're facing now."

"How far is it?"

"It's right through those trees. You could walk it."

The Maine state medical examiner arrived from Augusta an hour and a half later. As he stepped out of his car, carrying his kit, Maura immediately recognized the man with the white turban and neatly trimmed beard. Maura had first met Dr. Daljeet Singh at a pathology conference the year before, and they had dined together in February, when he'd attended a regional forensics meeting in Boston. Though not a tall man, his dignified bearing and traditional Sikh headdress made him seem more formidable than he really was. Maura had always been impressed by his air of quiet competence. And by his eyes; Daljeet had liquid brown eyes and the longest lashes she'd ever seen on a man.

They shook hands, a warm greeting between two colleagues who genuinely liked each other. "So what are you doing here, Maura? Not enough work for you in Boston? You have to come poach my cases?"

"My weekend's turned into a busman's holiday."

"You've seen the remains?"

She nodded, her smile fading. "There's a left iliac crest, partially buried. We haven't touched it yet. I knew you'd want to see it in situ first."

"No other bones?"

"Not so far."

"Well, then." He looked at the cleared field, as though steeling himself for the tramp through the dirt. She noticed that he'd come prepared with the right footwear: L.L. Bean boots that looked as if they were brand-new and about to get their first test on muddy terrain. "Let's see what the bulldozer turned up."

By now it was early afternoon, the heat so thick with humidity that Daljeet's face was quickly glazed with sweat. As they started across the clearing, insects swarmed in, taking bloody advantage of fresh meat. Detectives Corso and Yates from the Maine State Police had arrived twenty minutes earlier, and were pacing the field along with Ballard and Gresham.

Corso waved and called out: "Not the way to spend a beautiful Sunday, hey, Dr. Singh?"

Daljeet waved back, then squatted down to look at the ilium.

"This was an old homesite," said Maura. "There was a stone foundation here, according to the crew."

"But no coffin remains?"

"We didn't see any."

He looked across the landscape of muddy stones and uprooted weeds and tree stumps. "That bulldozer could have scattered bones everywhere."

There was a shout from Detective Yates: "I found something else!"

"Way over there?" said Daljeet, as he and Maura crossed the field to join Yates.

"I was walking by here, got my foot caught in that knot of blackberry roots," said Yates. "I tripped over it, and this kind of popped up from the dirt." As Maura crouched beside him, Yates gingerly eased apart a thorny tangle of uprooted canes. A cloud of mosquitoes rose from the damp soil, lighting on Maura's face as she stared at what was partially buried there. It was a skull. One hollow orbit stared up at her, pierced by tendrils of blackberry roots that had forced their way through openings that had once held eyes.

She looked at Daljeet. "You have a pruner?"

He opened his kit. Out came gloves, a rose pruner, and a garden trowel. Together they knelt in the dirt, working to free the skull. Maura clipped roots as Daljeet gently scooped away earth. The sun beat down, and the soil itself seemed to radiate heat. Maura had to pause several times to wipe away sweat. The insect repellant she had applied an hour ago was long gone, and blackflies were once again swarming around her face.

She and Daljeet set aside their tools and began to dig with their gloved hands, kneeling so close together that their heads bumped. Her fingers tunneled deeper into cooler soil, loosening its hold. More and more cranium emerged and she paused, staring down at the temporal bone. At the massive fracture now revealed.

She and Daljeet glanced at each other, both registering the same thought: *This was not a natural death.*

"I think it's loose now," said Daljeet. "Let's lift it out."

He laid out a plastic sheet, then reached deep into the hole. His hands emerged cradling the skull, the mandible partly anchored to it by helpful spirals of blackberry roots. He laid his treasure on the sheet.

For a moment, no one said anything. They were all staring at the shattered temporal bone.

Detective Yates pointed to the metallic glint of one of the molars. "Isn't that a filling?" he said. "In that tooth?"

"Yes. But dentists were using amalgam fillings a hundred years ago," said Daljeet.

"So it could still be an old burial."

"But where are the coffin fragments? If this was a formal burial, there should be a coffin. And there's this little detail." Daljeet pointed to the crush fracture. He looked up at the two detectives bending over his shoulder. "Whatever the age of these remains, I think you have a crime scene here."

The other men had crowded in around them, and suddenly the air felt as if all the oxygen had been sucked out of it. The buzz of mosquitoes seemed to grow to a pulsing roar. It's so warm, she thought. She rose to her feet and walked on unsteady legs toward the edge of the woods, where the canopy of oak and maple cast a welcome shade. Sinking onto a rock, she dropped her head in her hands, thinking: This is what I get for not eating breakfast.

"Maura?" called Ballard. "Are you okay?"

"It's just this heat. I need to cool down for a moment."

"Would you like some water? I have some

in my truck, if you don't mind drinking from the same bottle."

"Thank you. I could use some."

She watched as he headed toward his vehicle, the back of his shirt stained with wings of sweat. He didn't bother to pick his way delicately across the uneven field, but just forged ahead, boots tramping across broken soil. Purposeful. That's the way Ballard walked, like a man who knew what needed to be done, and simply got on with it.

The bottle he brought back to her was warm from sitting in the truck. She took a greedy gulp, water trickling down her chin. Lowering the bottle, she found Ballard watching her. For a moment she didn't notice the hum of insects, the murmur of men's voices as they worked yards away. Here, in the green shadows beneath the trees, she could focus only on him. On the way his hand brushed hers as he took the bottle back. On the soft light dappling his hair, and the web of laugh lines around his eyes. She heard Daljeet call her name, but she didn't answer, didn't turn away; neither did Ballard, who seemed just as trapped in the moment. She thought: One of us has got to break the spell. One of us has got to snap back out of it. But I can't seem to manage it.

"Maura?" Daljeet was suddenly standing right beside her; she hadn't even heard his approach. "We have an interesting problem," he said.

"What problem?"

"Come take another look at that ilium."

Slowly she rose to her feet, feeling steadier now, her head clear. The drink of water, the few moments in the shade, had given her a second wind. She and Ballard followed Daljeet back to the hip bone, and she saw that Daljeet had already cleared away some of the soil, exposing more of the pelvis.

"I got it down to the sacrum on this side," he said. "You can just see the pelvic outlet and the ischial tuberosity, here."

She dropped to a crouch beside him. Said nothing for a moment, just stared at the bone.

"What's the problem?" said Ballard.

"We need to expose the rest of this," she said. She looked up at Daljeet. "Do you have another trowel?"

He passed one to her; it was like the slap

of a scalpel handle in her palm. Suddenly she was at work, and all grim business. Kneeling side by side, trowels in hand, she and Daljeet cleared away more stony soil. Tree roots had woven through bony fossae, anchoring the bones to their grave, and they had to cut away the wiry tangle to free the pelvis. The deeper they dug, the faster her heart began to beat. Treasure hunters might dig for gold; she dug for secrets. For the answers that only a grave can reveal. With each trowelful of dirt they removed, more of the pelvis came into view. They worked feverishly now, tools probing deeper.

When at last they stared down at the exposed pelvis, they were both too stunned to speak.

Maura rose to her feet and walked back to look at the skull, still lying on the plastic sheet. Kneeling beside it, she pulled off her gloves and ran her bare fingers above the orbit, feeling the robust curve of the supraorbital ridge. Then she flipped over the skull, to examine the occipital protuberance.

This did not make sense.

She rocked back on her knees. Her blouse was sweat-soaked in the cloying air.

Except for the buzz of insects, the clearing had gone silent. Trees loomed on all sides, guarding this secret enclosure. Gazing at that impenetrable wall of green, she felt eyes staring back, as though the forest itself was watching her. Waiting for her next move.

"What's going on, Dr. Isles?"

She looked up at Detective Corso. "We have a problem," she said. "This skull—"

"What about it?"

"You see the heavy ridges here, above the eye sockets? And look back here, at the base of the skull. If you run your finger across it, you can feel a bump. It's called the occipital protuberance."

"So?"

"It's where the ligamentum nuchae attaches, anchoring the muscles from the back of the neck to the cranium. The fact that bump is so prominent tells me this individual had robust musculature. This is almost certainly a man's skull."

"What's the problem?"

"That pelvis over there is from a woman."

Corso stared at her. Turned to look at Dr. Singh.

"I completely agree with Dr. Isles," said Daljeet.

"But that would mean . . ."

"We have the remains of two different individuals here," said Maura. "One male, one female." She stood up and met Corso's gaze. "The question is, how many others are buried out here?"

For a moment, Corso seemed too startled to respond. Then he turned and slowly scanned the clearing, as though really seeing it for the first time.

"Chief Gresham," he said, "we're going to need volunteers. A lot of them. Cops, firemen. I'll call in our team from Augusta, but it won't be enough. Not for what we need to do."

"How many people are you talking about?"

"Whatever it takes to walk this site." Corso was staring at the surrounding trees. "We're going to comb every square inch of this place. The clearing, the woods. If there's more than two people buried here, I'm going to find them."

TWELVE

Jane Rizzoli had grown up in the suburb of Revere, just over the Tobin Bridge from downtown Boston. It was a working-class neighborhood of boxy homes on postage-stamp lots, a place where, every fourth of July, hot dogs sizzled on backyard grills and American flags were proudly displayed on front porches. The Rizzoli family had known its share of ups and downs, including a few terrible months when Jane was ten years old, and her father had lost his job. She'd been old enough to sense her mother's fear and absorb her father's angry desperation. She and her two brothers knew what it was like to live on that knife edge between comfort and ruin, and even though she enjoyed a steady paycheck, she could never quite silence the whispers of insecurity from her childhood. She would always think of herself as the girl from Revere who'd grown up dreaming of one day having a big house in a grander neighborhood, a house with enough bathrooms so she wouldn't have to pound on the door every morning, demanding her turn in the shower. It would have to have a brick chimney and a double front door and a brass knocker. The house she was now staring at from her car had all those features and more: the brass knocker, the double front door, and not one chimney, but two. Everything she'd dreamed about.

But it was the ugliest house she'd ever seen.

The other homes on this East Dedham street were what you'd expect to find in a comfortable middle-class neighborhood: two-car garages and neatly kept front yards. Late-model cars parked in driveways. Nothing fancy, nothing that demanded *look at me.* But this house—well, it didn't just demand your attention. It shrieked for it.

It was as if Tara, the plantation house from *Gone with the Wind,* had been whooshed up in a tornado and plopped

down on a city lot. It had no yard to speak
of, just a rim of land along the sides so narrow you could barely push a lawnmower
between the wall and the neighbor's fence.
White columns stood sentinel on a porch
where Scarlett O'Hara could have held
court in full view of the traffic on Sprague
Street. The house made her think of Johnny
Silva in the old neighborhood, and how he
had blown his first paycheck on a cherry-
red Corvette. "Trying to pretend he's not a
loser," her father had said. "Boy hasn't even
gotten around to moving outa his parents'
basement, and he buys himself a fancy
sports car. The biggest losers buy the
biggest cars."

Or build the biggest house in the neighborhood, she thought, staring at Tara-on-
Sprague-Street.

She maneuvered her belly out from behind the steering wheel. Felt the baby tap-
dance on her bladder as she walked up the
porch steps. First things first, she thought.
Ask to use the restroom. The doorbell didn't
just ring; it *bonged,* like a cathedral bell calling the faithful to worship.

The blond woman who opened the door
appeared to have wandered into the wrong

residence. Rather than Scarlett O'Hara, she was your classic Bambi—big hair, big boobs, body sausaged into a pink spandex exercise outfit. A face so unnaturally blank of expression that it had to be Botoxed.

"I'm Detective Rizzoli, here to see Terence Van Gates. I called earlier."

"Oh yeah, Terry's expecting you." A girlish voice, high and sweet. Okay in small doses, but after an hour, it would be like fingernails scraping across a chalkboard.

Rizzoli stepped into the foyer and was immediately confronted with a mammoth oil painting on the wall. It was Bambi dressed in a green evening gown, standing beside an enormous vase of orchids. Everything in this house seemed oversized. The paintings, the ceilings, the breasts.

"They're renovating his office building, so he's working from home today. Down the hall, on your right."

"Excuse me—I'm sorry, I don't know your name."

"Bonnie."

Bonnie, Bambi. Close enough.

"That would be . . . Mrs. Van Gates?" asked Rizzoli.

"Uh-huh."

Trophy wife. Van Gates had to be close to seventy.

"May I use your restroom? I seem to need one every ten minutes these days."

For the first time, Bonnie seemed to notice that Rizzoli was pregnant. "Oh, honey! Of course you can. The powder room's right there."

Rizzoli had never seen a bathroom painted candy-cane pink. The toilet sat high on a platform, like a throne, with a telephone mounted on the wall beside it. As if anyone would want to conduct business while, well, doing their business. She washed her hands with pink soap in the pink marble basin, dried them with pink towels, and fled the room.

Bonnie had vanished, but Rizzoli could hear the beat of exercise music, and the thumps of feet bouncing upstairs. Bonnie going through her exercise routine. I should get in shape one of these days too, thought Rizzoli. But I refuse to do it in pink spandex.

She headed down the hall in search of Van Gates's office. She peeked first into a vast living room with a white grand piano and a white rug and white furniture. White room, pink room. What came next? She passed another painting of Bonnie in the hallway, this time posed as a Greek goddess in a white gown, nipples showing through diaphanous fabric. Man, these people belonged in Vegas.

At last she came to an office. "Mr. Van Gates?" she said.

The man sitting behind the cherry desk looked up from his papers, and she saw watery blue eyes, a face gone soft and jowly with age, and hair that was—what *was* that shade? Somewhere between yellow and orange. Surely not intentional, just a dye job gone wrong.

"Detective Rizzoli?" he said, and his gaze fell to her abdomen. Got stuck there, as though he'd never seen a pregnant cop before.

Talk to me, not the belly. She crossed to his desk and shook his hand. Noticed the telltale transplant plugs dotting his scalp, sprouting hair like little tufts of yellow grass in a last desperate stand of virility. That's what you deserved for marrying a trophy wife.

"Sit down, sit down," he said.

She settled into a slick leather chair. Glancing around the room, she noticed that the decor in here was radically different from the rest of the house. It was done up in Traditional Lawyer, with dark wood and leather. Mahogany shelves were filled with law journals and textbooks. Not a whisper of pink. Clearly this was his domain, a Bonnie-free zone.

"I don't really know how I can help you, Detective," he said. "The adoption you're asking about was forty years ago."

"Not exactly ancient history."

He laughed. "I doubt you were even born then."

Was that a little poke? His way of saying she was too young to be bothering him with these questions?

"You don't recall the people involved?"

"I'm just saying that it was a long time ago. I would've been just out of law school then. Working out of a rented office with rented furniture and no secretary. Answered my own phone. I took every case that came in—divorces, adoptions, drunk driving. Whatever paid the rent."

"And you still have all those files, of course. From your cases back then."

"They'd be in storage."

"Where?"

"File-Safe, out in Quincy. But before we go any further, I have to tell you. The parties involved in this particular case requested absolute privacy. The birth mother did not want her name revealed. Those records were sealed years ago."

"This is a homicide case, Mr. Van Gates. One of the two adoptees is now dead."

"Yes, I know. But I fail to see what that has to do with her adoption forty years ago. How is it relevant to your investigation?"

"Why did Anna Leoni call you?"

He looked startled. Nothing he said after that could cover up that initial reaction, that expression of *uh-oh*. "Excuse me?" he said.

"The day before she was murdered, Anna Leoni called your law office from her room at the Tremont Hotel. We just got her phone record. The conversation lasted thirty-seven minutes. Now, you two must have talked about *something* during those thirty-seven minutes. You couldn't have kept the poor woman on hold all that time?"

He said nothing.

"Mr. Van Gates?"

"That—that conversation was confidential."

"Ms. Leoni was your client? You billed her for that call?"

"No, but—"

"So you're not bound by attorney-client privilege."

"But I am bound by another client's confidentiality."

"The birth mother."

"Well, she *was* my client. She gave up her babies on one condition—that her name never be revealed."

"That was forty years ago. She may have changed her mind."

"I have no idea. I don't know where she is. I don't even know if she's still alive."

"Is that why Anna called you? To ask about her mother?"

He leaned back. "Adoptees are often curious about their origins. For some of them it becomes an obsession. So they go on document hunts. Invest thousands of dollars and a lot of heartache searching for mothers who don't want to be found. And if they *do* find them, it's seldom the fairy-tale ending they expected. That's what she was looking for, Detective. A fairy-tale ending. Sometimes they're better off just forgetting it, and moving on with their lives."

Rizzoli thought of her own childhood, her own family. She had always known who she was. She could look at her grandparents, her parents, and see her own bloodline engraved on their faces. She was one of them, right down to her DNA, and no matter how much her relatives might annoy her or embarrass her, she knew they were hers.

But Maura Isles had never seen herself in the eyes of a grandparent. When Maura walked down a street, did she study the faces of passing strangers, searching for a hint of her own features? A familiar curve to the mouth or slope of the nose? Rizzoli could perfectly understand the hunger to know your own origins. To know that you're not just a loose twig, but one branch of a deeply rooted tree.

She looked Van Gates in the eye. "Who is Anna Leoni's mother?"

He shook his head. "I'll say it again. This is not relevant to your—"

"Let me decide that. Just give me the name."

"Why? So you can disrupt the life of a woman who may not want to be reminded of her youthful mistake? What does this have to do with the murder?"

Rizzoli leaned closer, placing both her hands on his desk. Aggressively trespassing on his personal property. Sweet little Bambis might not do this, but girl cops from Revere weren't afraid to.

"We can subpoena your files. Or I can ask you politely."

They stared at each other for a moment. Then he released a sigh of capitulation. "Okay, I don't need to go through this again. I'll just tell you, okay? The mother's name was Amalthea Lank. She was twenty-four years old. And she needed money—badly."

Rizzoli frowned. "Are you telling me she got paid for giving up her babies?"

"Well . . ."

"How much?"

"It was substantial. Enough for her to get a fresh start in life."

"How much?"

He blinked. "It was twenty thousand dollars, each."

"For each *baby*?"

"Two happy families walked away with a child. She walked away with cash. Believe me, adoptive parents pay a lot more today. Do you know how hard it is to adopt a healthy Caucasian newborn these days? There just aren't enough to go around. It's supply and demand, that's all."

Rizzoli sank back, appalled that a woman would sell her babies for cold hard cash.

"Now that's all I can tell you," said Van Gates. "If you want to find out more, well, maybe you cops should try talking to each other. You'd save a lot of time."

That last statement puzzled her. Then she remembered what he'd said only a moment earlier: *I don't need to go through this again.*

"Who else has asked you about this woman?" she said.

"You people all go about it the same way. You come in, threaten to make my life miserable if I don't cooperate—"

"It was another cop?"

"Yes."

"Who?"

"I don't remember. It was months ago. I must've blocked out his name."

"Why did he want to know?"

"Because she put him up to it. They came in together."

"Anna Leoni came in with him?"

"He was doing it for her. A favor." Van

Gates snorted. "We should all have cops doing us favors."

"This was several months ago? They came in to see you together?"

"I just said that."

"And you told her the mother's name?"

"Yeah."

"So why did Anna call you last week? If she already knew her mother's name?"

"Because she saw some photo in *The Boston Globe.* A lady who looks just like her."

"Dr. Maura Isles."

He nodded. "Ms. Leoni asked me directly, so I told her."

"Told her what?"

"That she had a sister."

THIRTEEN

The bones changed everything.

Maura had planned to drive home to Boston that evening. Instead she returned briefly to the cottage to change into jeans and a T-shirt, then drove back in her own car to the clearing. I'll stay a little longer, she thought, and leave by four o'clock. But as the afternoon wore on, as the crime scene unit arrived from Augusta and search teams began walking the grid that Corso had mapped out in the clearing, Maura lost track of the time. She took only one break, to wolf down a chicken sandwich that volunteers had delivered to the site. Everything tasted like the mosquito repellent she'd slathered all over her face, but she was so hungry she would have happily gnawed on a dry crust of bread. Her appetite sated, she once again pulled on gloves, picked up a trowel, and knelt down in the dirt beside Dr. Singh.

Four o'clock came and went.

The cardboard boxes began to fill with bones. Ribs and lumbar vertebrae. Femurs and tibias. The bulldozer had not, in fact, scattered the bones far. The female's remains were all located within a six-foot radius; the male's, bound together in a web of blackberry roots, were even more contained. There appeared to be only two individuals, but it took all afternoon to unearth them. Gripped by the excitement of the dig, Maura could not bring herself to leave, not when every shovelful of dirt she sifted might reveal some new prize. A button or a bullet or a tooth. As a Stanford University undergraduate, she had spent a summer working on an archaeological site in Baja. Though the temperatures there had soared well into the nineties, and her only shade was a broad-brimmed hat, she had worked straight into the hottest part of the day, driven by the same fever that afflicts treasure hunters who believe that the next artifact is only inches away. That fever was what she experienced now, kneeling among the ferns, swatting at blackflies. It was what kept her digging through the afternoon and into the evening as storm clouds moved in. As thunder rumbled in the distance.

That, and the quiet thrill she felt whenever Rick Ballard came near.

Even as she sifted through dirt, teased away roots, she was aware of him. His voice, his proximity. He was the one who brought her a fresh water bottle, who handed her the sandwich. Who stopped to place a hand on her shoulder and ask how she was doing. Her male colleagues at the M.E.'s office seldom touched her. Perhaps it was her aloofness, or some silent signal she gave off that told them she did not welcome personal contact. But Ballard did not hesitate to reach for her arm, to rest his hand on her back.

His touches left her flushed.

When the CSU team began packing up their tools for the day, she was startled to realize it was already seven, and daylight was fading. Her muscles ached, her clothes were filthy. She stood on legs trembling with weariness, and watched Daljeet tape shut the two boxes of remains. They each picked up a box and carried them across the field, to his vehicle.

"After today, I think you owe me dinner, Daljeet," she said.

"Restaurant Julien, I promise. Next time I'm down in Boston."

"Believe me, I plan to collect."

He loaded the boxes into his car and shut the door. Then they shook hands, filthy palm to filthy palm. She waved as he drove away. Most of the search team had already left; only a few cars remained.

Ballard's Explorer was among them.

She paused in the deepening dusk and looked at the clearing. He was standing near the woods, talking to Detective Corso, his back to her. She lingered, hoping that he would notice she was about to leave.

And then what? What did she want to happen between them?

Get out of here before you make an idiot of yourself.

Abruptly she turned and walked to her car. Started the engine and pulled away so quickly the tires spun.

Back in the cottage, she peeled off her soiled clothes. Took a long shower, lathering up twice to wash away every trace of the oily mosquito repellant. When she stepped out of the bathroom, she realized she had no more clean clothes to change into. She had planned on staying only one night in Fox Harbor.

She opened the closet door and gazed at Anna's clothes. They were all her size. What else was she going to wear? She pulled out a summer dress. It was white cotton, a little girlish for her taste, but on this warm and humid evening, it was just what she felt like wearing. Slipping the dress over her head, she felt the kiss of sheer fabric against her skin, and wondered when the last time was that Anna had smoothed this dress over her own hips, when had she last looped the sash around her waist. The creases were still there, marking the fabric where Anna had tied the knot. Everything I see and touch of hers still bears her imprint, she thought.

The ringing telephone made her turn and face the nightstand. Somehow she knew, even before she picked it up, that it was Ballard.

"I didn't see you leave," he said.

"I came back to the house to take a shower. I was such a mess."

He laughed. "I'm feeling pretty grungy myself."

"When are you driving back to Boston?"

"It's already so late in the day. I think I might as well just stay another night. What about you?"

"I don't really feel like driving back tonight, either."

A moment passed.

"Did you find a hotel room here?" she asked.

"I brought my tent and sleeping bag with me. I'm staying at a campground up the road."

It took her five seconds to make a decision. Five seconds to consider the possibilities. And the consequences.

"There's a spare room here," she said. "You're welcome to use it."

"I hate to barge in on you."

"The bed's just sitting here, Rick."

A pause. "That'd be great. But on one condition."

"What's that?"

"You let me bring you dinner. There's a take-out place down on Main Street. Nothing fancy, maybe just some boiled lobsters."

"I don't know about you, Rick. But in my book, lobsters definitely qualify as fancy."

"Do you want wine or beer?"

"Tonight feels like a beer night."

"I'll be there in about an hour. Save your appetite."

She hung up, and suddenly realized she was starving. Only moments ago, she'd been too tired to drive into town, and had considered skipping dinner and simply going to bed early. Now she was hungry, not just for food but for company as well.

She wandered the house, restless and driven by too many contradictory desires. Only a few nights ago, she had shared dinner with Daniel Brophy. But the church had long ago laid claim to Daniel, and she would never be in the running. Hopeless causes might be seductive, but they seldom brought you happiness.

She heard the rumble of thunder and went to the screen door. Outside, dusk had deepened to night. Though she saw no lightning flashes, the air itself seemed charged. Electric with possibilities. Raindrops began to patter on the roof. At first it was only a few hesitant taps, then the sky opened up like a hundred drummers pounding overhead. Thrilled by the storm's power, she stood on the porch and watched the rain pour down, and felt the welcome blast of cool air ripple her dress, lift her hair.

A pair of headlights cut through the silvery downpour.

She stood perfectly still on the porch, her heart pounding like the rain, as the car pulled up in front of the house. Ballard stepped out, carrying a large sack and a six-pack of beer. Head bent under the torrent, he splashed to the porch and up the steps.

"Didn't know I'd have to swim here," he said.

She laughed. "Come on, I'll get you a towel."

"Do you mind if I jump into your shower? I haven't had a chance to wash up yet."

"Go ahead." She took the grocery sack from him. "The bathroom's down the hall. There are clean towels in the cabinet."

"I'll get my overnight bag out of the trunk."

She carried the food into the kitchen and slid the beer into the refrigerator. Heard the screen door clap shut as he came back into the house. And then, a moment later, she heard the shower running.

She sat down at the table and released a deep breath. This is only dinner, she thought. A single night under the same roof. She thought of the meal she'd cooked for Daniel only a few days ago, and how different that evening had felt from the start. When she'd looked at Daniel, she'd seen the unattainable. *And what do I see when I look at Rick? Maybe more than I should.*

The shower was off. She sat very still, listening, every sense suddenly so acute she could feel the air whisper across her skin. Footsteps creaked closer, and suddenly he was there, smelling of soap, dressed in blue jeans and a clean shirt.

"I hope you don't mind eating with a barefoot man," he said. "My boots were too muddy to wear in the house."

She laughed. "Then I'll just go barefoot too. It'll feel like a picnic." She slipped out of her sandals and went to the refrigerator. "Are you ready for a beer?"

"I've been ready for hours."

She uncapped two bottles and handed one to him. Sipped hers as she watched him tilt his head back and take a deep gulp.

I will never see Daniel looking like this, she thought. Carefree and barefoot, his hair damp from a shower.

She turned and went to look in the grocery sack. "So what have you brought for dinner?"

"Let me show you." Joining her at the counter, he reached into the sack and took out various foil-wrapped packets. "Baked potatoes. Melted butter. Corn on the cob. And the main event." He produced a large Styrofoam container and flipped it open to reveal two bright red lobsters, still steaming.

"How do we get those open?"

"You don't know how to crack one of these critters?"

"I hope you do."

"Nothing to it." He pulled two nutcrackers out of the sack. "You ready for surgery, Doctor?"

"Now you're making me nervous."

"It's all in the technique. But first, we need to suit up."

"Excuse me?"

He reached in the sack and came out with plastic bibs.

"You've got to be kidding."

"You think restaurants give these things out just to make tourists look like idiots?"

"Yes."

"Come on, be a sport. It'll keep that nice dress clean." He circled around behind her and slipped the bib over her chest. She felt his breath in her hair as he fastened the ties behind her neck. His hands lingered there, a touch that made her shiver.

"It's your turn, now," she said softly.

"My turn?"

"I'm not going to be the only one wearing one of these ridiculous things."

He gave a sigh of resignation and tied a bib around his own neck. They looked at each other, wearing matching cartoon lobsters on their chests, and they both burst out laughing. Kept on laughing as they sank into chairs at the table. A few sips of beer on an empty stomach and I'm out of control, she thought. *And it feels so good.*

He picked up a nutcracker. "Now, Dr. Isles. Are we ready to operate?"

She reached for hers, holding it like a surgeon about to make the first incision. "Ready."

The rain pounded its steady drumbeat as they pulled off claws, cracked shells, and teased out sweet chunks of meat. They did not bother with forks but ate with their hands, their fingers slick with butter as they opened fresh bottles of beer and broke apart baked potatoes to expose the warm and yeasty flesh within. Tonight manners didn't matter; this was a picnic, and they sat barefoot at the table, licking their fingers. Stealing glances at each other.

"This is a lot more fun than eating with a knife and fork," she said.

"You've never eaten lobster with your bare hands before?"

"Believe it or not, this is the first time I've encountered one that wasn't already out of its shell." She reached for a napkin and wiped the butter from her fingers. "I'm not from New England, you know. I moved here only two years ago. From San Francisco."

"That surprises me somehow."

"Why?"

"You strike me as such a typical Yankee."

"Meaning?"

"Self-contained. Reserved."

"I try to be."

"Are you saying that it's not the real you?"

"We all play roles. I have my official mask at work. The one I wear when I'm Dr. Isles."

"And when you're with friends?"

She sipped her beer, then quietly set it down. "I haven't made that many friends in Boston, yet."

"It takes time, if you're an outsider."

An outsider. Yes, that's what she felt like, every day. She'd watch cops slap each other on the back. She heard them talk about barbecues and softball games to which she'd never be invited because she was not one of them, a cop. The M.D. behind her name was like a wall, shutting them out. And her doctor colleagues in the M.E.'s office, all of them married, didn't know what to do with her, either. Attractive divorcées were inconvenient, discomfiting. Either a threat or a temptation no one wanted to deal with.

"So what brought you to Boston?" he asked.

"I guess I needed to shake up my life."

"Career blahs?"

"No, not that. I was pretty happy at the medical school there. I was a pathologist at the university hospital. Plus I got the chance to work with all these bright young residents and students."

"So if it wasn't the job, it must have been the love life."

She looked down at the table, at the leavings of her dinner. "Good guess."

"This is where you tell me to mind my own business."

"I got divorced, that's all."

"Something you want to talk about?"

She shrugged. "What can I say? Victor was brilliant, incredibly charismatic—"

"Gee, I'm already jealous."

"But you can't stay married to someone like that. It's too intense. It burns out so fast you end up exhausted. And he . . ." She stopped.

"What?"

She reached for the beer. Took her time sipping it before she set it down. "He wasn't exactly honest with me," she said. "That's all."

She knew he wanted to know more, but he had picked up on that note of finality in her voice. *This far, no further.* He stood up and went to the refrigerator for two more beers. Popped off the caps and handed a bottle to her.

"If we're gonna talk about exes," he said, "we'll need a lot more beer than this."

"Let's not, then. If it hurts."

"Maybe it hurts because you *don't* talk about it."

"No one wants to hear about my divorce."

He sat down and met her gaze across the table. "I do."

No man, she thought, had ever focused on her so completely, and she could not look away. She found herself breathing deeply, inhaling the smell of rain and the rich animal scent of melted butter. She saw things in his face she had not noticed before. The streaks of blond in his hair. The scar on his chin, just a faint white line below his lip. The chipped front tooth. I've just met this man, she thought, but he looks at me as though he's known me forever. Faintly she heard her cell phone ringing in the bedroom, but did not want to answer it. She let it keep ringing until it fell silent. It was unlike her not to answer her phone, but tonight, everything felt different. *She* felt different. Reckless. A woman who ignored her phone and ate with her bare hands.

A woman who just might sleep with a man she scarcely knew.

The phone started ringing again.

This time, the urgency of that sound finally drew her attention. She could no longer ignore it. Reluctantly she stood up. "I guess I should answer that."

By the time she got to the bedroom, the phone had once again stopped ringing. She dialed up her voice mail and heard two different messages, both from Rizzoli.

"Doc, I need to talk to you. Call me back."

The second message, recorded in a more querulous voice: "It's me again. Why aren't you answering?"

Maura sat down on the bed. Couldn't help thinking, as she gazed at the mattress, that it was just big enough for two. She shook the thought from her head, took a deep breath, and dialed Rizzoli's number.

"Where are you?" Rizzoli demanded.

"I'm still in Fox Harbor. I'm sorry, I didn't get to the phone in time to answer it."

"Have you seen Ballard up there yet?"

"Yes, we just finished dinner. How did you know he was here?"

"Because he called me yesterday, asking where you'd gone. He sounded like he might head up that way."

"He's right in the other room. Do you want me to get him?"

"No, I want to talk to you." Rizzoli paused. "I went to see Terence Van Gates today."

Rizzoli's abrupt change in subject gave Maura a case of mental whiplash. "What?" she asked, bewildered.

"Van Gates. You told me he was the attorney who—"

"Yes, I know who he is. What did he tell you?"

"Something interesting. About the adoption."

"He actually talked to you about it?"

"Yeah, it's amazing how some people open up when you flash a badge. He told me your sister went to see him months ago. Just like you, she was trying to find her birth mother. He gave her the same runaround he gave you. Records were sealed, the mother wanted confidentiality, blah, blah, blah. So she returned with a friend, who finally convinced Van Gates it was in his best interests to give up the mother's name."

"And did he?"

"Yes, he did."

Maura had the phone pressed so hard to

her ear that she could hear her own pulse thumping in the receiver. She said, softly: "You know who my mother is."

"Yes. But there's something else—"

"Tell me her name, Jane."

A pause. "Lank. Her name is Amalthea Lank."

Amalthea. My mother's name is Amalthea.

Maura's breath whooshed out on a tide of gratitude. "Thank you! God, I can't believe I finally know—"

"Wait. I haven't finished."

The tone of Rizzoli's voice held a warning. Something bad was coming. Something that Maura would not like.

"What is it?"

"That friend of Anna's, the one who spoke to Van Gates?"

"Yes?"

"It was Rick Ballard."

Maura went very still. From the kitchen came the clatter of dishes, the hiss of running water. *I have just spent a whole day with him, and I suddenly learn I don't know what kind of man he really is.*

"Doc?"

"Then why didn't he tell me?"

"I know why he didn't."

"Why?"

"You'd better ask him. Ask him to tell you the rest of it."

When she returned to the kitchen, she saw that he had cleared the table and thrown the lobster shells in a trash bag. He was standing at the sink washing his hands and did not realize she was in the doorway, watching him.

"What do you know about Amalthea Lank?" Maura said.

He went rigid, his back still turned. A long silence passed. Then he reached for a dish towel and took his time drying his hands. *Buying time before he answers me,* she thought. But there was no excuse that she would accept, nothing he could say that could reverse the sense of distrust she now felt.

At last he turned to face her. "I was hoping you wouldn't find out. Amalthea Lank is not a woman you want to know, Maura."

"Is she my mother? Goddamn it, tell me that much."

A reluctant nod. "Yes. She is."

There, he'd said it. He'd confirmed it. Another moment passed while she absorbed the fact he had kept such important information from her. The whole time he was watching her with a look of concern.

"Why didn't you tell me?" she asked.

"I was thinking only of you, Maura. What's in your best interests—"

"The truth isn't in my best interests?"

"In this case, no. It isn't."

"What the hell is that supposed to mean?"

"I made a mistake with your sister—a serious one. She wanted so badly to find her mother, and I thought I could do her that favor. I had no idea it would turn out the way it did." He took a step toward her. "I was trying to protect you, Maura. I saw what it did to Anna. I didn't want the same thing to happen to you."

"I'm not Anna."

"But you're just like her. You're so much like her, it scares me. Not just the way you look, but the way you think."

She gave a sarcastic laugh. "So now you can read my *mind*?"

"Not your mind. Your personality. Anna was tenacious. When she wanted to know something, she wouldn't let go. And you'll just keep digging and digging, until you have an answer. The way you dug out there in the woods today. That wasn't your job, and it wasn't your jurisdiction. You had no reason to be out there at all, except for sheer curiosity. And stubbornness. You wanted to find those bones, so you did. That's how Anna was." He sighed. "I'm just sorry she found what she was digging for."

"Who was my mother, Rick?"

"A woman you don't want to meet."

It took a moment for Maura to fully register the significance of that answer. *Present tense.* "My mother is alive."

Reluctantly he nodded.

"And you know where to find her."

He didn't answer.

"Goddamn it, Rick!" she exploded. "Why don't you just *tell me*?"

He went to the table and sat down, as though suddenly too tired to continue the battle. "Because I know you're going to find it painful, hearing the facts. Especially because of who you are. What you do for a living."

"What does my job have to do with it?"

"You work with law enforcement. You help bring killers to justice."

"I don't bring anyone to justice. I just provide the facts. Sometimes the facts aren't what you cops want to hear."

"But you work on *our* side."

"No. The *victim's* side."

"All right, the victim's side. That's why you're not going to like what I tell you about her."

"You haven't told me a thing so far."

He sighed. "Okay. Maybe I should start off by telling you where she's living."

"Go on."

"Amalthea Lank—the woman who gave you up for adoption—is incarcerated at the Massachusetts Department of Corrections facility in Framingham."

Her legs suddenly unsteady, Maura sank into a chair across from him. Felt her arm smear across spilled butter that had congealed on the tabletop. Evidence of the cheerful meal they'd shared less than an hour ago, before her universe had tilted.

"My mother is in prison?"

"Yes."

Maura stared at him, and could not bring herself to ask the next obvious question, because she was afraid of the answer. But she had already taken the first step down this road, and even though she didn't know where it might take her, she couldn't turn back now.

"What did she do?" Maura asked. "Why is she in prison?"

"She's serving a life term," he said. "For a double homicide."

"That's what I didn't want you to know," said Ballard. "I saw what it did to Anna, knowing what her mother was guilty of. Knowing whose blood she had in her veins. That's a pedigree no one wants to have—a killer in the family. Naturally, she didn't want to believe it. She thought it had to be a mistake, that maybe her mother was innocent. And after she saw her—"

"Wait. Anna saw our mother?"

"Yes. She and I drove out together, to MCI–Framingham. The women's prison. It was another mistake, because that visit only made her more confused about her mother's guilt. She just couldn't accept the fact her mother was a monst—" He stopped.

A monster. My mother is a monster.

The rainfall had slowed to a gentle tap-

tap on the roof. Though the thunderstorm had passed, she could still hear its fading rumble as it swept out to sea. But inside the kitchen, all was silent. They sat facing each other across the table, Rick watching her with quiet concern, as though afraid she would shatter. He doesn't know me, she thought. I'm not Anna. I won't fall apart. And I don't need a goddamn keeper.

"Tell me the rest," she said.

"The rest?"

"You said Amalthea Lank was convicted of double homicide. When was this?"

"It was about five years ago."

"Who were the victims?"

"It's not an easy thing to tell you. Or an easy thing for you to hear."

"So far you've told me my mother is a murderer. I think I'm taking it pretty well."

"Better than Anna did," he admitted.

"So tell me who the victims were, and don't leave a goddamn thing out. It's the one thing I can't deal with, Rick, when people hide the truth from me. I was married to a man who kept too many secrets from me. That's what ended our marriage. I won't put up with it again, not from anyone. "

"Okay." He leaned forward, looking her in

the eye. "You want the details, then I'll be brutally honest about it. Because the details *are* brutal. The victims were two sisters, Theresa and Nikki Wells, ages thirty-five and twenty-eight, from Fitchburg, Massachusetts. They were stranded at the side of the road with a flat tire. It was late November, and there was a surprise snowstorm blowing. They must've felt pretty lucky when a car pulled over to give them a lift. Two days later, their bodies were found about thirty miles away, in a burned-down shed. A week after that, police in Virginia stopped Amalthea Lank for a traffic violation. Found out her car had stolen plates. Then they noticed smears of blood on the rear bumper. When police searched the car, they found the victims' wallets were in the trunk, as well as a tire iron with Amalthea's fingerprints. Later tests turned up traces of blood on it. Nikki's and Theresa's blood. The final piece of evidence was recorded on a gas station security camera up in Massachusetts. Amalthea Lank is seen on that recording filling a plastic container with gasoline. The gasoline she used to burn the victims' bodies." His gaze met hers. "There. I've been brutal. Is that what you wanted?"

"What was the cause of death?" she asked. Her voice strangely, chillingly calm. "You said the bodies were burned, but how were the women killed?"

He stared at her for a moment, as though not quite accepting her composure. "X-rays of the burned remains showed that the skulls of both women were fractured, most likely by that tire iron. The younger sister, Nikki, was struck so hard in the face that it caved in the facial bones, leaving nothing but a crater. That's how vicious a crime it was."

She thought about the scenario he had just presented. Thought about a snowy roadside and two stranded sisters. When a woman stops to help, they'd have every reason to trust their good samaritan, especially if she is older. Grayer. Women helping women.

She looked at Ballard. "You said Anna didn't believe she was guilty."

"I just told you what they presented at trial. The tire iron, the gas station video. The stolen wallets. Any jury would have convicted her."

"This happened five years ago. How old was Amalthea?"

"I don't remember. Sixty-something."

"And she managed to subdue and kill two women who are decades younger than she is?"

"Jesus, you're doing the same thing Anna did. Doubting the obvious."

"Because the obvious isn't always true. Any able-bodied person would fight back or run. Why didn't Theresa and Nikki?"

"They must have been taken by surprise."

"But *two* of them? Why didn't the other one run?"

"One of them wasn't exactly able-bodied."

"What do you mean?"

"The younger sister, Nikki. She was nine months pregnant."

FOURTEEN

Mattie Purvis did not know if it was day or night. She had no watch, so she could not keep track of the passing hours or days. That was the hardest part of all, not knowing how long she had been in this box. How many heartbeats, how many breaths she had spent all alone with her fear. She'd tried counting the seconds, then the minutes, but gave up after only five. It was a useless exercise, even if it served as a distraction from despair.

She'd already explored every square inch of her prison. Had found no weaknesses, no cracks she could dig into or widen. She had spread the blanket beneath her, a welcome padding on that hard wood. Had learned to use the plastic bedpan without too much splashing. Even while trapped in a box, life settles into a routine. Sleep. Sip water. Pee. All she really had to help her keep track of the passing time was her supply of food. How many Hershey bars she'd eaten, and how many were left.

There were still a dozen in the sack.

She slipped a fragment of chocolate into her mouth, but did not chew it. She let it melt to musky sweetness on her tongue. She had always loved chocolate, had never been able to walk past a candy store without stopping to admire the truffles displayed like dark jewels in their paper nests. She thought of bitter cocoa dust and tart cherry fillings and rum syrup oozing down her chin—a far cry from this simple candy bar. But chocolate was chocolate, and she savored what she had.

It would not last forever.

She looked down at the crumpled wrappings that littered her prison, dismayed that she had already consumed so much of the food. When it was gone, what happened next? Surely there was more coming. Why would her kidnapper supply her with food and water, only to let her starve to death days later?

No, no, no. I'm supposed to live, not die.

She lifted her face toward the air grate and sucked in deep breaths. I'm meant to live, she kept repeating to herself. Meant to live.

Why?

She sank back against the wall, that one word echoing in her head. The only answer she could come up with was: *ransom*. Oh, what a stupid kidnapper. You fell for Dwayne's illusion. The BMWs, the Breitling watch, the designer ties. *When you drive a machine like this, you're upholding an image*. She began to laugh hysterically. I've been kidnapped because of an image built on borrowed money. Dwayne can't afford to pay any ransom.

She pictured him walking into their house and finding her gone. He'll see that my car is in the garage, and the chair's on the floor, she thought. It won't make sense, until he sees the ransom note. Until he reads the demand for money. *You'll pay it, won't you?*

Won't you?

The flashlight suddenly dimmed. She snatched it up and banged it against her hand. It flickered brighter, just for a moment, then faded again. Oh god, the batteries. Idiot, you shouldn't have left it on so long! She rummaged in the grocery sack and ripped open a fresh package of batteries. They tumbled out, rolling in every direction.

The light died.

The sound of her own breathing filled the darkness. Whimpers of mounting panic. Okay, okay, Mattie, stop it. You know you've got fresh batteries. You just have to slide them in the right way.

She felt around on the floor, gathering up the loose batteries. Took a deep breath and unscrewed the flashlight, carefully setting the cap on her folded knee. She slid out the old batteries, set them off to the side. Every move she made was in pitch blackness. If she lost a vital part, she might never find it again without light. Easy, Mattie. You've changed flashlight batteries before. Just put them in, positive end first. One, two. Now screw on the cap . . .

Light suddenly beamed out, bright and beautiful. She gave a sigh and slumped back, as exhausted as though she'd just run a mile. You've got your light back, now save it. Don't run it down again. She turned off the flashlight and sat in darkness. This time her breathing was steady, slow. No panic. She might be blind, but she had her finger on the switch and could turn on the light any time. *I'm in control.*

What she could not control, sitting in the darkness, were the fears that now assailed her. By now Dwayne must know I've been kidnapped, she thought. He's read the note, or gotten the phone call. *Your money or your wife.* He'll pay it, of course he'll pay it. She imagined him frantically pleading with an anonymous voice on the phone. *Don't hurt her, please don't hurt her!* She imagined him sobbing at the kitchen table, sorry, very sorry, for all the mean things he'd said to her. For the hundred different ways he had made her feel small and inconsequential. Now he was wishing he could take it all back, wishing he could tell her how much she meant to him . . .

You're dreaming, Mattie.

She squeezed her eyes shut against an anguish so deep it seemed to reach in and grasp her heart in its cruel fist.

You know he doesn't love you. You've known it for months.

Wrapping her arms around her abdomen, she hugged herself and her baby. Curled into a corner of her prison, she could no longer block out the truth. She remembered his look of disgust as she'd stepped out of the shower one night, and he had stared at her belly. Or the evenings when she would come up behind him to kiss his neck, and he'd wave her away. Or the party at the Everetts' house two months ago, where she had lost track of him, only to find him in the backyard gazebo, flirting with Jen Hockmeister. There'd been clues, so many clues, and she had ignored them all because she believed in true love. Had believed it since the day she'd been introduced to Dwayne Purvis at a birthday party, and had known that he was the one, even if there were things about him that should have bothered her. Like the way he always split the check when they were dating, or the way he couldn't pass a mirror without fussing vainly with his hair. Little things that didn't matter in the long run because they had love to keep them together. That's what she'd told herself, pretty lies that were part of someone else's romance, maybe a romance she'd seen in the movies, but not hers. Not her life.

Her life was this. Sitting trapped in a box,

waiting to be ransomed by a husband who didn't want her back.

She thought about the real Dwayne, not the make-believe one, sitting in the kitchen reading the ransom note. *We have your wife. Unless you pay us a million dollars . . .*

No, that was way too much money. No sane kidnapper would ask that much. What were kidnappers asking these days for a wife? A hundred thousand dollars sounded far more reasonable. Even so, Dwayne would balk. He'd weigh all his assets. The Beemers, the house. What's a wife worth?

If you love me, if you ever loved me, you'll pay it. Please, please pay it.

She slid to the floor, hugging herself, withdrawing into despair. Her own private box, deeper and darker than any prison anyone could shut her into.

"Lady. Lady."

In mid-sob she froze, not certain she'd actually heard the whisper. Now she was hearing voices. She was going insane.

"Talk to me, lady."

She turned on the flashlight and aimed it overhead. That's where the voice had come from—the air grate.

"Can you hear me?" It was a man's voice. Low, mellifluous.

"Who are you?" she said.

"Did you find the food?"

"Who are you?"

"Be careful with it. You have to make it last."

"My husband will pay you. I know he will. Please, just let me out of here!"

"Are you having any pains?"

"What?"

"Any pains?"

"I just want to get out! Let me *out!*"

"When it's time."

"How long are you going to keep me in here? When are you going to let me out?"

"Later."

"What does that mean?"

No answer.

"Hello? Mister, *hello*? Tell my husband I'm alive. You tell him he *has* to pay you!"

Footsteps creaked away.

"Don't go!" she screamed. "Let me out!" She reached up and pounded on the ceiling. Shrieked: "You have to *let me out!*"

The footsteps were gone. She stared up at the grate. He said he'll be back, she thought. Tomorrow he'll be back. After Dwayne pays him, he'll let me out.

Then it occurred to her. *Dwayne*. The voice in the grate had not once mentioned her husband.

FIFTEEN

Jane Rizzoli drove like the Bostonian she was, her hand quick to hit the horn, her Subaru weaving expertly past double-parked cars as they worked their way to the Turnpike on-ramp. Pregnancy had not mellowed her aggression; if anything, she seemed more impatient than usual as traffic conspired to hold them up at every intersection.

"I don't know about this, Doc," she said, fingers drumming the steering wheel as they waited for a red light to count down. "This is just gonna screw around with your head. I mean, what good's it gonna do you to see her?"

"At least I'll know who my mother is."

"You know her name. You know the crime she committed. Isn't that enough?"

"No, it's not."

Behind them, a horn honked. The light had turned green.

"Asshole," said Rizzoli, and she roared through the intersection.

They took the Massachusetts Turnpike west to Framingham, Rizzoli's Subaru dwarfed by threatening convoys of big rigs and SUVs. After only a weekend on the quiet roads of Maine, it was a shock for Maura to be back on a busy highway, where one small mistake, one moment's inattention, was all it took to close the gap between life and death. Rizzoli's quick and fearless driving made Maura uneasy; she, who never took chances, who insisted on the safest car and double air bags, who never let her gas gauge fall below a quarter full, did not easily cede control. Not when two-ton trucks were roaring only inches from her window.

It wasn't until they'd exited the Turnpike, onto Route 126 through downtown Framingham, that Maura settled back, no longer poised to clutch the dashboard. But she faced other fears now, not of big rigs or hurtling steel. What she feared most was coming face-to-face with herself.

And hating what she saw.

"You can change your mind anytime," said Rizzoli, as though reading her thoughts. "You ask, and I'll turn the car around. We can go to Friendly's instead, have a cup of coffee. Maybe some apple pie."

"Do pregnant women ever stop thinking about food?"

"Not *this* pregnant woman."

"I'm not going to change my mind."

"Okay, okay." Rizzoli drove in silence for a moment. "Ballard came in to see me this morning."

Maura looked at her, but Rizzoli's gaze was fixed on the road ahead. "Why?"

"He wanted to explain why he never told us about your mother. Look, I know you're pissed at him, Doc. But I think he really was trying to protect you."

"Is that what he said?"

"I believe him. Maybe I even agree with him. I thought about keeping that information from you, too."

"But you didn't. You called me."

"The point is, I can see why he wouldn't want to tell you."

"He had no excuse for keeping that information from me."

"It's just a guy thing, you know? Maybe a cop thing, too. They want to protect the little lady—"

"So they hold back the truth?"

"I'm just saying, I understand where he's coming from."

"Wouldn't *you* be angry about it?"

"Sure as hell."

"So why are you defending him?"

"Because he's hot?"

"Oh, please."

"I'm just telling you he's really sorry about it. But I think he tried to tell you that himself."

"I wasn't in the mood for an apology."

"So you're just gonna stay mad at him?"

"Why are we discussing this?"

"I don't know. I guess it's the way he talked about you. Like something happened between you two up there. Did it?"

Maura felt Rizzoli watching her with those bright cop's eyes, and knew that if she lied, Rizzoli would see it.

"I don't need any complicated relation-ships right now."

"What's complicated about it? I mean, besides the fact you're pissed at him?"

"A daughter. An ex-wife."

"Men his age, they're all retreads. They're all going to have ex-wives."

Maura stared ahead at the road. "You know, Jane, not every woman is meant to be married."

"That's what I used to think, and look what happened to me. One day I can't stand the guy, the next day I can't stop thinking about him. I never thought it'd turn out this way."

"Gabriel's one of the good ones."

"Yeah, he's a straight-up guy. But the point is, he tried to pull the same stunt that Ballard did, that macho protection thing. And I was pissed at him. The point is, you can't always predict when a guy's a keeper."

Maura thought of Victor. Of her disaster of a marriage. "No, you can't."

"But you can start off by focusing on what's possible, on what has a chance. And forget the guys who'll never work out." Though they did not mention his name, Maura knew they were both thinking of

Daniel Brophy. The impossible, personified. A seductive mirage who could lure her through the years, the decades, into old age. Stranding her there all alone.

"This is the exit," said Rizzoli, turning off onto Loring Drive.

Maura's heart started to pound as she saw the sign for MCI–Framingham. *It's time to come face-to-face with who I really am.*

"You can still change your mind," said Rizzoli.

"We've already gone through this."

"Yeah, I just wanted you to know we can turn back."

"Would you, Jane? After a lifetime of wondering who your mother is, what she looks like, would you leave it at that? When you're so close to having every question you ever asked finally answered?"

Rizzoli turned to look at her. Rizzoli, who seemed always to be in motion, always at the eye of one storm or another, now regarded Maura with quiet understanding. "No," she said. "I wouldn't."

In the administrative wing of the Betty Cole Smith Building, they both presented their

IDs and signed in. A few minutes later, Superintendent Barbara Gurley came down to meet them at the front desk. Maura had expected an imposing prison commandant, but the woman she saw looked like a librarian, her short hair more gray than brown, her slim figure clad in a tan skirt and pink cotton blouse.

"Good to meet you, Detective Rizzoli," said Gurley. She turned to Maura. "And you're Dr. Isles?"

"Yes. Thank you for seeing me." Maura, too, reached out to shake hands. Found the other woman's grasp cool and reserved. She knows who I am, thought Maura. She knows why I'm here.

"Let's go up to my office. I've pulled her file for you."

Gurley led the way, moving with crisp efficiency. No wasted motion, no backward glance to see if the visitors were keeping up. They stepped into an elevator.

"This is a level four facility?" asked Rizzoli.

"Yes."

"Isn't that just medium security?" said Maura.

"We're developing a level six trial unit.

This is the only women's correctional unit in the state of Massachusetts, so for the moment, we're it. We have to deal with the whole spectrum of offenders."

"Even mass murderers?" asked Rizzoli.

"If they're female, and they're convicted of a crime, they come here. We don't have quite the same security issues that the men's facilities have to deal with. Also, our approach is a little different. We emphasize treatment and rehabilitation. A number of our inmates have mental health and substance abuse problems. Plus, there's the complicating fact that many of them are mothers, so we have to deal with all the emotional issues of maternal separation as well. There are a lot of children left crying when visiting hours end."

"What about Amalthea Lank? You have any special issues with her?"

"We have . . ." Gurley hesitated, her gaze fixed straight ahead. "A few."

"Like what?"

The elevator door opened and Gurley stepped out. "This is my office."

They passed through an anteroom. The two secretaries stared at Maura, then quickly dropped their gazes back to their computer screens. Everyone's trying to avoid meeting my eyes, she thought. What are they afraid I'll see?

Gurley led the visitors into her office and closed the door. "Please, sit down."

The room was a surprise. Maura had thought it would reflect Gurley herself, efficient and unadorned. But everywhere, there were photographs of smiling faces. Women holding babies, children posed with neatly parted hair and pressed shirts. A new bride and groom, surrounded by a flock of children. His, hers, ours.

"My girls," said Gurley, smiling at the wall of photos. "These are the ones who made the transition back to society. The ones who made the right choices and moved on with their lives. Unfortunately," she said, her smile fading, "Amalthea Lank will never be on this wall." She sat down behind her desk and focused on Maura. "I'm not sure your visit here is such a good idea, Dr. Isles."

"I've never met my birth mother."

"That's what concerns me." Gurley leaned back in her chair and studied Maura for a moment. "We all want to love our mothers. We want them to be special women because it makes *us* special, as their daughters."

"I don't expect to love her."

"What do you expect, then?"

That question made Maura pause. She thought of the imaginary mother she'd conjured up as a child, ever since her cousin had cruelly blurted out the truth: that Maura was adopted. That this was the reason why, in a family of blondes and towheads, she alone had black hair. She'd built a fairy-tale mother based on the darkness of her hair. An Italian heiress, forced to give up a daughter conceived in scandal. Or a Spanish beauty abandoned by her lover, tragically dead of a broken heart. Always, as Gurley had said, she'd imagined someone special, even extraordinary. Now she was about to confront not the fantasy but the real woman, and the prospect made her mouth go dry.

Rizzoli said to Gurley: "Why don't you think she should see her?"

"I'm only asking her to approach this visit with caution."

"Why? Is the inmate dangerous?"

"Not in the sense that she'll spring up

and physically attack anyone. In fact, she's quite docile on the surface."

"And beneath the surface?"

"Think of what she did, Detective. How much rage it must take to swing a crowbar with such force that you shatter a woman's skull? Now *you* answer that question: What lies beneath Amalthea's surface?" Gurley looked at Maura. "You need to go into this with your eyes open, and fully aware of whom you're dealing with."

"She and I may share the same DNA," said Maura. "But I have no emotional attachment to this woman."

"So you're just curious."

"I need to put this to rest. I need to move on."

"That's probably what your sister thought, too. You do know she came to visit Amalthea?"

"Yes, I've heard."

"I don't think it gave her any peace of mind. I think it only upset her."

"Why?"

Gurley slid a file across the desk toward Maura. "Those are Amalthea's psychiatric records. Everything you need to know about her is in there. Why don't you just read that instead? Read it, walk away, and forget about her."

Maura didn't touch the file. It was Rizzoli who picked up the folder and said: "She's under a psychiatrist's care?"

"Yes," said Gurley.

"Why?"

"Because Amalthea is a schizophrenic."

Maura stared at the superintendent. "Then why was she convicted of murder? If she's schizophrenic, she shouldn't be in prison. She should be in a hospital. "

"So should a number of our inmates. Tell it to the courts, Dr. Isles, because I've tried to. The system itself is insane. Even if you're flat-out psychotic when you commit murder, the insanity defense seldom sways a jury."

Rizzoli asked, softly: "Are you sure she *is* insane?"

Maura turned to Rizzoli. Saw that she was staring down at the inmate's psychiatric file. "Is there a question about her diagnosis?"

"I know this psychiatrist who's been seeing her. Dr. Joyce O'Donnell. She doesn't normally waste her time treating run-of-the-mill schizophrenics." She looked at Gurley. "Why is she involved in this case?"

"You sound disturbed about it," said Gurley.

"If you knew Dr. O'Donnell, you'd be disturbed too." Rizzoli clapped the folder shut. Took a deep breath. "Is there anything else Dr. Isles needs to know before she sees the prisoner?"

Gurley looked at Maura. "I guess I haven't talked you out of it, have I?"

"No. I'm ready to see her."

"Then I'll walk you down to visitor intake."

SIXTEEN

I can still change my mind.

That thought kept going through Maura's head as she walked through visitor processing. As she removed her watch and placed it, along with her handbag, in a locker. She could bring no jewelry or wallet into the visitors' room, and she felt naked without her purse, stripped of any proof of identity, of all the little plastic cards that told the world who she was. She closed the locker and the clang was a jarring reminder of the world she was about to enter: a place where doors slammed shut, where lives were trapped in boxes.

Maura had hoped this meeting would be private, but when the guard admitted her into the visiting room, Maura saw that privacy was an impossibility. Afternoon visiting hours had commenced an hour earlier, and the room was noisy with the voices of children and the chaos of reunited families. Coins clattered into a vending machine, which disgorged plastic-wrapped sandwiches and chips and candy bars.

"Amalthea's on her way down now," the guard said to Maura. "Why don't you find a seat?"

Maura went to an unoccupied table and sat down. The plastic tabletop was sticky with spilled juice; she kept her hands in her lap and waited, her heart hammering, her throat dry. The classic fight-or-flight response, she thought. Why the hell am I so nervous?

She rose and crossed to a sink. Filled a paper cup with water and gulped it down. Her throat still felt dry. This kind of thirst couldn't be quenched by mere water; the thirst, the quickened pulse, the sweating hands—it was all the same reflex, the body preparing itself for imminent threat. Relax, relax. You'll meet her, say a few words, satisfy your curiosity, and walk out. How hard can that be? She crushed the paper cup, turned, and froze.

A door had just opened and a woman entered, her shoulders squared, her jaw lifted in regal confidence. Her gaze settled on Maura and for a moment it locked there. But then, just as Maura thought: *It's her*, the woman turned, smiled, and opened her arms wide to embrace a child who was running toward her.

Maura halted in confusion, not knowing whether to sit down or remain standing. Then the door opened again, and the guard who had spoken to her earlier reappeared, leading a woman by the arm. A woman who did not walk but shuffled, her shoulders slumped forward, her head bent, as though obsessively searching the floor for something she'd lost. The guard brought her to Maura's table, pulled out a chair, and sat the prisoner down.

"There, now, Amalthea. This lady's come to see you. Why don't you have a nice talk with her, hmm?"

Amalthea's head remained bent, her gaze fixed on the tabletop. Tangled strands of hair fell across her face in a greasy curtain. Though heavily streaked with gray, clearly that hair had once been black. Like mine, thought Maura. Like Anna's.

The guard shrugged and looked at Maura. "Well, I'll just let you two visit, okay? When you're finished, give me a wave and I'll take her back."

Amalthea did not even glance up as the guard walked away. Nor did she seem to notice the visitor who had just sat down across from her. Her posture remained frozen, her face hidden behind that veil of dirty hair. The prison shirt hung loose on her shoulders, as though she was shrinking inside her clothes. Her hand, resting on the table, was rocking back and forth in a ceaseless tremor.

"Hello, Amalthea," said Maura. "Do you know who I am?"

No response.

"My name is Maura Isles. I . . ." Maura swallowed. "I've been looking for you for a very long time." *For all my life.*

The woman's head twitched sideways. Not in reaction to Maura's words, just an involuntary tic. A stray impulse sparking through nerves and muscles.

"Amalthea, I'm your daughter."

Maura watched, waiting for a reaction. Even longing to see one. In that moment, everything else in the room seemed to vanish. She did not hear the cacophony of children's voices or the quarters dropping into the vending machine or the scrape of chair legs across linoleum. All she saw was this tired and broken woman.

"Can you look at me? Please, *look* at me."

At last the head came up, moving in little jerks, like a mechanical doll whose gears have rusted. The unkempt hair parted, and the eyes focused on Maura. Fathomless eyes. Maura saw nothing there, not awareness. Not a soul. Amalthea's lips moved, but soundlessly. Just another twitching of muscles, without intent, without meaning.

A small boy toddled by, trailing the scent of a wet diaper. At the next table a dishwater blonde in prison denim was sitting with her head in her hands and quietly sobbing as her male visitor watched, expressionless. At that moment a dozen family dramas like Maura's were taking place; she was just one more bit player who couldn't see beyond the circle of her own crisis.

"My sister Anna came to see you," Maura said. "She looked just like me. Do you remember her?"

Amalthea's jaw was moving now, as

though chewing food. An imaginary meal that only she could taste.

No, of course she doesn't remember, thought Maura, gazing in frustration at Amalthea's blank expression. She doesn't register me, or who I am, or why I'm here. I'm shouting into an empty cave, and only my own voice is echoing back.

Determined to dredge up a reaction, any reaction, Maura said with what was almost deliberate cruelty: "Anna's dead. Your other daughter is dead. Did you know that?"

No answer.

Why the hell do I keep trying? There's nobody home in there. There's no light in those eyes.

"Well," said Maura. "I'll come back another time. Maybe you'll talk to me then." With a sigh, Maura stood and looked around for the guard. She spotted her at the other end of the room. Maura had just raised her hand in a wave when she heard the voice. A whisper so soft she might have imagined it:

"Go away."

Startled, Maura looked down at Amalthea, who was sitting in exactly the

same position, lips twitching, gaze still un-
focused.

Slowly, Maura sat back down. "What did
you say?"

Amalthea's gaze lifted to hers. And just
for an instant, Maura saw awareness there.
A gleam of intelligence. "Go away. Before
he sees you."

Maura stared. A chill clambered up her
spine, made the hairs on the back of her
neck bristle.

At the next table, the dishwater blonde
was still crying. Her male visitor stood up
and said, "I'm sorry, but you'll just have to
accept it. That's the way it is." He walked
away, back to his life on the outside where
women wore pretty blouses, not blue
denim. Where doors that locked could be
unlocked.

"Who?" Maura asked softly. Amalthea
didn't answer. "Who's going to see me,
Amalthea?" Maura pressed her. "What do
you mean?"

But Amalthea's gaze had clouded over.
That brief flash of awareness was gone, and
Maura was staring, once more, into a void.

"So, are we all done with the visit?" the
guard asked cheerfully.

"Is she always like this?" asked Maura, watching Amalthea's lips form soundless words.

"Pretty much. She has good days and bad days."

"She hardly spoke to me at all."

"She will, if she gets to know you better. Mostly keeps to herself, but sometimes she'll come out of it. Writes letters, even uses the phone."

"Whom does she call?"

"I don't know. Her shrink, I guess."

"Dr. O'Donnell?"

"The blond lady. She's been in a few times, so Amalthea's pretty comfortable with her. Aren't you, honey?" Reaching for the prisoner's arm, the guard said: "Come on, upsy daisy. Let's walk you back."

Obediently Amalthea rose to her feet and allowed the guard to guide her away from the table. She moved only a few steps, then stopped.

"Amalthea, let's go."

But the prisoner did not move. She stood as though her muscles had suddenly solidified.

"Honey, I can't wait all day for you. Let's go."

Slowly Amalthea turned. Her eyes were still vacant. The words she said next came out in a voice that was not quite human, but mechanical. A foreign entity, channeled through a machine. She looked at Maura.

"Now you're going to die, too," she said. Then she turned and shuffled away, back to her cell.

"She has tardive dyskinesia," said Maura. "That's why Superintendent Gurley tried to discourage me from visiting her. She didn't want me to see Amalthea's condition. She didn't want me to find out what they've done to her."

"What exactly did they do to her?" said Rizzoli. She was once again behind the wheel, guiding them fearlessly past trucks that made the road shake, that rattled the little Subaru with turbulence. "Are you saying they turned her into some kind of zombie?"

"You saw her psychiatric record. Her first doctors treated her with phenothiazines. That's a class of antipsychotic drugs. In older women, those drugs can have devastating side effects. One of them is called tardive dyskinesia—involuntary movements of the mouth and the face. The patient can't stop chewing or puffing her cheeks or sticking out her tongue. She can't control any of it. Think about what that's like. Everyone staring at you as you make weird faces. You're a freak."

"How do you stop the movements?"

"You can't. They should have discontinued the drugs immediately, as soon as she had the first symptoms. But they waited too long. Then Dr. O'Donnell came on the case. She was the one who finally stopped the drugs. Recognized what was happening." Maura gave an angry sigh. "The tardive dyskinesia is probably permanent." She looked out the window at the tightening traffic. This time she felt no anxiety, seeing tons of steel hurtling past. She was thinking instead of Amalthea Lank, her lips ceaselessly moving, as though whispering secrets.

"Are you saying she didn't need those drugs in the first place?"

"No. I'm saying they should have been stopped sooner."

"So is she crazy? Or isn't she?"

"That was their initial diagnosis. Schizophrenia."

"And what's your diagnosis?"

Maura thought about Amalthea's blank stare, her cryptic words. Words that made no sense except as a paranoid's delusion. "I would have to agree," she said. With a sigh, she leaned back. "I don't see myself in her, Jane. I don't see any part of me in that woman."

"Well, that's got to be a relief. Considering."

"But it's still there, that link between us. You can't deny your own DNA."

"You know the old saying, blood is thicker than water? It's bullshit, Doc. You don't have anything in common with that woman. She had you, and she gave you up at birth. That's that. Relationship over."

"She knows so many answers. Who my father is. Who I am."

Rizzoli shot her a sharp glance, then turned back to the road. "I'm going to give you some advice. I know you'll wonder where I'm coming from on this. Believe me, I'm not pulling this out of thin air. But that woman, Amalthea Lank, is someone you need to stay away from. Don't see her, don't talk to her. Don't even think about her. She's dangerous."

"She's nothing but a burned-out schizophrenic."

"I'm not so sure about that."

Maura looked at Rizzoli. "What do you know about her that I don't?"

For a moment Rizzoli drove without speaking. It was not the traffic that preoccupied her; she seemed to be weighing her response, considering how best to phrase her answer. "Do you remember Warren Hoyt?" she finally asked. Though she said the name without discernible emotion, her jaw had squared, and her hands had tightened around the steering wheel.

Warren Hoyt, thought Maura. *The Surgeon.*

That was what the police had dubbed him. He had earned that nickname because of the atrocities he'd inflicted on his victims. His instruments were duct tape and a scalpel; his prey were women asleep in their beds, unaware of the intruder who stood beside them in the darkness, anticipating the pleasure of making the first cut. Jane Rizzoli had been his final target, his opponent in a game of wits he'd never expected to lose.

But it was Rizzoli who brought him down with a single shot, her bullet piercing his spinal cord. Now quadriplegic, his limbs paralyzed and useless, Warren Hoyt's universe had shrunk to a hospital room, where the few pleasures left to him were those of the mind—a mind that remained as brilliant and dangerous as ever.

"Of course I remember him," said Maura. She had seen the result of his work, the terrible mutilation his scalpel had wrought in the flesh of one of his victims.

"I've been keeping tabs on him," said Rizzoli. "You know, just to reassure myself that the monster's still in his cage. He's still there, all right, on the spinal cord unit. And every Wednesday afternoon, for the last eight months, he's been getting a visitor. Dr. Joyce O'Donnell."

Maura frowned. "Why?"

"She claims it's part of her research in violent behavior. Her theory is that killers aren't responsible for their actions. That some bump on the noggin when they're kids makes them prone to violence. Naturally, defense attorneys have her on speed dial. She'd probably tell you that Jeffrey Dahmer was just misunderstood, that John Wayne Gacy just got his head knocked a few too many times. She'll defend anyone."

"People do what they're paid to do."

"I don't think she does it for the money."

"Then for what?"

"For the chance to get up close and personal to people who kill. She says it's her field of study, that she does it for science. Yeah, well, Josef Mengele did it for science, too. That's just the excuse, a way to make what she does respectable."

"What does she do?"

"She's a thrill seeker. She gets a kick out of hearing a killer's fantasies. She likes stepping into his head, taking a look around, seeing what he sees. Knowing what it feels like to be a monster."

"You make it sound like she's one of them."

"Maybe she'd like to be. I've seen letters she wrote to Hoyt while he was in prison. Urging him to tell her all the details about his kills. Oh yeah, she loves the details."

"A lot of people are curious about the macabre."

"She's beyond curious. She wants to

know what it's like to cut skin and watch a victim bleed. What it's like to enjoy that ultimate power. She's hungry for details the way a vampire's hungry for blood." Rizzoli paused. Gave a startled laugh. "You know, I just realized something. That's exactly what she is, a vampire. She and Hoyt feed off each other. He tells her his fantasies, she tells him it's okay to enjoy them. It's okay to get turned on by the thought of cutting someone's throat."

"And now she's visiting my mother."

"Yeah." Rizzoli looked at her. "I wonder what fantasies *they're* sharing."

Maura thought of the crimes Amalthea Lank had been convicted of. She wondered what had gone through her mind when she'd picked up the two sisters at the side of the road. Did she feel an anticipatory thrill, a heady shot of power?

"Just the fact O'Donnell finds Amalthea worth visiting should tell you something," said Rizzoli.

"What should it tell me?"

"O'Donnell doesn't waste her time on your everyday murderers. She doesn't care about the guy who shoots some 7-Eleven clerk during a robbery. Or the husband who gets pissed at his wife and shoves her down the stairs. No, she spends her time with the creeps who kill because they enjoy it. The ones who give that knife the extra twist, because they like the way it feels scraping against bone. She spends her time with the special ones. The monsters."

My mother, thought Maura. Is she a monster, too?

SEVENTEEN

Dr. Joyce O'Donnell's house in Cambridge was a large white colonial in a neighborhood of distinguished homes on Brattle Street. A wrought-iron fence enclosed a front yard with a perfect lawn and bark-mulched flower beds where landscape roses obediently bloomed. This was a disciplined garden, no disorder allowed, and as Maura walked up the path of granite pavers to the front door, she could already envision the house's occupant. Well groomed, neatly dressed. A mind as organized as her garden.

The woman who answered the door was just as Maura had imagined.

Dr. O'Donnell was an ash blonde with pale, flawless skin. Her blue Oxford shirt, tucked into pressed white slacks, was tailored to emphasize a trim waist. She regarded Maura with little warmth. Rather, what Maura saw in the other woman's eyes was the hard-edged gleam of curiosity. The gaze of a scientist regarding some new specimen.

"Dr. O'Donnell? I'm Maura Isles."

O'Donnell responded with a crisp handshake. "Come in."

Maura stepped into a house as coolly elegant as its owner. The only touches of warmth were the Oriental carpets covering dark teak floors. O'Donnell led the way from the foyer, into a formal sitting room where Maura settled uneasily on a couch upholstered in white silk. O'Donnell chose the armchair facing her. On the rosewood coffee table between them was a stack of files and a digital recorder. Though not turned on, the threat of that recorder was yet another detail that added to Maura's unease.

"Thank you for seeing me," said Maura.

"I was curious. I wondered what Amalthea's daughter might be like. I do know *of* you, Dr. Isles, but only what I read in the newspapers." She leaned back in the easy chair, looking perfectly comfortable.

Home advantage. She was the one with the favors to grant; Maura was merely a supplicant. "I know nothing about you personally. But I'd like to."

"Why?"

"I'm well acquainted with Amalthea. I can't help wondering if . . ."

"Like mother, like daughter?"

O'Donnell lifted one elegant eyebrow. "You said it, I didn't."

"That's the reason for your curiosity about me. Isn't it?"

"And what's the reason for yours? Why are you here?"

Maura's gaze shifted to a painting over the fireplace. A starkly modern oil streaked with black and red. She said: "I want to know who that woman really is."

"You know who she is. You just don't want to believe it. Your sister didn't, either."

Maura frowned. "You met Anna?"

"No, actually, I never did. But I got a call about four months ago, from a woman identifying herself as Amalthea's daughter. I was about to leave for a two-week trial in Oklahoma, so I couldn't meet with her. We simply talked on the phone. She'd been to visit her mother at MCI–Framingham, so she knew I was Amalthea's psychiatrist. She wanted to know more about her. Amalthea's childhood, her family."

"And you know all that?"

"Some of it is from her school records. Some from what she could tell me, when she was lucid. I know she was born in Lowell. When she was about nine, her mother died, and she went to live with her uncle and a cousin, in Maine."

Maura glanced up. "Maine?"

"Yes. She graduated from high school in a town called Fox Harbor."

Now I understand why Anna chose that town. I was following in Anna's footsteps; she was following our mother's.

"After high school, the records peter out," said O'Donnell. "We don't know where she moved from there, or how she supported herself. That's most likely when the schizophrenia set in. It usually manifests itself in early adulthood. She probably drifted around for years, and ended up the way you see her today. Burned out and delusional." O'Donnell looked at Maura. "It's a pretty grim picture. Your sister had a hard time accepting that was really her mother."

"I look at her and I see nothing familiar. Nothing of myself."

"But I see the resemblance. I see the same hair color. The same jaw."

"We look nothing alike."

"You really don't see it?" O'Donnell leaned forward, her gaze intent on Maura. "Tell me something, Dr. Isles. Why did you choose pathology?"

Perplexed by the question, Maura only stared at her.

"You could have gone into any field of medicine. Obstetrics, pediatrics. You could be working with live patients, but you chose pathology. Specifically, forensic pathology."

"What's the point of your question?"

"The point is, you're somehow attracted to the dead."

"That's absurd."

"Then why did you choose your field?"

"Because I like definitive answers. I don't like guessing games. I like to *see* the diagnosis under my microscope lens."

"You don't like uncertainty."

"Does anyone?"

"Then you could have chosen mathematics or engineering. So many other fields involve precision. Definitive answers. But there you are in the M.E.'s office, communing with corpses." O'Donnell paused. Asked, quietly: "Do you ever enjoy it?"

Maura met her gaze head-on. "No."

"You chose an occupation you don't enjoy?"

"I chose the challenge. There's satisfaction in that. Even if the task itself isn't pleasant."

"But don't you see what I'm getting at? You tell me you don't see anything familiar about Amalthea Lank. You look at her, and probably see someone horrifying. Or at least a woman who committed horrifying acts. There are people who look at you, Dr. Isles, and probably think the same thing."

"You can't possibly compare us."

"Do you know what your mother was convicted of?"

"Yes, I've been told."

"But have you seen the autopsy reports?"

"Not yet."

"I have. During the trial, the defense team asked me to consult on your mother's mental status. I've seen the photos, reviewed the evidence. You do know that the victims were two sisters? Young women stranded at the side of the road."

"Yes."

"And the younger one was nine months pregnant."

"I know all this."

"So you know that your mother picked up those two women on the highway. She drives them thirty miles away, to a shed in the woods. Crushes their skulls with a tire iron. And then she does something surprisingly—weirdly—logical. She drives to a service station and fills a can with gas. Returns to the shed and sets it on fire, with the two bodies inside." O'Donnell cocked her head. "Don't you find that interesting?"

"I find it sickening."

"Yes, but on some level, maybe you're feeling something else, something you don't even want to acknowledge. That you're intrigued by these actions, not just as an intellectual puzzle. There's something about it that fascinates you, even excites you."

"The way it obviously excites you?"

O'Donnell took no offense at that retort. Instead she smiled, easily acknowledging Maura's remark. "My interest is professional. It's my job to study acts of murder. I'm just wondering about the reasons for *your* interest in Amalthea Lank."

"Two days ago, I didn't know who my mother was. Now I'm trying to come to grips with the truth. I'm trying to understand—"

"Who you are?" O'Donnell asked softly.

Maura met her gaze. "I *know* who I am."

"Are you sure?" O'Donnell leaned closer. "When you're in that autopsy lab, examining a victim's wounds, describing a killer's knife thrusts, don't you ever feel just a whisper of a thrill?"

"What makes you think I would?"

"You are Amalthea's daughter."

"I'm an accident of biology. She didn't raise me."

O'Donnell settled back in the chair and studied her with coldly appraising eyes. "You're aware there's a genetic component to violence? That some families carry it in their DNA?"

Maura remembered what Rizzoli had told her about Dr. O'Donnell: *She's beyond curious. She wants to know what it's like to cut skin and watch a victim bleed. What it's like to enjoy that ultimate power. She's hungry for details, the way a vampire's hungry for blood*. Maura could now see that glint of hunger in O'Donnell's eyes. *This woman enjoys communing with monsters,* thought Maura. *And she's hoping she's found another one.*

"I came to talk about Amalthea," said Maura.

"Isn't that who we've been discussing?"

"According to MCI–Framingham, you've been to see her at least a dozen times. Why so often? Surely not for her benefit."

"As a researcher, I'm interested in Amalthea. I want to understand what drives people to kill. Why they take pleasure from it."

"You're saying she did it for pleasure?"

"Well, do *you* know why she killed?"

"She's clearly psychotic."

"The vast majority of psychotics don't kill."

"But you do agree that she is?"

O'Donnell hesitated. "She would appear to be."

"You don't sound sure. Even after all the visits you've made?"

"There's more to your mother than just psychosis. And there's more to her crime than meets the eye."

"What do you mean?"

"You say you already know what she did. Or at least, what the prosecution claims she did."

"The evidence was solid enough to convict her."

"Oh, there was plenty of evidence. Her license plate caught on camera at the service station. The women's blood on the tire iron. Their wallets in the trunk. But you probably haven't heard about this." O'Donnell reached for one of the files on the coffee table and handed it to Maura. "It's from the crime lab in Virginia, where Amalthea was arrested."

Maura opened the folder and saw a photo of a white sedan with a Massachusetts license plate.

"That's the car Amalthea was driving," said O'Donnell.

Maura turned to the next page. It was a summary of the fingerprint evidence.

"There were a number of prints found inside that car," said O'Donnell. "Both victims, Nikki and Theresa Wells, left their prints on the rear seat belt buckles, indicating they climbed into the backseat and strapped themselves in. There were fingerprints left by Amalthea, of course, on the steering wheel and gearshift." O'Donnell paused. "And then, there's the fourth set of fingerprints."

"A fourth set?"

"It's right there, in that report. They were found on the glove compartment. On both doors, and on the steering wheel. Those prints were never identified."

"It doesn't mean anything. Maybe a mechanic worked on her car and left behind his fingerprints."

"A possibility. Now look at the hair and fiber report."

Maura turned to the next page and saw that blond hairs had been found on the back seat. The hairs matched Theresa and Nikki Wells. "I see nothing surprising about this. We know the victims were in the car."

"But you'll notice that none of their hairs appear in the front seat. Think about it. Two women stranded at the side of the road. Someone pulls over, offers to give them a lift. And what do the sisters do? They *both* climb into the backseat. It seems a little rude, doesn't it? Leaving the driver all alone up in front. Unless . . ."

Maura looked up at her. "Unless someone else was already sitting in that front seat."

O'Donnell sat back, a satisfied smile on her lips. "That's the tantalizing question. A question that was never answered at trial. It's the reason I keep going back, again and again, to see your mother. I want to learn what the police never bothered to find out: Who was sitting in the front seat with Amalthea?"

"She hasn't told you?"

"Not his name."

Maura stared at her. "His?"

"I'm only guessing the sex. But I do believe that someone was in the car with Amalthea at the moment she spotted those two women on the road. Someone helped her control those victims. Someone who was strong enough to help her stack those bodies in the shed and helped her set them on fire." O'Donnell paused. "*He's* the one I'm interested in, Dr. Isles. He's the one I want to find."

"All your visits to Amalthea—they weren't even about her."

"Insanity doesn't interest me. Evil does."

Maura stared at her, thinking: Yes, it would. You enjoy getting close enough to brush against it, sniff it. Amalthea isn't what attracts you. She's only the go-between, the one who can introduce you to the real object of your desire.

"A partner," said Maura.

"We don't know who he is, or what he looks like. But your mother knows."

"Then why won't she say his name?"

"That's the question—why is she hiding him? Is she afraid of him? Is she protecting him?"

"You don't know if this person even exists. All you have are some unidentified fingerprints. And a theory."

"More than a theory. The Beast is real." O'Donnell leaned forward and said, quietly, almost intimately: "That's the name she used when she was arrested in Virginia. When the police there interrogated her. She said, quote: 'The Beast told me to do it,' unquote. *He* told her to kill those women."

In the silence that followed, Maura heard the sound of her own heart, like the quickening beat of a drum. She swallowed. Said, "We're talking about a schizophrenic. A woman who's probably having auditory hallucinations."

"Or she's talking about someone real."

"The *Beast*?" Maura managed a laugh. "A personal demon, maybe. A monster from her nightmares."

"Who leaves behind fingerprints."

"That didn't seem to impress the jury."

"They ignored that evidence. I was at that trial. I watched the prosecution build its case against a woman so psychotic, even the prosecution had to know she wasn't responsible for her actions. But she was the easy target, the easy conviction."

"Even though she was clearly insane."

"Oh, no one doubted she was psychotic and hearing voices. Those voices might've screamed at you to crush a woman's skull, to burn her body, but the jury still assumes you know right from wrong. Amalthea was a prosecutor's slam dunk, so that's what they did. They got it wrong. They missed *him*." O'Donnell leaned back in her chair. "And your mother is the only one who knows who he is."

It was almost six by the time Maura pulled up behind the medical examiner's building. Two cars were still parked in the lot— Yoshima's blue Honda and Dr. Costas's black Saab. There must be a late autopsy, she thought, with a twinge of guilt; today would have been her day on call, but she had asked her colleagues to cover for her.

She unlocked the back door, walked into the building, and headed straight to her office, meeting no one on the way. On her desk she found what she'd come in to retrieve: two folders, with an attached yellow Post-it note, on which Louise had written: *The files you requested*. She sat down at her desk, took a deep breath, and opened the first folder.

It was the file for Theresa Wells, the older sister. The cover sheet listed the victim's name and case number and the date of the postmortem. She didn't recognize the name of the pathologist, Dr. James Hobart, but then she had joined the medical examiner's office only two years ago, and this autopsy report was five years old. She turned to Dr. Hobart's typed dictation.

The deceased is a well-nourished female, age indeterminate, measuring five foot five inches in height and weighing one hundred fifteen pounds. Definitive ID established through dental X-rays; fingerprints unobtainable. Noted are extensive burn injuries to the trunk and extremities, with severe charring of skin and exposed areas of musculature. Face and front of torso are somewhat spared. Clothing remnants are in place, consisting of size eight Gap blue jeans with closed zipper and snaps still fastened, as well as charred white sweater and bra, hooks still fastened as well. Examination of the airways revealed no soot deposition, and blood carboxyhemoglobin saturation was minimal.

At the time her body was set afire, Theresa Wells was not breathing. The cause of death was apparent from Dr. Hobart's X-ray interpretation.

Lateral and AP skull films reveal depressed and comminuted right parietal fracture with four-centimeter-wide wedge-shaped fragment.

A blow to the head had most likely killed her.

At the bottom of the typed report, below Dr. Hobart's signature, Maura saw a familiar set of initials. Louise had transcribed the dictation. Pathologists might come and go, but in this office, Louise was forever.

Maura flipped through the next pages in the file. There was an autopsy worksheet listing all the X-rays that had been taken, which blood and fluid and trace evidence had been collected. Administrative pages recorded chain of custody, personal possessions, and the names of those present at the autopsy. Yoshima had been Hobart's assistant. She did not recognize the name of the Fitchburg police officer who'd attended the procedure, a Detective Swigert.

She flipped to the end of the file, to a photograph. Here she stopped, recoiling at the image. The flames had charred Theresa Wells's limbs, and had laid bare the muscles of her torso, but her face was strangely intact, and undeniably a woman's. Only thirty-five years old, thought Maura. Already I have outlived Theresa Wells by five years. She would be my age today, had she lived. Had her tire not gone flat on that day in November.

She closed Theresa's file and reached for the next one. Again she paused before opening the folder, reluctant to view the horrors it contained. She thought of the burn victim she herself had autopsied a year ago, and the odors that had permeated her hair and clothes even after she'd left the room. For the rest of that summer, she'd avoided lighting her backyard grill, unable to tolerate the smell of barbecued meat. Now, as she opened the file for Nikki Wells, she could almost smell that odor again, wafting back through her memory.

While Theresa's face had been largely spared by the fire, the same could not be said for her younger sister. The flames that had only partially consumed Theresa had focused all their rage instead on the flesh of Nikki Wells.

Subject is severely charred, with portions of the chest and abdominal wall completely burned away, revealing exposed viscera. Soft tissues of the face and scalp are burned away as well. Areas of cranial vault are visible, as are crush injuries of the facial bones. No fragments of clothing remain, but small metallic densities are visible on X-ray at the level of the fifth rib which may represent fasteners from a brassiere, as well as a single metallic fragment overlying the pubis. X-ray of abdomen also reveals additional skeletal remains representing a fetus, skull diameter compatible with gestation of about thirty-six weeks . . .

Nikki Wells's pregnancy would have been clearly evident to her killer. Yet her condition had brought her and her unborn child no pity, no concessions. Only a shared funeral pyre in the woods.

She turned the page. Paused, frowning, at the next sentence in the autopsy report:

Notably absent on X-ray are the fetus's right tibia, fibula, and tarsal bones.

An asterisk had been added in pen, with the scrawled note: "See addendum." She flipped to the attached page and read:

Fetal anomaly was noted in subject's outpatient obstetric record dated three months earlier. Ultrasound performed during second trimester revealed fetus was missing its right lower limb, most likely due to amniotic band syndrome.

A fetal malformation. Months before her death, Nikki Wells had been told that her baby would be born without its right leg, yet she had chosen to continue the pregnancy. To keep her baby.

The final pages in the file, Maura knew, would be the hardest to confront. She had no stomach for the photograph, but she forced herself to turn to it anyway. Saw blackened limbs and torso. No pretty woman here, no rosy glow of pregnancy, just a skull's visage, peering through a charred mask, the facial bones caved in by the killing blow.

Amalthea Lank did this. My mother. She crushed their skulls and dragged the bodies into a shed. As she poured gasoline over the corpses, as she struck the match, did she feel a thrill, watching the flames whoosh to life? Did she linger by the burning shed to inhale the stench of singed hair and flesh?

Unable to bear the image any longer, she closed the file. Turned her attention to the two large X-ray envelopes also lying on her desk. She carried them to the viewing box and inserted Theresa Wells's head and neck films under the clips. The lights flickered on, illuminating the ghostly shadows of bone. X-rays were far easier to stomach than photographs. Stripped of recognizable flesh, corpses lose their power to horrify. One skeleton looks like any other. The skull she now saw on the light box might be any woman's, loved one or stranger. She stared at the fractured cranial vault, at the triangle of bone that had been forced beneath the skull table. This had been no glancing blow; only a deliberate and savage swing of the arm could have driven that shard so deeply into the parietal lobe.

She took down Theresa's films, reached into the second envelope for a new pair of X-rays, and clipped them onto the light box. Another skull—this one Nikki's. Like her sister, Nikki had been struck in the head, but this blow had landed on the forehead, caving in the frontal bone, crushing both orbits so severely the eyes would have ruptured in their sockets. Nikki Wells must have seen the blow coming.

Maura removed the skull films and clipped up another pair of X-rays, showing Nikki's spine and pelvis, startlingly intact beneath the fire-ravaged flesh. Overlying the pelvis were the fetal bones. Though the flames had melded mother and child to a single charred mass, on X-ray, Maura could see they were separate individuals. Two sets of bones, two victims.

She saw something else, as well: a bright speck that stood out, even in the tangle of interlocking shadows. It was just a needle-thin sliver over Nikki Wells's pubic bone. A tiny shard of metal? Perhaps something from her overlying clothing—a zipper, a fastener—that had adhered to burned skin?

Maura reached into the envelope and

found a lateral torso view. She clipped it up beside the frontal view. The metallic sliver was still there on the lateral shot, but she could now see that it was not overlying the pubis; it seemed to be wedged within the bone.

She pulled all the X-rays from Nikki's envelope and clipped them up, two at a time. She spotted the densities that Dr. Hobart had seen on the chest X-ray, metallic loops that represented brassiere hook and eye fasteners. On the lateral films, those same loops of metal were clearly in the overlying soft tissue. She put up the pelvic films again and stared at that metallic sliver embedded in Nikki Wells's pubic bone. Although Dr. Hobart had mentioned it in his report, he had said nothing further about it in his conclusions. Perhaps he'd thought it a trivial finding. And why wouldn't he, in light of all the other horrors inflicted on this victim?

Yoshima had assisted Hobart at the autopsy; perhaps he would remember the case.

She left her office, headed down the stairwell, and pushed through the double doors, into the autopsy suite. The lab was deserted, the counters wiped clean for the night.

"Yoshima?" she called.

She pulled on shoe covers and walked through the lab, past the empty stainless steel tables, and pushed through yet another set of double doors, to the delivery bay. Swinging open the door to the cold locker, she glanced inside. Saw only the deceased, two white body pouches on side-by-side gurneys.

She closed the door and stood for a moment in the deserted bay, listening for voices, footsteps, anything to tell her that someone else was still in the building. But she heard only the rumble of the refrigerator and, faintly, the whine of an ambulance on the street outside.

Costas and Yoshima must have gone home for the night.

When she walked out of the building fifteen minutes later, she saw that the Saab and the Toyota were indeed gone; except for her black Lexus, the only other vehicles in the parking lot were the three morgue vans, stenciled with the words: OFFICE OF THE MEDICAL EXAMINER, COMMONWEALTH OF MASSACHUSETTS. Darkness had fallen, and her car sat isolated under a yellow pool of light cast by the streetlamp.

The images of Theresa and Nikki Wells still haunted her. As she walked toward the Lexus, she was alert to every shadow around her, to every stray noise, every hint of movement. A few paces from her car she came to a halt and stared at the passenger door. The hairs on the back of her neck suddenly stood up. The bundle of files she was carrying slid from her numb hands, papers scattering across the pavement.

Three parallel scratches marred her car's gleaming finish. A claw mark.

Get away. Get inside.

She spun around and ran back to the building. Stood at the locked door, fumbling through her keys. Where was it, where was the right one? Finally she found it, thrust it into the lock, and pushed through, slamming the door behind her. She threw her weight against it as well, as though to reinforce the barricade.

Inside the empty building, it was so quiet she could hear her own panicked breaths.

She ran down the hall to her office and locked herself inside. Only then, surrounded by all that was familiar, did she feel her pulse stop galloping, her hands stop shaking. She went to her desk, picked up the phone, and called Jane Rizzoli.

EIGHTEEN

"You did exactly the right thing. Backed the hell away and moved to a safe place," said Rizzoli.

Maura sat at her desk and stared at the creased papers that Rizzoli had retrieved for her from the parking lot. A now-untidy stack from Nikki Wells's file, smudged with dirt, trampled in panic. Even now, sitting safe in Rizzoli's company, Maura still felt the aftershocks.

"Did you find any fingerprints on my door?" Maura asked.

"A few. What you'd expect to find on any car door."

Rizzoli rolled a chair close to Maura's desk and sat down. Rested her hands on the shelf of her belly. Mama Rizzoli, pregnant and armed, thought Maura. Was there any less likely savior to come to my rescue?

"How long was your car in that parking lot? You said you arrived around six."

"But the scratches could have been made before I got here. I don't use the passenger door every day. Only if I'm loading groceries or something. I saw it tonight because of the way the car was parked. And it was right under the lamp."

"When was the last time you looked at that door?"

Maura pressed her hands to her temples. "I know it was fine yesterday morning. When I left Maine. I put my overnight bag in the front seat. I would have noticed the scratches then."

"Okay. So you drove home yesterday. Then what?"

"The car stayed in my garage all night. And then, this morning, I went to see you at Schroeder Plaza."

"Where did you park?"

"In that garage near police headquarters. The one off Columbus Ave."

"So it was in that parking garage all afternoon. While we were visiting the prison."

"Yes."

"That garage is fully monitored, you know."

"Is it? I didn't notice . . ."

"And then where did you go? After we got back from Framingham?"

Maura hesitated.

"Doc?"

"I went to see Joyce O'Donnell." She met Rizzoli's gaze. "Don't look at me like that. I had to see her."

"Were you going to tell me?"

"Of course. Look, I just needed to know more about my mother."

Rizzoli leaned back, mouth set in a straight line. She's not happy with me, thought Maura. She told me to stay away from O'Donnell and I ignored her advice.

"How long were you at her house?" Rizzoli asked.

"About an hour. Jane, she told me something I didn't know. Amalthea grew up in Fox Harbor. That's why Anna went to Maine."

"And after you left O'Donnell's house? What happened then?"

Maura sighed. "I came straight here."

"You didn't notice anyone following you?"

"Why would I bother to look? I have too many things on my mind."

They regarded each other for a moment, neither one speaking, the tension about her visit to O'Donnell still hanging between them.

"Did you know your security camera's broken?" Rizzoli said. "The one here in your parking lot."

Maura gave a laugh. A shrug. "Do you know how much our budget's been cut this year? That camera's been broken for months. You can almost see the wires hanging out."

"My point is, that camera would have scared off most vandals."

"Unfortunately, it didn't."

"Who else knows that camera's broken? Everyone who works in this office, right?"

Maura felt a stab of dismay. "I don't like what you're implying. A lot of people have noticed it's broken. Cops. Mortuary drivers. Anyone who's ever delivered a body here. You just have to look up and see it."

"You said there were two cars parked here when you arrived. Dr. Costas's and Yoshima's."

"Yes."

"And when you came out of the building, around eight, those cars were gone."

"They left before I did."

"Do you get along with both of them?"

Maura gave a disbelieving laugh. "You're kidding, right? Because these are ridiculous questions."

"I'm not crazy about having to ask them."

"Then why are you? You know Dr. Costas, Jane. And you know Yoshima. You can't treat them like suspects."

"They both walked through that parking lot. Right past your car. Dr. Costas left first, around six forty-five. Yoshima left sometime after that, maybe around seven fifteen."

"You've spoken to them?"

"They both told me they didn't see any scratches on your car. You'd think they would have seen it. Certainly Yoshima would, since he was parked right beside you."

"We've worked together for almost two years. I know him. So do you."

"We think we do."

Don't, Jane, she thought. Don't make me afraid of my own colleagues.

"He's worked in this building eighteen years," said Rizzoli.

"Abe's been here nearly as long. Louise has, too."

"Did you know Yoshima lives alone?"

"So do I."

"He's forty-eight years old, never married, and he lives by himself. Comes to work every day, and here you are, up close and personal. Both of you working with corpses. Dealing with some pretty grim stuff. That's got to forge a bond between you two. All the terrible things that only you and he have seen."

Maura thought of the hours that she and Yoshima had shared in that room with its steel tables and sharp instruments. He always seemed to anticipate her needs even before she did. Yes, there was a bond, of course there was, because they were a team. But after they stripped off the gowns and peeled off the shoe covers, they each walked out the door into their separate lives. They did not socialize; they'd never even shared a drink together after work. We're alike that way, she thought. Two solitary people who only meet over corpses.

"Look," said Rizzoli with a sigh, "I like Yoshima. I hate even bringing up the possibility. But it's something I have to consider, or I wouldn't be doing my job."

"Which is what? To make me paranoid? I'm scared enough as it is, Jane. Don't make me afraid of the very people I need to trust." Maura swept up the papers from her desk. "Have you finished with my car? I'd like to go home."

"Yeah, we're done with it. But I'm not so sure you should go home."

"What am I supposed to do?"

"There are other options. You could go to a hotel. You can sleep on my couch. I just spoke to Detective Ballard, and he mentioned he has a spare room."

"Why are you talking to Ballard?"

"He's been checking in with me every day about the case. Called about an hour ago, and I told him what happened to your car. He came right over to look at it."

"He's in the parking lot now?"

"Got here a little while ago. He's concerned, Doc. I am, too." Rizzoli paused. "So what do you want to do?"

"I don't know . . ."

"Well you've got a few minutes to think about it." Rizzoli heaved herself to her feet. "C'mon, I'll walk you out."

Now here was an absurd moment, thought Maura as they headed down the hallway together. I'm being protected by a woman who can barely push herself out of a chair. But Rizzoli made it clear that she was the one in charge, the one who'd assumed the role of guardian. She was the one who opened the door and stepped out first.

Maura followed her across the parking lot, to the Lexus, where Frost and Ballard were standing.

"Are you all right, Maura?" Ballard asked. The glow of the streetlamp cast his eyes in shadow; she looked up into a face whose expression she could not read.

"I'm fine."

"This could have turned out a lot worse." He looked at Rizzoli. "You told her what we think?"

"I told her she might not want to go home tonight."

Maura looked at her car. The three scratches stood out, even uglier than she'd remembered, like wounds left by a predator's claws. *Anna's killer is talking to me. And I never knew how close he came.*

Frost said, "CSU noticed a little ding on the driver's door."

"That's old. Someone bumped me in a parking lot a few months ago."

"Okay, so it's just the scratches. They pulled off a few fingerprints. They'll need yours, Doc. As soon as you can get a set over to the lab."

"Of course." She thought of all the fingers they'd inked in the morgue, all the cold flesh that was routinely pressed to cards. *They'll be getting mine ahead of the game. While I'm still alive.* She crossed her arms over her chest, feeling chilled despite the warm night. She thought of walking into her empty house, locking herself into her bedroom. Even with all those barricades, it was still just a house, not a fortress. A house with windows that were easily shattered, screens that could be cut with only a knife.

"You said it was Charles Cassell who scratched Anna's car." Maura looked at Rizzoli. "Cassell wouldn't have done *this*. Not to mine."

"No, he'd have no reason to. This is clearly meant as a warning to *you*." Rizzoli said, quietly: "Maybe Anna was a mistake."

I'm the one. I'm the one who should have died.

"Where do you want to go, Doc?" asked Rizzoli.

"I don't know," Maura said. "I don't know what to do . . ."

"Well, may I suggest you not stand around out here?" said Ballard. "Where everyone can watch you?"

Maura glanced at the sidewalk. Saw the silhouettes of people who'd been drawn by the flashing lights of the police cruiser. People whose faces she could not see because they were in shadow, while she stood here, lit like the star performer beneath the street-lamp's glare.

Ballard said, "I have a spare bedroom."

She did not look at him, but kept her gaze focused, instead, on those faceless shadows. Thinking: This is happening too fast. Too many decisions are being made on the spur of the moment. Choices I may come to regret.

"Doc?" said Rizzoli. "What do you think?"

At last Maura looked at Ballard. And she felt, once again, that disturbing tug of attraction. "I don't know where else to go," she said.

* * *

He drove right behind her, so close that his headlights glared in her rearview mirror, as though he was afraid she might pull away, might try to lose him in the dense tangle of traffic. He stayed close even as they headed into the quieter suburb of Newton, even as she circled his block twice, the way he had instructed, to confirm no car was following them. When at last she came to a stop in front of his house, he was almost immediately standing at her window, tapping on the glass.

"Pull into my garage," he said.

"I'll be taking your space."

"That's okay. I don't want your car sitting on the street. I'll open the bay door."

She turned into the driveway and watched as the door rumbled open to reveal an orderly garage where tools hung on a pegboard and built-in shelves held rows of paint cans. Even the concrete floor seemed to gleam. She eased into the bay, and the door immediately rolled shut behind her, closing off any view of her car from the street. For a moment she sat listening to the ticks of her cooling engine, and braced herself for the evening ahead. Only moments ago, returning to her own house had seemed unsafe, unwise. Now she wondered if this choice was any wiser.

Ballard opened her car door. "Come on in. I'll show you how to arm the security system. Just in case I'm not here to do it."

He led her into the house and up a short hallway to the foyer. Pointed to a keypad mounted near the front door.

"I had this updated only a few months ago. First you punch in the security code, then you press arm. Once you've armed it, if anyone opens a door or a window, it'll trigger an alarm so loud it'll make your ears ring. It also automatically notifies the security company, and they'll call the house. To disarm it, you punch in the same code, then hit off. Is that clear so far?"

"Yes. Do you want to tell me the code?"

"I was just getting to that." He glanced at her. "You realize, of course, that I'm about to hand you the numerical key to my house."

"Are you wondering if you can trust me?"

"Just promise not to pass it along to your unsavory friends."

"Lord knows I have plenty of those."

"Yeah." He laughed. "And they probably

all carry badges. Okay, the code is twelve seventeen. My daughter's birthday. Think you can remember that, or do you want to write it down?"

"I'll remember it."

"Good. Now go ahead and arm it, since I think we're in for the night."

As she punched in the numbers, he stood so close beside her she could feel his breath in her hair. She pressed arm and heard a soft beep. The digital readout now said: system armed.

"Fortress secure," he said.

"That was simple enough." She turned and found him watching her so intently, she had the urge to step back, if only to reestablish a safe distance between them.

"Did you get any dinner?" he asked.

"I never got around to it. So much was happening tonight."

"Come on, then. I can't let you go hungry."

His kitchen looked exactly the way she expected it would, with sturdy maple cabinets and butcher-block countertops. Pots and pans hung in orderly array from a ceiling rack. No extravagant touches, just the workspace of a practical man.

"I don't want you to go to any trouble," she said. "Eggs and toast would be fine."

He opened the refrigerator and took out a carton of eggs. "Scrambled?"

"I can do it, Rick."

"How about you make us some toast? The bread's right over there. I'd like one, too."

She took two bread slices from the package and dropped them into the toaster. Turned to watch as he stood by the stove, scrambling eggs in a bowl, and remembered their last meal together, both of them barefoot, laughing. Enjoying each other's company. Before Jane's phone call had made her wary of him. And if Jane hadn't called that night, what would have happened between them? She watched him pour the eggs into a pan and turn up the burner. Felt her face flush, as though he'd lit another flame inside her as well.

She turned and looked instead at the refrigerator door, where photos of Ballard and his daughter were displayed. Katie as an infant in her mother's arms. As a toddler, sitting in a high chair. A progression of images, leading to a photo of a blond teenager with a grudging smile.

"She's changing so fast," he said. "I can't believe those photos are all the same kid." She glanced over her shoulder at him. "What did you decide to do about that joint in her locker?"

"Oh, that." He sighed. "Carmen grounded her. Even worse, she's said no TV for a month. Now I'm going to have to lock up my own set, just to make sure Katie doesn't sneak over here and watch it while I'm not at home."

"You and Carmen are good about keeping a united front."

"There's not much choice, really. No matter how bitter the divorce is, you have to stand together, for the kid's sake." He turned off the stove and slid steaming eggs onto two plates. "You never had children?"

"No, fortunately."

"Fortunately?"

"Victor and I wouldn't have managed to stay as civil as you two."

"It's not as easy as it looks. Especially since . . ."

"Yes?"

"We manage to keep up appearances. That's all."

They set the table, laid out plates of eggs

and toast and butter, and sat down facing each other. The subject of their failed marriages had left them subdued. We are both still recovering from emotional wounds, she thought. No matter how attracted we are to each other, this is the wrong time to get involved.

But later, as he walked her upstairs, she knew the same possibilities were surely dancing in both their heads.

"Here's your room," he said, opening the door to Katie's bedroom. She walked in and confronted Britney Spears's come-hither eyes, gazing down from a giant poster on the wall. Britney dolls and CDs lined the bookshelves. This room is going to give me nightmares, thought Maura.

"You have your own bathroom, through that door," he said. "There should be a spare toothbrush or two in the cabinet. And you can use Katie's bathrobe."

"She won't mind?"

"She's with Carmen this week. She won't even know you're here."

"Thank you, Rick."

He paused, as though waiting for her to say something more. Waiting for words that would change everything.

"Maura," he said.

"Yes?"

"I'll take care of you. I just want you to know that. What happened to Anna—I won't let it happen to you." He turned to leave. Said, softly: "Good night," and closed the door behind him.

I'll take care of you.

Isn't that what we all want? she thought. Someone to keep us safe. She'd forgotten what it felt like, to be watched over. Even when she'd been married to Victor, she had never felt protected by him; he'd been too self-absorbed to watch over anyone but himself.

Lying in bed, she listened to the clock ticking on the nightstand. To Ballard's footsteps creaking in the room next door. Slowly the house settled into silence. She watched the hours advance on the clock. Midnight. One A.M. And still she couldn't sleep. Tomorrow she would be exhausted.

Is he lying awake, too?

She hardly knew this man, just as she'd hardly known Victor when she'd married him. And what a mess that had turned out to be, three years of her life thrown away, all because of chemistry. Sparks. She did not trust her own judgment when it came to men. The one man you most want to sleep with may be the worst choice of all.

Two A.M.

The beams of a car's headlights slid past the window. An engine purred on the street. She tensed, thinking: It's nothing, probably just a neighbor coming home late. Then she heard the creak of footsteps on the porch. She held her breath. Suddenly the darkness was shrieking. She shot up in bed.

The security alarm. Someone is in the house.

Ballard pounded on her door. "Maura? *Maura?*" he yelled.

"I'm okay!"

"Lock your door! Don't come out."

"Rick?"

"Just stay in the room!"

She scrambled out of bed and locked the door. Crouched there, hands covering her ears against the alarm's shriek, unable to hear anything else. She thought of Ballard, moving down the staircase. Imagined a house full of shadows. Someone waiting below. *Where are you, Rick?* She could hear nothing except that piercing alarm. Here in the darkness she was both blind and deaf to whatever might be moving toward her door.

The shrieks suddenly ceased. In the silence that followed, she could finally hear her own panicked breaths, the pounding of her heart.

And voices.

"Jesus Christ!" Rick was yelling. "I could have shot you! What the hell were you thinking?"

Now a girl's voice. Hurt, angry. "You chained the door! I couldn't get in to shut off the alarm!"

"Don't you yell at me."

Maura opened her door and stepped out into the hallway. The voices were louder now, both raised in fury. Looking over the banister, she saw Rick standing below, shirtless in blue jeans, the gun he'd carried downstairs now tucked in his waistband. His daughter was glaring at him.

"It's two in the morning, Katie. How did you get over here?"

"My friend drove me."

"In the middle of the night?"

"I came to get my backpack, okay? I forgot I needed it tomorrow. I didn't want to wake up Mom."

"Tell me who this friend is. Who drove you?"

"Well, he's gone now! The alarm probably freaked him out."

"It's a boy? Who?"

"I'm not going to get him in trouble, too!"

"Who is this boy?"

"Don't, Dad. Just *don't.*"

"You stay down here and talk to me. Katie, don't go up there—"

Footsteps thumped up the steps and suddenly halted. Katie stood frozen on the stairway, staring at Maura.

"Get back down here!" Rick yelled.

"Yeah, Dad," Katie murmured, her gaze still on Maura. "Now I know why you chained the door on me."

"Katie!" Rick paused, suddenly cut off by the ringing telephone. He turned to answer it. "Hello? Yeah, this is Rick Ballard. Everything's okay here. No, you don't need to send a man out. My daughter came home and didn't shut off the alarm system in time . . ."

The girl was still staring at Maura with open hostility. "So you're his new girlfriend."

"Please, you don't need to get upset

about this," Maura said quietly. "I'm not his girlfriend. I just needed a place to sleep for the night."

"Oh, right. So why not with my dad?"

"Katie, it's the truth—"

"Nobody in this family ever tells the truth."

Downstairs, the phone rang again. Again Rick answered it. "Carmen. Carmen, calm down! Katie's right here. Yeah, she's fine. Some boy drove her over to pick up her backpack . . ."

The girl shot a last poisonous glance at Maura, and went back down the stairs.

"It's your mother calling," Rick said.

"Are you going to tell her about your new girlfriend? How can you *do* this to her, Dad?"

"We need to have a talk about this. You need to accept the fact your mother and I aren't together anymore. Things have changed."

Maura went back into the bedroom and shut the door. While she got dressed, she could hear them continue to argue downstairs. Rick's voice, steady and firm, the girl's sharp with rage. It took Maura only moments to change clothes. When she came downstairs, she found Ballard and his daughter sitting in the living room. Katie was curled up on the couch like an angry porcupine.

"Rick, I'm going to leave now," Maura said.

He rose to his feet. "You can't."

"No, it's okay. You need time alone with your family."

"It's not safe for you to go home."

"I won't go home. I'll check into a hotel. Really, I'll be perfectly fine."

"Maura, wait—"

"She wants to leave, *okay*?" Katie snapped. "So just let her go."

"I'll call you when I get to the hotel," said Maura.

As she backed out of his garage, Rick came out and stood by the driveway, watching her. Their gazes met through her car window, and he stepped forward, as though to try once again to persuade her to stay, to return to the safety of his house.

Another pair of headlights swung into view. Carmen's car pulled over to the curb, and she stepped out, blond hair in disarray, her nightgown peeking out from beneath a bathrobe. Another parent roused from bed by this errant teenager. Carmen shot a look in Maura's direction, then said a few words to Ballard and walked into the house. Through the living room window, Maura saw mother and daughter embrace.

Ballard lingered in the driveway. Looked toward the house, then back at Maura, as though pulled in two directions.

She made the decision for him. She put the car into gear, stepped on the gas, and drove away. The last glimpse she had of him was in her rearview mirror, as he turned and walked into the house. Back to his family. Even divorce, she thought, cannot erase all the bonds forged by years of marriage. Long after the papers are signed, decrees notarized, the ties still remain. And the most powerful tie of all is written in a child's flesh and blood.

She released a deep breath. Felt, suddenly, cleansed of temptation. Free.

As she'd promised Ballard, she did not go home. Instead she headed west, toward Route 95, which traced a wide arc along the outskirts of Boston. She stopped at the first roadside motel she came to. The room she checked into smelled of cigarettes and Ivory soap. The toilet had a "sanitized" paper band across the lid, and the wrapped cups in the bathroom were plastic. Traffic noise from the nearby highway filtered in through thin walls. She could not remember the last time she had stayed in a motel so cheap, so run-down. She called Rick, just a curt thirty-second phone call to let him know where she was. Then she shut off her cell phone and climbed in between fraying sheets.

That night she slept more soundly than she had in a week.

NINETEEN

Nobody likes me, everybody hates me, think I'll go eat worms. Worms, worms, worms.

Stop thinking about that!

Mattie closed her eyes and gritted her teeth, but she could not block out the melody of that insipid children's song. It played again and again in her head, and always it came back to those worms.

Except I won't be eating them; they'll be eating me.

Oh, think about something else. Nice things, pretty things. Flowers, dresses. White dresses with chiffon and beads. Her wedding day. Yes, think about that.

She remembered sitting in the bride's room at St. John's Methodist Church, staring at herself in the mirror and thinking: Today is the best day of my life. I'm marrying the man I love. She remembered her mother coming into the room to help her with the veil. How her mother had bent close and said, with a relieved sigh: "I never thought I'd see this day." The day a man would finally marry her daughter.

Now, these seven months later, Mattie thought about her mother's words and how they had not been particularly kind. But on that day, nothing had dampened her joy. Not the nausea of morning sickness, or her killer high heels, or the fact that Dwayne drank so much champagne on their wedding night that he fell asleep in their hotel bed before she'd even come out of the bathroom. Nothing mattered, except that she was Mrs. Purvis, and her life, her real life, was finally about to begin.

And now it's going to end here, in this box, unless Dwayne saves me.

He will, won't he? He does want me back?

Oh, this was worse than thinking about worms eating her. Change of subject, Mattie!

What if he doesn't want me back? What if he was hoping all along that I'd just go away, so he can be with that woman? What if he's the one who . . .

No, not Dwayne. If he wanted her dead, why keep her in a box? Why keep her alive?

She took a deep breath, and her eyes filled with tears. She wanted to live. She'd do anything to live, but she didn't know how to get herself out of this box. She'd spent hours thinking about how to do it. She had pounded on the walls, kicked again and again against the top. She'd thought about taking apart the flashlight, maybe using its parts to build—what?

A bomb.

She could almost hear Dwayne laughing at her, ridiculing her. Oh right, Mattie, you're a real MacGyver.

Well, what am I supposed to do?

Worms . . .

They squirmed back into her thoughts. Into her future, slithering under her skin, devouring her flesh. They were out there waiting in the soil right outside this box, she thought. Waiting for her to die. Then they would crawl in, to feast.

She turned on her side and trembled.

There has to be a way out.

TWENTY

Yoshima stood over the corpse, his gloved hand wielding a syringe with a sixteen-gauge needle. The body was a young female, so gaunt that her belly drooped like a sagging tent across the hip bones. Yoshima spread the skin taut over her groin and angled the needle into the femoral vein. He drew back on the plunger and blood, so dark it was almost black, began to fill the syringe.

He did not look up as Maura came into the room, but stayed focused on his task. She watched in silence as he withdrew the needle and transferred the blood into various glass tubes, working with the calm efficiency of someone who had handled countless tubes of blood from countless corpses.

If I'm the queen of the dead, she thought, then Yoshima is surely the king. He has undressed them, weighed them, probed their groins and necks for veins, deposited their organs in jars of formalin. And when the autopsy is done, when I am finished cutting, he is the one who picks up the needle and thread and sews their incised flesh back together again.

Yoshima cut the needle and deposited the used syringe in the contaminated trash. Then he paused, gazing down at the woman whose blood he had just collected. "She came in this morning," he said. "Boyfriend found her dead on the couch when he woke up."

Maura saw the needle tracks on the corpse's arms. "What a waste."

"It always is."

"Who's doing this one?"

"Dr. Costas. Dr. Bristol's in court today." He wheeled a tray to the table and began laying out instruments. In the awkward silence, the clang of metal seemed painfully loud. Their exchange had been businesslike as usual, but today Yoshima was not looking at her. He seemed to be avoiding her gaze, shying away from even a glance in her direction. Shying, too, from any mention of what had happened in the parking lot last night. But the issue was there, hanging between them, impossible to ignore.

"I understand Detective Rizzoli called you at home last night," she said.

He paused, his profile to her, his hands motionless on the tray.

"Yoshima," she said, "I'm sorry if she implied in any way—"

"Do you know how long I've worked in the medical examiner's office, Dr. Isles?" he cut in.

"I know you've been here longer than any of us."

"Eighteen years. Dr. Tierney hired me right after I got out of the army. I served in their mortuary unit. It was hard, you know, working on so many young people. Most of them were accidents or suicides, but that goes with the territory. Young men, they take chances. They get into fights, they drive too fast. Or their wives leave them, so they reach for their weapon and shoot themselves. I thought, at least I can do something for them, I can treat them with the respect due a soldier. And some of them were just kids, barely old enough to grow beards. That was the upsetting part, how young they were, but I managed to deal with it. The way I deal with it here, because it's my job. I can't remember the last time I called in sick." He paused. "But today, I thought about not coming in."

"Why?"

He turned and looked at her. "Do you know what it's like, after eighteen years working here, to suddenly feel like I'm a suspect?"

"I'm sorry that's how she made you feel. I know she can be brusque—"

"No, actually, she wasn't. She was very polite, very friendly. It was the *nature* of her questions that made me realize what was going on. *What's it like working with Dr. Isles? Do you two get along?*" Yoshima laughed. "Now, why do you suppose she asked me that?"

"She was doing her job, that's all. It wasn't an accusation."

"It felt like one." He went to the countertop and began lining up jars of formalin for tissue samples. "We've worked together almost two years, Dr. Isles."

"Yes."

"There's never been a time, at least that I'm aware of, that you've been unhappy with my performance."

"Never. There's no one I'd rather work with than you."

He turned and faced her. Under the harsh fluorescent lights, she saw how much gray peppered his black hair. She had once thought him to be in his thirties. With that placidly seamless face and slender build, he'd seemed somehow ageless. Now, seeing the troubled lines around his eyes, she recognized him for what he was: a man quietly slipping into middle age. *As I am.*

"There wasn't a moment," she said, "not an *instant,* when I thought you might have—"

"But now you *do* have to think about it, don't you? Since Detective Rizzoli's brought it up, you have to consider the possibility that I vandalized your car. That I'm the one stalking you."

"No, Yoshima. I don't. I refuse to."

His gaze held hers. "Then you're not being honest with yourself, or with me. Because the thought's got to be there. And as long as the smallest ounce of mistrust is there, you're going to be uneasy with me. I can feel it, you can feel it." He stripped off his gloves, turned, and began writing the deceased's name on labels. She could see the tension in his shoulders, in the rigid muscles of his neck.

"We'll get past this," she said.

"Maybe."

"Not maybe. We will. We have to work together."

"Well, I guess that's up to you."

She watched him for a moment, wondering how to recapture the cordial relationship they had once enjoyed. Perhaps it wasn't so cordial after all, she thought. I just assumed it was, while all this time, he's hidden his emotions from me, just as I hide mine. What a pair we are, the poker-faced duo. Every week tragedy passes across our autopsy table, but I have never seen him cry, nor has he seen me cry. We just go about the business of death like two workers on the factory floor.

He finished labeling the specimen jars and turned back to see she was still standing behind him. "Did you need anything, Dr. Isles?" he asked, and his voice, like his expression, revealed no hint of what had just passed between them. This was the Yoshima she had always known, quietly efficient, poised to offer his assistance.

She responded in kind. She removed X-rays from the envelope she'd carried into the room and mounted Nikki Wells's films on the light box. "I'm hoping you remember this case," she said, and flipped on the switch. "It's from five years ago. A case out in Fitchburg."

"What's the name?"

"Nikki Wells."

He frowned at the X-ray. Focused, immediately, on the collection of fetal bones overlying the maternal pelvis. "This was that pregnant woman? Killed with her sister?"

"You do remember it, then."

"Both the bodies were burned?"

"That's right."

"I remember, it was Dr. Hobart's case."

"I've never met Dr. Hobart."

"No, you wouldn't have. He left about two years before you joined us."

"Where is he working now? I'd like to talk to him."

"Well, that would be hard. He's dead."

She frowned at him. "What?"

Sadly, Yoshima shook his head. "It was so hard on Dr. Tierney. He felt responsible, even though he had no choice."

"What happened?"

"There were some . . . problems with Dr. Hobart. First he lost track of a few slides. Then he misplaced some organs, and the family found out. They sued our office. It was a big mess, a lot of bad publicity, but Dr. Tierney stood by him. Then some drugs went missing from a bag of personal effects, and he had no choice. He asked Dr. Hobart to resign."

"What happened then?"

"Dr. Hobart went home and swallowed a handful of Oxycontin. They didn't find him for three days." Yoshima paused. "That was the autopsy no one here wanted to do."

"Were there questions about his competence?"

"He may have made some mistakes."

"Serious ones?"

"I'm not sure what you mean."

"I'm wondering if he missed this." She pointed to the X-ray. To the bright sliver embedded in the pubic bone. "His report on

Nikki Wells doesn't explain this metallic density here."

"There are other metallic shadows on that film," noted Yoshima. "I can see a bra hook here. And this looks like a snap."

"Yes, but look at the lateral view. This sliver of metal is *in* the bone. Not overlying it. Did Dr. Hobart say anything about it to you?"

"Not that I recall. It's not in his report?"

"No."

"Then he must not have thought it was significant."

Which meant it had probably not been brought up during Amalthea's trial, she thought. Yoshima returned to his tasks, positioning basins and buckets, assembling paperwork on his clipboard. Though a young woman lay dead only a few feet away, Maura's attention was not on the fresh corpse, but on the X-ray of Nikki Wells and her fetus, their bones melded together by fire into a single charred mass.

Why did you burn them? What was the point? Had Amalthea felt pleasure, watching the flames consume them? Or was she hoping those flames would consume something else, some trace of herself that she did not want to be found?

Her focus moved from the arc of fetal skull to the bright shard embedded in Nikki's pubis. A shard as thin as . . .

A knife's edge. A broken-off fragment from a blade.

But Nikki had been killed with a blow to the head. Why use a knife on a victim whose face you have just crushed with a crowbar? She stared at that metallic sliver, and its significance suddenly struck her—a significance that sent a chill streaking up her spine.

She crossed to the phone and hit the intercom button. "Louise?"

"Yes, Dr. Isles?"

"Can you connect me with Dr. Daljeet Singh? The medical examiner's office in Augusta, Maine."

"Hold on." Then, a moment later: "I've got Dr. Singh on the line."

"Daljeet?" said Maura.

"No, I haven't forgotten about that dinner I owe you!" he answered.

"I may owe *you* a dinner, if you can answer this question for me."

"What's that?"

"Those skeletal remains we dug up in Fox Harbor. Have you identified them yet?"

"No. It may take a while. There are no missing persons reports on file in either Waldo or Hancock County that would match these remains. Either these bones are very old, or these people were not from the area."

"Have you requested an NCIC search yet?" she asked. The National Crime Information Center, administered through the FBI, maintained a searchable database of missing persons cases from across the country.

"Yes, but since I can't narrow it down to any particular decade, I got back pages of names. Everything on record for the New England area."

"Maybe I can help you narrow down your search parameters."

"How?"

"Specify just the missing persons cases from 1955 to 1965."

"Can I ask how you came up with that particular decade?"

Because that's when my mother was living in Fox Harbor, she thought. *My mother, who has killed others.*

But all she said was: "An educated guess."

"You're being very mysterious."

"I'll explain it all when I see you."

For once, Rizzoli was letting Maura drive, but only because they were in Maura's Lexus, heading north toward the Maine Turnpike. During the night, a storm front had blown in from the west, and Maura had awakened to the sound of rain drumming her roof. She'd made coffee, read the newspaper, all the usual things she did on a typical morning. How quickly old routines reasserted themselves, even in the face of fear. Last night she had not stayed in a motel, but had returned home. Had locked all her doors and left the porch light burning, a meager defense against the threats of the night, yet she had slept through the storm's bluster, and had awakened feeling back in control of her own life.

I've had enough of being afraid, she thought. I won't let it drive me again from my own house.

Now, as she and Rizzoli headed toward Maine, where even darker rain clouds loomed, she was ready to fight back, ready to turn the tables. *Whoever you are, I'm going to track you down and find you. I can be a hunter, too.*

It was two in the afternoon when they arrived at the Maine medical examiner's building in Augusta. Dr. Daljeet Singh met them in reception and walked them downstairs to the autopsy lab, where the two boxes of bones were waiting on a countertop.

"This hasn't been my highest priority," he admitted as he shook out a plastic sheet. It settled with a soft whish on the steel table, like parachute silk. "They've probably been buried for decades; a few more days won't make much difference."

"Did you get back the new search results from NCIC?" asked Maura.

"This morning. I printed up the list of names. It's on that desk there."

"Dental X-rays?"

"I've downloaded the files they emailed me. Haven't had a chance yet to review them. I thought I'd wait till you two got here." He opened the first cardboard box and began removing bones, gently setting them on the plastic sheet. Out came a skull, its cranium caved in. A dirt-stained pelvis and long bones and chunky spine. A bundle of ribs, which clattered together like a bamboo wind chime. It was otherwise silent in Daljeet's lab, as stark and bright as Maura's autopsy suite in Boston. Good pathologists are by nature perfectionists, and he now revealed that aspect of his personality. He seemed to dance around the table, moving with almost feminine grace as he arranged the bones in their anatomic positions.

"Which one is this?" asked Rizzoli.

"This is the male," he said. "Femoral length indicates he was somewhere in the range of five foot ten to six feet tall. Obvious crush fracture of the right temporal bone. Also, there's an old Colles fracture, well healed." He glanced at Rizzoli, who looked perplexed. "That's a broken wrist."

"Why do you doctors do that, anyway?"

"What?"

"Call it some fancy name. Why don't you just call it a broken wrist?"

Daljeet smiled. "Some questions have no easy answers, Detective Rizzoli."

Rizzoli looked at the bones. "What else do we know about him?"

"There are no apparent osteoporotic or arthritic changes of the spine. This was a young adult male, Caucasian. Some dental work here—silver amalgam fillings numbers eighteen and nineteen."

Rizzoli pointed to the cratered temporal bone. "Is that the cause of death?"

"That would certainly qualify as a fatal blow." He turned and looked at the second box. "Now, to the female. She was found about twenty yards away."

On the second autopsy table, he again spread out a plastic sheet. Together, he and Maura laid out the next collection of remains in their anatomical positions, like two fussy waiters arranging a place setting for dinner. Bones clattered against the table. The dirt-encrusted pelvis. Another skull, smaller, the supraorbital ridges more delicate than the man's. Leg bones, arm bones, sternum. A bundle of ribs, and two paper sacks containing loose carpal and tarsal bones.

"So here's our Jane Doe," said Daljeet, surveying the finished arrangement. "I can't tell you the cause of death here, because there's nothing to go on. She appears to be young, also Caucasian. Twenty to thirty-five years old. Height around five foot three, no old fractures. Dentition's very good. A little chip here, on the canine, and a gold crown on number four."

Maura glanced at the X-ray viewing box, where two films were mounted. "Are those their dental films?"

"Male's on the left, female on the right." Daljeet went to the sink to wash the dirt from his hands and yanked out a paper towel. "So there you have it, John and Jane Doe."

Rizzoli picked up the printout of names that NCIC had emailed to Daljeet that morning. "Jesus. There are dozens of entries here. So many people missing."

"And that's only for the New England region. Caucasians between the ages of twenty and forty-five."

"All these reports are from the 1950s and '60s."

"That's the time frame Maura specified." Daljeet crossed to his laptop computer. "Okay, let's take a look at some of the X-rays they sent." He opened the file that had been emailed to him from NCIC. A row of icons appeared, each labeled with a case number. He clicked on the first icon, and an X-ray filled the screen. A crooked line of teeth, like tumbling white dominoes.

"Well, this certainly isn't one of ours," he said. "Look at the teeth on this one! It's an orthodontist's nightmare."

"Or an orthodontist's gold mine," said Rizzoli.

Daljeet closed that image, and clicked on the next icon. Another X-ray, this one with a gaping space between incisors. "I don't think so," he said.

Maura's attention drifted back to the table. To the bones of the unnamed woman. She stared down at the skull with its gracile brow line and delicate zygomatic arch. A face of gentle proportions.

"Well, *hello,*" she heard Daljeet say. "I think I recognize these teeth."

She turned to look at the computer screen. Saw an X-ray of lower molars and the bright glow of dental fillings.

Daljeet rose from his chair and crossed to the table where the male skeleton was laid out. He picked up the mandible and carried it back to the computer to compare.

"Amalgam filling numbers eighteen and

nineteen," he noted. "Yes. Yes, that matches . . ."

"What's the name on that X-ray?" Rizzoli asked.

"Robert Sadler."

"Sadler . . . Sadler . . ." Rizzoli flipped through the pages of computer printouts. "Okay, I found the entry. Sadler, Robert. Caucasian male, age twenty-nine. Five foot eleven, brown hair, brown eyes." She looked at Daljeet, who nodded.

"That's compatible with our remains."

Rizzoli continued reading. "He was a building contractor. Last seen in his home-town of Kennebunkport, Maine. Reported missing July third, 1960, along with his . . ." She paused. Turned to look at the table where the female's bones had been laid out. "Along with his wife."

"What was her name?" asked Maura.

"Karen. Karen Sadler. I have the case number for you."

"Give it to me," said Daljeet, turning back to the computer. "Let's see if her X-rays are here." Maura stood close behind him, star-ing over his shoulder as he clicked on the correct icon, and an image appeared on the screen. It was an X-ray taken when Karen

Sadler was alive and sitting in her dentist's chair. Anxious, perhaps, about the prospect of a cavity and the inevitable drilling that would result. She could not have imagined, as she'd clamped down on the cardboard wing to hold the unexposed film in place, that this same image her dentist captured that day would be glowing, years later, on a pathologist's computer screen.

Maura saw a row of molars, and the bright metallic glow of a crown. She crossed to the X-ray light box, where Daljeet had clipped up the panograph he'd taken of the unidentified woman's teeth. She said, softly, "It's her. These bones are Karen Sadler's."

"So we have a double match," said Daljeet. "Both husband and wife."

Behind them, Rizzoli flipped through the printouts, looking for Karen Sadler's missing persons report. "Okay, here she is. Caucasian female, age twenty-five. Blond hair, blue eyes . . ." She suddenly stopped. "There's something wrong here. You'd better check those X-rays again."

"Why?" said Maura.

"Just check them again."

Maura studied the panograph, then

turned to look at the computer screen. "They are a match, Jane. What's the problem?"

"You're missing another set of bones."

"Whose bones?"

"A fetus." Rizzoli looked at her, a stunned expression on her face. "Karen Sadler was eight months pregnant."

There was a long silence.

"We found no other remains," Daljeet said.

"You could have missed them," said Rizzoli.

"We sifted the soil. Thoroughly excavated that grave site."

"Scavengers might have dragged them away."

"Yes, that's always possible. But this *is* Karen Sadler."

Maura went to the table and stared down at the woman's pelvis, thinking about another woman's bones, glowing on an X-ray light box. *Nikki Wells was pregnant, too.*

She swung the magnifying lens over the table and switched on the light. Focused the lens over the pubic ramus. Reddish dirt had crusted over the symphysis, where the two rami met, joined by leathery cartilage.

"Daljeet, could I have a wet Q-tip or gauze? Something to wipe this dirt away."

He filled a basin of water and tore open a packet of Q-tips. He set them on the tray beside her. "What are you looking for?"

She didn't answer him. Her attention was focused on dabbing away that coating of dirt, on revealing what lay beneath. As the crust melted, her pulse quickened. The last fleck of dirt suddenly fell away. She stared at what was now revealed beneath the magnifier. Straightening, she looked at Daljeet.

"What is it?" he said.

"Take a look. It's right at the edge, where the bones articulate."

He bent to look through the lens. "You mean that little nick? Is that what you're talking about?"

"Yes."

"It's pretty subtle."

"But it's there." She took a deep breath. "I brought an X-ray. It's in my car. I think you should look at it."

Rain battered her umbrella as she walked out to the parking lot. As she pressed the unlock button on her key ring, she couldn't avoid glancing at the scratches on her passenger door. A claw mark meant to scare her. *All it did is make me angry. Ready to fight back.* She took the envelope out of the backseat and sheltered it under her coat as she carried it into the building.

Daljeet looked bewildered as he watched her clip Nikki Wells's films onto the light box. "What is this case you're showing me?"

"A five-year-old homicide in Fitchburg, Massachusetts. The victim's skull was crushed and her body later burned."

Daljeet frowned at the X-ray. "Pregnant female. The fetus looks close to term."

"But this is what caught my eye." She pointed to the bright sliver embedded in Nikki Wells's pubic symphysis. "I think it's the broken edge of a knife blade."

"But Nikki Wells was killed with a tire iron," said Rizzoli. "Her skull was smashed in."

"That's right," said Maura.

"Then why use a knife as well?"

Maura pointed to the X-ray. To the fetal bones curled over Nikki Wells's pelvis. "That's why. That's what the killer really wanted."

For a moment Daljeet didn't speak. But

she knew, without his saying a word, that he understood what she was thinking. He turned back to the remains of Karen Sadler. He picked up the pelvis. "A midline incision, straight down the abdomen," he said. "The blade would hit bone, right where this nick is . . ."

Maura thought of Amalthea's knife, slicing down a young woman's abdomen with a stroke so decisive the blade stops only when it collides with bone. She thought of her own profession, where knives played such a large part, and of the days she spent in the autopsy lab, slicing skin and organs. *We are both cutters, my mother and I. But I cut dead flesh, and she cut the living.*

"That's why you didn't find fetal bones in Karen Sadler's grave," said Maura.

"But your other case—" He gestured toward the X-ray of Nikki Wells. "That fetus wasn't taken. It was burned with the mother. Why make an incision to extract it, and then kill it anyway?"

"Because Nikki Wells's baby had a congenital defect. An amniotic band."

"What's that?" asked Rizzoli.

"It's a membranous strand that sometimes stretches across the amniotic sac," said Maura. "If it wraps around a fetus's limb, it can constrict blood flow, even amputate the limb. The defect was diagnosed during Nikki's second trimester." She pointed to the X-ray. "You can see the fetus is missing its right leg beneath the knee."

"That's not a fatal defect?"

"No, it would have survived. But the killer would have seen the defect immediately. She would have seen it wasn't a perfect baby. I think that's why she didn't take it." Maura turned and looked at Rizzoli. Could not avoid confronting the fact of Rizzoli's pregnancy. The swollen belly, the estrogenic flush of her cheeks. "She wanted a perfect baby."

"But Karen Sadler's wouldn't have been perfect either," Rizzoli pointed out. "She was only eight months pregnant. The lungs wouldn't be mature, right? It would need an incubator to survive."

Maura looked down at Karen Sadler's bones. She thought of the site from which they had been recovered. Thought, too, of the husband's bones, buried twenty yards away. But not in the same grave— a separate spot. Why dig two different

holes? Why not bury husband and wife together?

Her mouth suddenly went dry. The answer left her stunned.

They were not buried at the same time.

TWENTY-ONE

The cottage huddled beneath rain-heavy tree branches, as though cringing from their touch. When Maura had first seen it the week before, she had thought the house merely depressing, a dark little box slowly being strangled by encroaching woods. Now, as she gazed at it from her car, the windows seemed to stare back like malevolent eyes.

"This is the house where Amalthea grew up," said Maura. "It wouldn't have been hard for Anna to track down that information. All she had to do was check Amalthea's high school records. Or search an old phone book for the name Lank." She looked at Rizzoli. "The landlady, Miss

Clausen, told me Anna asked specifically about renting this house."

"So Anna must have known Amalthea once lived here."

And like me, she was hungry to know more about our mother, thought Maura. To understand the woman who gave us life, and then abandoned us.

Rain pounded on the car roof and slid in silvery sheets down the windshield.

Rizzoli zipped up her slicker and pulled the hood over her head. "Well, let's go in and take a look, then."

They dashed through the rain and scrambled up the steps to the porch, where they shook water from their raincoats. Maura produced the key she'd just picked up at Miss Clausen's real estate office and thrust it into the lock. At first it would not turn, as though the house was fighting back, determined not to let her enter. When at last she managed to open the door, it gave a warning creak as it swung open, resisting her to the end.

Inside it was even gloomier and more claustrophobic than she had remembered. The air was sour with the smell of mildew, as though the dampness outside had seeped through the walls into the curtains, the furniture. The light through the window cast the living room in sullen shades of gray. This house does not want us here, she thought. It does not want us to learn its secrets.

She touched Rizzoli's arm. "Look," she said, pointing to the two bolts and the brass chains.

"Brand-new locks."

"Anna had them installed. It makes you wonder, doesn't it? Who she was trying to lock out."

"If it wasn't Charles Cassell." Rizzoli crossed to the living room window and gazed out at a curtain of leaves dripping with rain. "Well, this place is awfully isolated. No neighbors. Nothing but trees. I'd want a few extra locks, too." She gave an uneasy laugh. "You know, I never did like it, out in the woods. Bunch of us went camping once, in high school. Drove up to New Hampshire and laid our sleeping bags out around the campfire. I didn't sleep a wink. I kept thinking: How do I know what's out there, watching me? Up in the trees, hiding in the bushes."

"Come on," said Maura. "I want to show

you the rest of the house." She led the way to the kitchen, and flipped the wall switch. Fluorescent lights flickered on with an ominous hum. The harsh glare brought out every crack, every buckle in the ancient linoleum. She looked down at the black and white checkerboard pattern, yellowed with wear, and thought about all the spilled milk and tracked-in mud that, over the years, had surely left their microscopic traces on this floor. What else had seeped into these cracks and seams? What terrible events had left their residue?

"These are brand-new dead bolts, too," said Rizzoli, standing at the back door.

Maura crossed to the cellar door. "This is what I wanted you to see."

"Another bolt?"

"But see how tarnished this one is? It isn't new. This bolt's been here a long time. Miss Clausen said it was already on the door when she bought the property at auction twenty-eight years ago. And here's the strange part."

"What?"

"The only place this door leads is down to the cellar." She looked at Rizzoli. "It's a dead end."

"Why would anyone need to lock this door?"

"That's what I wondered."

Rizzoli opened the door, and the smell of damp earth rose from the darkness. "Oh man," she muttered. "I hate going down into cellars."

"There's a light chain, right over your head."

Rizzoli reached up and gave the chain a tug. The bulb came on, its anemic glow spilling down a narrow stairway. Below were only shadows. "You sure there's no other way into this cellar?" she asked, peering down into shadow. "A coal hatch or something?"

"I walked all around the outside of this house. I didn't see any outside doors leading into the cellar."

"Have you been down there?"

"I didn't see any reason to." *Until today.*

"Okay." Rizzoli pulled a mini Maglite from her pocket and took a deep breath. "I guess we should take a look."

The lightbulb swayed above them, tilting shadows back and forth as they descended creaky stairs. Rizzoli moved slowly, as though testing each step before she trusted her weight to it. Never before had Maura known Rizzoli to be so tentative, so cautious, and that apprehension was fueling her own. By the time they reached the bottom of the stairs, the door to the kitchen seemed far above them, in another dimension.

The bulb at the bottom of the stairs had burned out. Rizzoli swept her Maglite across a floor of packed earth, damp from seeping rainwater. The beam revealed a stack of paint cans and a rolled-up carpet, moldering against one wall. In a corner sat a crate filled with bundles of kindling for the living room fireplace. Nothing here seemed out of the ordinary, nothing justified the sense of threat that Maura had felt at the top of the stairs.

"Well, you're right," said Rizzoli. "There doesn't seem to be another way out of here."

"Just that door up there, to the kitchen."

"Which means the bolt doesn't make any sense. Unless . . ." Rizzoli's beam suddenly came to a halt on the far wall.

"What is it?"

Rizzoli crossed the cellar and stood staring. "Why is this thing here? What would anyone use it for?"

Maura moved closer. Felt a chill clamber up her spine when she saw what Rizzoli's Maglite was shining on. It was an iron ring, lodged in one of the massive cellar stones. *What would anyone use this for?* Rizzoli had asked. The answer made Maura step away, repelled by the visions it conjured up.

This is not a cellar; it's a dungeon.

Rizzoli's flashlight jerked upward. "Someone's inside the house," she whispered.

Through the pounding of her own heart, Maura heard the floor creaking above them. Heard heavy footsteps move through the house. Approach the kitchen. A silhouette suddenly loomed in the doorway, and the flashlight beam that flooded down was so bright, Maura had to turn away, blinded.

"Dr. Isles?" a man called.

Maura squinted up into the light. "I can't see you."

"Detective Yates. CSU just got here, too. You want to take us through the house before we start?"

Maura released a sharp breath. "We're coming up."

By the time Maura and Rizzoli emerged

from the cellar, there were four men standing in the kitchen. Maura had met Maine state detectives Corso and Yates the week before, at the clearing in the woods. Two CSU techs, who introduced themselves merely as Pete and Gary, had joined them, and they all paused for a round of handshakes.

Yates said, "So is this some kind of treasure hunt?"

"No guarantees we'll find anything," said Maura.

Both CSU techs were looking around the kitchen, scanning the floor. "This linoleum looks pretty beat up," said Pete. "What period of time are we looking at?"

"The Sadlers vanished forty-five years ago. The suspect would still have been living here, with her cousin. After they left, the house went empty for years, before it got sold at auction."

"Forty-five years ago? Yeah, this linoleum could be that old."

"I know the carpet in the living room's more recent, only about twenty years old," Maura said. "We'd have to pull it up to check that floor."

"We haven't tried this on anything older

than fifteen years. This would be a new record for us." Pete glanced at the kitchen window. "Won't be dark for at least another two hours."

"Then let's start in the cellar," said Maura. "It's dark enough down there."

They all pitched in to haul various equipment from the van: video and still cameras and tripods, boxes with protective gear and aerosol sprayers and distilled water, an Igloo cooler containing bottles of chemicals, and electrical cords and flashlights. All these they carried down the narrow steps into the cellar, which suddenly felt cramped as six people and camera gear crowded in. Only half an hour earlier, Maura had regarded this same gloomy space with uneasiness. Now, as she watched the men matter-of-factly set up tripods and uncoil electrical cords, the room lost its power to frighten her. This is only damp stone and packed earth, she thought. There are no ghosts down here.

"I don't know about this," said Pete, turning the bill of his Sea Dogs baseball cap backward. "You've got a dirt floor here. It's going to have a high iron content. Could light up everywhere. That's gonna be hard to interpret."

"I'm more interested in the walls," said Maura. "Smears, spatter patterns." She pointed to the block of granite with the iron ring. "Let's start with that wall."

"We'll need a baseline photo first. Let me set up the tripod. Detective Corso, can you mount the ruler up on that wall right there? It's luminescent. It'll give us a frame of reference."

Maura looked at Rizzoli. "You should go upstairs, Jane. They're going to start mixing the Luminol. I don't think you should be exposed to it."

"I didn't think it was that toxic."

"Still, you shouldn't take the chance. Not with the baby."

Rizzoli sighed. "Yeah, okay." Slowly she headed up the steps. "But I hate missing a light show." The cellar door swung shut behind her.

"Man, shouldn't she be on maternity leave already?" Yates said.

"She has another six weeks to go," said Maura.

One of the techs laughed. "Like that woman cop in *Fargo,* huh? How do you chase down a perp when you're that knocked up?"

Through the closed cellar door, Rizzoli yelled: "Hey, I may be knocked up, but I'm not deaf!"

"She's also armed," said Maura.

Detective Corso said, "Can we get started here?"

"There are masks and goggles in that box," said Pete. "You all might want to pass those around."

Corso handed a respirator and a pair of goggles to Maura. She slipped them on and watched as Gary began measuring chemicals.

"We're going with a Weber prep," he said. "It's a little more sensitive, and I think it's safer to use. This stuff is irritating enough on the skin and eyes."

"Are those stock solutions you're mixing?" asked Maura, her voice muffled through the mask.

"Yeah, we keep 'em stored in the lab refrigerator. Mix all three together in the field, along with distilled water." He capped the jar and gave it a vigorous shake. "Anyone here wear contact lenses?"

"I do," said Yates.

"Then you might want to step out, Detective. You're gonna be more sensitive, even wearing those goggles."

"No, I wanna watch."

"Then stay back when we start spraying." He gave the bottle one more swirl, then decanted the contents into a spray bottle. "Okay, we're ready to rock. Let me snap a photo first. Detective, can you move away from that wall?"

Corso stepped to the side and Pete pressed the shutter release cable. The flash went off as the camera captured a baseline image of the wall they were about to spray with Luminol.

"You want the lights off now?" said Maura.

"Let Gary get in position first. Once it's dark, we're gonna be stumbling around here. So everyone just pick a spot and stay there, okay? Only Gary moves."

Gary crossed to the wall and held up the spray bottle containing Luminol. With his goggles and mask, he looked like a pest exterminator, about to squirt some offending roach.

"Hit the lights, Dr. Isles."

Maura reached out to the flood lamp beside her and switched it off, plunging the cellar into pitch blackness.

"Go ahead, Gary."

They could hear the hiss of the spray bottle. Flecks of greenish-blue suddenly glowed in the darkness, like stars in the night sky. Now a ghostly circle appeared, seeming to float in the darkness, unattached. The iron ring.

"It may not be blood at all," said Pete. "Luminol reacts with a lot of things. Rust, metals. Bleach solutions. That iron ring would probably glow anyway, whether there's blood on it or not. Gary, can you move aside while I get this shot? This is going to be a forty-second exposure, so just stand tight." When the shutter finally clicked, he said: "Lights, Dr. Isles."

Maura fumbled in the darkness for the flood lamp switch. When the light came on, she was staring at the stone wall.

"What do you think?" asked Corso.

Pete shrugged. "Not too impressive. There's going to be a lot of false positives down here. You've got soil staining all those rocks. We'll try the other walls, but unless you see a handprint or a major splatter, it's not going to be easy to pick up blood against this background."

Maura noticed Corso glancing at his watch. It had been a long drive for both Maine state detectives, and she could see he was starting to wonder if this was a waste of time.

"Let's keep going," she said.

Pete moved the tripod and positioned his camera lens to focus on the next wall. He clicked off a flash photo, then said, "Lights."

Again, the room went pitch black.

The spray bottle hissed. More blue-green flecks magically appeared like fireflies twinkling in the darkness as the Luminol reacted with oxidized metals in the stone, producing pinpoints of luminescence. Gary sprayed a fresh arc across the wall, and a new swath of stars appeared, eclipsed by his shadowy outline as he moved past. There was a loud thump, and the silhouette suddenly lurched forward.

"Shit."

"You okay, Gary?" said Yates.

"Hit my shin against something. The stairs, I think. Can't see a goddamn thing in this . . ." He stopped. Then murmured: "Hey, guys. Look at this."

As he moved aside, a patch of blue-green floated into view, like a ghostly pool of ecto-plasm.

"What the hell is that?" said Corso.

"Light!" called Pete.

Maura turned on the lamp. The blue-green pool vanished. In its place she saw only the wooden staircase leading up to the kitchen.

"It was on that step there," said Gary. "When I tripped, it caught some of the spray."

"Let me reposition this camera. Then I want you to move up to the top of those stairs. Think you can feel your way down if we turn off the lights?"

"I don't know. If I go slowly enough—"

"Spray the steps as you come down."

"No. No, I think I'm gonna start from the bottom and go up. I don't like the idea of backing down the stairs in the dark."

"Whatever you're comfortable with." The camera flash went off. "Okay, Gary. I've got my baseline. Whenever you're ready."

"Yeah. You can hit the light, Doc."

Maura turned off the lamp.

Once again, they heard the hiss of the spray bottle dispersing its fine mist of Luminol. Near the ground, a splash of blue-green appeared, then above it another splash, like ghostly pools of water. They could hear Gary's heavy breathing through his mask, and the creak of the steps as he backed up the stairs, spraying the whole time. Step after step lit up, forming an intensely luminous cascade.

A waterfall of blood.

There was nothing else that this could be, she thought. It was smeared across every step, trickles of it streaking down the sides of the staircase.

"Jesus," murmured Gary. "It's even brighter up here, on the top step. Looks like it came from the kitchen. Seeped under the door and dripped down the stairs."

"Everyone stay right where you are. I'm taking the shot. Forty-five seconds."

"It might be dark enough outside now," said Corso. "We can start on the rest of the house."

Rizzoli was waiting for them in the kitchen as they came up the stairs, hauling their equipment. "Sounds like it was quite a light show," she said.

"I think we're about to see even more," said Maura.

"Where do you want to start spraying now?" Pete asked Corso.

"Right here. The floor nearest the cellar door."

This time, Rizzoli did not leave the room when the lights went off. She backed off and watched from a distance as the mist of Luminol was sprayed across the floor. A geometric pattern suddenly glowed at their feet, a blue-green checkerboard of old blood trapped in the linoleum's repeating pattern. The checkerboard grew like blue fire spreading across a landscape. Now it streaked up one vertical surface, into broad swipes and smears, into arcs of bright droplets.

"Turn on the lights," said Yates, and Corso flipped the switch.

The smears vanished. They stared at the kitchen wall, which no longer glowed blue. At worn linoleum with its repeating pattern of black and white squares. They saw no horror here, just a room with yellowed flooring and tired appliances. Yet everywhere they had looked, only a moment ago, they had seen blood screaming at them.

Maura stared at the wall, the image of what she'd seen there still burned in her memory. "That was arterial spray," she said softly. "This is the room where it happened. This is where they died."

"But you saw blood in the cellar as well," said Rizzoli.

"On the steps."

"Okay. So we know at least one victim is killed in this room, since there's arterial spray on that wall there." Rizzoli paced across the kitchen, unruly curls hiding her eyes as she focused on the floor. She stopped. "How do we know there aren't other victims? How do we know this blood is from the Sadlers?"

"We don't."

Rizzoli crossed to the cellar and opened the door. There she stood for a moment, gazing down the dark stairway. She turned and looked at Maura. "That cellar has a dirt floor."

A moment passed in silence.

Gary said, "We have GPR gear in the van. We used it two days ago, on a farm out in Machias."

"Bring it into the house," said Rizzoli. "Let's take a look at what's under that dirt."

TWENTY-TWO

GPR, or ground-penetrating radar, uses electromagnetic waves to probe beneath the ground's surface. The SIR System-2 machine that the techs unloaded from the van had two antennae, one to send out a pulse of high frequency electromagnetic energy into the ground, the other to measure the echoing waves bounced back by subsurface features. A computer screen would display the data, showing the various strata as a series of horizontal layers. As the techs carried the equipment down the steps, Yates and Corso marked off one-meter intervals on the cellar floor to form a search grid.

"With all this rain," said Pete, unrolling

electrical cable, "the soil's going to be pretty damp."

"Does that make a difference?" asked Maura.

"GPR response varies depending on the subsurface water content. You need to adjust the EM frequency to account for it."

"Two hundred megahertz?" asked Gary.

"It's where I'd start. You don't want to go any higher, or we'll get too much detail." Pete connected cables to the backpack console and powered up the laptop. "That's going to be something of a problem out here, especially with all these woods around us."

"What do the trees have to do with it?" Rizzoli asked.

"This house is built on a wood lot. There's probably a number of cavities under here, left over from decayed roots. That's going to confuse the picture."

Gary said, "Help me get on this backpack."

"How's that? You need to adjust the straps?"

"No, they feel fine." Gary took a breath and looked around the cellar. "I'll start at that end."

As Gary moved the GPR across the earthen floor, the subsurface profile appeared on the laptop screen in undulating stripes. Maura's medical training had made her familiar with ultrasounds and CT scans of the human body, but she had no idea how to interpret these ripples on the screen.

"What are you seeing?" she asked Gary.

"These dark areas here are positive radar echoes. Negative echoes show up as white. We're looking for anything anomalous. A hyperbolic reflection, for example."

"What's that?" said Rizzoli.

"It'll look like a bulge, pushing up these various layers. Caused by something buried underground, scattering the radar waves in all directions." He stopped, studying the screen. "Okay, here, see this? We've got something about three meters deep that's giving off a hyperbolic reflection."

"What do you think?" asked Yates.

"Could be just a tree root. Let's mark it and keep going."

Pete tapped a stake into the ground to mark the spot.

Gary moved on, following the grid lines back and forth, as radar echoes rippled across the laptop screen. Every so often he'd stop, call out for another stake to be planted, marking another spot they would recheck on the second walk-through. He had turned and was coming back along the middle of the grid when he suddenly halted.

"Now this is interesting," he said.

"What do you see?" asked Yates.

"Hold on. Let me try this section again." Gary backed up, moving the GPR across the section he had just probed. Inched forward again, his gaze fixed on the laptop. Again he stopped. "We've got a major anomaly here."

Yates moved in close. "Show me."

"It's less than a meter's depth. A big pocket right here. See it?" Gary pointed to the screen, where a bulge distorted the radar echoes. Staring down at the ground, he said: "There's something right here. And it's not very deep." He looked at Yates. "What do you want to do?"

"You got shovels in the van?"

"Yeah, we've got one. Plus a couple of trowels."

Yates nodded. "Okay. Let's bring them down here. And we're going to need some more lights."

"There's another flood lamp in the van. Plus more extension cords."

Corso started up the stairs. "I'll get them."

"I'll help," said Maura, and she followed him up the steps to the kitchen.

Outside, the heavy rain had lightened to a drizzle. They rooted through the CSU van, found the spade and extra lighting gear, which Corso carried into the house. Maura closed the van door and was about to follow him with the box of excavation hand tools when she saw headlights glimmering through the trees. She stood in the driveway, watching as a familiar pickup truck came down the road and pulled up next to the van.

Miss Clausen stepped out, an oversize slicker dragging behind her like a cape. "Thought you'd be finished by now. I was wondering why you didn't bring back my key."

"We're going to be here for a while."

Miss Clausen eyed the vehicles in the driveway. "I thought you just wanted to take another look around. What's the crime lab doing here?"

"This is going to take us a little longer than I thought. We may be here all night."

"Why? Your sister's clothes aren't even here anymore. I boxed 'em up for you so you can take them home."

"This isn't just about my sister, Miss Clausen. The police are here about something else. Something that happened a long time ago."

"How long ago?"

"It would have been about forty-five years ago. Before you even bought the house."

"Forty-five years? That'd be back when . . ." The woman paused.

"When what?"

Miss Clausen's gaze suddenly fell on the box of excavation tools that Maura was holding. "What are the trowels for? What are you doing in my house?"

"The police are searching the cellar."

"Searching? You mean they're *digging* down there?"

"They may have to."

"I didn't give you permission to do that." She turned and thumped up the porch, her slicker dragging behind her on the steps.

Maura followed her inside, trailing after her into the kitchen. She set the box of tools on the counter. "Wait. You don't understand—"

"I don't want anyone tearing up my cellar!" Miss Clausen yanked open the cellar door and glared down at Detective Yates, who was holding a shovel. Already he had dug into the earthen floor, and a mound of dirt was piled up near his feet.

"Miss Clausen, let them do their jobs," said Maura.

"I own this house," the woman yelled down the steps. "You can't dig down there unless I give my permission!"

"Ma'am, we promise we'll fill in the hole when we're done," said Corso. "We're just going to take a little look here."

"Why?"

"Our radar shows a major bounce-back."

"What do mean, *bounce-back*? What's down there?"

"That's what we're trying to find out. If you'd just let us continue."

Maura tugged the woman away from the cellar and closed the door. "Please let them work. If you refuse, they'll just be forced to get a warrant."

"What the hell got them digging down there in the first place?"

"Blood."

"What blood?"

"There's blood all over this kitchen."

The woman's gaze dropped to the floor, scanning the linoleum. "I don't see any."

"You can't see it. It takes a chemical spray to make it visible. But believe me, it's here. Microscopic traces of it on the floor, splattered on that wall. Running under the cellar door and down the steps. Someone tried to wash it away by mopping the floor, wiping down the walls. Maybe they thought they got rid of it all, because they couldn't see it anymore. But the blood is still here. It seeps into crevices, into cracks in the wood. It remains for years and years and you can't erase it. It's trapped in this house. In the walls themselves."

Miss Clausen turned and stared at her. "Whose blood?" she asked softly.

"That's what the police would like to know."

"You don't think I had anything to do with—"

"No. We think the blood is very old. It was probably here when you bought the house."

The woman looked dazed as she sank into a chair at the kitchen table. The hood of her slicker had slipped off her head, revealing a porcupine's ruff of gray hair. Slouching in that oversize raincoat, she seemed even smaller, older. A woman already shrinking into her grave.

"No one will want to buy this house from me now," she murmured. "Not when they hear about this. I won't be able to give the damn thing away."

Maura sat down across from her. "Why did my sister ask to rent this house? Did she tell you?"

No reply. Miss Clausen was still shaking her head, looking stunned.

"You said she saw that for sale sign out on the road. And she called you at the realty office."

At last a nod. "Out of the blue."

"What did she say to you?"

"She wanted to know more about the property. Who'd lived here, who'd owned it before me. Said she was looking around at real estate in the area."

"Did you tell her about the Lanks?"

Miss Clausen stiffened. "You know about them?"

"I know they used to own this house. There was a father and son. And the man's niece, a girl named Amalthea. Did my sister ask about them, too?"

The woman took a breath. "She wanted to know. I understood that. If you're thinking of buying a house, you'd want to know who built it. Who lived here." She looked at Maura. "This is about them, isn't it? The Lanks."

"You grew up in this town?"

"Yeah."

"So you must have known the Lank family."

Miss Clausen did not immediately respond. Instead she rose and pulled off her raincoat. Took her time hanging it up on one of the hooks near the kitchen door. "He was in my class," she said, her back still turned to Maura.

"Who was?"

"Elijah Lank. I didn't know his cousin Amalthea very well, because she was five years behind us in school—just a kid. But we all knew Elijah." Her voice had dropped to nearly a whisper, as though she was reluctant to say the name aloud.

"How well did you know him?"

"As well as I needed to."

"It doesn't sound as if you liked him very much."

Miss Clausen turned and looked at her. "It's hard to like people who scare the hell out of you."

Through the cellar door, they could hear the thud of the shovel hitting soil. Digging deeper into the house's secrets. A house that, even years later, still bore silent witness to something terrible.

"This was a small town, Dr. Isles. Not like it is now, with all these new folks coming in from away, buying up summer places. Back then, it was just locals, and you got to know people. Which families are good, and which ones you should stay away from. I figured that out about Elijah Lank when I was fourteen years old. He was one of the boys you stayed the hell away from." She moved back to the table and sank into a chair, as though exhausted. Stared at the Formica surface, as though looking into a pool at her own reflection. A reflection of a fourteen-year-old girl, afraid of the boy who lived on this mountain.

Maura waited, her gaze on that bowed head with its stiff brush of gray hair. "Why did he scare you?"

"I wasn't the only one. We were all afraid of Elijah. After . . ."

"After what?"

Miss Clausen looked up. "After he buried that girl alive."

In the silence that followed, Maura could hear the murmur of men's voices as they dug deeper into the cellar floor. She could feel her own heart throbbing against her ribs. Jesus, she thought. What are they going to find down there?

"She was one of the new kids in town," said Miss Clausen. "Alice Rose. The other girls'd sit behind her and make comments. Tell jokes about her. You could say all kinds of mean things about Alice and get away with it, because she couldn't hear you. She never knew we were making fun of her. I know we were being cruel, but that's the sort of thing kids do when they're fourteen. Before they learn to put themselves in someone else's shoes. Before they get a taste of it themselves." She sighed, a sound of regret for childhood transgressions, for all the lessons learned too late.

"What happened to Alice?"

"Elijah said it was just a joke. He said he always planned to pull her out after a few hours. But can you imagine what it was like, being trapped inside a hole? So terrified that you wet yourself? And no one can hear you screaming. No one knows where you are except the boy who put you in there."

Maura waited, silent. Afraid to hear the story's ending.

Miss Clausen saw the apprehension in her eyes and shook her head. "Oh, Alice didn't die. It was the dog saved her. He knew where she was. Kept barking his fool head off, led people right to the spot."

"Then she survived."

The woman nodded. "They found her late that night. By then, she'd been in the hole for hours. When they pulled her out, she was barely speaking. Like a zombie. A few weeks later, her family moved away. I don't know where they went."

"What happened to Elijah?"

Miss Clausen gave a shrug. "What do you think happened? He kept insisting it was just a prank. The sort of thing the rest of us kids were doing to Alice every day in school. And it's true, we all tormented her.

We all made her miserable. But Elijah, he took it to the next level."

"He wasn't punished?"

"When you're only fourteen, you get a second chance. Especially when people need you at home. When your dad's drunk half the day, and there's a nine-year-old cousin living in the same house."

"Amalthea," said Maura softly.

Miss Clausen nodded. "Imagine being a little girl in this house. Growing up in a family of beasts."

Beasts.

The air suddenly felt charged. Maura's hands had gone cold. She thought of Amalthea Lank's ravings. *Go away, before he sees you.*

And she thought of the scratch mark clawed into her car door. *The sign of the Beast.*

The cellar door creaked open, startling Maura. She turned and saw Rizzoli standing in the doorway.

"They've hit something," Rizzoli said.

"What is it?"

"Wood. Some kind of panel, about two feet down. They're trying to clear away the dirt now." She pointed to the box of trowels on the counter. "We'll need those."

Maura carried the box down the cellar steps. She saw that piles of excavated earth now ringed the perimeter of their trench, extending almost six feet long.

The size of a coffin.

Detective Corso, who now wielded the shovel, glanced up at Maura. "Panel feels pretty thick. But listen." He banged the shovel against the wood. "It's not solid. There's an air space underneath."

Yates said, "You want me to take over now?"

"Yeah, my back's about to give out." Corso handed over the shovel.

Yates dropped into the trench, his shoes thudding onto the wood. A hollow sound. He attacked the dirt with grim determination, flinging it onto a rapidly growing mound. No one spoke as more and more of the panel emerged. The two flood lamps slanted their harsh light across the trench, and Yates's shadow bounced like a marionette on the cellar walls. The others watched, silent as grave robbers eagerly awaiting their first glimpse into a tomb.

"I've cleared one edge here," said Yates,

breathing hard, his shovel scraping across wood. "Looks like some kind of crate. I've already dinged it with the shovel. I don't want to damage the wood."

"I've got the trowels and brushes," said Maura.

Yates straightened, panting, and clambered out of the hole. "Okay. Maybe you can clear off that dirt on top. We'll get some photos before we pry it open."

Maura and Gary dropped into the trench, and she felt the panel shudder under their weight. She wondered what horrors lay beneath the stained planks, and had a terrible vision of the wood suddenly giving way, of plunging into decayed flesh. Ignoring her pounding heart, she knelt down and began to sweep dirt away from the panel.

"Hand me one of those brushes, too," said Rizzoli, about to jump into the trench as well.

"Not you," said Yates. "Why don't you just take it easy?"

"I'm not handicapped. I hate standing around doing nothing."

Yates gave an anxious laugh. "Yeah, well, we'd hate seeing you go into labor down there. And I wouldn't want to have to explain it to your husband, either."

Maura said, "There's not much maneuvering room down here, Jane."

"Well, let me reposition these lamps for you. So you can see what you're doing."

Rizzoli moved a flood lamp, and suddenly light beamed down on the corner where Maura was working. Crouched on her knees, Maura used the brush to clear soil from the planks, uncovering pinpoints of rust. "I'm seeing old nail heads here," she said.

"I've got a crowbar in the car," said Corso. "I'll get it."

Maura kept brushing away dirt, uncovering the rusted heads of more nails. The space was cramped, and her neck and shoulders began to ache. She straightened her back. Heard a clank behind her.

"Hey," said Gary. "Look at this."

Maura turned and saw that Gary's trowel had scraped up against an inch of broken pipe.

"Seems to come straight up through the edge of this panel," said Gary. With bare fingers, he gingerly probed the rusted protrusion and broke through a clot of dirt crust-ing the top. "Why would you stick a pipe into a . . ." He stopped. Looked at Maura.

"It's an air hole," she said.

Gary stared down at the planks under his knees. Said, softly: "What the hell's inside this thing?"

"Come out of the hole, you two," said Pete. "We're going to take photos."

Yates reached down to help Maura out and she stepped back from the trench, feeling suddenly light-headed from rising too quickly to her feet. She blinked, dazed by the flashes of the camera. By the surreal glare of floodlights and the shadows dancing on the walls. She went to the cellar steps and sat down. Only then remembered that the step she was now resting on was impregnated with ghostly traces of blood.

"Okay," said Pete. "Let's open it."

Corso knelt beside the trench and worked the tip of the crowbar under one corner of the lid. He strained to pry up the panel, eliciting a squeal of rusty nail heads.

"It's not budging," said Rizzoli.

Corso paused and wiped his sleeve across his face, leaving a streak of dirt on his forehead. "Man, my back's gonna pay for this tomorrow." Again he positioned the tip of the crowbar under the lid. This time he was able to jam it farther in. He sucked in a deep breath and threw his weight against the fulcrum.

The nails screeched free.

Corso tossed aside the crowbar. He and Yates both reached into the trench, grasped the edge of the lid, and lifted. For a moment, no one said a word. They all stared into the hole, now fully revealed under the glare of flood lamps.

"I don't get it," said Yates.

The crate was empty.

They drove home that night, down a highway glistening with rain. Maura's windshield wipers swept a slow, hypnotic beat across misted glass.

"All that blood in the kitchen," said Rizzoli. "You know what it means. Amalthea's killed before. Nikki and Theresa Wells weren't her first victims."

"She wasn't alone in that house, Jane. Her cousin Elijah lived there, too. It could have been him."

"She was nineteen years old when the

Sadlers vanished. She had to know what was happening in her own kitchen."

"It doesn't mean she's the one who did it."

Rizzoli looked at her. "You believe O'Donnell's theory? About the Beast?"

"Amalthea is schizophrenic. Tell me how someone with a mind that disordered manages to kill two women, and then goes through the very logical step of burning their bodies, destroying the evidence?"

"She didn't do that good a job of covering her tracks. She got caught, remember?"

"The police in Virginia got lucky. Catching her on a routine traffic stop wasn't an example of brilliant detective work." Maura stared ahead at fingers of mist curling across the empty highway. "She didn't kill those women all by herself. There had to be someone else helping her, someone who left fingerprints in her car. Someone who's been with her from the very beginning."

"Her cousin?"

"Elijah was only fourteen when he buried that girl alive. What kind of boy would do something like that? What kind of man does he grow into?"

"I hate to imagine."

"I think we both know," said Maura. "We both saw the blood in that kitchen."

The Lexus hummed down the road. The rain had ceased, but the air still steamed, misting over the windshield.

"If they did kill the Sadlers," said Rizzoli, "then you've got to wonder . . ." She looked at Maura. "What did they do with Karen Sadler's baby?"

Maura said nothing. She kept her gaze on the highway, driving straight down that road. No detours, no side trips. *Just keep driving.*

"You know what I'm getting at?" said Rizzoli. "Forty-five years ago, the Lank cousins killed a pregnant woman. The baby's remains are missing. Five years later, Amalthea Lank shows up in Van Gates's office in Boston, with two newborn daughters to sell."

Maura's fingers had gone numb on the steering wheel.

"What if those babies weren't hers?" Rizzoli said. "What if Amalthea isn't really your mother?"

TWENTY-THREE

Mattie Purvis sat in the dark, wondering how long it took a person to starve to death. She was going through her food too fast. Only six Hershey bars, half a packet of saltines, and a few strips of beef jerky were left in the grocery sack. I have to ration it, she thought. I have to make it last long enough to . . .

To what? Die of thirst instead?

She bit off a precious chunk of chocolate, and was sorely tempted to take a second bite, but managed to hold on to her willpower. Carefully, she rewrapped the rest of the bar for later. If I get truly desperate, there's always the paper to eat, she thought. Paper was edible, wasn't it? It's made of wood, and hungry deer eat the bark off trees, so there must be some nutritional value to it. Yes, save the paper. Keep it clean. Reluctantly, she returned the partially eaten chocolate bar to the sack. Closing her eyes, she thought of hamburgers and fried chicken and all the forbidden foods she had denied herself ever since Dwayne had said that pregnant women reminded him of cows. Meaning *she* reminded him of a cow. For two weeks afterwards, she'd eaten nothing but salads, until one day she'd felt dizzy and had sat right down on the floor in the middle of Macy's. Dwayne had turned red-faced as worried ladies gathered around them, asking again and again if his wife was all right. He kept waving them away while he'd hissed at Mattie to get up. Image was everything, he always liked to say, and there was Mr. BMW with his cow of a wife in her maternity stretch pants, wallowing on the floor. *Yes, I am a cow, Dwayne. A big, beautiful cow carrying your baby. Now come and save us, goddamn it. Save us, save us.*

A footstep creaked overhead.

She looked up as her captor approached. She had come to recognize his tread, light and cautious as a stalking cat's. Each time he'd visited, she'd pleaded with him to release her. Each time, he had just walked away, leaving her in this box. Now her food was running low, and the water, too.

"Lady."

She didn't answer. Let him wonder, she thought. He'll worry whether I'm okay and he'll have to open the box. He has to keep me alive or he won't get his precious ransom.

"Talk to me, lady."

She stayed silent. Nothing else has worked, she thought. Maybe this will scare him. Maybe now he'll let me out.

A thump on the dirt. "Are you there?"

Where else would I be, you asshole?

A long pause. "Well. If you're already dead, there's no point digging you up. Is there?" The footsteps moved away.

"Wait! *Wait!*" She turned on the flashlight. Began pounding on the ceiling. "Come back, goddamn it! Come back!" She listened, heart thudding. Almost laughed with relief when she heard the creak of his approach. How pitiful was this? She was reduced to begging for his attention, like an ignored lover.

"You're awake," he said.

"Have you talked to my husband? When is he going to pay you?"

"How are you feeling?"

"Why don't you ever answer my questions?"

"Answer mine first."

"Oh, I'm feeling just *dandy!*"

"What about the baby?"

"I'm running out of food. I need more food."

"You have enough."

"Excuse me, but I'm the one down here, not you! I'm starving. How are you going to get your money if I'm dead?"

"Stay calm, lady. Rest. Everything's going to be all right."

"Everything is so *not* right!"

No answer.

"Hello? *Hello?*" she yelled.

The footsteps were moving away now.

"Wait!" She pounded on the ceiling. "Come back!" She beat on the wood with both fists. Rage suddenly consumed her, a rage like nothing she had ever known before. She screamed, "You can't do this to me! I'm not an *animal!*" She collapsed against the wall, hands bruised and throbbing, body wracked with sobs. Sobs of fury, not defeat. "Fuck you," she said. "Fuck you. And fuck Dwayne. And fuck all the other assholes in this world!"

Exhausted, she collapsed onto her back. Drew her arm across her eyes, wiping away tears. *What does he want from us? By now, Dwayne must have paid him. So why am I still down here? What is he waiting for?*

The baby gave a kick. She pressed her hand against her belly, a calming touch transmitted through the skin that separated them. She felt her womb tighten, the first quiver of a contraction. *Poor thing. Poor . . .*

Baby.

She went very still, thinking. Remembering all the conversations through the air grate. *Never about Dwayne. Never about money. That made no sense. If the asshole wanted money, Dwayne is the person he has to go to. But he doesn't ask about my husband. He doesn't talk about Dwayne. What if he hasn't even called him? What if he hasn't asked for any ransom at all?*

Then what does he want?

The flashlight dimmed. The second set of batteries was dying. Two more fresh sets to go, and then she'd be in permanent darkness. This time she did not panic as she reached into the grocery sack and tore open a new package. *I've done this before; I can do it again.* She unscrewed the back, calmly slid out the old batteries, and inserted the new. Bright light beamed out, a temporary reprieve from the long goodnight she feared was coming.

Everybody dies. But I don't want to die buried in this box, where no one will ever find my bones.

Save the light, save the light as long as you can. She flicked off the switch and lay in the darkness as fear closed in and wrapped its tentacles tighter. *No one knows,* she thought. *No one knows I'm here.*

Stop it, Mattie. Keep it together. You're the only one who can save yourself.

She turned onto her side and hugged herself. Heard something roll across the floor. One of the spent batteries, useless now.

What if no one knows I've been kidnapped? What if no one knows I'm still alive?

She wrapped her arms around her belly and thought about every conversation she'd had with her captor. *How are you feeling?* That's what he always asked, how was she feeling? As if he cared. As if anyone who stuck a pregnant woman in a box gave a damn how she was feeling. But he always asked the question, and she always pleaded with him to let her out.

He's waiting for a different answer.

She drew her knees closer and her foot hit something that went rolling away. She sat up and turned on the flashlight. Began scrambling around for all the loose batteries. She had four old ones, plus two fresh ones still in the package. Plus the two in the flashlight. She flicked off the switch again. Save the light, save the light.

In darkness, she began to untie her shoe.

TWENTY-FOUR

Dr. Joyce P. O'Donnell walked into the homicide unit's conference room looking as though she owned the place. Her sleek St. John's suit had probably cost more than Rizzoli's entire clothing budget for a year. Three-inch heels emphasized her already statuesque height. Although three cops were watching her as she sat down at the table, she revealed not a flicker of discomfort. She knew how to take control of a room, a skill that Rizzoli could not help envying, even though she despised the woman.

The dislike was clearly mutual. O'Donnell cast one icy glance at Rizzoli, then her gaze moved on past Barry Frost, before she finally turned her full attention on Lieutenant

Marquette, the homicide unit's ranking officer. Of course she would focus on Marquette; O'Donnell didn't waste her time with
underlings.

"This is an unexpected invitation, Lieutenant," she said. "I don't often get asked
to Schroeder Plaza."

"Detective Rizzoli was the one who suggested it."

"Even more unexpected, then. Considering."

Considering we play for opposite teams,
thought Rizzoli. I catch the monsters; you
defend them.

"But as I told Detective Rizzoli on the
phone," O'Donnell continued, "I can't help
you unless you help me. If you want me to
help you find the Beast, you have to share
what information you have."

In answer, Rizzoli slid a folder to O'Donnell. "That's what we know about Elijah
Lank so far." She saw the eager gleam in
the psychiatrist's eyes as she reached for
the folder. This was what O'Donnell lived
for: a glimpse of a monster. A chance to get
close to the beating heart of evil.

O'Donnell opened the file. "His high
school record."

"From Fox Harbor."

"An IQ of 136. But only average grades."

"Your classic underachiever." *Capable of great things if he applies himself,* one teacher had written, not realizing where Elijah Lank's achievements would take him. "After his mother died, he was raised by his father, Hugo. The father never held down a job for long. Apparently spent most of his days with a bottle, and died of pancreatitis when Elijah was eighteen."

"And this is the same household Amalthea grew up in."

"Yeah. She came to live with her uncle when she was nine, after her mother died. No one even knows who her father was. So there you have the Lank family of Fox Harbor. A drunk uncle, a sociopathic cousin, and a girl who grows up schizophrenic. Just your nice wholesome American family."

"You called Elijah sociopathic."

"What else would you call a boy who buries his classmate alive, just for the fun of it?"

O'Donnell turned to the next page. Anyone else reading that file would wear an expression of horror, but the look on her face was one of fascination.

"The girl he buried was only fourteen," said Rizzoli. "Alice Rose was the new kid in school. She was also hearing impaired, which is why the other kids tormented her. And probably why Elijah chose her. She was vulnerable, easy prey. He invited her up to his house, then led her through the woods to a pit he'd dug. He threw her inside, covered the hole with boards, and piled rocks on top. When questioned about it later, he said the whole thing was a prank. But I think he honestly meant to kill her."

"According to this report, the girl came out of it unharmed."

"Unharmed? Not exactly."

O'Donnell looked up. "But she did survive it."

"Alice Rose spent the next five years of her life being treated for severe depression and anxiety attacks. When she was nineteen, she climbed into a bathtub and slit her wrists. As far as I'm concerned, Elijah Lank is responsible for her death. She was his first victim."

"Can you prove there are others?"

"Forty-five years ago, a married couple named Karen and Robert Sadler vanished from Kennebunkport. Karen Sadler was eight months pregnant at the time. Their remains were found just last week, in that same plot of land where Elijah buried Alice Rose alive. I think the Sadlers were Elijah's kills. His and Amalthea's."

O'Donnell had gone very still, as though she was holding her breath.

"You're the one who first suggested it, Dr. O'Donnell," said Lieutenant Marquette. "You said Amalthea had a partner, someone she'd called the Beast. Someone who helped her kill Nikki and Theresa Wells. That's what you told Dr. Isles, isn't it?"

"No one else believed my theory."

"Well, now we do," said Rizzoli. "We think the Beast is her cousin, Elijah."

O'Donnell's eyebrow lifted in amusement. "A case of *killing cousins*?"

"It wouldn't be the first time that cousins have killed together," pointed out Marquette.

"True," O'Donnell said. "Kenneth Bianchi and Angelo Buono—the Hillside Stranglers—they were cousins."

"So there's a precedent," said Marquette. "Cousins as killing partners."

"You didn't need me to tell you that."

"You knew about the Beast before anyone else did," said Rizzoli. "You've been trying to find him, to contact him through Amalthea."

"But I haven't succeeded. So I don't see how I can help you find him. I don't even know why you asked me here, Detective, since you have so little regard for my research."

"I know Amalthea talks to you. She wouldn't say a word to me when I saw her yesterday. But the guards told me she does talk to *you*."

"Our sessions are confidential. She's my patient."

"Her cousin isn't. He's the one we want to find."

"Well, where was his last known location? You must have some information you can start with."

"We have almost none. Nothing on his whereabouts in decades."

"Do you even know that he's alive?"

Rizzoli sighed. Admitted: "No."

"He'd be nearly seventy years old now, wouldn't he? That's getting a little geriatric for a serial killer."

"Amalthea is sixty-five," said Rizzoli. "Yet no one ever doubted that she killed Theresa and Nikki Wells. That she crushed their skulls, soaked their bodies in gasoline, and lit them on fire."

O'Donnell leaned back in her chair and regarded Rizzoli for a moment. "Tell me why Boston PD is even pursuing Elijah Lank. These are old murders—not even your jurisdiction. What's your interest in this?"

"Anna Leoni's murder may be tied in."

"How?"

"Just before she was murdered, Anna was asking a lot of questions about Amalthea. Maybe she learned too much." Rizzoli slid another file to O'Donnell.

"What's this?"

"You're familiar with the FBI's National Crime Information Center? It maintains a searchable database of missing persons from across the country."

"Yes, I'm aware of NCIC."

"We submitted a search request using the key words *female* and *pregnant*. That's what we got back from the FBI. Every case they have in their database, back to the 1960s. Every pregnant woman who's vanished in the continental U.S."

"Why did you specify pregnant women?"

"Because Nikki Wells was nine months

pregnant. Karen Sadler was eight months pregnant. Don't you find that awfully coincidental?"

O'Donnell opened the folder and confronted pages of computer printouts. She looked up in surprise. "There are dozens of names in here."

"Consider the fact that thousands of people go missing every year in this country. If a pregnant woman vanishes every so often, it's only a blip against that bigger background; it won't raise any red flags. But when one woman a month vanishes, over a forty-year span, then the total numbers start to add up."

"Can you link any of these missing persons cases to Amalthea Lank or her cousin?"

"That's why we called you. You've had over a dozen sessions with her. Is there anything she's told you about her travels? Where she's lived, where she's worked?"

O'Donnell closed the folder. "You're asking me to breach patient-doctor confidentiality. Why would I?"

"Because the killing isn't over. It hasn't stopped."

"My patient can't kill anyone. She's in prison."

"Her partner isn't." Rizzoli leaned forward, closer to the woman she so thoroughly despised. But she needed O'Donnell now, and she managed to quell her revulsion. "The Beast fascinates you, doesn't he? You want to know more about him. You want to get inside his head, know what makes him tick. You like hearing all the details. That's why you should help us. So you can add one more monster to your collection."

"What if we're both wrong? Maybe the Beast is just a figment of our imaginations."

Rizzoli looked at Frost. "Why don't you turn on that overhead projector?"

Frost rolled the projector into position and flipped on the power switch. In this age of computers and PowerPoint slide shows, an overhead projector felt like Stone Age technology. But she and Frost had opted for the quickest, most straightforward way to make their case. Frost now opened a folder and took out multiple transparencies on which they'd recorded data points in various colors of marker ink.

Frost slid a sheet onto the overhead projector. A map of the U.S. appeared on the screen. Now he overlaid the map with the first transparency. Six black dots were added to the image.

"What do the dots signify?" O'Donnell asked.

"Those are NCIC case reports from the first six months of 1984," said Frost. "We chose that year because it's the first full year the FBI's computerized database went active. So the data should be pretty complete. Each one of those dots represents a report of a missing pregnant woman." He aimed a laser pointer at the screen. "There's a certain amount of geographical scatter there, one case up there in Oregon, one in Atlanta. But notice this little cluster down here in the southwest." Frost circled the relevant corner of the map. "One woman missing in Arizona, one in New Mexico. Two in Southern California."

"What am I supposed to make of that?"

"Well, let's take a look at the next six-month period. July through December, 1984. Maybe it'll become clearer."

Frost laid the next transparency over the map. A new set of dots was added, these marked in red.

"Again," he said, "You'll see some scatter around the country. But notice we have another cluster." He sketched a circle around a group of three red dots. "San Jose, Sacramento, and Eugene, Oregon."

O'Donnell said, softly: "This is getting interesting."

"Wait until you see the next six months," said Rizzoli.

With the third transparency, yet another set of dots was added, these in green. By now the pattern was unmistakable. A pattern that O'Donnell stared at with disbelieving eyes.

"My god," she said. "The cluster keeps moving."

Rizzoli nodded. Grimly she faced the screen. "From Oregon, it heads northeast. During the next six months, two pregnant women vanish from Washington state, then a third one disappears one state over, in Montana." She turned and looked at O'Donnell. "It doesn't stop there."

O'Donnell rocked forward in her chair, her face alert as a cat about to pounce. "Where does the cluster move next?"

Rizzoli looked at the map. "Through that summer and fall, it moves straight east to

Illinois and Michigan, New York and Massachusetts. Then it makes an abrupt drop to
the south."

"Which month?"

Rizzoli glanced at Frost, who shuffled
through the printouts. "The next case
shows up in Virginia, on December four-
teenth," he said.

O'Donnell said, "It's moving with the
weather."

Rizzoli looked at her. "What?"

"The weather. See how it moved across
the upper Midwest during the summer
months? By fall, it's in New England. And
then, in December, it suddenly goes south.
Just as the weather turns cold."

Rizzoli frowned at the map. Jesus, she
thought. The woman's right. Why didn't we
see that?

"What happens next?" asked O'Donnell.

"It makes a complete circle," said Frost.
"Moves across the south, Florida to Texas.
Eventually heads back to Arizona."

O'Donnell rose from her chair and
crossed to the screen. She stood there for a
moment, studying the map. "What was the
time cycle again? How long did it take to
complete that circuit?"

"That time, it took three and a half years to circle the country," said Rizzoli.

"A leisurely pace."

"Yeah. But notice how it never stays in one state for long, never harvests too many victims in a single area. It just keeps moving, so the authorities never see the pattern, never realize it's been going on for years and years."

"What?" O'Donnell turned. "The cycle repeats?"

Rizzoli nodded. "It starts all over again, retracing the same route. The way old nomadic tribes used to follow the buffalo herds."

"Authorities never noticed the pattern?"

"Because these hunters never stop moving. Different states, different jurisdictions. A few months in one region and then they're gone. Onto the next hunting ground. Places they return to again and again."

"Familiar territory."

"*Where we go depends upon where we know. And where we know depends upon where we go,*" Rizzoli said, quoting one of the principles of geographic criminal profiling.

"Have any bodies turned up?"

"None of these have. These are the cases that remain open."

"So they must have burial caches. Places to conceal victims, dispose of bodies."

"We're assuming they'd be out-of-the-way places," said Frost. "Rural areas, or bodies of water. Since none of these women have been found."

"But they found Nikki and Theresa Wells," said O'Donnell. "Those bodies weren't buried, but burned."

"The sisters were found November twenty-fifth. We went back and checked the weather records. There was an unexpected snowstorm that week—eighteen inches fell in a single day. It took Massachusetts by surprise, closing down a number of roads. Maybe they couldn't get to their usual burial spot."

"And that's why they burned the bodies?"

"As you pointed out, the vanishings seem to move with the weather," said Rizzoli. "As it turns cold, they head south. But that November, New England was caught by surprise. No one expected such an early snowfall." She turned to O'Donnell. "There's your Beast. Those are his footprints on that map.

I think Amalthea was with him every step of the way."

"What are you asking me to do, a psychological profile? Explain why they killed?"

"We know why they did it. They weren't killing for pleasure, or for thrills. These are not your usual serial killers."

"Then what was their motive?"

"Absolutely mundane, Dr. O'Donnell. In fact, their motive is probably boring to a monster hunter like you."

"I don't find murder boring in the least. Why do you think they killed?"

"Did you know there are no employment records for either Amalthea or Elijah? We can't find any evidence that either of them held down a job or paid into Social Security, or filed an income tax report. They owned no credit cards, had no bank accounts. For decades, they were invisible people, living on the outermost fringes of society. So how did they eat? How did they pay for food and gas and lodging?"

"Cash, I assume."

"But where does the cash come from?" Rizzoli turned to the map. "That's how they made their living."

"I don't follow you."

"Some people catch fish, some people pick apples. Amalthea and her partner were harvesters, too." She looked at O'Donnell. "Forty years ago, Amalthea sold two newborn daughters to adoptive parents. She was paid forty thousand dollars for those babies. I don't think they were hers to give."

O'Donnell frowned. "Are you talking about Dr. Isles and her sister?"

"Yes." Rizzoli felt a twinge of satisfaction when she saw O'Donnell's stunned expression. This woman had no idea what she was dealing with, thought Rizzoli. The psychiatrist who so regularly consorts with monsters has been taken by surprise.

"I examined Amalthea," said O'Donnell. "I concurred with the other psychiatrists—"

"That she was psychotic?"

"Yes." O'Donnell released a sharp breath. "What you're showing me here—this is a different creature entirely."

"Not insane."

"I don't know. I don't know what she is."

"She and her cousin killed for money. For cold hard cash. That sounds a lot like sanity to me."

"Possibly . . ."

"You get along with murderers, Dr.

O'Donnell. You talk to them, spend hours with people like Warren Hoyt." Rizzoli paused. "You understand them."

"I try to."

"So what kind of killer is Amalthea? Is she a monster? Or just a businesswoman?"

"She's my patient. That's all I care to say."

"But you're questioning your diagnosis right now, aren't you?" Rizzoli pointed to the screen. "*That's* logical behavior, what you see there. Nomadic hunters, following their prey. Do you still think she's insane?"

"I repeat, she's my patient. I need to protect her interests."

"We're not interested in Amalthea. It's the other one we want. Elijah." Rizzoli moved closer to O'Donnell, until they were almost face-to-face. "He hasn't stopped hunting, you know."

"What?"

"Amalthea has been in custody for almost five years, now." Rizzoli looked at Frost. "Show the data points since Amalthea Lank was arrested."

Frost removed the earlier transparencies and placed a new one on the map. "The month of January," he said. "A pregnant woman vanishes in South Carolina. In February, it's a woman in Georgia. In March, it's Daytona Beach." He laid down another sheet. "Six months later, it's happening in Texas."

"Amalthea Lank was in prison all those months," said Rizzoli. "But the abductions continued. The Beast didn't stop."

O'Donnell stared at the relentless march of data points. One dot, one woman. One life. "Where are we now in the cycle?" she asked softly.

"A year ago," said Frost, "it reached California and began heading north again."

"And now? Where is it now?"

"The last reported abduction was a month ago. In Albany, New York."

"Albany?" O'Donnell looked at Rizzoli. "That means . . ."

"By now, he's in Massachusetts," said Rizzoli. "The Beast is coming to town."

Frost turned off the overhead projector and the sudden shut-off of the fan left the room eerily silent. Though the screen was now blank, the image of the map seemed to linger, burned into everyone's memories. The ringing of Frost's cell phone seemed all the more startling in that quiet room.

Frost said, "Excuse me," and left the room.

Rizzoli said to O'Donnell: "Tell us about the Beast. How do we find him?"

"The same way you'd find any other flesh-and-blood man. Isn't that what you police do? You already have a name. Go from there."

"He has no credit card, no bank account. He's hard to track."

"I'm not a bloodhound."

"You've been talking to the one person closest to him. The one person who might know how to find him."

"Our sessions were confidential."

"Does she ever refer to him by name? Does she give any hint at all that it's her cousin, Elijah?"

"I'm not at liberty to share any private conversations I had with my patient."

"Elijah Lank isn't your patient."

"But Amalthea is, and you're trying to build a case against her as well. Multiple charges of homicide."

"We're not interested in Amalthea. *He's* the one I want."

"It's not my job to help you catch your man."

"What about your goddamn civic respon-
sibility?"

"Detective Rizzoli," said Marquette.

Rizzoli's gaze stayed on O'Donnell.
"Think about that map. All those dots, all
those women. He's here, now. Hunting for
the next one."

O'Donnell's gaze dropped to Rizzoli's
bulging abdomen. "Then I guess you'd better be careful, Detective. Shouldn't you?"

Rizzoli watched in rigid silence as O'Donnell reached for her briefcase. "I doubt I
could add much, anyway," she said. "As
you said, this killer is driven by logic and
practicality, not lust. Not enjoyment. He
needs to make a living, plain and simple.
His chosen occupation just happens to be a
little out of the ordinary. Criminal profiling
won't help you catch him. Because he's not
a monster."

"And I'm sure you'd recognize one."

"I've learned to. But then, so have you."
O'Donnell turned to the door. Stopped and
glanced back with a bland smile. "Speaking
of monsters, Detective, your old friend asks
about you, you know. Every time I visit
him."

O'Donnell didn't need to say his name;

they both knew she was talking about Warren Hoyt. The man who continued to surface in Rizzoli's nightmares, whose scalpel
had carved the scars in her palms nearly
two years ago.

"He still thinks about you," said O'Donnell. Another smile, quiet and sly. "I just
thought you'd like to know that you're remembered." She walked out the door.

Rizzoli felt Marquette's gaze, watching for
her reaction. Waiting to see if she'd lose it,
right there and then. She was relieved when
he too walked out of the room, leaving her
alone to pack up the overhead projector.
She gathered up the transparencies, un-
plugged the machine, and wound up the
cord into tight coils, all her anger directed at
that cord as she wrapped it around her
hand. She wheeled the projector out into
the hallway and almost collided with Frost,
who was just snapping his cell phone shut.

"Let's go," he said.

"Where?"

"Natick. They've got a missing woman."

Rizzoli frowned at him. "Is she . . ."

He nodded. "She's nine months pregnant."

TWENTY-FIVE

"You ask me," said Natick Detective Sarmiento, "this is just another Laci Peterson case. Marriage off the rails, husband's got a mistress in the wings."

"He admits he's got a girlfriend?" asked Rizzoli.

"Not yet, but I can smell it, you know?" Sarmiento tapped his nose and laughed. "Scent of the other woman."

Yeah, he probably *could* smell it, thought Rizzoli as Sarmiento led her and Frost past desks with glowing computer screens. He looked like a man familiar with the scent of the ladies. He had the walk, the confident strut of the cool guy, right arm swinging out from years of wearing a gun on his hip, that telltale arc that shouted *cop*. Barry Frost had never picked up that swagger. Next to the strapping, dark-haired Sarmiento, Frost looked like a pale clerk with his trusty pen and notebook.

"Missing woman's name is Matilda Purvis," said Sarmiento, pausing at his desk to pick up a folder, which he handed to Rizzoli. "Thirty-one years old, Caucasian. Married seven months to Dwayne Purvis. He owns the BMW dealership here in town. Saw his wife last Friday, when she dropped in to see him at work. Apparently they had an argument, because witnesses said the wife left crying."

"So when did he report her missing?" asked Frost.

"On Sunday."

"It took him two days to get around to it?"

"After the fight, he said he wanted to let things cool down between them, so he stayed in a hotel. Didn't return home till Sunday. Found the wife's car in the garage, Saturday's mail still in the box. Figured something was wrong. We took his report Sunday night. Then this morning, we saw that alert you sent out, about pregnant women going missing. I'm not sure this one fits your pattern. Looks more to me like your classic domestic blowup."

"You checked out that hotel he stayed in?" asked Rizzoli.

Sarmiento responded with a smirk. "Last time I spoke to him, he was having trouble remembering which one it was."

Rizzoli opened the folder and saw a photo of Matilda Purvis and her husband, taken on their wedding day. If they'd been married only seven months, then she was already two months pregnant when this photo had been taken. The bride was sweet-faced, with brown hair, brown eyes, and girlishly round cheeks. Her smile reflected pure happiness. It was the look of a woman who had just fulfilled her lifelong dream. Standing beside her, Dwayne Purvis looked weary, almost bored. The photo could have been captioned: *Trouble ahead.*

Sarmiento led the way down a corridor, and into a darkened room. Through a one-way window, they could see into the adjoining interview room, unoccupied at the moment. It had stark white walls, a table and three chairs, a video camera mounted high in one corner. A room designed to sweat out the truth.

Through the window they saw the door swing open, and two men entered. One of them was a cop, barrel-chested and balding, a face with no expression, just a blank. The kind of face that made you anxious for a glimpse of emotion.

"Detective Ligett's going to handle it this time," murmured Sarmiento. "See if we get anything new out of him."

"Have a seat," they heard Ligett say. Dwayne sat down, facing the window. From his point of view it was just a mirror. Did he realize there were eyes watching him through the glass? His gaze seemed to focus, for an instant, directly on Rizzoli. She suppressed the urge to step back, to recede deeper into the darkness. Not that Dwayne Purvis looked particularly threatening. He was in his early thirties, dressed casually in a button-down white shirt, no tie, and tan chinos. On his wrist was a Breitling watch—a bad move on his part, to walk in for police questioning flashing a piece of jewelry that a cop couldn't afford. Dwayne had the bland good looks and cocky self-assurance that some women might find attractive—if they liked men who flaunted pricey watches.

"Must sell a lot of BMWs," she said.

"Mortgaged up to his ears," said Sarmiento. "Bank owns the house."

"Policy on the wife?"

"Two hundred fifty thousand."

"Not enough to make it worth killing her."

"Still, it's two hundred fifty G's. But without a body, he'll have a hard time collecting. So far, we don't have one."

In the next room, Detective Ligett said: "Okay, Dwayne, I just want to go back over a few details." Ligett's voice was as flat as his expression.

"I've already talked to that other policeman," said Dwayne. "I forgot his name. The guy who looks like that actor. You know, Benjamin Bratt."

"Detective Sarmiento?"

"Yeah."

Rizzoli heard Sarmiento, standing beside her, give a pleased little grunt. Always nice to hear you look like Benjamin Bratt.

"I don't know why you're wasting your time here," said Dwayne. "You should be out there, looking for my wife."

"We are, Dwayne."

"How is this helping?"

"You never know. You never know what

little detail you might remember that will make a difference in the search." Ligett paused. "For instance."

"What?"

"That hotel you checked into. You remember the name of it yet?"

"It was just some hotel."

"How'd you pay for it?"

"This is irrelevant!"

"You use a credit card?"

"I guess."

"You guess?"

Dwayne huffed out a sound of exasperation. "Yeah, okay. It was my credit card."

"So the name of the hotel should be on your statement. All we have to do is check."

A silence. "Okay, I remember, now. It was the Crowne Plaza."

"The one in Natick?"

"No. It was out in Wellesley."

Sarmiento, standing beside Rizzoli, suddenly reached for the telephone on the wall. He murmured into it: "This is Detective Sarmiento. I need the Crowne Plaza Hotel, in Wellesley . . ."

In the interrogation room, Ligett said, "Wellesley's kind of far from home, isn't it?"

Dwayne sighed. "I needed some breathing room, that's all. A little time to myself. You know, Mattie's been so clingy lately. Then I have to go to work, and everyone there wants a piece of me, too."

"Rough life, huh?" Ligett said it straight, without a hint of the sarcasm he had to be feeling.

"Everyone wants a deal. I've gotta smile through my teeth at customers who're asking me for the moon. I can't give them the moon. A fine machine like a BMW, they have to expect to pay for it. And they all have the money, that's what kills me. They have the money, and they still want to suck every last cent out of my hide."

His wife is missing, possibly dead, thought Rizzoli. And he's pissed off about Beemer bargain hunters?

"That's why I lost my temper. That's what the argument was all about."

"With your wife?"

"Yeah. It wasn't about *us.* It's the business. Money's been tight, you know? That's all it was. Things are just tight."

"The employees who saw that argument—"

"Which employees? Who did you talk to?"

"There was a salesman and a mechanic. They both said your wife looked pretty upset when she left."

"Well, she's pregnant. She gets upset at the craziest things. All those hormones, it sends 'em out of control. Pregnant women, you just can't reason with them."

Rizzoli felt her cheeks flush. Wondered if Frost thought the same thing about *her.*

"Plus, she's tired all the time," Dwayne said. "Cries at the drop of a hat. Her back hurts, her feet hurt. Has to run to the bathroom every ten minutes." He shrugged. "I think I deal with it pretty well. Considering."

"Sympathetic guy," said Frost.

Sarmiento suddenly hung up the phone and stepped out. Then, through the window, they saw him stick his head into the interrogation room and motion to Ligett. Both detectives left the room. Dwayne, now left alone at the table, looked at his watch, shifted in his chair. Gazed at the mirror and frowned. He pulled out a pocket comb and fussed with his hair until every strand was perfect. The grieving husband, getting camera-ready for the five o'clock news.

Sarmiento slipped back into the room

with Rizzoli and Frost, and gave them a knowing wink. "Gotcha," he whispered.

"What do you have?"

"Watch."

Through the window, they saw Ligett reenter the interrogation room. He closed the door and just stood gazing at Dwayne. Dwayne went very still, but the pulse in his neck was visibly bounding above his shirt collar.

"So," said Ligett. "You wanna tell me the truth now?"

"About what?"

"Those two nights in the Crowne Plaza Hotel?"

Dwayne gave a laugh—an inappropriate response, under the circumstances. "I don't know what you mean."

"Detective Sarmiento just spoke to the Crowne Plaza. They confirm you were a guest those two nights."

"Well, you see? I told you—"

"Who was the woman who checked in with you, Dwayne? Blond, pretty. Had breakfast with you both mornings in the dining room?"

Dwayne fell silent. He swallowed.

"Your wife know about the blonde? Is that what you and Mattie were arguing about?"

"No—"

"So she didn't know about her?"

"No! I mean, that's not why we argued."

"Sure it is."

"You're trying to put the worst possible spin on this!"

"What, the girlfriend doesn't exist?" Ligett moved closer, getting right up in Dwayne's face. "She's not going to be hard to find. She'll probably call *us.* She'll see your face on the news and realize she's better off stepping right up to the plate with the truth."

"This has got nothing to do with—I mean, I know it looks bad, but—"

"Sure does."

"Okay." Dwayne sighed. "Okay, I kind of strayed, all right? Lot of guys do, in my position. It's hard when your wife's so huge you can't do it with her anymore. There's that big belly sticking out. And she's just not interested."

Rizzoli stared rigidly ahead, wondering if Frost and Sarmiento were glancing her way. Yeah, here I am. Another one with a big belly. And a husband who's out of town.

She stared at Dwayne and imagined Gabriel sitting in that chair, saying those words. Jesus, don't do this to yourself, she thought, don't screw around with your own head. It's not Gabriel, but a loser named Dwayne Purvis who got caught with a girlfriend and couldn't deal with the consequences. *Your wife finds out about the chickie on the side, and you're thinking: bye bye to Breitling watches and half the house and eighteen years of child support. This asshole is definitely guilty.*

She looked at Frost. He shook his head. Both of them could see this was just a replay of an old tragedy they'd seen a dozen times before.

"So did she threaten divorce?" asked Ligett.

"No. Mattie didn't know anything about her."

"She just shows up at work and picks a fight?"

"It was stupid. I told Sarmiento all about it."

"Why did you get mad, Dwayne?"

"Because she drives around with a goddamn flat tire and doesn't even notice it! I mean, how dense can you be not to notice that you're scraping your rim? The other salesman saw it. Brand-new tire, and it's shredded, just ripped to hell. I see that and I guess I yelled at her. And she gets all teary-eyed, and that just irritates me more, because it makes me feel like a jerk."

You *are* a jerk, thought Rizzoli. She looked at Sarmiento. "I think we've heard enough."

"What'd I tell you?"

"You'll let us know if anything new develops?"

"Yeah, yeah." Sarmiento's gaze was back on Dwayne. "It's easy when they're this dumb."

Rizzoli and Frost turned to leave.

"Who knows how many miles she was driving around with it like that?" Dwayne was saying. "Hell, it might already have been flat when she got to the doctor's office."

Rizzoli suddenly halted. Turning back to the window, she frowned at Dwayne. Felt her pulse suddenly pounding in her temple. *Jesus. I almost missed it.*

"Which doctor is he talking about?" she asked Sarmiento.

"A Dr. Fishman. I spoke to her yesterday."

"Why did Mrs. Purvis see her?"

"Just a routine OB appointment, nothing unusual about it."

Rizzoli looked at Sarmiento. "Dr. Fishman is an obstetrician?"

He nodded. "She has an office in the Women's Clinic. Over on Bacon Street."

Dr. Susan Fishman had been up most of the night at the hospital, and her face was a map of exhaustion. Her unwashed brown hair was pulled back in a ponytail, and the white lab coat she wore over the rumpled scrub suit had pockets so loaded down with various examination tools that the fabric seemed to be dragging her shoulders toward the floor.

"Larry from security brought over the surveillance tapes," she said as she escorted Rizzoli and Frost from the clinic reception desk into a rear hallway. Her tennis shoes squeaked across the linoleum. "He's getting the video equipment set up in the back room. Thank god no one expects me to do it. I don't even have a VCR at home."

"Your clinic still has the recordings from a week ago?" asked Frost.

"We have a contract with Minute Man Security. They keep the tapes for at least a week. We asked them to, given all the threats."

"What threats?"

"This is a pro-choice clinic, you know. We don't perform any abortions on site, but just the fact we call ourselves a *women's* clinic seems to tick off the right-wing crowd. We like to keep an eye on who comes into the building."

"So you've had problems before?"

"What you'd expect. Threatening letters. Envelopes with fake anthrax. Assholes hanging around, taking photos of our patients. That's why we keep that video camera in the parking lot. We want to keep an eye on everyone who comes near our front door." She led them down another hallway, decorated with the same cheerfully generic posters that seemed to adorn every obstetrician's office. Diagrams on breast-feeding, on maternal nutrition, on the "five danger signs that you have an abusive partner." An anatomical illustration of a pregnant woman, the contents of her abdomen revealed in cross section. It made Rizzoli uncomfortable walking beside Frost, with that poster looming on the wall, as though her own anatomy was up there on display. Bowel, bladder, uterus. Fetus curled up in a tangle of limbs. Only last week, Matilda Purvis had walked past this very poster.

"We're all heartsick about Mattie," said Dr. Fishman. "She's just the sweetest person. And she's so thrilled about the baby."

"At her last appointment, everything was fine?" asked Rizzoli.

"Oh, yes. Strong fetal heart tones, good position. Everything looked great." Fishman glanced back at Rizzoli. Asked, grimly: "You think it's the husband?"

"Why do you ask?"

"Well, isn't it usually the husband? He only came in with her once, way at the beginning. Acted bored the whole visit. After that, Mattie would show up alone for her appointments. That's the tip-off for me. If you make a baby together, you damn well ought to show up together. But that's just my opinion." She opened a door. "This is our conference room."

Larry from Minute Man Security Systems was waiting in the room for them. "I've got that video ready to show you," he said. "I narrowed it down to the time frame you're interested in. Dr. Fishman, you'll need to watch the footage. Tell us when you spot your patient on the video."

Fishman sighed and settled into a chair in front of the monitor. "I've never had to look at one of these before."

"Lucky you," said Larry. "Most of the time they're pretty boring."

Rizzoli and Frost sat down on either side of Fishman. "Okay," said Rizzoli. "Let's see what you've got."

Larry hit PLAY.

On the monitor, a long view of the clinic's main entrance appeared. A bright day, sunlight glinting off a row of cars parked in front of the building.

"This camera's mounted on top of a lamppost in the parking lot," said Larry. "You can see the time there, at the bottom. Two oh five P.M."

A Saab swung into view and pulled into a stall. The driver's door opened and a tall brunette climbed out. She strolled toward the clinic and vanished inside.

"Mattie's appointment was at one thirty," said Dr. Fishman. "Maybe you should back up the film a little."

"Just keep watching," said Larry. "There. Two thirty p.m. Is that her?"

A woman had just stepped out of the building. She paused for a moment in the sunshine, and ran her hand across her eyes, as though she was dazzled by the light.

"That's her," said Fishman. "That's Mattie."

Mattie started walking away from the building now, moving in that duck waddle so characteristic of heavily pregnant women. She took her time, digging through her purse for her car keys as she walked, distracted, not paying attention. Suddenly she stopped and glanced around with a bewildered look, as though she'd forgotten where she left her car. Yes, this was a woman who might not notice that her tire was flat, thought Rizzoli. Now Mattie turned and walked in a completely different direction, vanishing from the camera's view.

"Is that all you have?" asked Rizzoli.

"That's what you wanted, isn't it?" said Larry. "Confirmation of the time she left the building?"

"But where's her car? We don't see her getting into her car."

"Is there some question that she didn't?"

"I just want to see her leave the parking lot."

Larry rose and went to the video system. "There's one other angle I can show you, from a camera that's way on the other side of the lot," he said, changing the tape. "But I don't think it helps much, because it's so far away." He picked up the remote and again pressed PLAY.

Another view appeared. This time only one corner of the clinic building was visible; most of the screen was filled with parked cars.

"This parking lot's shared with the medical-surgery clinic across the way," said Larry. "That's why you see so many cars here. Okay, look. Isn't that her?"

In the distance, Mattie's head was visible as she moved along a row of cars. Now she ducked out of sight. A moment later, a blue car backed out of its stall and rolled out of the frame.

"That's all we've got," said Larry. "She comes out of the building, gets in her car, drives away. Whatever happened to her, it didn't happen in our lot." He reached for the remote.

"Wait," said Rizzoli.

"What?"

"Go back."

"How far?"

"About thirty seconds."

Larry pressed REWIND and digital pixels briefly scrambled on the monitor, then re-formed into an image of parked cars. There was Mattie, ducking into her car. Rizzoli rose from her chair, crossed to the monitor, and stared as Mattie drove away. As a flash of white appeared, gliding across one corner of the frame, in the same direction as Mattie's BMW.

"Stop," said Rizzoli. The image froze, and Rizzoli touched the screen. "There. That white van."

Frost said, "It's moving parallel to the vic's car." *The victim*. Already assuming the worst about Mattie's fate.

"So what?" said Larry.

Rizzoli looked at Fishman. "Do you recognize that vehicle?"

The doctor shrugged. "It's not as if I pay attention to cars at all. I'm clueless about makes and models."

"But have you seen this white van before?"

"I don't know. To me it looks like every other white van."

"Why are you interested in that van?" said Larry. "I mean, you can see her get safely into her car and drive away."

"Rewind it," said Rizzoli.

"You want to play this part again?"

"No. I want to go back further." She looked at Fishman. "You said her appointment was for one thirty?"

"Yes."

"Go back to one o'clock."

Larry pressed the remote. On the monitor, pixels scrambled, then rearranged themselves. The time at the bottom said 1:02.

"Close enough," said Rizzoli. "Let's play it."

As the seconds ticked forward, they watched cars roll in and out of view. Saw a woman pull two toddlers from their car seats and walk across the lot, little hands grasped firmly in hers.

At 1:08, the white van appeared. It cruised slowly down the row of cars, then vanished out of camera range.

At 1:25, Mattie Purvis's blue BMW drove into the lot. She was partially hidden by the row of cars between her and the camera, and they saw only the top of her head as she emerged from her car, as she walked down the row toward the building.

"Is that enough?" said Larry.

"Keep running."

"What are we looking for?"

Rizzoli felt her pulse quicken. "That," she said softly.

The white van was back on the screen. It cruised slowly up the row of cars. Stopped between the camera and the blue BMW.

"Shit," said Rizzoli. "It's blocking our view! We can't see what the driver's doing."

Seconds later, the van moved on. They had not caught even a glimpse of the driver's face; nor had they seen the license plate.

"What was that all about?" said Dr. Fishman.

Rizzoli turned and looked at Frost. She didn't have to say a word; they both understood what had happened in that parking lot. *The flat tire. Theresa and Nikki Wells had a flat tire as well.*

This is how he finds them, she thought. A clinic parking lot. Pregnant women walking in to visit their doctors. A quick slash of the tire, and then it's just a waiting game. Follow your prey as she drives out of the lot. When she pulls over, there you are, right behind her.

Ready to offer your assistance.

As Frost drove, Rizzoli sat thinking about the life nestled inside her. About how thin was the wall of skin and muscle that cradled her baby. A blade would not have to cut very deep. A quick incision, straight down the abdomen, from breast bone to pubis, without concern about scars, because there would be no healing, no worries about the mother's health. She is just a disposable husk, peeled open for the treasure she contains. She pressed her hands to her belly and felt suddenly sickened by the thought of what Mattie Purvis might, at that moment, be enduring. Surely Mattie had not entertained such grotesque images while she'd stared at her own reflection. Perhaps she'd looked at the stretch marks spidering across her abdomen and felt a sense of bereavement about losing her attractiveness. A sense of grief that when her husband looked at her, it was now with disinterest, not lust. Not love.

Did you know Dwayne was having an affair?

She looked at Frost. "He'll need a broker."

"What?"

"When he gets his hands on a new baby, what does he do with it? He must bring it to a go-between. Someone who seals the adoption, draws up the papers. And pays him the cash."

"Van Gates."

"We know he did it for her at least once before."

"That was forty years ago."

"How many other adoptions has he arranged since then? How many other babies has he placed with paying families? There's got to be money in it." *Money to keep the trophy wife in pink spandex.*

"Van Gates is not going to cooperate."

"Not a chance in hell. But we know what to watch for, now."

"The white van."

Frost drove for a moment in silence. "You know," he said, "if that van does show up at his house, it probably means . . ." His voice trailed off.

That Mattie Purvis is already dead, thought Rizzoli.

TWENTY-SIX

Mattie braced her back against one wall, placed her feet against the other wall, and pushed. Counted the seconds until her legs were quivering and sweat beaded her face. *Come on, five more seconds. Ten.* She went limp, panting, her calves and thighs tingling with a pleasant burn. She had scarcely used them in this box, had spent too many hours curled up and wallowing in self-pity as her muscles degenerated to mush. She remembered the time she'd caught the flu, a bad flu that had laid her flat on her back, feverish and shaking. A few days later she had climbed out of bed and felt so weak she had to crawl to the bathroom. That's what lying around too long did to you: It robbed you of your strength. Soon she'd need those muscles; she had to be ready when he came back.

Because he *would* come back.

That's enough rest. Feet against the wall again. Push!

She grunted, sweat blooming on her forehead. She thought of the movie *GI Jane,* and how sleek and toned Demi Moore had looked as she'd lifted weights. Mattie held that image in her head as she pushed against her prison walls. Visualize muscles. And fighting back. And beating the bastard.

With a gasp, she once again relaxed against the wall and rested there, breathing deep as the ache in her legs subsided. She was about to repeat the exercise when she felt the tightening in her belly.

Another contraction.

She waited, holding her breath, hoping it would pass quickly. Already it was easing off. Just the womb trying out its muscles, as she was trying out hers. It wasn't painful, but it was a sign that her time was coming.

Wait, baby. You have to wait a little longer.

TWENTY-SEVEN

Once again, Maura was shedding all the proof of her own identity. She placed her purse in the locker, added to it her watch, her belt, and her car keys. But even with my credit card and driver's license and Social Security number, she thought, I still don't know who I really am. The only person who knows that answer is waiting for me on the other side of the barrier.

She entered the visitor trap, took off her shoes and placed them on the counter for inspection, then passed through the metal detector.

A female guard was waiting for her. "Dr. Isles?"

"Yes."

"You requested an interview room?"

"I need to speak to the prisoner alone."

"You'll still be monitored visually. You understand that?"

"As long as our conversation is private."

"It's the same room where prisoners meet with their attorneys. So you'll have privacy." The guard led Maura through the public day room and down a corridor. There she unlocked a door and waved her through. "We'll bring her to the room. Have a seat."

Maura stepped into the interview room and confronted a table and two chairs. She sat down in the chair facing the door. A Plexiglas window looked into the hallway, and two surveillance cameras peered from opposite corners of the room. She waited, her hands sweating despite the air-conditioning. Glanced up, startled, to see Amalthea's dark, flat eyes staring at her through the window.

The guard escorted Amalthea into the room and sat her in a chair. "She's not talking much today. I don't know that she's going to say a thing to you, but here she is." The guard bent down, fastened a steel cuff around Amalthea's ankle, and attached it to the table leg.

"Is that really necessary?" asked Maura.

"It's just regulation, for your safety." The guard straightened. "When you're done, press that button there, on the wall intercom. We'll come get her." She gave Amalthea's shoulder a pat. "Now, you talk to the lady, okay, honey? She's come all this way just to see *you.*" She gave Maura a silent glance of *good luck,* and left, locking the door behind her.

A moment passed.

"I was here last week to visit you," said Maura. "Do you remember?"

Amalthea hunched in her chair, eyes cast down at the table.

"You said something to me as I was about to leave. You said, *now you're going to die, too.* What did you mean by that?"

Silence.

"You were warning me off, weren't you? Telling me to leave you alone. You didn't want me digging into your past."

Again, silence.

"No one is listening to us, Amalthea. It's just you and me in this room." Maura placed her hands on the table, to show she had no tape recorder, no notepad. "I'm not a policeman. I'm not a prosecutor. You can say whatever you want to me, and we're the only ones who'll hear it." She leaned closer, said quietly: "I know you can understand every word I'm saying. So look at me, god-damn it. I've had enough of this game."

Though Amalthea did not lift her head, there was no missing the sudden tension in her arms, the twitch of her muscles. *She's listening, all right. She's waiting to hear what I have to say next.*

"That was a threat, wasn't it? When you told me I was going to die, you were telling me to stay away, or I'd end up like Anna. I thought it was just psychotic babbling, but you meant it. You're protecting him, aren't you? You're protecting the Beast."

Slowly, Amalthea's head lifted. Dark eyes met hers in a gaze so cold, so empty, that Maura drew back, skin prickling.

"We know about him," said Maura. "We know about you both."

"What do you know?"

Maura had not expected her to speak. That question was whispered so softly she wondered if she'd actually heard it. She swallowed. Drew in a deep breath, shaken by the black void of those eyes. No insanity there, just emptiness.

"You're as sane as I am," said Maura. "But

you don't dare let anyone know that. It's so much easier to hide behind a schizophrenic's mask. Easier to play the psychotic, because people always leave the crazy ones alone. They don't bother to interrogate you. They don't dig any deeper, because they think it's all delusion anyway. And now they don't even medicate you, because you're so good at faking the side effects." Maura forced herself to stare deeper into that void. "They don't know the Beast is real. But you do. And you know where he is."

Amalthea sat perfectly still, but tautness had crept into her face. The muscles had tightened around her mouth, and stood out in cords down her throat.

"It was your only option, wasn't it? Pleading insanity. You couldn't argue away the evidence—the blood on your tire iron, the stolen wallets. But convince them you're psychotic, and maybe you'd avoid any further scrutiny. Maybe they wouldn't find out about all your other victims. The women you killed in Florida and Virginia. Texas and Arkansas. States with the death penalty." Maura leaned even closer. "Why don't you just give him up, Amalthea? After all, he let *you* take the blame. And he's still out there killing. He's going on without you, visiting all the same places, the same hunting grounds. He's just abducted another woman, in Natick. You could stop him, Amalthea. You could put an end to it."

Amalthea seemed to be holding her breath, waiting.

"Look at you, sitting here in prison." Maura laughed. "What a loser you are. Why should you be in here when Elijah's free?"

Amalthea blinked. In an instant, all rigidity seemed to melt from her muscles.

"Talk to me," pressed Maura. "There's no one else in this room. Just you and me."

The other woman's gaze lifted to one of the video cameras mounted in the corner.

"Yes, they can see us," said Maura. "But they can't hear us."

"Everyone can hear us," whispered Amalthea. She focused on Maura. The fathomless gaze had turned cold, collected. And frighteningly sane, as though some new creature had suddenly emerged, staring out through those eyes. "Why are you here?"

"I want to know. Did Elijah kill my sister?"

A long pause. And, strangely, a gleam of amusement in those eyes. "Why would he?"

"You know why Anna was murdered. Don't you?"

"Why don't you ask me a question I know the answer to? The question you really came to ask me." Amalthea's voice was low, intimate. "This is about you, Maura, isn't it? What is it *you* want to know?"

Maura stared at her, heart pounding. A single question swelled like an ache in her throat. "I want you to tell me . . ."

"Yes?" Just a murmur, soft as a voice in Maura's head.

"Who was really my mother?"

A smile twitched on Amalthea's lips. "You mean you don't see the resemblance?"

"Just tell me the truth."

"Look at me. And look in the mirror. There's your truth."

"I don't recognize any part of you in me."

"But I recognize myself in *you.*"

Maura gave a laugh, surprising herself that she could even manage it. "I don't know why I came. This visit is a waste of my time." She shoved back her chair and started to rise.

"Do you like working with the dead, Maura?"

Startled by the question, Maura paused, half out of her chair.

"It's what you do, isn't it?" said Amalthea. "You cut them open. Take out their organs. Slice their hearts. Why do you do it?"

"My job requires it."

"Why did you choose that job?"

"I'm not here to talk about myself."

"Yes you are. This is all about you. About who you really are."

Slowly Maura sat back down. "Why don't you just tell me?"

"You slit open bellies. Dip your hands in their blood. Why do you think we're any different?" The woman had been moving forward so imperceptibly that Maura was startled to suddenly realize how close Amalthea was to her. "Look in the mirror. You'll see me."

"We're not even the same species."

"If that's what you want to believe, who am I to change your mind?" Amalthea stared, unflinching, at Maura. "There's always DNA."

The breath went out of Maura. A bluff, she thought. Amalthea's waiting to see if I'll call her on it. If I really want to know the truth. DNA doesn't lie. With a swab of her mouth, I could have my answer. I could have my worst fears confirmed.

"You know where to find me," said Amalthea. "Come back when you're ready for the truth." She stood, her ankle cuff clanking against the table leg, and stared up at the video camera. A signal to the guard that she wanted to leave.

"If you're my mother," said Maura, "then tell me who my father is."

Amalthea glanced back at her, the smile once again on her lips. "Haven't you guessed?"

The door opened, and the guard poked her head in. "Everything okay in here?"

The transformation was stunning. Just an instant before, Amalthea had looked at Maura with cold calculation. Now that creature vanished, replaced by a dazed husk of a woman who tugged on her ankle manacle, as though bewildered why she could not free herself. "Go," she mumbled. "Wanna—wanna go."

"Yes, honey, of course we'll go." The guard looked at Maura. "I guess you're all done with her?"

"For now," said Maura.

*   *   *

Rizzoli had not expected a visit from Charles Cassell, so she was surprised when the desk sergeant called to inform her that Dr. Cassell was waiting for her in the lobby. When she stepped out of the elevator and saw him, she was shocked by the change in his appearance. In just a week, he seemed to have aged ten years. Clearly he had lost weight, and his face was now gaunt and colorless. His suit jacket, though no doubt expensively tailored, seemed to hang, shapeless, on his drooping shoulders.

"I need to talk to you," he said. "I need to know what's going on."

She nodded to the desk officer. "I'll take him upstairs."

As she and Cassell stepped inside the elevator, he said: "No one is telling me anything."

"You realize, of course, that that's standard during an active investigation."

"Are you going to charge me? Detective Ballard says it's just a matter of time."

She looked at him. "When did he tell you that?"

"Every goddamn time I hear from him. Is

that the strategy, Detective? Scare me, bully me into cutting a deal?"

She said nothing. She had not known about Ballard's continuing phone calls to Cassell.

They stepped off the elevator and she brought him to the interview room, where they sat at a corner of the table, facing each other.

"Did you have something new to tell me?" she asked. "Because if not, there's really no reason for this meeting."

"I didn't kill her."

"You've said that before."

"I don't think you heard me the first time."

"Is there something else you want to tell me?"

"You checked my airline travel, didn't you? I gave you that info."

"Northwest Airlines confirms you were on that flight. But that still leaves you without an alibi for the night of Anna's murder."

"And that incident with the dead bird in her mailbox—did you even bother to confirm where I was when that happened? I know I wasn't in town. My secretary can tell you that."

"Still, you understand it doesn't prove

your innocence. You could have hired someone else to wring a bird's neck and deliver it to Anna's mailbox."

"I'll freely admit the things I *did* do. Yes, I followed her. I drove by her house maybe half a dozen times. And yes, I *did* hit her that night—I'm not proud of that. But I never sent any death threats. I never killed any bird."

"Is that all you came to say? Because if that's it—" She started to rise.

To her shock, he reached out and grasped her arm, his grip so hard she instantly reacted in self-defense. She grabbed his hand and twisted it away.

He gave a grunt of pain and sat back, looking stunned.

"You want me to break your arm?" she said. "Just try that little trick again."

"I'm sorry," he murmured, staring at her with stricken eyes. Whatever anger he'd managed to summon up during this exchange suddenly seemed to drain right out of him. "God, I'm sorry . . ."

She watched him huddle in his chair and she thought: This grief is real.

"I just need to know what's going on," he

said. "I need to know you're *doing* something."

"I'm doing my job, Dr. Cassell."

"All you're doing is investigating *me*."

"That's not true. This is a broad-based investigation."

"Ballard said—"

"Detective Ballard is not in charge—I am. And trust me, I'm looking at every possible angle."

He nodded. Took a deep breath and straightened. "That's really what I wanted to hear, that everything's being done. That you're not overlooking anything. No matter what you think of me, the honest-to-god truth is, I *did* love her." He ran his hand through his hair. "It's terrible, when people leave you."

"Yes, it is."

"When you love someone, it's only natural to want to hold on to them. You do crazy things, desperate things—"

"Even murder?"

"I didn't kill her." He met Rizzoli's gaze. "But yes. I would have killed *for* her."

Her cell phone rang. She rose from the chair. "Excuse me," she said and left the room. It was Frost on the phone. "Surveillance just spotted a white van at the Van Gates residence," he said. "It cruised by the house about fifteen minutes ago, but didn't stop. There's a chance the driver spotted our boys, so they've moved down the street a ways."

"Why do you think it's the right van?"

"The plates were stolen."

"What?"

"They got a look at the license number. The plates were pulled off a Dodge Caravan three weeks ago, out in Pittsfield."

Pittsfield, she thought, right across the state border from Albany.

Where a woman vanished just last month.

She stood with the receiver pressed to her ear, her pulse starting to hammer. "Where's that van now?"

"Our team sat tight and didn't follow it. By the time they heard back about the plates, it was gone. It hasn't come back."

"Let's change out that car and move it to a parallel street. Bring in a second team to watch the house. If the van comes by again, we can do a leapfrog tail. Two cars, taking turns."

"Right, I'm headed over there now."

She hung up. Turned to look into the interview room where Charles Cassell was still sitting at the table, his head bowed. Is that love or obsession I'm looking at? she wondered.

Sometimes, you couldn't tell the difference.

TWENTY-EIGHT

Daylight was fading when Rizzoli cruised up Dedham Parkway. She spotted Frost's car and pulled up behind him. Climbed out of her car and slid into his passenger seat.

"And?" she said. "What's going on?"

"Not a damn thing."

"Shit. It's been over an hour. Did we scare him off?"

"There's still a chance it wasn't Lank."

"White van, stolen plates from Pittsfield?"

"Well, it didn't hang around. And it hasn't been back."

"When's the last time Van Gates left the house?"

"He and the wife went grocery shopping around noon. They've been home ever since."

"Let's cruise by. I want to take a look."

Frost drove past the house, moving slowly enough for her to get a good long gander at Tara-on-Sprague-Street. They passed the surveillance team, parked at the other end of the block, then turned the corner and pulled over.

Rizzoli said: "Are you sure they're home?"

"Team hasn't seen either one of them leave since noon."

"That house looked awfully dark to me."

They sat there for a few minutes, as dusk deepened. As Rizzoli's uneasiness grew. She'd seen no lights on. Were both husband and wife asleep? Had they slipped out without the surveillance team seeing them?

What was that van doing in this neighborhood?

She looked at Frost. "That's it. I'm not going to wait any longer. Let's pay a visit."

Frost circled back to the house and parked. They rang the bell, knocked on the door. No one answered. Rizzoli stepped off the porch, backed up the walkway, and gazed up at the southern plantation facade with its priapic white columns. No lights were on upstairs, either. The van, she thought. It was here for a reason.

Frost said, "What do you think?"

Rizzoli could feel her heart starting to punch, could feel prickles of unease. She cocked her head, and Frost got the message: *We're going around back.*

She circled to the side yard and swung open a gate. Saw just a narrow brick walkway, abutted by a fence. No room for a garden, and barely room for the two trash cans sitting there. She stepped through the gate. They had no warrant, but something was wrong here, something that was making her hands tingle, the same hands that had been scarred by Warren Hoyt's blade. A monster leaves his mark on your flesh, on your instincts. Forever after, you can feel it when another one passes by.

With Frost right behind her, she moved past dark windows and a central air-conditioning unit that blew warm air against her chilled flesh. Quiet, quiet. They were trespassing now, but all she wanted was a peek in the windows, a look in the back door.

She rounded the corner and found a small backyard, enclosed by a fence. The rear gate was open. She crossed the yard to that gate and looked into the alley beyond it. No one there. She started toward the house and was almost at the back door when she noticed it was ajar.

She and Frost exchanged a look. Both their weapons came out. It had happened so quickly, so automatically, that she did not even remember having drawn hers. Frost gave the back door a push, and it swung open, revealing an arc of kitchen tiles.

And blood.

He stepped in and flipped the wall switch. The kitchen lights came on. More blood shrieked at them from the walls, the countertops, the cacophony so powerful that Rizzoli reeled back as though shoved. The baby in her womb gave a sudden kick of alarm.

Frost stepped out of the kitchen, into the hallway. But she stood frozen, staring down at Terence Van Gates, who lay like a glassy-eyed swimmer floating in a pool of red. *The blood's not even dry yet.*

"Rizzoli!" she heard Frost yell. "The wife—she's still alive!"

She almost slipped as she ran, big-bellied and clumsy, from the kitchen. The hallway was a continuous scroll of terror. A trail of arterial spray and cast-off droplets pulsed across the wall. She followed the trail into the living room, where Frost knelt, barking into his radio for an ambulance while he pressed one hand against Bonnie Van Gates's neck. Blood seeped out between his fingers.

Rizzoli dropped to her knees beside the fallen woman. Bonnie's eyes were open wide, rolled back in terror, as though she could see Death himself, hovering right above, waiting to welcome her.

"I can't stop it!" said Frost as blood continued to dribble past his fingers.

Rizzoli grabbed a slipcover from the couch armrest and wadded it up in her fist. She leaned forward to press the makeshift dressing to Bonnie's neck. Frost withdrew his hand, releasing a pulse of blood just before Rizzoli clamped down on the wound. The bunched fabric was immediately saturated.

"Her hand's bleeding, too!" said Frost.

Glancing down, Rizzoli saw a steady dribble of red coursing from Bonnie's slashed palm. *We can't stop it all . . .*

"Ambulance?" she asked.

"On its way."

Bonnie's hand shot up and grabbed at Rizzoli's arm.

"Lie still! Don't move!"

Bonnie jerked, both hands in the air now, like a panicked animal clawing at her attacker.

"Hold her down, Frost!"

"Jesus, she's strong."

"Bonnie, stop it! We're trying to help you!"

Another thrash, and Rizzoli lost her grip. Warmth sprayed across her face, and she tasted blood. Gagged on its coppery heat. Bonnie twisted onto her side, legs jerking like pistons.

"She's seizing!" said Frost.

Rizzoli forced Bonnie's cheek against the carpet and clamped the dressing back on the wound. Blood was everywhere now, sprayed across Frost's shirt, soaking into Rizzoli's jacket as she fought to maintain pressure on the slippery skin. So much blood. Jesus, how much could a person lose?

Footsteps thudded into the house. It was the surveillance team, who'd been parked up the street. Rizzoli did not even look up as the two men barreled into the room. Frost yelled at them to hold down Bonnie. But there was little need now; the seizures had faded to agonal shudders.

"She's not breathing," said Rizzoli.

"Roll her on her back! Come on, come on."

Frost put his mouth against Bonnie's and blew. Came up, his lips rimmed in blood.

"No pulse!"

One of the cops planted his hands on the chest and began compressions. One-one-thousand, two-one-thousand, palms buried in Bonnie's Hollywood cleavage. With each thrust, only a trickle leaked from the wound. There was so little blood left in her veins to circulate, to nourish vital organs. They were pumping a dry well.

The ambulance team arrived with their tubes and monitors and bottles of IV fluid. Rizzoli moved back to give them room, and suddenly felt so dizzy she had to sit down. She sank into an armchair and lowered her head. Realized she was sitting on white fabric, probably smearing it with blood from her clothes. When she raised her head again, she saw that Bonnie had been intubated. Her blouse was torn open and her brassiere cut away. EKG wires crisscrossed her chest. Only a week ago, Rizzoli had thought of that woman as a Barbie doll, dumb and plastic in her tight pink blouse and spike-heeled sandals. Plastic was exactly what she looked like now, her flesh waxy, her eyes without a glimmer of a soul. Rizzoli spotted one of Bonnie's sandals, lying a few feet away, and wondered if she had tried to flee in those impossible shoes. Imagined her frantic clack-clacking down the hall as she trailed sprays of red, as she struggled in those spike heels. Even after the EMTs had wheeled Bonnie away, Rizzoli was still staring at that useless sandal.

"She's not going to make it," said Frost.

"I know." Rizzoli looked at him. "You've got blood on your mouth."

"You should look at yourself in the mirror. I'd say we've both been fully exposed."

She thought of blood and all the terrible things it might carry. HIV. Hepatitis. "She seemed pretty healthy," was all she could say.

"Still," said Frost. "You being pregnant and all."

So what the hell was she doing here, steeped in a dead woman's blood? I should be at home in front of the TV, she thought, with my swollen feet propped up. This is not the life for a mother. It's not a life for anyone.

She tried to launch herself out of the chair. Frost held out his hand to her, and for the first time, she took it, allowing him to pull her to her feet. Sometimes, she thought, you've got to accept a helping hand. Sometimes you've got to admit you can't do it all by yourself. Her blouse was stiff, her hands caked brown. Crime scene personnel would be arriving soon, and then the press. Always the goddamn press.

It was time to clean up and get to work.

Maura stepped out of her car, into a disorienting assault of camera lenses and thrusted microphones. Cruiser lights flashed blue and white, illuminating a crowd of bystanders gathered near the perimeter of police tape. She did not hesitate, did not give the media any chance to close in on her as she walked briskly toward the house and nodded at the cop guarding the scene.

He returned her nod with a puzzled look. "Uh—Dr. Costas is already here—"

"So am I," she said, and ducked under the tape.

"Dr. Isles?"

"He's inside?"

"Yeah, but—"

She kept walking, knowing that he would not challenge her. Her air of authority brought her access that few cops dared question. She paused in the front door to pull on gloves and shoe covers, necessary fashion accessories when blood is involved. Then she stepped inside, where crime scene techs gave her barely a glance. They all knew her; they had no reason to question her presence. She walked, unimpeded, from the foyer into the living room and saw bloodstained carpet and scattered medical debris from the ambulance team. Syringes, torn wrappings, and wads of soiled gauze littered the floor. No body.

She started down a hallway, where violence had left its record on the walls. On one side, bursts of arterial spray. On the other, more subtle, the cast-off droplets of the pursuer's blade.

"Doc?" Rizzoli was standing at the other end of the hallway.

"Why didn't you call me?" said Maura.

"Costas is taking this one."

"So I just heard."

"You don't need to be here."

"You could have told me, Jane. You could have let me know."

"This one isn't yours."

"This involves my sister. It concerns *me*."

"That's why it's not your case." Rizzoli moved toward her, her gaze unwavering. "I don't have to tell you this. You already know it."

"I'm not asking to be M.E. on this one. What I resent is not being called about it."

"I didn't get the chance, okay?"

"That's the excuse?"

"But it's true, goddamn it!" Rizzoli waved at the blood on the walls. "We've got two vics here. I haven't eaten dinner. I haven't showered the blood outta my hair. For god's sake, I don't even have time to pee." She turned. "I have better things to do than explain myself to you."

"Jane."

"Go home, Doc. Let me do my job."

"Jane! I'm sorry. I shouldn't have said all that."

Rizzoli turned back to face her, and Maura saw what she had failed to register until that moment. The hollow eyes, the sagging shoulders. *She is barely standing.*

"I'm sorry, too." Rizzoli looked at the blood-spattered wall. "We missed him by *that much,*" she said, bringing thumb and forefinger together. "We had a team on the street, watching the house. I don't know how he spotted the car, but he drove right on by, and came in the back gate instead." She shook her head. "Somehow he knew. He knew we were looking for him. That's why Van Gates was a problem . . ."

"*She* warned him."

"Who?"

"Amalthea. It had to be her. A phone call, a letter. Something passed out through one of the guards. She's protecting her partner."

"You think she's rational enough to do that?"

"Yes, I do." Maura hesitated. "I went to visit her today."

"When were you going to tell me?"

"She knows secrets about me. She has the answers."

"She hears voices, for god's sake."

"No, she doesn't. I'm convinced she's perfectly sane, and she knows exactly what she's doing. She's protecting her partner, Jane. She'll never give him up."

Rizzoli regarded her for a moment in silence. "Maybe you'd better come see this. You need to know what we're up against."

Maura followed her to the kitchen and halted in the doorway, stunned by the carnage she saw in that room. Her colleague, Dr. Costas, was crouching over the body. He glanced up at Maura with a look of puzzlement.

"I didn't realize you were coming in on this," he said.

"I'm not. I just needed to see . . ." She stared at Terence Van Gates and swallowed hard.

Costas rose to his feet. "This one was bloody efficient. No defense wounds, no indication the victim had any chance to put up a fight. A single slash, just about ear to ear. Approached from behind. Incision starts higher on the left, crosses the trachea, and trails a little lower on the right side."

"A right-handed attacker."

"And strong, too." Costas bent down and gently tilted the head backward, revealing an open ring of glistening cartilage. "We're all the way to vertebral column here." He released the head and it rolled forward, incised edges once again kissing together.

"An execution," she murmured.

"Pretty much."

"The second victim—in the living room—"

"The wife. She died in the ER an hour ago."

"But that execution wasn't so efficient," said Rizzoli. "We think the killer took out the man first. Maybe Van Gates was expecting the visit. Maybe he even let him into his kitchen, thinking it was business. But he didn't expect the attack. There were no defense wounds, no signs of a struggle. He turned his back on the killer, and went down like a slaughtered lamb."

"And the wife?"

"Bonnie was a different story." Rizzoli stared down at Van Gates, at the dyed tufts of transplanted hair, symbols of an old man's vanity. "I think Bonnie walked in on them. She comes into the kitchen and sees the blood. Sees her husband sitting here on the floor, his neck almost severed. The killer's in here too, still holding the knife. The air conditioner's going, and all the windows are shut tight. Double-paned, for insulation.

So our team parked down the street, they wouldn't hear her screams. If she even managed to scream."

Rizzoli turned to look at the doorway leading to the hall. Paused as though she saw the dead woman herself standing there.

"She sees the killer coming at her. But unlike her husband, she fights back. All she can do, as that knife comes at her, is grab it by the blade. It cuts right into the palm of her hand, through skin, tendons, all the way to bone. It slices so deep the artery's severed."

Rizzoli pointed through the doorway, at the hallway beyond. "She runs that way, her hand spurting blood. He's right behind her, and corners her in the living room. Even then she fights back, tries to fend off the blade with her arms. But he makes one more cut, across her throat. Not as deep as the incision in her husband's neck, but it's deep enough." Rizzoli looked at Maura. "She was alive when we found her. That's how close we came."

Maura stared down at Terence Van Gates, slumped against the cabinet. She thought of the little house in the woods where two cousins had formed their poisonous bond. *A bond that endures even now.*

"You remember what Amalthea said to you, the first day you went to visit her?" said Rizzoli.

Maura nodded. *Now you're going to die, too.*

"We both thought it was just psychotic rambling," said Rizzoli. She looked down at Van Gates. "It seems pretty clear now that it was a warning. A threat."

"Why? I don't know any more than you do."

"Maybe it's because of who you *are,* Doc. Amalthea's daughter."

An icy wind swept up Maura's spine. "My father," she said softly. "If I really am her daughter, then who is my father?"

Rizzoli didn't say Elijah Lank's name; she didn't need to.

"You're the living proof of their partnership," said Rizzoli. "Half your DNA is his."

She locked her front door and turned the dead bolt. Paused there, thinking of Anna and all the brass bolts and chains that had

adorned the little house in Maine. I'm turning into my sister, she thought. Soon I'll be
cowering behind barricades, or fleeing my
own home for a new city, a new identity.

Headlights trailed across the closed curtains of her living room. She glanced out
and saw a police cruiser glide by. Not
Brookline this time, but a patrol car with
BOSTON POLICE DEPARTMENT emblazoned on
the side. Rizzoli must have requested it, she
thought.

She went into the kitchen and mixed herself a drink. Nothing fussy tonight, not her
usual cosmopolitan, just orange juice and
vodka and ice. She sat at the kitchen table
and sipped it, ice cubes rattling in her glass.
Drinking alone; not a good sign, but what
the hell. She needed the anesthesia,
needed to stop thinking of what she'd seen
tonight. The air conditioner hissed its cool
breath from the ceiling. No open windows
tonight; everything was locked and secure.
The cold glass chilled her fingers. She set it
down and looked at her palm, at the pale
blush of capillaries. *Does their blood run in
my veins?*

The doorbell rang.

Her head snapped up; she turned toward

the living room, her heart beating a quick-step, every muscle in her body rigid. Slowly she rose to her feet and moved soundlessly down the hall to the front door. Paused there, wondering how easily a bullet might penetrate that wood. She eased toward the side window and glanced out to see Ballard standing on her porch.

With a sigh of relief, she opened the door.

"I heard about Van Gates," he said. "Are you okay?"

"A little shaken up. But I'm fine." *No I'm not. My nerves are shot, and I'm drinking alone in my kitchen.* "Why don't you come in?"

He had never been inside her house. He stepped in, closed the door, and eyed the dead bolt as he locked it. "You need to get a security system, Maura."

"I've been planning to."

"Do it soon, okay?" He looked at her. "I can help you choose the best one."

She nodded. "I'd appreciate the advice. Would you like a drink?"

"Not tonight, thanks."

They went into the living room. He paused, looking at the piano in the corner. "I didn't know you played."

"Since I was a kid. I don't practice nearly enough."

"You know, Anna played too . . ." He stopped. "I guess you might not know that."

"I didn't know that. It's so eerie, Rick, how every time I learn something new about her, she seems more and more like me."

"She played beautifully." He went to the piano, lifted the keyboard cover, and plunked out a few notes. Closed the cover again, and stood staring down at the gleaming black surface. He looked at her. "I'm worried about you, Maura. Especially tonight, after what happened to Van Gates."

She sighed and sank onto the couch. "I've lost control of my life. I can't even sleep with my windows open anymore."

He sat down, too. Chose the chair facing her, so that if she raised her head, she would have to look at him. "I don't think you should be alone here tonight."

"This is my house. I'm not going to leave."

"Then don't leave." A pause. "Do you want me to stay with you?"

Her gaze lifted to his. "Why are you doing this, Rick?"

"Because I think you need watching over."

"And you're the one to do it?"

"Who else is going to? Look at you! You live such a solitary life, all by yourself in this house. I think about you alone here, and it scares me, what could happen. When Anna needed me, I wasn't there. But I can be here for you." He reached out and took her hands. "I can be here whenever you need me."

She looked down at his hands, covering hers. "You loved her, didn't you?" When he didn't answer, she looked up and met his gaze. "Didn't you, Rick?"

"She needed me."

"That's not what I asked."

"I couldn't stand by and let her get hurt. Not by that man."

I should have seen it from the beginning, she thought. It was always there, in the way he looked at me, the way he touched me.

"If you'd seen her that night, in the ER," he said. "The black eye, the bruises. I took one look at her face, and I wanted to beat the shit out of whoever did it. There aren't many things that'll make me lose it, Maura, but any man who hurts a woman—" He took a sharp breath. "I wasn't going to let that happen to her again. But Cassell wouldn't let go. He kept calling her, stalking her, so I had to step in. I helped her install some locks. Started dropping by every day, to check on her. Then one night, she asked me to stay for dinner, and . . ." He gave a defeated shrug. "That's how it started. She was scared, and she needed me. It's instinct, you know. Maybe a cop's instinct. You want to protect."

Especially when she's an attractive woman.

"I tried to keep her safe, that's all." He looked at her. "So, yes. I ended up falling in love with her."

"And what is this, Rick?" She looked at his hands, still grasping hers. "What's happening here? Is this for me, or for her? Because I'm not Anna. I'm not her replacement."

"I'm here because *you* need me."

"This is like a replay. You've cast yourself in the same role, as the guardian. And I'm just the understudy who happened to step into Anna's part."

"It's not like that."

"What if you'd never known my sister, if

you and I were just two people who'd met at a party? Would you still be here?"

"Yes. I would be." He leaned toward her, his hands tight around hers. "I know I would be."

For a moment they sat in silence. I want to believe him, she thought. It would be so easy to believe him.

But she said, "I don't think you should stay here tonight."

Slowly he straightened. His eyes were still on hers, but there was distance between them now. And disappointment.

She rose to her feet; so did he.

In silence they walked to the front door. There he paused and turned to her. Gently he lifted his hand to her face and cupped her face, a touch she did not flinch away from.

"Be careful," he said, and walked out.

She locked the door behind him.

TWENTY-NINE

Mattie ate the last strip of beef jerky. She gnawed it like a wild animal feeding on desiccated carrion, thinking: Protein for strength. For victory! She thought of athletes preparing for marathons, honing their bodies for the performance of their lives. This would be a marathon, too. One chance to win.

Lose, and you're dead.

The jerky was like leather, and she almost gagged as she swallowed it, but she managed to wash it down with a gulp of water. The second jug was almost empty. I'm down to the bitter end, she thought; I can't hold out much longer. And now she had a new worry: Her contractions were starting to get uncomfortable, like a fist squeezing down. It didn't qualify as painful yet, but it was a harbinger of things to come.

Where was he, goddamn it? Why had he left her alone so long? With no watch to track the time, she didn't know if it had been hours or days since his last visit. She wondered if she had made him angry when she'd yelled at him. Was this her punishment? Was he trying to scare her a little, make her understand that she had to be polite and show him some respect? All her life, she'd been polite, and look where it had gotten her. Polite girls got pushed around. They got stuck at the end of the line, where no one paid them any attention. They got married to men who promptly forgot they even existed. Well, I'm through being polite, she thought. If I ever get out of here, I'm going to grow a spine.

But first I have to get out of here. And that means I have to *pretend* to be polite.

She took another sip of water. Felt strangely sated, as though she'd feasted and drunk wine. Bide your time, she thought. He'll come back.

Wrapping the blanket around her shoulders, she closed her eyes.

And woke up in the grip of a contraction.

Oh no, she thought, this one hurts. This one definitely hurts. She lay sweating in the dark, trying to remember her Lamaze classes, but they seemed like a lifetime ago. Someone else's lifetime.

Breathe in, breathe out. Cleanse . . .

"Lady."

She went rigid. Stared up toward the grate, where the voice had whispered. Her pulse hammered. *Time to act, GI Jane.* But lying in the darkness, breathing in her own scent of terror, she thought: I'm not ready. I'll never be ready. Why did I ever think I could do this?

"Lady. Talk to me."

This is your one chance. Do it.

She took a deep breath. "I need help," she whimpered.

"Why?"

"My baby . . ."

"Tell me."

"It's coming. I'm having pains. Oh, please let me out! I don't know how much longer it will be . . ." She gave a sob. "Let me out. I need to get out. My baby's coming."

The voice fell silent.

She clung to the blanket, afraid to breathe, afraid to miss his softest whisper.

Why didn't he answer? Had he left again? Then she heard the thud, and a scraping.

A shovel. He was starting to dig.

One chance, she thought. I have just this one chance.

More thuds. The shovel moved in longer strokes, scooping away dirt, the scrapes as jarring as the screech of chalk on a board. She was breathing fast now, her heart banging in her chest. Either I live or die, she thought. It all gets decided now.

The scraping stopped.

Her hands were ice, fingers chilled as they clutched the blanket to her shoulders. She heard wood creak, and then the hinges gave a squeal. Dirt spilled into her prison, into her eyes. *Oh god, oh god, I won't be able to see. I need to see!* She turned away to protect her face against the earth trickling onto her hair. Blinked again and again to clear the grit from her eyes. With her head down, she could not see him standing above her. And what did he see, staring down into the pit? His captive huddled under a blanket, dirty, defeated. Wracked by the pains of childbirth.

"It's time to come out," he said, this time

not through a grate. A quiet voice, utterly ordinary. How could evil sound so normal?

"Help me." She gave a sob. "I can't jump all the way up there."

She heard wood grate against wood, and felt something bump down beside her. A ladder. Opening her eyes, she looked up and saw only a silhouette against stars. After the pitch blackness of her prison, the night sky seemed awash in light.

He turned on a flashlight, aiming it down at the rungs. "It's only a few steps," he said.

"It hurts so much."

"I'll take your hand. But you have to step onto the ladder."

Sniffling, she rose slowly to her feet. Swayed and dropped back down to her knees. She had not stood up in days, and it shocked her now, how weak she felt despite her attempts to exercise, despite the adrenaline now pumping through her blood.

"If you want to get out," he said, "you have to stand up."

She groaned and staggered back to her feet, unsteady as a newborn calf. Her right hand was still inside the blanket, clutching it to her chest. With her left hand, she grasped the ladder.

"That's it. Climb."

She stepped onto the lowest rung and paused to steady herself before she reached up with her free hand for the next rung. Took another step. The hole was not deep; just a few more rungs and she'd be out of it. Already, her head and shoulders were at his waist.

"Help me," she pleaded. "Pull me up."

"Let go of the blanket."

"I'm too cold. Please, pull me up!"

He laid his flashlight on the ground. "Give me your hand," he said, and bent toward her, a faceless shadow, one tentacle extended toward her.

That's it. He's close enough.

His head was just above hers now, within striking distance. For an instant she faltered, repulsed by the thought of what she was about to do.

"Stop wasting my time, " he ordered. *"Do it!"*

Suddenly it was Dwayne's face she imagined staring down at her. Dwayne's voice berating her, scorn shoveled upon scorn. *Image is everything, Mattie, and look at you!* Mattie the cow clinging to her ladder, afraid to save herself. Afraid to save her baby. *You just aren't good enough for me anymore.*

Yes I am. YES I AM!

She let the blanket go. It slid off her shoulders, uncovering what she had been clutching beneath it: her sock, bulging with the eight flashlight batteries. She brought her arm up, swinging the sock like a mace, the arc propelled by sheer rage. Her aim was wild, clumsy, but she felt the satisfying *whump* as batteries slammed into skull.

The shadow reeled sideways and toppled.

In seconds she was up the ladder and scrambling out of the hole. Terror did not make you clumsy; it sharpened your senses, made you quick as a gazelle. In the split second after her feet touched solid ground, she registered a dozen details at once. A quarter moon peeking out from behind branches that arched across the sky. The smell of soil and damp leaves. And trees, everywhere trees, a ring of towering sentinels that blocked out all but a narrow dome of stars overhead. *I'm in a forest.* In one sweeping gaze she took all this in, made a split-second decision, and sprinted toward what looked like a gap between those trees. She found herself suddenly hurtling down a steep gully, crashing through brambles and whip-thin saplings that did not snap in two but lashed back at her face in vengeance.

She landed on her hands and knees. Scrambled back to her feet in an instant and was running again, but with a limp now, her right ankle twisted and throbbing. I'm making too much noise, she thought, I'm loud as a trampling elephant. Don't stop, don't stop—he could be right behind me. Just keep moving!

But she was blind in these woods, with just the stars and that pitiful excuse of a moon to show her the way. No light, no landmarks. No idea where she was or in which direction help might lie. She knew nothing of this place, and was as lost as a wanderer in a nightmare. She fought her way through underbrush, heading instinctively downhill, letting gravity decide which direction she should take. Mountains lead to valleys. Valleys lead to streams. Streams lead to people. Oh hell, it sounded good, but was it true? Already her knees were stiffening up, the aftermath of the fall she'd taken. Another tumble and she might not be able to walk at all.

And now another pain gripped her. It brought her up short, catching her in mid-breath. A contraction. She doubled over, waiting for it to pass. When at last she could straighten again, she was drenched in sweat.

Something rustled behind her. She whirled and faced a wall of impenetrable shadow. She felt evil closing in. All at once she was running away from it, tree branches slashing her face, panic shrieking at her. *Faster. Faster!*

On the downhill slope she lost her footing and began to tumble, and would have slammed belly first onto the ground if she had not caught herself on a sapling. *Poor baby, I almost landed on you!* She heard no sound of pursuit, but she knew he had to be right behind her, tracking her. Terror sent her hurtling on, through a web of interlocking branches.

Then the trees magically evaporated. She broke through a last tangle of vines and her feet slammed onto packed earth. Stunned and gasping, she stared across ripples of reflected moonlight. A lake. A road.

And, in the distance, perched on a point, the silhouette of a small cabin.

She took a few steps and stopped, groaning as another contraction gripped her in its fist, squeezing so tightly she could not breathe, could do nothing but crouch there in the road. Nausea flooded her throat. She heard water slap against the shore, and the cry of a bird on the lake. Dizziness washed over her, threatening to drag her down to her knees. *Not here! Don't stop here, so exposed on the road.*

She staggered forward, the contraction easing now. Pushed herself onward, the cabin a shadowy hope. She started to run, her knee throbbing with every slap of her shoe against the dirt road. Faster, she thought. He can see you here against the lake's reflection. Run before the next pain clamps down. How many minutes until the next one? Five, ten? The cabin looked so far away.

She was pushing herself all out, now, legs pumping, air roaring in and out of her lungs. Hope was like rocket fuel. *I'm going to live. I'm going to live.*

The cabin windows were dark. She rapped on the door anyway, not daring to shout for fear her voice would carry back up the road, up the mountain. There was no answer.

She hesitated only a second. *To hell with being a good girl. Just break the goddamn window!* She grabbed a rock near the front door and slammed it against a pane, and the sound of breaking glass shattered the night's silence. With the rock, she batted away the few remaining shards, reached in, and unlocked the door.

Breaking and entering, now. Go, GI Jane!

Inside she smelled cedar and stale air. A vacation house that had been closed up and neglected too long. Glass crunched under her shoes as she hunted for a wall switch. An instant after the lights came on, she realized: He'll see it. *Too late now. Just find a phone.*

She looked around the room and saw a fireplace, stacked wood, furniture with plaid upholstery, but no phone.

She ran into the kitchen and spotted a handset on the counter. Picked it up and was already dialing 911 when she realized there was no dial tone. The line was dead.

In the living room, broken glass skittered across the floor.

He's in the house. Get out. Get out now.

She slipped out the kitchen door and quietly closed it behind her. Found herself standing in a small garage. Moonlight filtered in through a single window, just bright enough for her to make out the low silhouette of a rowboat cradled in its trailer. No other cover, no place to hide. She backed away from the kitchen door, shrinking as far into the shadows as she could. Her shoulder bumped up against a shelf, rattling metal, stirring the smell of long-gathered dust. She reached out blindly along the shelf for a weapon and felt old paint cans, their lids caked shut. Felt paint brushes, the hairs shellacked solid. Then her fingers closed around a screwdriver, and she snatched it up. Such a pitiful weapon, about as lethal as a nail file. The runt cousin of all screwdrivers.

The light under the kitchen door rippled. A shadow moved across the glowing crack. Stopped.

So did her breathing. She backed toward the garage bay door, her heart battering its way to her throat. Only one choice left.

She reached down for the handle and pulled. The door squealed as it slid up the tracks, a shriek announcing: *Here she is! Here she is!*

Just as the kitchen door flew open, she scrambled out under the bay door and ran into the night. She knew he could see her moving along that pitilessly exposed shore. She knew she could not outpace him. Yet she struggled forward along the moon-silvered lake, the mud sucking at her shoes. She heard him moving closer through the clattering cattail reeds. Swim, she thought. Into the lake. She veered toward the water.

And suddenly doubled over as the next contraction seized her. This was pain like none she had ever known. It dropped her to her knees. She splashed down into ankle-deep water as the pain crescendoed, clamping her so tightly in its jaws that for a moment her vision went black and she felt herself tilting sideways, toppling. She tasted mud. Writhed, coughing, onto her back, as helpless as an overturned tortoise. The contraction faded. The stars slowly brightened in the sky. She could feel water caressing her hair, lapping at her cheeks. Not cold at all, but warm as a bath. She heard the splash of his footsteps, the snapping of reeds. Watched the cattails part.

And then he was there, standing above her, towering against the sky. Here to claim his prize.

He knelt beside her, and the water's reflection glinted in his eyes in pinpoints of light. What he held in his hand gleamed as well: a knife's silvery streak. He seemed to know, as he crouched over her body, that she was spent. That her soul was only waiting for release from its exhausted shell.

He grasped the waistband of her maternity slacks and pulled it down, revealing the white dome of her belly. And still she did not move, but lay catatonic. Already surrendered, already dead.

He placed one hand on her abdomen; with the other, he grasped the knife, lowering the blade toward bared flesh, bending toward her to make the first cut.

Water fountained up in a silvery splash as her hand suddenly shot up from the mud. As she aimed the tip of the screwdriver toward his face. Muscles taut with fury, she drove it upward, the pathetic little weapon suddenly launched with lethal aim at his eye.

This is for me, asshole!

And this is for my baby!

She thrust deep, felt the weapon penetrate bone and brain, until the handle lodged in the socket and could sink no deeper.

He dropped without uttering a sound.

For a moment she could not move. He had fallen across her thighs, and she could feel the heat of his blood soaking through her clothes. The dead are heavy, so much heavier than the living. She pushed, grunting with the effort, repulsed by the touch of him. At last she rolled him away and he splashed onto his back among the reeds.

She stumbled to her feet and staggered toward higher ground. Away from the water, away from the blood. She collapsed farther up on the bank, dropping onto a bed of grass. There she lay as the next contraction came and went. And the next, and the next. Through pain-dimmed eyes she watched the quarter moon wheel across the heavens. Saw the stars fade and a pink glow seep into the eastern sky.

As the sun lifted over the horizon, Mattie Purvis welcomed her daughter into the world.

THIRTY

Turkey vultures traced lazy circles in the sky, the black-winged heralds of fresh carrion. The dead do not long escape Mother Nature's attention. The perfume of decomposition draws blowflies and beetles, crows and rodents, all converging on Death's bounty. And how am I any different? Maura thought, as she headed down the grassy bank toward the water. She too was drawn to the dead, to poke and prod cold flesh like any scavenger. This was such a beautiful place for so grim a task. The sky was a cloudless blue, the lake like silvered glass. But at the water's edge, a white sheet draped what the vultures, circling above, were so eager to feast on.

Jane Rizzoli, standing with Barry Frost

and two Massachusetts State Police officers, stepped forward to meet Maura.
"Body was lying in a couple inches of water,
over in those cattails. We pulled it up onto
the bank. Just wanted you to know it's been
moved."

Maura stared down at the draped corpse,
but did not touch it. She was not quite
ready to confront what lay beneath the
plastic sheet. "Is the woman all right?"

"I saw Mrs. Purvis in the ER. She's a little
banged up, but she'll be fine. And the
baby's doing great." Rizzoli pointed toward
the bank, where tufts of feathery grass
grew. "She had it right over there. Managed
it all by herself. When the park ranger drove
by around seven, he found her sitting at the
side of the road, nursing the baby."

Maura stared up the bank and thought of
the woman laboring alone under the open
sky, her cries of pain unheard, while twenty
yards away, a corpse cooled and stiffened.
"Where did he keep her?"

"In a pit, about two miles from here."

Maura frowned at her. "She made it all
this way on foot?"

"Yeah. Imagine running in the dark,
through the trees. And doing it while you're

in labor. Came down that slope there, out of the woods."

"I can't imagine."

"You should see the box he kept her in, like a coffin. Buried alive for a week—I don't know how she came out of it still sane."

Maura thought of young Alice Rose, trapped in a pit all those years ago. Just one night of despair and darkness had haunted her for the rest of her short life. In the end, it had killed her. Yet Mattie Purvis had emerged not only sane, but prepared to fight back. To survive.

"We found the white van," said Rizzoli.

"Where?"

"It's parked way up on one of the maintenance roads, about thirty, forty yards away from the pit where he buried her. We never would have found her there."

"Have you found any remains yet? There must be victims buried nearby."

"We've just started to look. There's a lot of trees, a large area to search. It'll take time for us to comb that whole hill for graves."

"All these years, all those missing women. One of them could be my . . ."

Maura stopped, and looked up at the trees

on the slope. *One of them could be my mother. Maybe I don't have a monster's blood in my veins at all. Maybe my real mother has been dead all these years. Another victim, buried somewhere in those woods.*

"Before you make any assumptions," said Rizzoli, "you need to see the corpse."

Maura frowned at her. Looked down at the shrouded body lying at her feet. She knelt and reached for a corner of the sheet.

"Wait. I should warn you—"

"Yes?"

"It's not what you're expecting."

Maura hesitated, her hand hovering over the sheet. Insects hummed, greedy for access to fresh meat. She took a breath and peeled back the cover.

For a moment she didn't say a word as she stared at the face she'd just exposed. What stunned her was not the ruined left eye, or the screwdriver handle jammed deep into the orbit. That gruesome detail was merely a feature to be noted, mentally filed away as she would file a dictated report. No, it was the face that held her attention, that horrified her.

"He's too young," she murmured. "This man's too young to be Elijah Lank."

"I'd guess he's about thirty, thirty-five."

Maura released a shocked breath. "I don't understand . . ."

"You do see it, don't you?" Rizzoli asked quietly. "Black hair, green eyes."

Like mine.

"I mean, sure, there could be a million guys with hair and eyes that color. But the resemblance . . ." She paused. "Frost saw it, too. We all saw it."

Maura pulled the sheet over the corpse and stepped back, retreating from the truth which had stared so undeniably from the dead man's face.

"Dr. Bristol's on his way now," said Frost. "We didn't think you'd want to do this autopsy."

"Then why did you call me?"

"Because you said you wanted to be in the loop," said Rizzoli. "Because I promised I would. And because . . ." Rizzoli looked down at the draped body. "Because you'd find out sooner or later who this man was."

"But we don't know who he was. You think you see a resemblance. That's not proof."

"There's more. Something we just learned this morning."

Maura looked at her. "What?"

"We've been trying to track down Elijah Lank's whereabouts. Searching for any place his name may have popped up. Arrests, traffic tickets, anything. This morning we got a fax from a county clerk in North Carolina. It was a death certificate. Elijah Lank died eight years ago."

"Eight years ago? Then he wasn't with Amalthea when she killed Theresa and Nikki Wells."

"No. By then, Amalthea was working with a new partner. Someone who stepped in to take Elijah's place. To continue the family business."

Maura turned and stared at the lake, its water now blindingly bright. I don't want to hear the rest of this, she thought. I don't want to know.

"Eight years ago, Elijah died of a heart attack in a Greenville hospital," said Rizzoli. "He showed up in the emergency room complaining of chest pain. According to their records, he was brought to the ER by his family."

Family.

"His wife, Amalthea," said Rizzoli. "And their son, Samuel."

Maura took a deep breath and smelled both decay and the scent of summer in the air. Death and life mingled in a single perfume.

"I'm sorry," said Rizzoli. "I'm sorry you had to find out. There's still a chance we're wrong about this man, you know. There's still a chance he's not related to them at all."

But they weren't wrong, and Maura knew it.

I knew it when I saw his face.

When Rizzoli and Frost walked into J.P. Doyle's that evening, the cops standing around the bar greeted them with a loud and boisterous round of applause that made Rizzoli flush. Hell, even the guys who didn't particularly like her were applauding in comradely acknowledgment of her success, which at that moment was being trumpeted on the five o'clock news playing on the TV above the bar. The crowd began to stomp in unison as Rizzoli and Frost approached the counter, where the grinning bartender had already set out two drinks for them. For Frost, a shot of whiskey, and for Rizzoli . . .

A large glass of milk.

As everyone burst out laughing, Frost leaned over and whispered in her ear: "You know, my stomach's kind of upset. Wanna trade drinks?"

The funny thing was, Frost really *did* like milk. She slid her glass his way, and asked the bartender for a Coke.

As their fellow cops came around to shake their hands and slap high fives, she and Frost ate peanuts and sipped their virtuous drinks. She missed having her usual Adams ale. Missed a lot of things tonight— her husband, her beer. Her waistline. Still, this was a good day. It's always a good day, she thought, when a perp goes down.

"Hey, Rizzoli! The bets are up to two hundred bucks you're having a girl, a hundred twenty on a boy."

She glanced sideways and saw Detectives Vann and Dunleavy standing beside her at the bar. The fat Hobbit and the skinny one, holding up their twin pints of Guinness.

"So what if I have both?" she asked. "Twins?"

"Huh," said Dunleavy. "We didn't consider that."

"So who wins then?"

"I guess no one."

"Or everyone?" said Vann.

The two men stood pondering that question for a while. Sam and Frodo, stuck on the Mount Doom of dilemmas.

"Well," said Vann, "I guess we should add another category."

Rizzoli laughed. "Yeah, you guys do that."

"Great work, by the way," said Dunleavy. "Just watch, next thing, you're gonna be in *People* magazine. A perp like that, all those women. What a story."

"You want the honest truth?" Rizzoli sighed and set down her Coke. "We can't take the credit."

"No?"

Frost looked over at Vann and Dunleavy. "Wasn't us brought him down. It was the vic."

"Just a housewife," said Rizzoli. "A scared, pregnant, ordinary housewife. Didn't need a gun or a billy club, just a goddamn sock filled with batteries."

Up on the TV, the local news was over, and the bartender flipped the channel to

HBO. A movie with women in short skirts. Women who had waistlines.

"So what about that Black Talon?" asked Dunleavy. "How did that tie in?"

Rizzoli was quiet for a moment as she sipped her Coke. "We don't know yet."

"You find the weapon?"

She caught Frost looking at her, and felt a ripple of uneasiness. That was the detail that troubled them both. They had found no gun in the van. There had been knotted cords and blood-caked knives. There'd been a neatly kept notebook with the names and phone numbers of nine other baby brokers around the country; Terence Van Gates had not been the only one. And there'd been records of cash payments made to the Lanks through the years, a mother lode of information that would keep investigators busy for years. But the weapon that had killed Anna Leoni was not in the van.

"Oh, well," said Dunleavy. "Maybe it'll turn up. Or he got rid of it."

Maybe. Or maybe we're still missing something.

It was dark when she and Frost left Doyle's. Instead of going home, she drove back to Schroeder Plaza, the conversation with Vann and Dunleavy still weighing on her mind, and sat down at her desk, which was covered by a mountain of files. On top were the records from NCIC, several decades' worth of missing persons reports compiled during their hunt for the Beast. But it was Anna Leoni's murder that had set the whole search in motion, like a pebble dropped into water, launching ever wider ripples. Anna's murder was what had led them to Amalthea, and eventually to the Beast. Yet Anna's death remained a question still unresolved.

Rizzoli cleared away the NCIC files, working her way down to the folder on Anna Leoni. Though she had read and reread everything in this file, she leafed through it again, rereading the witness statements, the autopsy, the reports from hair and fiber, fingerprints, and DNA. She came to the ballistics report, and her gaze lingered over the words *Black Talon.* She remembered the starburst shape of the bullet in Anna Leoni's skull X-ray. Remembered, too, the track of devastation it had left in her brain.

A Black Talon bullet. Where was the gun that had fired it?

She closed the folder and looked down at the cardboard box that had been sitting beside her desk for the last week. It contained the files that Vann and Dunleavy had lent her, on the murder of Vassily Titov. He'd been the only other Boston-area victim of a Black Talon bullet in the last five years. She took the folders from that box and piled them on her desk, sighing when she saw how high the stack was. Even a slam-dunk investigation generates reams of paper. Vann and Dunleavy had summed up the case for her earlier, and she had read enough of their files to satisfy herself that they had indeed made a good arrest. The subsequent trial and speedy conviction of Antonin Leonov only reinforced that belief. Yet here she was, reviewing the files again, on a case which left no room for doubt that the right man had been convicted.

Detective Dunleavy's final report was thorough and convincing. Leonov had been under police surveillance for a week, in anticipation of a delivery of Tajikistan heroin. While the two detectives had watched from their vehicle, Leonov had pulled up in front of Titov's residence, knocked on the front door, and was admitted. Moments later, two gunshots were fired inside the house. Leonov walked out, climbed into his car, and was about to drive away when Vann and Dunleavy closed in and arrested him. Inside the house, Titov was found dead in the kitchen, two Black Talons in his brain. Ballistics later confirmed both bullets had been fired by Leonov's weapon.

Open and shut. The perp convicted, the weapon in police custody. Rizzoli could see no link at all between the deaths of Vassily Titov and Anna Leoni, except for the use of Black Talon bullets. Increasingly rare ammunition, but not enough to constitute any real connection between the murders.

Yet she continued flipping through the files, reading through the dinner hour. By the time she reached the last folder, she was almost too tired to tackle it. I'll get this over and done with, she thought, then pack up the files and put this issue to bed.

She opened the folder and found a report on the search of Antonin Leonov's warehouse. It contained Detective Vann's description of the raid, a list of Leonov's arrested employees, along with an accounting of everything confiscated, from crates and cash to bookkeeping records. She skimmed down until she reached the list of officers on the scene. Ten Boston PD cops. Her gaze froze on one particular name, a name she hadn't noticed when she'd read the report a week ago. *Just a coincidence. It doesn't necessarily mean . . .*

She sat and thought about it for a moment. She remembered a drug raid she'd been in on as a young patrol officer. Lots of noise, lots of excitement. And confusion— when a dozen adrenaline-hyped cops converge on a hostile building, everyone's nervous, everyone's looking out for himself. You may not notice what your fellow cop is doing. What he's slipping into his pocket. Cash, drugs. A box of bullets that would never be missed. It's always there, that temptation to take a souvenir. A souvenir you might later find useful.

She picked up the phone and called Frost.

THIRTY-ONE

The dead were not good company.

Maura sat at her microscope, staring through the eyepiece at sections of lung and liver and pancreas—bits of tissue sliced from a suicide victim's mortal remains, preserved under glass, and stained a gaudy pink and purple with a hematoxylin-eosin preparation. Except for the occasional clink of the slides, and the faint hiss of the air-conditioning vent, the building was quiet. Yet it was not empty of people; in the cold room downstairs, half a dozen silent visitors lay zipped into their shrouds. Undemanding guests, each with a story to tell, but only to those willing to cut and probe.

The phone rang on her desk; she let the

after-hours office recording pick up. *Nobody here but the dead. And me.*

The story Maura now saw beneath her microscope lens was not a new one. Young organs, healthy tissues. A body designed to live many more years, had the soul been willing, had some inner voice only whispered to the despairing man: *Now, wait a minute, heartbreak is temporary. This pain will pass, and you'll find another girl to love someday.*

She finished the last slide and set it in the box. Sat for a moment, her mind not on the slides she had just reviewed, but on another image: a young man with dark hair and green eyes. She had not watched his autopsy; that afternoon, while he had been split open and dissected by Dr. Bristol, she had remained upstairs in her office. But even as she'd dictated reports and flipped through microscope slides late into the evening, she had been thinking about him. *Do I really want to know who he is?* She still hadn't decided. Even as she rose from her desk, as she gathered her purse and an armful of files, she was uncertain of her answer.

Again, the phone rang; again, she ignored it.

Walking down the silent hallway, she passed closed doors and deserted offices. She remembered another evening when she had walked out of this empty building, to find the claw mark scratched into her car, and her heart started to beat a little faster.

But he's gone, now. The Beast is dead.

She stepped out the rear exit, into a night soft with summery warmth. She paused beneath the building's outside lamp to scan the shadowy parking lot. Drawn by the glow of the light, moths swarmed around the lamp and she heard wings fluttering against the bulb. Then, another sound: the closing of a car door. A silhouette walked toward her, taking on form and features as it moved into the lamp's glow.

She gave a sigh of relief when she saw it was Ballard. "Were you waiting for me?"

"I saw your car in the lot. I tried calling you."

"After five, I let the machine pick up."

"You weren't answering your cell phone, either."

"I turned it off. You don't need to keep checking on me, Rick. I'm fine."

"Are you, really?"

She sighed as they walked to her car. She looked up at the sky, where stars were washed pale by city lights. "I have to decide what to do about the DNA. Whether I really want to know the truth."

"Then don't do it. It doesn't matter if you are related to them. Amalthea has nothing to do with who *you* are."

"That's what I would have said before." *Before I knew whose bloodlines I might share. Before I knew I might come from a family of monsters.*

"Evil isn't hereditary."

"Still, it's not a good feeling, knowing I might have a few mass murderers in my family."

She unlocked her door and climbed in behind the wheel. Had just thrust her key in the ignition when Ballard leaned into the car.

"Maura," he said. "Have dinner with me."

She paused, not looking at him. Just stared at the green glow of the dashboard lights as she considered his invitation.

"Last night," he said, "you asked me a question. You wondered whether I'd still be interested in you if I'd never loved your sister. I don't think you believed my answer."

She turned to look at him. "There's no way to really know, is there? Because you *did* love her."

"So give me the chance to know *you*. I didn't just imagine it, up there in the woods. You felt it, I felt it. There *was* something between us." He leaned in closer. Said, softly, "It's only dinner, Maura."

She thought of the hours she had just spent working in that sterile building, with only the dead to keep her company. Tonight, she thought, I don't want to be alone. I want to be with the living.

"Chinatown's right up the street," she said. "Why don't we go there?"

He slid into the passenger seat beside her, and they looked at each other for a moment. The glow of the parking lot lamp slanted across his face, casting half of it in shadow. He reached out to touch her cheek. Then his arm came around to pull her closer, but she was already there, leaning into him, ready to meet him halfway. More than halfway. His mouth found hers, and she heard herself sigh. Felt him draw her into the warmth of his arms.

The explosion rocked her.

She flinched as Rick's window imploded, as glass stung her cheek. She opened her eyes again to stare at him. At what was left of his face, now bloody pulp. Slowly his body slumped toward her. His head landed on her thighs, and the heat of his blood soaked into her lap.

"Rick. *Rick!*"

A movement outside drew her stunned gaze. She looked up, and from out of the darkness, a figure in black emerged, moving toward her with robotic efficiency.

Coming to kill me.

Drive. Drive.

She shoved at Rick's body, struggling to move him off the gearshift, his ruined face oozing blood, turning her hands slippery. She managed to yank the gear into reverse, and hit the gas.

The Lexus lurched backward, out of the stall.

The shooter was somewhere behind her, moving in.

Sobbing with the effort, she pushed Rick's face off the gearshift and her fingers sank into bloodied meat. She jammed the gear into drive.

The rear window exploded, and she cringed as glass showered her hair.

She floored the accelerator. The Lexus screeched forward. The shooter had cut off her nearest parking lot exit; there was only one direction she could go now, toward the adjoining parking lot for the Boston University Medical Center. The two lots were separated only by a curb. She drove straight toward that curb, bracing herself for the bump. Felt her chin snap forward, her teeth slam together, as her tires bounced up over the concrete.

Another bullet flew; the windshield disintegrated.

Maura ducked as shattered glass rained onto the dashboard, pelleting her face. The Lexus careened forward, out of control. She glanced up to see the lamppost straight ahead. Unavoidable. She closed her eyes just before the air bag exploded. She was slammed back against her seat.

Slowly she opened her eyes, stunned. Her horn blasted, unceasing. It did not stop, even as she rolled away from the collapsed air bag, even as she shoved open her door and tumbled out, onto the pavement.

She staggered to her feet, ears ringing

from the horn's continuing blare. Managed to duck behind the cover of a nearby parked car. Legs unsteady, she forced herself to keep moving along that row of cars, until she suddenly came to a stop.

A wide expanse of open pavement lay in front of her.

She dropped to her knees behind a tire and peered around the bumper. Felt the blood freeze in her veins as she saw the dark figure stride out of the shadows, relentless as a machine, moving toward the smashed Lexus. It stepped beneath the pool of light cast by the streetlamp.

Maura saw the glint of blond hair, the streak of a ponytail.

The shooter yanked open the passenger door and leaned inside to look at Ballard's body. Suddenly her head popped up again and she stared, head swiveling, her gaze sweeping the parking lot.

Maura ducked back behind the wheel. Her pulse throbbed in her temples, her breaths were gulps of panic. She looked toward the empty pavement, starkly lit by another streetlamp. Beyond it, across the street, was the bright red EMERGENCY sign for the Medical Center ER. She had only to make it across that open pavement, and then across Albany Street. Already, the blare of her car horn must be attracting the attention of hospital personnel.

So close. Help is so close.

Heart banging, she rocked onto the balls of her feet. Afraid to move, afraid to stay. Slowly she eased forward and peered around the tire.

Black boots were planted right on the other side of the car.

Run.

In an instant she was sprinting straight for that open pavement. No thought of evasive moves, no dodging left and right, just all-out panicked flight. The red EMERGENCY sign glowed ahead of her. I can make it, she thought. I can—

The bullet was like a slam to her shoulder. It sent her pitching forward, sprawling onto blacktop. She tried to rise to her knees, but her left arm collapsed beneath her. What's wrong with my arm, she thought, why can't I use my arm? Groaning, she rolled onto her back and saw the glare of the parking-lot lamp shining above her.

The face of Carmen Ballard moved into view.

"I killed you once," Carmen said. "Now I have to do it all over again."

"Please. Rick and I—we never—"

"He wasn't yours to take." Carmen raised her gun. The barrel was a dark eye, staring at Maura. "Fucking whore." Her hand tensed, about to squeeze off the killing shot.

Another voice suddenly cut in—a man's. "Drop the weapon!"

Carmen blinked in surprise. Glanced sideways.

Standing a few yards away was a hospital security guard, his gun trained on Carmen. "Did you hear me, lady?" he barked. "Drop it!"

Carmen's aim wavered. She glanced down at Maura, then back at the guard, her rage, her hunger for revenge, battling with the reality of the consequences.

"We were never lovers," said Maura, her voice so weak she wondered if Carmen could hear it through the far-off bleat of the car horn. "Neither were they."

"Liar." Carmen's gaze snapped back to Maura. "You're just like her. He left me because of her. He left me."

"That wasn't Anna's fault—"

"Yes it was. And now it's yours." She kept her focus on Maura, even as tires screeched to a stop. Even as a new voice yelled:

"Officer Ballard! Drop the weapon!"

Rizzoli.

Carmen glanced sideways, a last calculating look as she weighed her choices. Two weapons were now trained on her. She had lost; no matter what she chose, her life was over. As Carmen stared back down at her, Maura could see, in her eyes, the decision she'd made. Maura watched as Carmen's arms straightened, steadying her aim on Maura, the barrel poised for its final blast. She watched Carmen's hands tighten around the grip, preparing to squeeze off the killing shot.

The blast shocked Maura. It knocked Carmen sideways; she staggered. Fell.

Maura heard pounding footsteps, a crescendo of sirens. And a familiar voice murmuring,

"Oh, Jesus. Doc!"

She saw Rizzoli's face hovering above her. Lights pulsed on the street. All around her shadows approached. Ghosts, welcoming her to their world.

THIRTY-TWO

Seeing it from the other side now. As a patient, not a doctor, the ceiling lights flickering past her as the gurney rolled down the hall, as the nurse in a bouffant cap glanced down, concern in her eyes. The wheels squeaked and the nurse panted a little as she pushed the gurney through double doors, into the operating room. Different lights glared overhead now, harsher, blinding. Like the lights of the autopsy room.

Maura closed her eyes against them. As the OR nurses transferred her to the table, she thought of Anna, lying naked beneath identical lamps, her body carved open, strangers peering down at her. She felt Anna's spirit hovering above her, watching, just as Maura had once stared down at

Anna. *My sister,* she thought as the pento-barbital slid into her veins, as the lights faded. *Are you waiting for me?*

But when she awakened, it wasn't Anna she saw; it was Jane Rizzoli. Slats of daylight glowed through the partially closed blinds, casting bright horizontal bars across Rizzoli's face as she leaned toward Maura.

"Hey, Doc."

"Hey," Maura whispered back.

"How're you feeling?"

"Not so good. My arm . . ." Maura winced.

"Looks like it's time for more drugs." Rizzoli reached over and pressed the nurse's call button.

"Thank you. Thank you for everything."

They fell silent as the nurse came in to inject a dose of morphine into the IV. The silence lingered after the nurse had left, and the drug began to work its magic.

Maura said, softly: "Rick . . ."

"I'm sorry. You do know he's . . ."

I know. She blinked back tears. "We never had a chance."

"She wasn't about to let you have a chance. That claw mark in your car door—that was all about him. About staying away from her husband. The slashed screens, the dead bird in the mailbox—all the threats Anna blamed on Cassell—I think that was Carmen, trying to scare Anna into leaving town. Into leaving her husband alone."

"But then Anna came back to Boston."

Rizzoli nodded. "She came back, because she learned she had a sister."

Me.

"So Carmen finds out that the girlfriend's back in town," said Rizzoli. "Anna left that message on Rick's answering machine, remember? The daughter heard it and told her mother. There goes any hope Carmen had of a reconciliation. The other woman was moving in again, on *her* territory. *Her* family."

Maura remembered what Carmen had said: *He wasn't yours to take.*

"Charles Cassell said something to me, about love," said Rizzoli. "He said, there's a kind of love that never lets go, no matter what. It sounds almost romantic, doesn't it? Till death do us part. Then you think about how many people get killed because a lover won't let go, won't give up."

By now, the morphine had spread through her bloodstream. Maura closed her eyes, welcoming the drug's embrace. "How did you know?" she murmured. "Why did you think of Carmen?"

"The Black Talon. That's the clue I should have followed all along—that bullet. But I got thrown off the track by the Lanks. By the Beast."

"So did I," whispered Maura. She felt the morphine dragging her toward sleep. "I think I'm ready, Jane. For the answer."

"The answer to what?"

"Amalthea. I need to know."

"If she's your mother?"

"Yes."

"Even if she is, it doesn't mean a thing. It's just biology. What do you gain by that knowledge?"

"The truth." Maura sighed. "At least I'll know the truth."

The truth, thought Rizzoli as she walked to her car, is seldom what people really want to hear. Wouldn't it be better to hold on to the thinnest sliver of hope that you are not the spawn of monsters? But Maura had asked for the facts, and Rizzoli knew they would be brutal. Already, searchers had found two sets of women's remains buried on the forested slope, not far from where Mattie Purvis had been confined. How many other pregnant women had known the terrors of that same box? How many had awakened in the darkness and had clawed, shrieking, at those impenetrable walls? How many had understood, as Mattie had, that a terrible finale waited in store for them once their usefulness, as living incubators, was over?

Could I have survived that horror? I'll never know the answer. Not until I'm the one in the box.

When she reached her car in the parking garage, she found herself checking all four tires to confirm they were intact, found herself scanning the cars around her, searching for anyone who might be watching. This is what the job does to you, she thought; you begin to feel evil all around you, even when it's not there.

She climbed into her Subaru and started the engine. Sat for a moment as it idled, as the air blowing from the vents slowly cooled down. She reached into her purse for the cell phone, thinking: I need to hear Gabriel's voice. I need to know that I am not Mattie

Purvis, that my husband *does* love me. The way I love him.

Her call was answered on the first ring. "Agent Dean."

"Hey," she said.

Gabriel gave a startled laugh. "I was about to call you."

"I miss you."

"That's what I was hoping you'd say. I'm heading to the airport now."

"The airport? Does that mean—"

"I'm catching the next flight to Boston. So how about a date with your husband tonight? Think you can pencil me in?"

"In permanent ink. Just come home. Please, come home."

A pause. Then he said, softly: "Are you okay, Jane?"

Unexpected tears stung her eyes. "Oh, it's these goddamn hormones." She wiped her face and laughed. "I think I need you right now."

"You hold that thought. Because I'm on my way."

Rizzoli was smiling as she drove toward Natick to visit a different hospital, a different patient. The other survivor in this tale of slaughter. These are two extraordinary women, she thought, and I'm privileged to know them both.

Judging by all the TV vans in the hospital parking lot, and all the reporters milling near the lobby entrance, the press, too, had decided that Mattie Purvis was a woman worth knowing. Rizzoli had to walk through a gantlet of reporters to get into the lobby. The tale of the lady buried in the box had set off a national news frenzy. Rizzoli had to flash her ID to two different security guards before finally being allowed to knock on Mattie's hospital room door. When she heard no answer, she stepped into the room.

The TV was on, but with the sound off. Images flickered onscreen, unwatched. Mattie lay in bed, eyes closed, looking nothing like the well-scrubbed young bride in the wedding photo. Her lips were bruised and swollen; her face was a map of nicks and scratches. A coiled IV tube was taped to a hand which had scabbed fingers and broken nails. It looked like the claw of a feral creature. But the expression on Mattie's face was serene; it was a sleep without nightmares.

"Mrs. Purvis?" said Rizzoli softly.

Mattie opened her eyes and blinked a few times before she fully focused on her visitor. "Oh. Detective Rizzoli, you're back again."

"I thought I'd check in on you. How're you feeling today?"

Mattie gave a deep sigh. "So much better. What time is it?"

"Nearly noon."

"I've slept all morning?"

"You deserve it. No, don't sit up, just take it easy."

"But I'm tired of being flat on my back." Mattie pushed back the covers and sat up, uncombed hair falling in limp tangles.

"I saw your baby through the nursery window. She's beautiful."

"Isn't she?" Mattie smiled. "I'm going to call her Rose. I've always liked that name."

Rose. A shiver went through Rizzoli. It was just a coincidence, one of those unexplainable convergences in the universe. *Alice Rose. Rose Purvis.* One girl long dead, the other just beginning her life. Yet another thread, however fragile, that connected the lives of two girls across the decades.

"Did you have more questions for me?" Mattie asked.

"Well, actually . . ." Rizzoli pulled a chair next to the bed and sat down. "I asked you so many things yesterday, Mattie. But I never asked you how you did it. How you managed."

"Managed?"

"To stay sane. To not give up."

The smile on Mattie's lips faded. She looked at Rizzoli with wide, haunted eyes and murmured: "I don't know how I did it. I never imagined I could ever . . ." She stopped. "I wanted to live, that's all. I wanted my baby to live."

They were quiet for a moment.

Then Rizzoli said: "I should warn you about the press. They're all going to want a piece of you. I had to walk through a whole mob of them outside. So far, the hospital's managed to keep them away from you, but when you get home, it's going to be a different story. Especially since . . ." Rizzoli paused.

"Since what?"

"I just want you to be prepared, that's all. Don't let anyone rush you into something you don't want to do."

Mattie frowned. Then her gaze lifted to the muted TV, where the noon news was playing. "He's been on every channel," she said.

On the screen, Dwayne Purvis stood before a sea of microphones. Mattie reached for the TV remote and turned up the volume.

"This is the happiest day of my life," Dwayne said to the crowd of reporters. "I have my wonderful wife and daughter back. It's been an ordeal I can't even begin to describe. A nightmare that none of you could possibly imagine. Thank God, thank *God* for happy endings."

Mattie pressed the off button. But her gaze remained on the blank TV. "It doesn't feel real," she said. "It's like it never happened. That's why I can sit here and be so calm about it, because I don't believe I was really there, in that box."

"You were, Mattie. It's going to take time for you to process it. You might have nightmares. Flashbacks. You'll step into an elevator, or look into a closet, and suddenly you'll feel like you're back in the box again. But it will get better, I promise you. Just remember that—it does get better."

Mattie looked at her with glistening eyes. "You know."

Yes, I know, thought Rizzoli, her hands closing over the scars on her palms. They were the evidence of her own ordeal, her own battle for sanity. *Survival is only the first step.*

There was a knock on the door. Rizzoli stood up as Dwayne Purvis walked in, carrying an armful of red roses. He went straight to his wife's bedside.

"Hey, babe. I would have come up sooner, but it's a zoo down there. They all wanted interviews."

"We saw you on TV," said Rizzoli. Trying to sound neutral, though she could not look at him without remembering the interview at the Natick police station. Oh, Mattie, she thought. You can do better than this man.

He turned to look at Rizzoli, and she saw his tailored shirt, his neatly knotted silk tie. The scent of his aftershave overwhelmed the fragrance of the roses. "So how'd I do?" he asked eagerly.

She told the truth. "You looked like a real pro on TV."

"Yeah? It's amazing, all the cameras out there. This has got everyone so excited."

He looked at his wife. "You know, hon, we need to document everything. Just so we have a record of it."

"What do you mean?"

"Like, right now. This moment. We should have a picture of this moment. Me bringing you flowers as you lie in your hospital bed. I've already got pictures of the kid. Had the nurse bring her up to the window. But we need to get close-ups. You holding her, maybe."

"Her name is Rose."

"And we don't have any of you and me together. We definitely need a few photos of us. I brought a camera."

"My hair isn't combed, Dwayne. I'm a mess. I don't want any pictures."

"Come on. They're all asking for 'em."

"Who is? Who are the pictures for?"

"That's something we can decide later. We can take our time, weigh all the offers. The story's worth so much more if it comes with photos." He pulled a camera from his pocket and handed it to Rizzoli. "Here, you mind taking the picture?"

"It's up to your wife."

"It's okay, it's okay," he insisted. "Just take the picture." He leaned in close to Mattie and extended the bouquet of roses to her. "How about this? Me handing her the flowers. It'll look great." He smiled, teeth gleaming, the loving husband sheltering his wife.

Rizzoli looked at Mattie. She saw no protest in her gaze, just a strange, volcanic gleam that she could not interpret. She raised the camera, centered the couple in the viewfinder, and pressed the shutter release.

The flash went off, just in time to capture the image of Mattie Purvis whacking her husband across the face with the bouquet of roses.

THIRTY-THREE

Four weeks later

There was no playacting this time, no pretense of madness. Amalthea Lank walked into the private interview room and sat down at the table, and the look she aimed at Maura was clear-eyed and perfectly sane. Her previously disheveled hair was now pulled back in a tidy ponytail, thrusting her features into stark prominence. Staring at Amalthea's high cheekbones, her direct gaze, Maura wondered: Why did I refuse to see it before? It's so obvious. I am looking at my own face twenty-five years from now.

"I knew you'd come back," said Amalthea. "And here you are."

"Do you know why I'm here?"

"You've gotten back the test results, haven't you? Now you know I was telling the truth. Even if you didn't want to believe me."

"I needed proof. People lie all the time, but DNA doesn't."

"Still, you must have known the answer. Even before your precious lab test came back." Amalthea leaned forward in the chair and regarded her with an almost intimate smile. "You have your father's mouth, Maura. Do you know that? And you have my eyes, my cheekbones. I see Elijah and me right there, on your face. We're family. We have the same blood. You, me, Elijah. And your brother." She paused. "You do know that's who he was?"

Maura swallowed. "Yes." *The one baby you kept. You sold my sister and me, but you kept your son.*

"You never told me how Samuel died," said Amalthea. "How that woman killed him."

"It was self-defense. That's all you need to know. She had no choice but to fight back."

"And who is this woman, Matilda Purvis? I'd like to know more about her."

Maura said nothing.

"I saw her picture on TV. She didn't look so special to me. I don't see how she could have done it."

"People do anything to survive."

"Where does she live? What street? They said on TV that she's from Natick."

Maura stared into her mother's dark eyes and suddenly felt a chill. Not for herself, but for Mattie Purvis. "Why do you want to know?"

"I have a right to know. As a mother."

"A mother?" Maura almost laughed. "Do you really think you deserve that title?"

"But I am his mother. And you're Samuel's sister." Amalthea leaned closer. "It's our right to know. We're his family, Maura. There's nothing in this life that's thicker than blood."

Maura stared into eyes so eerily like her own, and she recognized the matching intelligence there, even the gleam of brilliance. But it was a light that had gone askew, a twisted reflection in a shattered mirror.

"Blood means nothing," said Maura.

"Then why are you here?"

"I came because I wanted to get one last

look at you. And then I'm going to walk away. Because I've decided that, no matter what the DNA may say, you're not my mother."

"Then who is?"

"The woman who loved me. You don't know how to love."

"I loved your brother. I could love you." Amalthea reached across the table and caressed Maura's cheek. Such a gentle touch, as warm as a real mother's hand. "Give me the chance," she whispered.

"Good-bye, Amalthea." Maura stood up and pressed the button to call the guard. "I'm finished here," she said into the intercom. "I'm ready to leave."

"You'll come back," said Amalthea.

Maura did not look at her, did not even glance over her shoulder as she walked out of the room. As she heard Amalthea call out behind her: "Maura! You *will* come back."

In the visitors' locker room, Maura stopped to reclaim her purse, her driver's license, her credit cards. All the proof of her identity. But I already know who I am, she thought.

And I know who I am not.

Outside, in the heat of a summer afternoon, Maura paused and took a deep breath. She felt the day's warmth cleanse the taint of prison from her lungs. Felt, too, the poison of Amalthea Lank wash out of her life.

In her face, her eyes, Maura wore the proof of her parentage. In her veins flowed the blood of murderers. But evil was not hereditary. Though she might carry its potential in her genes, so too did every child ever born. *In this, I am no different. We are all descended from monsters.*

She walked away from that building of captive souls. Ahead was her car, and the road home. She did not look back.